Roby's Moonlit Night
Sweet McKenna Book Four

Christine Young

Chapter One

Scotland 1749

The full moon hung low in the darkening sky. Silver light from the huge orb cast eerie shadows that danced and flirted across the ground. Mist and murky air clung to the path Roby McKenna and Kit Stuart rode. The air smelled like autumn and tasted of smoke. Dried leaves coated the forest floor crunching beneath the horse's hooves. They were almost to Paisley, a small town near Glasgow. No breeze or sounds filled the forest, as the land was unusually quiet, foreboding as if challenging something bad to enter into the domain.

Roby felt as if something very significant in his life was about to happen. Beneath his shirt the skin on his body prickled. All the hairs on the back of his neck stood on end. The sensations blasted through him, leaving a trace of excitement as well as anticipation. His lungs rushed to bring in air.

He and Kit had been away for two years. Home soil, Scotland awaited them. They were both eager to reach the highlands see family along with friends. These feelings signaled something different. The McKenna castle was about a day and half's ride north of Inverness. While the travel to America was challenging, the land as well as the natives intriguing, neither man accomplished their goal. He was two and seven as was Kit with no mate in sight.

Well, what had he expected? Perhaps he just wanted an adventure he could tell tales about when he grew old and his muscles were weak. When he finally did find the perfect woman to have children with, he could keep all entertained around the fire on a cold winter's night with regales of his exploits in that rugged land so far away.

"What do you suppose that is?" Kit pointed to what appeared to be gallows rising from the ground.

The dark black structure stood out as silhouette in front of the brilliant light of the full moon, which encompassed the scene. Eerie sensations swept Roby to his core. Shivers swept up his spine. The noose dangled below the high beam. On the platform a small figure stood, a cowl thrown over the head, arms bound in front. Another smaller form danced around the other. The animal chattered hysterically. When the tiny beast saw him, it launched itself forward, swinging on tree branches, noisily claiming its displeasure.

"Appears to be a hanging," Roby said as curiosity caused him to spur his horse forward and faster. His heart raced with the knowledge he needed to stop whatever was going on here. This seemed passing strange. The victim was either a woman or a child. The animal landed on his shoulder, covering his eyes with its hands, babbling angrily. When it let go, it pointed seeming to think he should do something about the situation.

Absently he cradled the animal, a monkey, in his arms, making hushing noises as he tried to calm her. He chuckled softly as he noticed the dress the monkey wore.

"Too small to be a man. Why would someone be hanging a woman in the middle of the night?" Kit followed behind keeping pace with him. "In the middle of nowhere for that matter. What the devil? Did you just catch yourself a monkey?" Kit asked not bothering to hide his laughter.

Roby nodded a soft chuckle escaping him. "Guess so."

At the sight coupled with the realization a woman was about to dangle from that noose, Roby's gut clenched, his fingers tightened around the animal. Something wrong was happening here. He meant to find out what it was. If at all possible, he meant to correct it.

"Hello there." A man stepped down from the gallows, waving his hand. "Nice evening now, isn't it? Care to bear witness?"

"There's going to be a hanging here? How could this possibly be a nice evening when someone, a woman, is going to die," Roby asked, his voice filled with sarcasm as he brought his thoroughbred to a halt in front of the wizened man. This was not right.

"Might not be a hanging. Not if one of you fine *laddies* wants to marry this *lass*." His wide grin showed yellowed teeth. The scent of garlic emanated from him. He looked back to the trembling woman standing on the platform. "Either you lads up for the task? When cleaned up I heard she's a pretty little thing. Now," he stuffed his hands in his pockets, "now, she's a tiny bundle of filth. Several baths might uncover what the grime is hiding."

She was shaking, most likely terrified. Still, she held her head high, her narrow shoulders straight as if she defied the very act that was about to be perpetrated against her. Nothing she could have done could possibly warrant her execution. Roby found he wanted to see her, see if she could be a pretty little thing. No other way to put what he was feeling. He was intrigued.

"Marry? As in wed?" Kit laughed as he leaned forward on the saddle horn to get a better look. "Not a chance. What about you, Roby? You want to wed this *wee lassie* to rescue her? Believe the animal would go along with her. The start of a family."

"What did she do?" Roby asked, his mind focused on the slight sway of the girl's body as she tried to hold herself still.

She looked as if her knees would buckle at any moment. This had to be some kind of horrible travesty of justice. She certainly would not, could not have murdered someone unless it was in self-defense. The monkey leapt from his arms rushing to the woman. She bent down. The animal perched on her shoulder, pointing her bony finger at the hangman.

The man cackled. There was no other term to describe the noise. "Got caught eatin' a rabbit on Lord Bigley's land. He doesn't take to anyone poaching in his forest. Always says what's his is his and it's goin' to remain that way. Punishment he doles out is always harsher than it should be. She spent a month in the filthy pen he keeps outside his house near the barn before he finally decided that hanging was the best punishment, a life for a life."

"You don't say," Kit spoke, a bit of insolence in his voice. His horse nervously side-stepped.

Roby sickened at the thought a human life could be compared at the same value as a rabbit. The woman shifted from one foot to the other before she seemed to lock her knees to keep from falling, her body trembling hard. Even while she waited execution she stroked her pet, seeming to calm the animal.

"Why marriage?" Roby snorted, still disgusted. "Doesn't change the manner of the crime in any way. Doesn't mean it won't happen again."

"Well, the old Lord Bigley believes that a woman should be molded by a man. It's his right to shape her into the woman she should be. If she's wed, well then, she won't be gettin' herself into any more trouble. She won't have to ferret out her food. She'll be provided for now, won't she? You wouldn't let your woman starve, now, would you? She'll do what her man tells her to do. She'll have a protector, a man to keep her to the straight and narrow so to speak."

"I see," Roby spoke softly his gaze still riveted on the woman as well as the monkey standing so very resolutely on the gallows waiting for his answer. He was her last hope.

"You do?" Kit asked, his head swirling to look at Roby, sounding as if he wanted a better explanation. "What the devil do you see?"

"So..." Roby's gaze ran over the woman's petite frame, taking note of her. It seemed upon hearing the conversation her chin rose higher. She was a proud lady. Hardly had the air about her of someone who would be reduced to fending for her food. "Allow me to get this straight. If one of us marries this lady, she will be set free. Her life will be spared?"

The words on Roby's part were more musings than questions. He could wed her then set her free after they were far enough away from this place. No one would *ken* the difference.

"That's what I said wasn't it?" the man asked irritably, rubbing first his head as if he tried to clear his brains before his hand found his crotch to do the same in his lower regions.

Roby chuckled before he wondered if he just lost all common sense. When he spoke, he was surprised by how clear and strong his voice was. Stunned about how certain he was. This was something he'd never thought to do or that he would do what Kit did. Run the other way. He felt this strange calling toward her, a need to know her, to learn more about her. Very slowly and softly, he spoke, "I'll marry the *lass*. Does she have a name?"

"You will?" Kit's voice exploded through the silence of the evening. He sounded shocked as well as appalled. "You've lost your ever blessed mind, Roby McKenna. What will Connal and Wynnie say? They will be mortified, might even disown you. You are meant to wed your mate not some poor waif along with her monkey you found awaiting execution."

"For eating a rabbit." One eyebrow arched heavenward. "Besides," he said unemotionally, "I'm not wedding the animal."

"Yes."

"My parents will bless the union if they believe it's what I want. I do want to marry this woman. Don't ask me why but I do. There is something about her that calls to me, to my soul, my heart as well. Don't understand why. Just that she does." As every second passed, he became more and more positive this was something he had to do. Wedding this lady he'd never seen before wasn't foolishness. It was written in the stars.

"Then, I'll just be gettin' out my bible. Come over this way. You can stand up here on the hangin' platform with the little lady. You stand right beside her now." The man pointed at Kit. "You come stand beside your friend. We'll be the two witnesses. Don't need more than that."

"Shouldn't you at least take the cowl off her head and untie her?" Roby asked, his voice bland.

He would do it himself if the man didn't agree. He didn't want the marriage to precede any farther until this little matter was taken care of to his satisfaction. He would see the woman he married.

"Well, sir, if you saw her before the ceremony, you might have a change of heart. Wouldn't want that now, would we?" he cackled. "Don't want to see the *wee* little *lassie* hang for being hungry. In this instance, I've got no choice or say in the matter. If I didn't do my duty by Bigley, I'd most likely find myself up there too."

"My mind won't change."

With both hands, Roby gently removed the cowl. Stepping back, he stared into dark mesmerizing eyes that met his gaze with intensity. He wished he could see their color. She was gazing up at him, her small pert nose in the air, a defiant chin along with full sensual lips. Her hair hung to her waist tangled and matted, her face smudged with dirt. From what little he could see of her, her waist was trim, her breasts small and her hips curved femininely. However, the stench emanating from her was nearly unbearable. He grinned at her, knowing now he'd lost all sense of reality. With the full moon lighting the view behind them, the panorama had taken on an ethereal quality.

Still, she stood her ground. He reached to his boot, bringing up a knife. When moonlight glinted on the steel blade, with a stifled gasp she backed away. "I'm not going to hurt you, just get rid of this rope binding your hands. Don't think we should get married with you all trussed up." He paused, gently touching her cheek with his knuckles. "Do you wish to marry me, *lass*? If you don't...?"

She nodded after turning to look at the noose. He heard the swiftly drawn breath of air. Smiled. He decided she would do quite nicely even though he had no earthly idea what awaited him.

Thankfully, the ceremony was nothing more than do you take this woman to be your wife? When he said yes, the old man closed up the bible and grabbed some papers from the pocket of his coat.

"Is that all?" Roby asked fairly unsure if the wedding was actually legal and binding. "You need to ask the lady. If you don't, I won't consider myself wed. Don't want her to think she was forced in any way. I want to hear the words, I do, from her lips."

At that moment he thought of kissing those lips, tasting her. Quickly, his thoughts backed up. Not until she had the bath he intended for her as soon as there was a small measure of privacy.

"Alright then, if you insist. Doesn't actually matter what she thinks though. Does it? Do you take this man?"

"Yes."

"Now, see, that was a waste of time. You got to sign these papers then everything will be in order. Don't go annulling this marriage or divorcing her unless you want to see her swinging up there. This all is legally binding. Lord Bigley has a far reach. He won't be likin' anything like that."

The man found a semi-flat rock then smoothed the document out before handing him a pen, the bottle of ink already on the rock as if the man knew someone would come along to claim this woman as his own. Roby looked to Kit then back as he shrugged his shoulders in resignation. What was done was done. He would make the best of this wherever it took them. Kit was going to hand him an earful as soon as he got him alone, which wasn't going to happen anytime soon since he now possessed a wife.

A very dirty and smelly wife.

With a flourish he signed his name then watched the lady do the same. For a moment he wondered if she would have preferred hanging to marriage. Well, he did ask her.

"Very well then. The two of you are married. Let no man put asunder." The minister guffawed again finishing the loud noise with a snort. The man stepped back. He collected his belongings then handed the document to the newlyweds. "Now, the two of you have a nice evening. Don't stop until you get to the other side of the river. That's where you'll be off Bigley's land." With another snort ending with a chortle, he mounted a nearby donkey. He vanished into the darkness and rising mist.

Roby looked from the document he held in his hand then to the lady. He stuffed the parchment in his saddlebags. "Guess we're married. Let's get out of here. Can you ride?"

She nodded.

"Good, one less thing for me to worry about." With his hands around her waist, he lifted her easily onto his horse before mounting behind her. She weighed next to nothing. The monkey followed, resting in her arms. "You ever say anything?"

He felt her stiffen against him. "No, well maybe you'll warm up to me after a while. I certainly hope so. I'd like the two of us to be friends."

The devil but she was his wife. They would be more than friends. They would be lovers.

Kit wasn't speaking either. Roby could hear his thoughts clearly in his head as he wondered about the same things Kit was thinking. Ten minutes passed then another ten. They waded their horses across the stream to the opposite side, following the water until they reached a sheltered glen to set up camp.

"We're going to stay here for the night. Why don't you go into Paisley? Find yourself a willing woman for the evening. In the morning you can get my new wife something else to wear. I'll meet you back here tomorrow after daybreak. I want some privacy to acquaint myself with this lady."

"You're going to...?" It seemed Kit didn't want to finish the question. "Sure, a new dress if I can find one."

"As long as it's clean, I don't care what it is. When we get to Glasgow, we can buy a few more things for her. She's going to need boots and a warm cloak to name some of the items. As we head north it's going to get colder."

"Probably needs a bit of everything," Kit said, a mocking smile lighting his face.

Kit seemed to be enjoying this pickle he got himself into. The thing was, Roby wasn't the least bit worried.

He watched Kit ride away. Kit didn't put up an argument, just grinned as if he knew what was going to happen. What Kit was thinking wasn't going to happen, at least not tonight. That was a good thing he supposed. Now, he needed to figure out just how to proceed with the woman who wouldn't speak, along with her monkey who seemed to have a great deal to say.

After dismounting he helped her to her feet. She smelled god-awful. Her first order of business was a bath. He hoped she wouldn't put up a fight. If she did, he would hog-tie her before tossing her in the small pond. He stifled the small chuckle threatening to erupt at the absurdity. If she fought him, he would bathe her himself.

"In case you're wondering, you wed Roby McKenna." *Of the clan Chattan and by the way I'm a shape shifter*. "And you are?"

For a second then another she looked at her feet. He figured she still wasn't going to talk. So be it, at least she didn't rattle on about nothing important. A silent female might be nice, practical in many different ways. He didn't need conversation.

"My name is Phillipa MacPherson. And this is Hypatia. She's named after an ancient philosopher."

He was brought back from his inward thinking by the sound of her voice. "Ah, my fair lady does talk." He wasn't going to ask her anything else, at least not until he could breathe when she was nearby. Rummaging in his saddlebags, he brought out a towel along with a fat bar of soap. She might need it all. "Here you go." He nodded to the pond. "You're going to take a bath."

"Where will you be?" Her voice quavered as she took the items, holding them close to her chest as if they would protect her from him. Her eyes were wide dark pools in a pale face.

"Right here. Need to make sure you don't decide to run off. I rescued you. For some reason I can't fathom, I don't want that nullified. You're my wife. I'll protect you from now on."

No, he certainly didn't want her to leave. In fact, he realized he truly did want to get to know this woman better. Needed to know what brought her to this point of nearly no return. "The monkey, Hypatia, can sit on the rock while you clean yourself."

"Will you turn your back?"

"When you undress, of course. I promise I won't stare at you."

Though, more than getting to know her better, he did want to see what she looked like naked. After all, she was his wife. Soon enough, he would see all of her. It would be his pleasure, hopefully hers as well to be seen in the buff. For now, the last thing he wanted was to frighten her.

While she marched to the pond appearing to be walking to her execution, Roby busied himself with starting a fire then setting up the tent they would sleep inside tonight. Hypatia now sat on a nearby rock, staring at him. When all of her body was beneath the water, he picked up her discarded clothing. He tossed them one at a time into the fire. Instantly, the air around him changed, becoming sweeter smelling as the soiled rags she called clothing burned to nothing. When he looked her way, she was washing her hair. She ducked beneath the surface. Foamy white bubbles coated the top of the pond. He looked her way just as she was hesitantly backing from the water. When she turned slightly to see her way, he caught sight of her breasts. The air he inhaled jabbed in his throat. Her body was not as he'd thought. Good heavens, she must have bound her breasts. They were luscious curves that would spill deliciously from a man's hands, his large hands, crested with tight buds he wanted to taste.

He pulled one of his shirts from the saddlebag. When he reached her, she had the towel wrapped around her. He grinned pleased with her scent, the stench was now replaced with the smell of strong lye soap and woman. She was clean.

"Where are my clothes?"

Hastily, he shrugged his shoulders in a futile attempt to make light of his actions. "Burned them. You can put this on until Kit brings you something else to wear tomorrow morning."

"You burned them? That's all I had to wear." Her voice wavered yet she didn't sound angry just desolate.

"They weren't good for anything else. Don't tell me you intended to put them on after your bath."

"Was planning on washing them first." To his ears she now sounded indignant.

"Foolhardy idea." He went about fixing a pot of coffee then pulled out a loaf of bread as well as an assortment of meat and cheeses. He held up a chunk of bread. "Hungry?"

"Why is that?" she was standing with her hands on her hips, her wet hair dripping onto her shoulders. She was shivering from the chill of the autumn air.

"Why are you hungry? Wouldn't know the answer to that question. Would you?" he asked grinning, understanding exactly what she'd been talking about. "Like bread?"

"Why foolhardy?" She appeared to want to stomp her tiny shoeless foot but thought better of the action.

It didn't seem she was going to give up. He was enjoying her voice immensely. It was low, throaty, a seductive burr in her accent coupled with rich low tones that seemed to travel straight to his loins. He could well imagine how she might whisper to him when he was giving her pleasure. Not a bad thing to think about one's wife. At this point in time, he was hardly in the position to bed this woman he knew almost nothing about. He needed to like this lady he rescued from certain death before he took her to his bed.

"Foolhardy because first, there is no way you could rid the cloth of the stench by a mere washing. Second, because you would be wearing them wet and you would most likely freeze to death or take sick. The nights are chilly. Now put that shirt on then you can come sit by the fire. The heat will help dry your hair." He handed her his comb thinking he would like to comb her hair out for her. Perhaps in the future if they had one.

If there would be a future for them...

He certainly hoped there would be. For Roby there were no regrets about this night.

When next he saw her, she wore his shirt. "Thank you." She sat on a rock near the fire, his comb in hand. Her hesitancy didn't surprise him. In order to live, she was putting an awful lot of trust into the hands of a stranger.

He watched her grimace as she constantly tugged at the tangles. Her arms must be tired from the work. He almost laughed before realizing this had to be a harrowing experience for her. Only an hour or so ago, she'd been standing on the gallows expecting to die. If he had not come along when he did, she would be gone from this earth.

"I am hungry as well as tired." Her arms dropped to her sides. "I'll work on this mess later."

He handed her a chunk of bread along with a couple of slices of cheese. "If you want, I can comb your hair. Used to do it for my sister all the time. Do you trust me, *lass*?"

Briefly, his thoughts sped to Crissie. Where was she now? He hoped she wasn't with Walker Endicott. Well, he would find out soon enough.

She looked as if that was the last thing she wanted. He watched her let out a long deep sigh. Sounding a bit reluctant, she said, "Yes, I would like that if you don't mind."

While she ate, he sat behind her. She was nestled between his thighs. As he worked, she slowly began to relax. He felt her exhaustion, nearly bone deep. There were so many questions he needed to ask her. Wondered if she would answer.

He didn't ask.

"You can have as much to eat as you like," he told her as he bent close to her ear to tell her, wondering how she would react to this unasked-for closeness.

The shiver coursing through her thin frame was a good sign to him. The quivering wasn't from fear. Instead, it was her reaction to the warmth of his breath on her skin. While he wasn't going to rush her, he did want a true marriage. Time would prove to be in his favor. Although he didn't intend to wait forever.

She ate more then, "Thank you. You're very kind. It was delicious. Why did you agree to marry me?"

He paused in thought, setting the comb back in the saddlebag before he answered. "I don't know." He was shaking his head bemused at his spontaneous actions of this evening. "At the time I wondered if I had cobwebs for brains. In the end, I could not bear to see a woman hang for wanting to feed herself." He couldn't tell her how something about her called to him, enchanted him. If he said anything in that vein, she wouldn't believe him.

"A kind heart, do people take advantage of you often?"

She was stroking her hand along Hypatia's back. The little monkey looked asleep, if not that, then content.

"Never," he murmured laughing, watching the way she moved.

She was slim, too slim. After what she'd been through, that was to be expected having spent the last month penned up. He liked the way she carried herself, the way her eyes shimmered in the light cast by the flames. Firelight danced across her face, casting it in shadows one moment, a warm glow the next.

"Confident as well." She sipped at her coffee; her eyes focused on his mouth. "You're a *verra bonnie mon*. I'm sure the ladies tell you that quite often. Do you often have coffee?"

For a moment he forgot to breathe. "Not in those words. Kit and I learned to enjoy the coffee when we were in America. Would you prefer tea?"

"I see."

"Do you?" he questioned wondering how much life experience this young lady had.

Everything about her spoke of innocence yet she didn't voice innocent thoughts. He would feel very foolish if he assumed something that wasn't true. He decided to leave all judgments concerning the lady to the back of his mind after that let time tell the story. She would show her true colors soon enough. He would deal with her as his wife.

"You can call me Pippa. My friends do."

He laughed softly then once more bending close to her neck, "You consider me a friend already? Suppose it's better than being your enemy. What happened to your friends when you were caught?"

He pushed her drying hair to one side. The breath from his words brushed across her nape. He'd like to taste her there. Knew it was too soon.

"A friend in a husband would be nice. I've never thought about a husband except the one I *dinna* want."

This time the shudder he felt against him was not a good sensation as he sensed her fear shuffle into him, become part of him. He didn't understand how he felt her emotions intuitively.

"The one you don't want?" he asked a bit puzzled but willing to wait until she wanted to tell him more. "That wouldn't be me, would it?"

"No, I'm not speaking of you."

"You want me for a husband?"

For some reason he needed that answer to be yes now and for always.

"Yes, considering the alternative," she told him sounding sincere. She turned slanting him a bemused smile. "Truly, dying was not something I was looking forward to."

He was sure she evaded his question then wondered who the alternative husband was. Again, in time she would tell him. Patience should be his friend. Demanding answers now would get him nowhere. "How," he asked, deciding to change the direction of their conversation, "did you end up fending for yourself?"

As she lifted her slim shoulders in a very feminine shrug, the tips of her breasts caught the fabric of his shirt. The rosy crests were dark beneath fine lawn fabric. When she stood to stretch her muscles, the silhouette of her legs and hips were clearly visible. She was made with lush curves, bounty that would fill her very new husband's hands. In time, in time he would reap the benefits of this hasty marriage. She might not be his mate. Even if she wasn't, they would do well together.

"Five years ago..." She sat down again, smoothing the fabric along her legs, pulling it tight against her breasts, "I ran away. Couldn't stay where I was one moment longer." Absently she fed the little monkey pieces of cheese and bread.

"How old were you then?" Mesmerized and fascinated by her he craved more information.

Her hands clasped in front of her, she looked down, her lashes fluttering against her cheekbones. "Fourteen. I was fourteen the day I left. I gathered up a few necessities, took the coin I had in my room then never looked back. I've been on my own since. Of course, the money ran out very soon."

He let the breath he'd been holding out in a loud whoosh. "Fourteen you say?"

The reason must have been drastic. She survived though. Roby found he was proud of her, the tenacity she showed.

"I suppose you'd be wantin' to know why." She looked up at him then, firelight glowing warm across her high cheekbones.

"Whenever you want to tell me. I am your husband. While I probably can't undo all the wrongs that may or may not have been heaped against you, I can always try. My family, the clan, is powerful. Perhaps we can help."

He understood trust was fragile, giving of all her secrets to a man she barely knew would take time.

He was willing to wait however long it took.

"I would like that, Roby McKenna." She waited for a time, staring into the fire. "You spoke of a sister. Are there other siblings?" she asked as she poured herself another cup of coffee.

It seemed she wanted to change the subject again. He couldn't blame her. She already divulged quite a bit about her journey to this place in time. "Just another brother who is married. When I left, his wife was increasing. My sister has one child also. By now they might have more."

"And Kit? What about him and where is he tonight?"

"He's a Stuart. His father married my father's sister. As to his whereabouts," Roby cleared his throat unsure of how much to tell her.

She should remember he went into town. Perhaps she didn't hear.

"Cousins, I gather. You think he's found himself a willing *lass* to spend the evening with? While you are stuck with me, a wife you didn't want, he's dallying in a warm bed."

Again and again, she stunned him with her honesty combined with her knowledge about the ways of men. "Yes, Kit has a way with the ladies. Houston is one of his brothers, the oldest, then Kit and Riley is the baby of the bunch. The youngest would take grave offense if he were to hear any one call him the baby. He's nearly two and twenty."

"I'm an only child. Always wanted a brother or a sister. Guess it wasn't to be. However, I do have a cousin whom I despise, Harry Finchbottom."

A cousin she despised. He guessed there was more to this story also. "I see. Should I feel sorry for you or him?"

She laughed. The sound was low not a high-pitched giggle of most girls. He liked the way she laughed, the sound as well as the tenor. He wanted to hear more laughter.

"I'd like to say most assuredly for him. In two years, I'm hoping that will be *verra* true. Until then it's sorry for me you should be feeling. Except now that I've found you, or more accurately that you found me, perhaps my luck has changed for the better."

"Now that you've survived the hangman's noose and you are clean as well, don't think I'll be feeling sorry for you right now. You've married me. True enough that fact might prove to bring you good fortune."

"I've had food too. You fed me as well as saved my life. I'm *verra* glad you came along, Roby McKenna, arrogant man that you are. Mayhap arrogance in a man is a good quality. I've yet to figure that one out."

"I like to call it self-assurance. Has a better ring to it." Roby was laughing, thoroughly enjoying his wife of a few hours.

He was pleased he came along too. The first fat raindrop fell, hissing and sizzling on the flames. Before the coming deluge could soak them, he finished constructing the shelter he started earlier that they would use tonight, hoping she would not put up a fuss at the sleeping conditions. He was not going to get soaked while he had a tent to share with this lady who seemed to entrance him with her husky voice as well as her body.

"Come." He held out his hand, studying her for any sign of reluctance. "You must be exhausted. Today along with the previous ones must have been trying for you. We should go to bed now. Tomorrow will come soon enough. We've a long way to travel before we reach McKenna territory."

She didn't acknowledge his invitation for a few seconds seeming to mull over his words as well as the tent. He watched her let out a slow puff of air, seeming resigned as she looked from the fire then back to him. "Are you going to stick your rod inside me now? Claim your conjugal rights?"

~ * ~

By the look on Roby's face, she guessed she shocked him to the core. Bluntly honest perhaps was not appropriate with a brand-new husband. He stuffed his hands through his hair as he looked at the full moon still hovering in the sky. Drops of rain splattered and hissed on the hot rocks surrounding the fire pit. Seconds turned into minutes before he answered.

"No, Pippa, not tonight. You've *naught* to worry over."

Her voice deepened as she tried for a calm she truly didn't feel. "I'd just as soon get it over with if you *dinna* mind. Isn't it what husband's do? What they want to do?"

If he did do it tonight, they would be done. She would be his wife in every way. After that, she would no longer fear the marriage bed with him.

"You think I would only want to make love to my wife once? Is that what you're saying?" he asked unremarkably as his gaze seemed to fasten on her lips then her bosom.

Once more he sounded shocked to his very core by her blatant but very necessary honesty. She meant to proceed this way in everything.

She nodded while she looked at her feet. "Isn't once enough?" she asked still moving one foot around in circles.

She knew she changed from the confident woman of a few seconds ago to shy. Her voice shaking, she asked, "Are you telling me you would want to do it more than one time?"

His grin unnerved her to the tips of her toes, his even teeth flashing white in the moonlight catching more light from the dying fire. She was pleased they weren't yellowed and rotten. "Once with the right woman, one's wife, is never enough. Ah, Pippa, once we do make love you will want to do it with me all the time. You will ask me to take your warm body into my arms to fill you with my shaft as well as my seed."

She felt the color drain from her face. "I *dinna* think that will be true, Roby McKenna. Don't know what would make you think something so preposterous." Just the way he smiled, the way his gaze lingered on her eyes then swept slowly the length of her clear to her toes unnerved her, heating her to an inferno. She smoothed the shirt she wore. Curled her toes in the grass.

"What crazy notions you have. Who made you think making love was something to do only once with one's husband?" he asked stepping so close to her she felt the heat radiating from his all-male body. He smelled of the same lye soap she'd used coupled with himself.

He was rubbing tiny circles with his thumb on the underside of her wrist. The strange contact sent spirals of heat coursing through her. A strange ache simmered between her legs. She didn't understand any of this. "*Ye* should not be doing that. It's not seemly." Her voice shook.

"It is very appropriate with one's wife." He brought her hand to his lips, kissed each knuckle before turning it over and pressing a tender kiss to her palm. "We shall go to sleep now. I promise you I won't stick my rod inside you tonight, hmm... You've nothing to worry about."

"Are you a *mon* who keeps his word?"

"*Aye*, come along now."

She nodded, unable to think of anything to say at that. She wasn't at all sure if she was relieved or disappointed in what he told her. Roby McKenna was nothing like Harry Finchbottom in face or form. Perhaps the act would not be as repulsive as she previously thought it would be. She would have to give the idea some consideration.

He let her go inside first. As she bent over, she was very aware of the shirt creeping up her bare legs. She tugged on the tails as she crawled inside, hoping to keep a tiny bit of modesty. It was all to no avail when she heard his words from behind her.

"You've very nice legs, long and slender. Your bottom is quite nice too," he told her, his voice so soft and throaty it sounded unnatural to her.

Heat flared on her face, on all of her body. She wanted to tell him his legs were nice, too, but she hadn't seen them without his trousers. Perhaps they weren't as nice as she imagined them to be. She realized she would like to do just that.

Look at his naked legs.

More heat. More funny sensations spiraled through her. *I am a foolish ninny to be thinking things such as this.*

Once she was settled, he crept inside followed by Hypatia who settled in a far corner as if she understood that would be her new place. She pulled the covers to her chin, felt him settle beneath them also. Next to her, so close she fought for each breath, he felt big and hot. She liked the sensation. He made her feel safe. Pippa wasn't at all sure how she was going to manage to fall asleep. Heat from his large well-muscled manly frame so close to hers was overwhelming all her senses. She didn't contemplate why.

His arm wrapped around her as he pulled her even closer. "Hush, don't protest. I won't hurt you. Relax and fall asleep. If I hold you, we'll both be warmer."

Her voice was a hushed tremble deep and low. "I don't see how a girl can sleep with you lying there all big and…" she gulped tiny bits of air. "You're not wearing your shirt."

He laughed softly as she felt his warm breath sweep across her cheek. "I am making concessions for you along with your tender sensibilities. I don't sleep in my trousers either. For you I'm wearing them."

She was on her side, spooned up tight against him, her thoughts a hazy muddle of confusion in her head. Afraid but liking the way she felt so close to him, she pushed back against him, feeling the length of his legs against hers. At the intimate contact, his big hand tightened on her waist, his fingers pressing into her. She closed her eyes. Listened to the patter of the rain on the canvas of the tent while she tried to tamp down the unnatural feelings that were zooming through her at a wild and reckless pace.

Heard more night sounds.

Listened to the wind.

This was the first time in so very long that she slept near to someone other than by herself. The fear was always so close and clear that it always cramped her stomach. She never knew what would happen to her during the night, nights at times that seemed to last an eternity. She always said silent prayers that the sun would rise. When it did, she would still be the same Pippa.

Not much time passed before she felt Roby relax. The hand holding her body so close to his no longer stroked her. She wondered if she could go to sleep now that he seemed to be sleeping soundly. Wondered what the next days and months would bring. She should tell him that he should be afraid for his life now that he was her husband. If her cousin ever discovered she was alive and wed to someone else, he would act to change both those facts. While Harry would not kill her right away, he would certainly see to it after he forced a marriage between them after he inherited all that was hers. That fact meant that Roby could not continue to live.

She had a lot of telling to do.

Guilt battered her as she recalled everything.

A man like Roby McKenna deserved to know what he would be facing since he made that fatal leap of marriage to a woman awaiting death. Nothing for her changed. She still awaited death, this time at the hands of her cousin instead of the hangman. For her savior's sake she should not have agreed to the marriage.

She should not have divulged the private information about his rod either. He would think she was a hussy or worse. What was worse than a hussy? She didn't know. Truth of the matter was that Harry told her he was going to do that to her until she was increasing. When it happened, she would have to marry him. What Harry didn't know was that nothing he did to her would make her wed him.

He was a vile, loathsome man.

From the bottom of my heart, I despise you, Harry Finchbottom.

Pippa didn't want to think about Harry using Robby against her, to make her succumb to his plans. Not understanding exactly what was happening, she wriggled against the man behind her, pressing against him for the warmth he so sweetly offered. She discovered he was clasping her tightly, squeezing her waist. He was still breathing deeply, still sleeping. Could men do that in their sleep? The warmth of his fingers moved up her ribcage then downward to caress and squeeze her hip. Without thought, she pushed back against him one more time, felt something hard against her bottom.

Closing her eyes, she tried to put the strange and wondrous new feelings she was experiencing to the back of her head. Now he was trailing a fingertip along her arm then back down. A tiny unexpected sound rippled up from deep inside of her. To no avail, she tried to reposition herself so she wasn't as close to him. His breath tickled the back of her neck just before the palm of his hands brushed across the tip of one breast.

"Roby, what are you doing?" she asked the question even though she was sure he was still asleep.

"Sleeping," he whispered and once again the warmth of his breath whispered across the nape of her neck sending a myriad of shivers up then down her spine only to settle and throb deep in her most feminine parts.

"No, you're not."

"Go to sleep, Pippa. Morning is going to come soon enough. Don't want you falling off my horse because you're too exhausted to do anything else."

"You go to sleep too," she whispered as he once again pulled her closer, his large leg covered hers.

She found herself well and truly pinned against the man. *Baw* he told her, promised her he wasn't going to stick his rod inside her tonight. What did he think to be doing at this time? Everything felt wondrous and unique to her. Truth be told, she didn't want him to stop.

"I'm sleeping now," he murmured against her ear just before his teeth tugged on the lobe nearly sending her jumping out of her skin.

"You're making me very hot."

"Hot is good. You can sleep better if you're warm."

His hand cupped her breast, his thumb rubbing lightly across the hardened tip.

"I cannot sleep if you keep doing those things to my body. I *dinna ken* what you're about, but you need to stop."

The long whoosh of air coupled with a groan that sounded as if he was in pain surprised her. Her words stopped him from doing whatever it was he was doing. His hand settled on the rise of her hip but didn't move again.

She wished he hadn't stopped. Now she was hot and wet as well as unable to fall asleep, the sensations in her body were so strong, pulsing and throbbing. She wished he would touch her more. Liked what he'd been doing. Pippa decided she would tell him as much tomorrow morning as soon as she found the chance to do so.

When she woke, the sun was shining. She found she was alone under the tent. Even Hypatia had abandoned her. Kit's and Roby's voices she heard outside. She couldn't quite hear what they were saying, just heard the warm rumble of men's voices she wasn't afraid of. Fearing Roby McKenna was just not possible. Not when she liked him so much. As she also trusted him, she understood he would look after her.

He saved her.

She owed him.

Unsure of Kit, however, she decided to watch him closely, needed to take the measure of the man before she acknowledged him as she did Roby. The tread of boots on the ground neared her sleeping space. She looked up when the flap opened.

"Good, you're awake. Did you sleep well?" he asked his grin wide as if he remembered the way he touched her. She certainly did. She wanted more of the same.

"I did after you stopped tormenting me," she said looking up into his handsome face and hearing the soft chuckle humming from the back of his throat.

Suddenly, she recalled she was lying. Before she slept, she wished for him to caress her more. She heard her little friend's chatter behind him.

"Torment?" he queried lifting one of his marvelous black brows into a perfect arch above gray eyes that shimmered molten steel. "You cannot fool me. I heard the soft little sighs of pleasure leaving your lips. The sound was a gift I'll never forget. It was our wedding night after all. A husband couldn't ask for more."

"Was that pleasure you were gifting me with?"

She caught her bottom lip between her teeth. She'd heard such things could happen. She'd also heard of the pain of being forced. Pippa supposed she'd been lucky over the last five years.

Until she'd been caught with the rabbit.

His chuckle was warm, all-knowing. "You know it was."

He handed her the clothing Kit brought for her. "You can dress in these. He wasn't able to purchase a dress. However, the pants and shirt will have to do for now. As soon as you're dressed, come get something to eat and drink."

"Will there be more of that pleasure stuff tonight?" she asked then immediately thought she should not have done so when she saw the expression on his face.

The shock turned to a wide grin, immediately relieving her of the notion that she was a foolish woman for saying something so forward.

"If you ask, you shall receive."

With more laughter following him, he left, the flap falling into place as she picked up the clothing to examine the pieces. He brought a shirt and trousers for her then apologized. What he didn't know was that shirts and trousers were her preferred form of clothing. She was pretty sure she hadn't worn a dress since the day before she left her home.

Inside the tent she scrambled to rid herself of his shirt then quickly donned the clothing he gave her. When she stepped outside, the air was brisk. She ran her hands along her arms in a feeble attempt to warm herself. The coffee smelled good, the bacon sizzling on the campfire even better. She couldn't remember when she had two meals so close together.

A few minutes later she joined the two men. "I'm in heaven," she murmured as she sipped her first cup of coffee while she chewed on a piece of crispy bacon, in her mind cooked to perfection. "Such bounty, I forgot normal people eat more than every couple of days. Thank you,

Roby McKenna."

"You don't have to keep thanking me." He looked from his plate of food to stare into her eyes. "I do believe I'm going to be the biggest benefactor in this relationship of ours. You enthrall me, please me very much." He brushed her cheek with the back of his knuckles.

"How so?" Kit asked still seeming displeased over what happened last evening in the moonlit night. "You need more than just sex for a marriage to work."

Pippa saw that Roby sent his cousin a blistering glance. "You know nothing of our relationship, Kit Stuart. I trust you to keep a civil tongue around my wife."

The air she inhaled punched her throat. For several seconds she looked away, trying not to retaliate with words that would serve only to hurt Roby. She would never want that even though his cousin didn't seem to care. The man was too quick to judge. She set her plate down suddenly, not quite so hungry.

"Don't let Kit get to you, Pippa. He's only trying to look out for me. He has only good intentions. Don't you, Kit? Now, before we leave here, I want you to eat everything on your plate. I didn't fill it so full as to give you too much. I *ken* you haven't eaten much for the last five years." He slanted a pointed look toward his cousin.

She did try to eat and managed most of the food even though it had lost the marvelous taste it should have had. Actually, the food tasted of sawdust.

It was another half hour before they were riding again. Once more she sat in front of Roby. Kit rode ahead as if he meant to give them privacy. She wasn't all that sure what she needed privacy for, but it was nice to have her new husband all to herself. Hypatia swung from tree branch to tree branch until seemingly tired she settled on Roby's shoulder.

Finally able to relax, she leaned against Roby's broad chest. "Ah, *lass* take this time for more rest. If you fall asleep, I'll make sure you don't fall off."

She turned slightly, looking up at him. "You have silver eyes that are rimmed with light blue. They are striking." There were several blank seconds then, "Your lashes are far too long for a man. 'Tis not fair."

"You, my sweet wife, possess the most beguiling green eyes with golden flecks I've ever seen. Last night when I..." he cleared his throat as if thinking better of what he meant to say, "When I first looked at your face, I wondered what color they were as I wondered at the color of your hair. Chestnut, I would say. Delightful. Very lovely."

"Flatterer," she murmured as she wondered why he was being so sweet to her.

They rode in silence for a while, Pippa trying to decide what part of her life she should tell Roby first. She could hardly blurt out everything all at once. Yet she had to find someplace to start. Not wanting to travel over ground she already walked on, she remained silent.

It was a few minutes after she decided she would start by explaining why she ran away when his hand brushed across her nipple. Just as it had last night, the caress sent unbelievable sensations raging straight to her core, in that secret part of her between her legs, at the juncture of her thighs. She gasped in a gulp of air as his fingers pinched lightly. As he switched his attention to her other breast, she pushed back against him, feeling that same hard part of him as she felt last night. She knew what it was as well as what it meant because Harry took great delight in embarrassing her and taunting her with his rod. While he never raped her, she understood if she stayed where he could get at her for much longer, he would force her.

So, she did the only thing she could do.

She left.

Pippa let her head fall against his chest. His lips made tiny forays down her neck, sipping and nibbling. She turned her head toward him. His lips swept so very lightly against hers she wasn't at all sure they made contact. Now, she understood he was kissing her as his tongue touched her bottom lip, moved lightly across it.

"I find I cannot keep my hands to myself," he murmured beside her ear so only she could hear.

"You are a devil and a bad *mon*, Roby McKenna," she said softly as he continued the exploration that made her want more. Told her she needed something else even while she didn't have the foggiest notion what that something else was.

"How can I be a bad man for giving my wife pleasure, for watching her eyes simmer with the passion she wants to bestow on me?"

"I *dinna ken* any of this. Don't understand what you're speaking of." She did understand that she liked all the delicious raw feelings he generated in her. "All I know is that I don't want you to stop."

He pulled his hand away when Kit turned to ride back to them. "Did you want to bypass Glasgow or go into the city to get her more clothes?"

"What do you think, Pippa? Would you be more comfortable wearing a dress?" he asked, as he seemed to be staring at her mouth.

The kiss they shared was brief and so *verra* hot. She wanted more and wished Kit to leave them alone again.

She swept her tongue across her bottom lip as his hand tightened at her waist before creeping just a bit higher to rest beneath her breast. Pippa didn't understand why every contact with this man sent her senses reeling.

"I'm fine with what I'm wearing. You did say there is one change of clothing. That is more than I'm used to."

It wasn't entirely true. During her stay with the gypsies, she'd wanted for nothing, even companionship. She'd thought herself in love. Now she knew what she felt for the boy, Aaron Rosmara, was temporary infatuation. With time the feeling would have faded. She would have to tell Roby about him as well as the few kisses they shared.

"When we reach home, you're going to get used to more, much, much more. I will bring the modiste from the village to fit you," he murmured close to her ear again, lightly grazing the tip with his teeth. "I want to give you anything your heart desires."

Kit let out a snort that to her ears was one of disgust. She stiffened realizing Kit knew exactly what his cousin was about. Roby chuckled sending waves of shivers down her arms. He was wicked, seemed to love to torment her in his devil's own way.

The next village is about two hours away. We can stop early or we can spend the night on the ground," Kit said, waiting impatiently for an answer.

It was abundantly clear he meant to ride ahead as well as out of hearing range of any conversation they might have. That was fine with her. Kit had a way of disarming her, making her uncomfortable in her skin. While Pippa understood Kit's obvious contempt surrounding her, he shouldn't take his feelings out on his cousin.

"Let's stay at the inn. If I recall correctly, it's the Drum and Ox, a pleasant place, clean with good food. I for one would like to sleep on a bed with my new wife beside me," he taunted his cousin while his hand settled firmly on her waist.

He was sending her a message. While she couldn't fathom why or what it meant, she set the question aside for the time being.

She watched. She assumed Roby observed Kit as he spurred his horse faster. "Will he come back do you think?"

"As soon as he's worked off some of the anger he's feeling. As of yet, he hasn't come to terms with our marriage. In time he will." Roby allowed a long hiss of air to escape from his lungs. "I'm sorry for how he's acting and all. You deserve to be treated better. You've done nothing wrong."

"I assume it's because you married a convicted criminal to save her from death that he is in such a bad simmer," she spoke softly understanding the words had to be said.

"No."

"Then why?"

"Because the two of us spent the better part of two years looking for our soul mates. We left the highlands to do so. Neither one of us was successful in that endeavor then out of the blue I decide to wed someone I've never spoken to. Speak o' the devil, the lass is a highlander. I had to come home to find my eternal woman. What he doesn't understand is that there is a strange and unique connection between the two of us. A bond I would like to come to understand better. I've a mind to believe you might indeed be that soul mate I've been searching the world for."

"Oh." It was her turn to be shocked.

Searching the world?

"Is that all you've got to say now that I've laid all my thoughts bare for you to demolish if you so choose?" He laughed then and pulled her close, teasing her with his male arrogance taking liberties that were best left to private intimate settings.

"I feel a connection of sorts with you too." She lowered her lashes, staring at his big hand that still held one of her breasts inside it. "I've never truly been close to a man before but everywhere you touch me, I want you to never stop." This was when she should mention Aaron Rosmara, tell him about the few kisses he stole.

"You have the most bountiful breasts. I want to stroke them, tease and taunt them until the tips harden into tight buds. More than anything I have this incessant urge that I cannot rid myself of to suck them deep into my mouth until you cry out in ecstasy."

Truly, he was the devil's own spawn. She swallowed the lump in her throat so she could speak. Still had trouble saying the words. "What would you say if I was so brazen as to tell you that I want the same?" She paused to garner more courage to tell him honestly how she felt. "I would like to know how that would feel."

"I would tell you we can't get to that inn fast enough."

She sat up straighter, touched his forearm, marveling in its width, in the hard muscles her fingers surrounded. She tried to pull it away before she sighed softly before giving up. "We've things we should talk about before we carry this any farther. You might not want to stay married to me if you know the truth about my past. Kit might well be correct in his assumption that I'm using you because I am. We both understand that fact. The difference is that you don't *ken* why."

~ * ~

"What does the letter say?" Wynnie asked impatiently as she paced the main room in the north tower where she and Connal had lived for the past thirty years. She was impatient to see her son again. He'd been away for two long years. They both missed him, were eager to tell him of all that transpired as well as hear all about his adventure in America.

"Says if all goes well, he'll be home in two weeks," Connal said as he set the letter on the table so he could pull his wife into his arms.

He kissed her quickly as she pushed away from him knowing all too well the conversation would end if she allowed him to have his way

27

with her. It always did. "*Ye* are too impatient, lady of my heart, my eternal love. Our son will be home soon enough, aggravating us as he always manages to do."

"Did he say if he found his mate?" she queried allowing Connal to hold her close to him again, trusting he would take this no farther while they still had things to talk about.

She set her head on his chest, heard the steady beat of his heart against her cheek. The sound was wonderful to her. The years with Connal had been good ones. Now, she was eager to see her son fulfilled, to find his mate, to sire children.

"Says neither he nor Kit found someone they can call their eternal love. It seems my meeting with you so soon in my adult life proved me to be a lucky man. If you had not been running for your *verra* life, you would *nay* have run into my arms."

"You were a *verra* bad man then, Connal McKenna. First, you threatened to lock me away in a tower prison with mice as my companions. When that wasn't going to work for you, I found myself locked in your chambers with a different kind of rat to contend with."

"You wound me, Madam." Instead of placing his hand on his heart, he cupped her breast in his hand with obvious intentions.

He was not satisfied. Lightly and oh so tenderly, Connal brushed his mouth across hers, nibbling at the corners then sweeping his tongue across her bottom lip urging her to open for him. She met his with her own, touched the tip then explored the dark warm recess inside that which he offered.

His hand closed more tightly over her breast, stroking the sensitive underside through the fabric of her gown. Teasing and coaxing her to his will. It never took much wheedling for him to get his way. They both paused for breath.

"I'm sorry to hear the news. The boys had high expectations when they left."

They all understood they journeyed from the highlands with more than one reason. It was no longer safe for any of the clan to shift and run wild among the heather. For young men freedom is a heady notion. One that can only be *coshed* with time.

"Wynnie, they wanted adventure along with their freedom probably more so than the idea of finding their mates. I suppose they needed to find out what kind of men they were. Those two could not do that here where everything they wanted was given to them."

She hit him on the shoulder. "Are you telling me I spoiled my son?"

"Along with your daughter and other son. I'm as much to blame as you. We both adored them, needed them to have everything they wished for. The journey was good for both men. I'm certain of that. They will come back wiser and braver than when they left."

"Are you now? So sure of yourself?" she asked looking to the bed and perhaps a small dalliance before they went downstairs for their evening meal. She would be amenable if he showed her that he wanted her other than the swift kiss they just shared.

"I am just as sure as the fact that I should carry you to our bed. No, on second thought now I take a few seconds to reconsider," he stopped talking for a few moments. "I've the urge to make love to my wife on the soft fur rug in front of the fire."

"You would be making assumptions. What makes you think I would be amenable to such a situation, Laird McKenna?" She laughed as he further explored her, sucked in air when he found more tender sensitive places. "You're a bold one."

"You adore my boldness."

"*Aye.*"

With the tip of his finger, he touched her nose then kissed the same spot. "By the wild passion I see simmering in the crystal-clear depth of your eyes, I know for a fact you are wanting me. By the way your pulse is thundering right here where my thumb rests so I can tell what your body is saying to mine, I know your body is weeping for me. I *ken* you want me just as I *ken* I want you." He told her as he swept her into his arms, his mouth pressed gently against hers.

"Love me, Connal McKenna, as you always do."

"I will *lass.* After that, we'll think of our son and pray for his safe return."

Chapter Two

"As to why you ran away?" he asked, wishing the past was not obviously an integral part of what he believed would be their future. Perhaps that fact was true of all couples. The past fashioned every person into who they are now. "I would that you tell me about what happened to you, at least as much as you feel comfortable revealing. Sometimes, I'm a patient man. Sometimes, I am not."

"You deserve to learn everything about that time of my life. By rescuing me from the gallows you put your life in danger. I'm figuring that you also put your family in danger too. From what you tell me, they will be willing to fight for me. Perhaps," she stopped to think further on what she meant to say, "perhaps not Kit. He's formed his opinion of me. That opinion is not good. For the moment, nothing will change his mind. I don't know how. I will have to prove myself to him."

"Why is that?" he asked as he set his chin on her forehead, pondering what she told him.

He understood Kit's reticence, prayed the rest of the family would not formulate the same misgivings when her full story was revealed to them.

They still had over an hour to go before they reached the Drum and Ox Inn and Tavern. He contemplated her statement figuring it was a dire situation that had caused her to flee. She had courage or perhaps there was more fear driving her that day. He also wondered if flight had anything to do with the alternate man who might have become her husband.

Surely not at fourteen.

Men did wed women that young but never for a good reason.

Hence, he could only assume it was for a bad reason. Assumptions were usually dangerous.

"Harry Finchbottom," she said softly. "My cousin along with his parents coveted my estate, my inheritance. They meant to take everything away from me. I couldn't allow that to happen."

"Was their no last will and testament?"

"There was," she murmured, speaking so softly he had to bend closer to hear, "but my parents neglected to name a guardian." She was looking at her hands as they fisted in her lap. "I believe they would have named Connal McKenna guardian. Our families were not close but father talked about him as a good man. He just didn't get around to cementing that proposition."

"My father? As your guardian? That would have made this arrangement of ours awkward. I'm assuming your parents were no longer with you at the time," he spoke softly as he tried to fill in any pieces of this tale that she wasn't explaining.

He figured he would have to do all of that before they got to the bottom of her difficulties.

"As they didn't believe they would perish so soon, no they didn't name a guardian. It was an accident that took them in their prime. Took their lives before it was their time."

"Was it really an accident or one staged to appear as an unlucky mishap resulting in your parents' death?"

He'd heard of such things, vaguely remembered hearing of the MacPhersons and their loss of life. The story did not concern him, so he paid little attention. His gut instinct at the time had been to question the validity of such a thing. It seemed contrived. He well recalled the family that descended on the MacPherson manor, taking over the running of the estate. Some of the crofters moved to McKenna land asking if they could work for Laird McKenna instead of the MacPhersons.

"I don't know." Lifting her slim shoulders a dejected look turned her mouth downward, "Grief took away all rational thought from my mind. Mourning their loss, I walked around in a stupor as the Finchbottoms slowly took over everything in my life. I had no say in anything concerning me."

"So, you had no guardian named in the will."

He tried to clarify all she said in his mind. What a dastardly mistake. Parents could be so dumb never thinking their precious daughter would reap the misfortune from their neglect.

"They were not my lawful guardians. In any case they assumed the title in lieu of my parents overlooking that part in their will. My parents would have never named them. Father despised his younger brother who was a wastrel, a gambler at heart. Perhaps there had been love between them once. For me, when mother and father died any love that might have existed for them was gone."

"I believe I'm beginning to understand more than you've actually explained to me. Do go on."

Hoping to hear more of her story he waited as he remembered other encounters from his past. There was more here than either one of them comprehended.

She closed her eyes though, leaning against him. To Roby it appeared she was finished speaking for the time being. When he urged the big stallion, he rode a bit faster. He felt her breasts against his hand as they bounced, enticingly brushing his arm giving him good reason to dream of other delights. Just as he enjoyed everything about Pippa, he enjoyed the feel of her bountiful breasts along with the way they swayed as he watched. Once they were closer to Kit, he slowed his horse, walking the animal.

Only a few minutes later, she spoke, "Harry and my guardian decided that he should marry me. That way the inheritance would legally fall into their hands. Until I turned twenty-one, they would control everything."

"He was the alternate husband?" he asked glad that she felt ready to reveal more of her story. When she turned once more to look at him, her lips were full as well as moist. He wanted to kiss her again, mate his tongue with hers. There would be plenty of time for that.

Her small body shuddered against him. All of her was small except for her abundant bubbies. Keeping his hands to himself was becoming more difficult with each passing mile. Of course, he wasn't exactly keeping his hands to himself. He was, in his mind, exhibiting tremendous restraint especially in lieu of the fact she told him she liked what he was doing.

"Harry Finchbottom was supposed to become my husband. As far as the three of them were concerned the sooner the wedding took place the better. Harry didn't want to wait at all."

"You were only fourteen." *Barely able to reproduce.*

He didn't like the direction his thoughts were taking. He couldn't imagine a fourteen-year-old, scarcely a woman, *nay*, not a woman at all but still a child beneath a rutting bastard such as Harry Finchbottom. If he was ever sure of anything in his life, her cousin was indeed a rutting bastard who had no problem forcing a young girl out of greed for what was not his.

"This is true."

Her breath whispered from her lips, the same lips he wanted to kiss only a few seconds past while he condemned another man for coveting her. There was a difference in this, he reminded himself.

"He didn't want to wait for what he sought, planned on taking me with or without benefit of marriage since he understood I would refuse him at the altar."

"How old is your cousin Harry?"

The thought of some lecherous old man forcing this sweet woman a child left him scarred from the inside out. Brilliantly if not at grave danger to herself, she weathered the storm.

"Five years ago, he was three and twenty. I'm tired," she spoke softly clearly indicating she was ending the conversation for now.

"One more question if you're not overtired. While I'm thinking of it."

Not that he would ever forget her question she asked just before they went to bed last night.

"Can't guarantee I'll answer it."

"No, if you wish to wait, you may. I was just wondering if this Harry Finchbottom is the man who told you he would stick his rod inside you."

There he asked the question he knew the answer to. He wanted to hear her tell him that what he thought was true. While he waited for the answer, his fist tightened around the reins he was holding, the other around her waist.

"He is and he's the reason I fled, looking over my shoulder as I ran, sure that he would know where I was and find me. Told me he would come to me that night. What choice did I have?"

With that said, she fell silent, resting her slim shoulders against his chest.

After they reached McKenna land and were settled, he would take Kit or perhaps Brady if Kit wasn't willing, for a visit to see this man, this Harry Finchbottom. Taking full measure of the man was high on his list of things he would do to set everything right for Pippa.

Roby knew the moment Pippa fell asleep. Her body molded against his, fit his to perfection. They were made for each other, two peas in a single pod. Another half hour and they would arrive at their destination.

Harry Finchbottom, what to do about the man? He could hardly murder him, for words spoken five years ago. Although, he'd like to do just that. The Finchbottoms probably spent as much of her inheritance as they could legally get their hands on. If he had his way, they would pay every groat they spent, so far, back to Pippa.

If he understood all Pippa told him, Harry, when he discovered the marriage, would plan to kill him. For the second part, he would marry Phillipa before he got rid of her also. That, he decided, summed the scenario up nicely to the benefit of the Finchbottoms. Well, he wasn't planning on getting murdered nor was it in his plans to leave Pippa's holdings to these scoundrels.

When Kit discovered Pippa asleep, he let Roby catch up to him. For the next few miles, they rode in silence taking full measure of each other. Roby searched his mind for words to convince Kit of Pippa's true character, could find none that would do the job. He figured the convincing would come with the passage of time.

The sky darkened. A storm was brewing, would divulge itself with the evening. By the look of it, there would be wind and rain, perhaps even thunder and lightning. He was glad they decided to stop at the inn. Braving the elements and risking Pippa's health was not high on his list of priorities. Tonight, he wanted her snuggled against him. She needed to sleep with no worries. He meant to give her that element most people took for granted. Last night he'd been left with no other choice but to sleep on the ground. He could hardly take her to an inn the way she appeared, good God the way she smelled.

"You seem pleased with yourself," Kit said as he seemed to study him with dark brows furrowed together, his silver toned gaze searching him for truths. "You think she's the one for you?"

Roby let his breath out slowly. *Yes.* "Possibly." He didn't intend to say too much too soon. "Do you recall how my father met Wynnie? It was a coincidence just as this was."

"Heard the stories from my *dah.*"

"As did I. The meeting was chance if you recall. Neither one was looking for or expecting to find their mate that dark night in late October. It did take Connal a few hours to come to the realization Wynnie was for him, only him. He acted. He wed her quickly so she couldn't escape or be taken from him."

"I hardly think this is the same thing," Kit said, the sarcasm in his voice couldn't be missed.

"You're right this is different. Pippa and I are different people. This story is mine to tell. I don't understand why I feel as I do, but we..." he stopped to figure out the right words to explain, "I feel as if I've known her all my life. At first, I doubted. My mind and heart were crying out to save her. If I didn't, I understood that I would regret doing nothing for the rest of my life."

"You were an impulsive fool," Kit said some laughter in his voice, as if he was beginning to understand what drove him.

He tightened his hand circling her waist. "Aye, I am a blind fool where Pippa is concerned. She will run me around her little finger if I allow her to do so. However," he held up his hand to stop Kit's next words, "it will please me to give her whatever she so desires."

"She is using you," Kit said.

"Yes, she is. So far, she has told me everything I've asked of her. "Perhaps I am using her too."

"Not possible."

"Oh, but it is. She's innocent, a virgin. I'm taking advantage of her every opportunity that presents itself. I've teased her with gentle coaxing to give me whatever I ask of her."

"Under the circumstances of your meeting, what you're telling me is impossible. Since you obviously, at least from what you haven't said, didn't have a wedding night. So, your coaxing lacks your usual charm and tenacity."

Very softly, "We did of sorts. I don't yet consider us wed in the way of the clan, so no." Oh, he did recall every tiny sigh, the soft curves she allowed him to explore. There would be more exploration tonight. If all went as he planned, he would teach her how to kiss her husband. As he did that, she would teach him all that pleased her.

"Take the devil, what's that supposed to mean? A wedding night of sorts?" Two dark brows formed flawless arches.

Roby grinned at his favorite cousin as he eased his hand along Pippa's waist. He wasn't about to divulge secrets, their secrets. She moaned softly once more nestling in as close as she could get to his body, trusting him explicitly.

"Private?"

"Very private. When we arrive at the Drum and Ox, I want to be left alone with Pippa. She's exhausted. I'm certain the hasty bath in the cold water was far from satisfactory for her. I suppose you will wish to find a willing lass to share your bed as well as the evening with."

"We will part ways at the inn at least until the morning. What do you think your mother and father are going to think of your new wife when they hear the story of your acquaintance and marriage? A woman sentenced to hang?" He ended with the pointed barb.

"They will understand I had no choice in the matter." *No choice.* "Father would have done anything in his power to rescue mother from the clutches of her father. In fact, we both *ken* he did wed her before he knew for certain they were destined to be together. His soul mission was to protect Wynnie."

I will protect you with my life.

"When you discover your mate, Kit, you will *ken* what the rest of us comprehend to be true. The feelings surrounding you and your life

36

partner are more instinct than knowledge. There was no way I could have walked away from her. Nor will I ever."

Kit waved his hand in a certain manner of disdain appearing certain he had cobwebs for brains. He didn't. No, he was a man falling in love, deeply in love if he didn't miss his guess. Kit would know the feelings sometime when he least expected it. That thought blindsided him. Finding one's mate seemed to work out that way, at least for the McKennas, Stuarts as well. Kit's own mother and father lived in the same proximity for years. One day, the same day Connal discovered Wynnie, Alistair and Brenna realized they were mates. So they could sleep together that night, they handfasted. Houston, Kit's older brother was conceived very soon if not that first time.

As the day passed, the wind seemed to pick up speed. The storm brewed on the horizon. Little whirls of dust danced around them. Clouds grew to enormous sizes as the tops reached higher and higher toward the heavens. Without saying anything they increased the tempo. Pippa seemed to realize what was happening too.

She woke.

Yawned.

Stretched. She felt altogether too pleasant against him. In response his male parts hardened in anticipation of nicer moments to come. Her silent invitation to him was sweet. During the hours she slept his hand slipped beneath the shirt she wore. His fingers were pressed against her bare flesh. She didn't seem to notice. If she did, she didn't object.

I like the way you touch me.

Are you going to put your rod inside me?

Oh, how I'd like to do just that.

He hoped she would continue to tell him exactly what she thought as well as how she was feeling. He never met a woman who was so honest that it stole his breath. Honesty would go so very far in building their happiness. He moved his hand up then down her belly, hoping she would acknowledge his presence there.

"You are making me hot again, Roby McKenna, but you know that don't you? You wicked man."

Kit cleared his throat before riding on ahead of them. Perhaps she should temper those thoughts for when it was just the two of them.

With his thumb beneath her chin, he turned her head. "Did you embarrass yourself?"

"*Aye,* I blurted what was on my mind without paying attention to who would hear. I was thinking only of you and me along with your hand where it shouldn't be."

"Kiss me," he whispered as he bent to touch her mouth with his.

The sensation was hot and sweet. She learned to use her tongue. He groaned when she moved her warmth across his lips then hesitantly sought entrance. Opening for her, he yearned to see how she would proceed.

Pippa did not fail.

He taught her well.

She kissed him deep and long and hot until he ran his fingers through her hair then kissed her back, taking over the kiss. His hands supported her. His fingers sought the tips of her breasts, touching, caressing until the tiny whimper he looked for rippled from her mouth in intoxicating streams into his.

"Please," she whispered as he drew away for a moment so they could both breathe.

"Please what?" he chuckled softly as he stole her lips one more time to spread more sweet hot sensations through her.

She punched his shoulder just before her fingers wound into his hair, just before her body melted into his. He groaned his joy, his awareness that she would soon be entirely his.

He pressed his lips against the pulse on her slim white neck, the place where the throbbing of her heart beat rapidly, wildly impatient for more of this sweetness.

She punched him again. "I don't know but I would be willing to bet that you do."

"You're quite surprising."

"As are you. I never thought a person could do such things while riding a horse. I would think we should both have fallen off by now."

"I imagine we could experiment. See what else could be accomplished."

His mind unraveled with possibilities that could not happen until he completely made her his.

"Suppose you could but not with me," she told him tartly while her nimble fingers caressed the back of his neck.

"*Och, dinna* say you want me to do these things with a woman other than my wife."

"I didn't mean that."

He kissed her one more time, not a gentle slow kiss but a hard fast one that aroused him nearly as much as the earlier kiss.

Roby pulled away grinning like a besotted fool as he absorbed the hungry passion he read in her ever-darkening green eyes as well as the blush painted hotly on her cheeks "What you're asking for is best accomplished in private. We're almost to the inn. I'll teach you more about the carnal delights a man can gift his wife. Within his arms he turned her yet he didn't remove his hand from her breast until they were nearly at the inn.

With great reluctance he helped her adjust the clothing he trifled with so he could reach his ultimate goal.

"There you go. You're as good as new." Now, his entire forearm possessively fastened her to his chest as he galloped the rest of the way to the inn. Her breasts bouncing against him so thoroughly, she placed her hands on them in what seemed to him an effort to hold them still.

"Does it hurt?" he asked curiously.

"Does what hurt?"

"The way your breasts bounce."

Her gasp surprised him as he thought he might have embarrassed her with the question.

"*Aye.*"

"Then we will take this at a more leisurely pace," he told her as he slowed his big stallion.

When he pulled up in front of the inn, Kit was waiting for them. Quickly dismounting, he helped Pippa, holding onto her for a few seconds, his hands cupping her rounded bottom before he allowed her feet to touch ground.

"You are a wicked man, Roby McKenna as well you *ken*."

She was breathless. Her words sweet to his ears because he understood what he did pleased her. By the look in her eyes, his touches satisfied her a great deal.

"Only around you, my saucy wife."

He took her hand in his, placing it on his arm as he ushered her up the steps to the building.

Inside, a huge fireplace took up a major portion of a wall in the main room. Delicious smells wafted from the kitchen. He heard her stomach growl. While they ate a fairly large breakfast, they had nothing to satisfy their hunger since. He was famished but he wasn't sure if the hunger was more for a delightful interlude with his wife than for the aroma's filling his nostrils.

The innkeeper greeted them. As they stepped farther inside, "Two rooms for the night?"

"Yes, for mine and my wife's we'd like a hot bath immediately along with the best Bordeaux you have in your wine cellar. In about an hour send up whatever you are serving for dinner. We'll be ready by then."

The man led the way up the stairs then down a hallway. Kit's room was next to theirs.

"I will see the two of you in the morning," Kit said before disappearing inside.

"What will he do?" Pippa asked.

"What we both used to do best. He will continue in the tradition we began together as lads."

Chuckling softly as if remembering times before, Roby opened the door while standing back to let her walk in.

The room was large. Two large brocaded chairs were arranged in front of a fireplace. A red chaise lounge occupied a sidewall. The flames licked upward, casting a warm glow in the fading light of the day. She held out her hands to warm them. From lowered lashes she studied Roby, wondering what he meant by what they did best as well as continuing the tradition.

She seemed thoughtful, meditating about nothing or something. The knock on the door startled him from his musings as it did her. Pippa turned at the same time he did.

"Must be your bath water."

She nodded while he wondered if she was as nervous as he. "The small hip tub was brought into the room along with steaming water to fill it with. There were two bars of soap. One smelled of lavender the other was rose scented. Roby wondered which one she would choose.

"What about you?" she asked.

"I'll be back in ten minutes for my bath."

~ * ~

A hot bath.

Her slow build of confidence vanished. Here they were, together, alone in their second day of wedded bliss. He'd yet to bed his bride. Pippa couldn't help but wonder if he found her lacking in some way. He told her that her breasts were abundantly large. Were they too big? On the other hand, she told him many things about her past, the troubles surrounding her, yet for some reason and somewhere on the ride to this very spot, he decided he wanted a real wedding before he made her entirely his woman. A true and valid marriage ceremony could be many days from this one. Did he mean to wait until then to bed her?

With her fingers clasped beneath her chin, she watched him stride from the room. His confidence shook her to her very soul. She wasn't sure if she was thankful he was giving her ten minutes of privacy or disappointed.

When everyone, including Roby disappeared out the door, she stripped off her clothing. Settling into the warm water, she realized how different this was from the chill of the water she'd been bathing in for the last five years except those she spent with Callum. So much, she gave up so very much to leave her home behind in the hands of her money grasping cousin and his father. For the first time in as long as it seemed she could remember she had hope for her life.

Her stomach rumbled hungrily. The clock on the shelf ticked away the seconds. If she didn't hurry and make use of her time, he would be in the room. Vulnerable and naked he would see her. She wasn't sure if she cared as the time for that to happen naturally would come soon enough. Choosing the lavender scented soap, she quickly washed her body then her hair. Dipping beneath the surface she rinsed. A look at the clock told her she had two minutes left.

Stepping out of tub, she wrapped the towel around her just as the door was opening. She gasped, surprised to see Kit. Just to make sure she wasn't imagining his sudden appearance she blinked.

"What are you doing here?"

Her words wobbled as she stepped back, bumped into a chair where she promptly sat down. He was striding toward her, his face grim, promising some curt words of significance she was sure she didn't want to hear.

"To give you a message directly from me to you," he said, bracing his strong arms on the sides of the chair where she sat.

There was no escape, no way to hide from him. He was a man just as powerful and determined as her husband. She understood his dislike for her. Her breath drew into her lungs in a thin ragged stream.

"Yes." The word came out in a tiny squeak of fear while she pushed her still damp body against the chair.

"If you hurt Roby in any way, you'll answer to me." There was no denying the menace or the threat in his words. "Do you understand?" he asked, one finger beneath her chin as he made sure she saw the anger simmering in his silver eyes, eyes so like Roby's.

She swept her tongue across her lips. "I wouldn't expect anything different. As I *ken* you love your cousin dearly. I don't intend to hurt him." *I care for him too much to do that.*

She was suddenly struck by the word care; knew her feelings ran deeper than the mild word. Just didn't know how deep those feelings actually went. For a moment she considered love.

"See that you don't. You won't like the consequences."

Hypatia leapt on his head, the small monkey's fingers winding into his hair, chattering angrily.

"Hypatia, stop it!"

The monkey swung down and sat on her lap. Pippa stroked her fur. "Hush, he means no harm to me."

Pippa knew what she said wasn't true. Kit would throttle her if he thought he could get away with it.

He left as abruptly as he arrived. She found herself shivering, unsure if it was his threat or the fact that her hair was dripping down her back. The time was up, ten minutes had come and gone. Roby would be in the room any second. Keeping the towel wrapped around, her she found the set of clean clothes he left on a chair. With speed she dressed and was buttoning the last button on her shirt when he walked inside.

"You're dressed." He sounded disappointed.

She turned intending to smile at him. "Just now. Do you want me to leave while you take your bath? I saved a bucket of clean water for you. It's no longer all that hot."

The grin sliding across his well-chiseled manly features that never failed to make her smile flashed even white teeth, while the silver of his eyes turned to fire, giving her a hitch in her breath. A muscle ticked along his jaw. "No, if I had my wish, we could have shared the bath."

"You should have asked." She blurted the words before she realized what she implied.

His grin grew if that was possible. "Next time I won't forget to delve more thoroughly into what your wishes might be." He set the tray carrying the food and wine on the table near the fire. "If you like, you can start without me."

"I'll use the time to dry my hair."

She turned from him, knowing he was going to undress. Knew she wanted to peek at him. More than anything she wished to see him naked. Her entire being cried out for her to see what he looked like with not a stitch to cover him. He would be so finely built the sight would steal her breath. Pippa just knew that to be true. With that thought the breath she sucked into her lungs sputtered to its death before the miniature speck reached its destination.

Fool, ye are a fool, Pippa MacPherson—McKenna.

"You can watch if you like." He stood behind her, his bare hands on her shoulders. Once again, she tried to suck in a breath of air. Again, the attempt failed. The fine trembling his touch generated covered the length of her body.

"I would not want to embarrass you," she spoke softly even while he pushed her hair aside, even as his soft gentle mouth touched upon the nape of her neck, as his tongue traced a tiny path downward before taking his time to head upward hinting at something she knew he would reveal when it pleased him.

"Didn't take you for a coward."

His teeth tugged gently on the lobe of her ear before soothing the spot with his tongue.

"I'm not."

She didn't take him up on his suggestion. Couldn't.

"Maybe tomorrow then."

"Maybe tomorrow," she parroted in a whisper she could scarcely hear.

The heat of his big body vanished. The splash as he sat down in the tub nearly had her turning around for a tiny view. She laughed at herself. All she would see would be his knees sticking above the rim. They would be *verra bonnie* knees. Without giving in to the temptation presented to her, she found his comb. Idly gliding the comb through the long tresses, she continued to muse about what he looked like naked. Her eyes crossed when she thought on all his manly parts mainly that part of him that was so very different from her. She'd never seen a naked man before.

He would be splendid.

She just knew it.

Jerked back from her wayward thoughts by the glass of wine in front of her along with the large hand holding it for her to take, she gasped a bit of air.

"Y-you're finished."

"Disappointed?" he asked as he arched a brow in speculation.

"I've never had wine," she told him as she accepted the glass from him.

"Tiny sips," he told her. "Tiny sips. It might go to your head. Would you like me to finish combing out your hair?"

The thought of his fingers running through her hair unraveled ever nerve she possessed. "N-no." She was stuttering again realizing she needed to steady those same nerves that weren't having any trouble unraveling. "You did such a fine job last night there is no reason. The tangles have all but vanished into thin air." She did sip the wine then another small sip as he suggested.

"What do you think?" He gestured toward her glass, "Of the wine?"

She sipped again, smiled, "I like it but not as much as I like looking at you."

His grin widened as he leaned close to her. His scent was male and warm. He used her lavender soap but somehow the aroma didn't smell feminine on him.

"Did you sneak a peek at me, lass, when I was vulnerable?"

"Vulnerable, you? Pifle. Of course, I didn't," she was so quick to reply to him it generated more laughter from him.

"That's too bad. I was thinking about you looking at me. Hoping you would share how you felt about what you witnessed."

Roby had been busy with more than just his quick tongue just now. While he was teasing, he ladled up two bowls of stew, which he was now bringing to her, the scent heavenly. After he set hers nearby, he cut two huge slices of bread before lathering each one with butter that melted on contact.

Her stomach growled again.

When her mouth was full of hot bread and butter, he asked with an innocent undertone as if he didn't *ken* her mouth was full, "What have you been doing for the last five years? Seems I comprehend the back story, what caused you to run. Would you consider telling me how you survived on your own for so long."

For a moment the bread stuck in the back of her mouth. She coughed, drank too much wine so she could wash down the bread. Coughed again. With her faltering senses calmed, she spoke, "I wondered when you would ask me about that. I've not one reason to keep the truth from you. It's just that it's so hard for me to talk about. Not something I wish to remember. If I even think about my past, the thoughts leave me bone weary as well creating a depression I've trouble not falling into. They stole my life from me. One might say I made the choice to leave.

However, from my standpoint there was no other option."

"Certainly, I can understand why you wouldn't want to recall past horrific events. Wondered too if you would be more forthcoming. Eat your dinner, *lass*. Relax. We have the rest of our lives together for the telling. As for eating, I don't want to stop early tomorrow or the next few days. Want to spend as much time as possible on the road. So, it's important you take your fill tonight as well as tomorrow at breakfast. Would like to put my feet on McKenna land as soon as possible. I've missed my home."

"They are not all horrific."

She recalled Aaron Rosmara, his gentle sweetness. She met him when the gypsies adopted her. He was the same age. They learned to laugh together. He kissed her for the first time one night when a storm was raging while they were huddled inside his wagon. Her feelings for him were not the same as what she felt for Roby. His kisses did not stir the same deep longing nor did they generate the inferno flaming inside.

Although, his kisses were pleasant.

"No, don't suppose they were," he conceded pensively, an unusual glint in eyes as if he processed what she'd just been thinking. "So, you did have a few good times."

At his words earlier, words of hearth and home, the stab of homesickness sweeping through her startled her. With difficulty she swallowed the bite of food in her mouth. After a smaller drink of wine she said, "When I first left Clearborne Manor, I used to think about my life before I was fourteen when my world as I knew it crashed down around my feet. The time before was idyllic when mother and father lived. I missed terribly the only home and family I ever knew, the laughter as well as the love. After a couple of years, I became contented and resigned myself to my loss, understanding nothing would ever be the same. Nothing would bring them back to me. Life changed for me, never truly for the best until I met you. Although the last years were better."

She ate thoughtfully wondering just how much of her mundane tale he wanted to hear. At best it would bore him to tears. She wasn't at all certain her story was worth the telling.

As if reading what was in her mind, Roby spoke, "Everything,

Pippa, I want to learn all that I can about you before you left as well as after. You can tell me about your parents along with what you enjoyed best. I've a strange feeling I've met you before. I can't seem to remember though."

She laughed softly as she placed her hand on his forearm. "My story would bore you to tears."

What she really meant was that she didn't want him feeling sorry for her. Didn't need that from him as he told her, she survived. There could be nothing better than that. Survival.

"Never," he spoke softly seemingly from the heart. "Nothing about your tale would bore me. I want to hear everything."

Those words brought her to a place of reflection. If they were meant to be together, he deserved the knowledge. With a heartfelt sigh, she spoke. "If you insist."

"I do."

"Very well, I'm sure it's a yawn I'll be seeing from your beautiful mouth soon. It cannot be helped or avoided. Perhaps I could have another glass of wine." Pippa wondered if she was stalling for time.

He laughed. The chortle warmed her heart. With one brow arched toward the ceiling, "Beautiful mouth?" He did pour both more wine.

"Yes. Don't you ever forget that. Now hush so I can finish what you want me to start." For courage she drew in a long deep breath of air. "The day I left I was lucky. An old man driving a cart came upon me. His beard reached his belly. It was pure snow white. His skin was wrinkled with age from the sun and the wind. His eyes, Robby, his eyes were the most startling, silver rimmed with blue. Now that I think on it, they remind me of your eyes. A coincidence or not I don't know, will most likely never know. In any case, I thought he could see into my mind, read my thoughts along with my deepest fears and joys. By the time he passed on, I was sure he understood more about me than I'd ever told him. Mayhap he understood things about me I didn't know."

"What happened to him?" Pippa heard the eagerness and sudden attentiveness in his voice. "When did he pass on?"

She lifted her shoulders as she stared at the potatoes in her stew, playing with her spoon. "He died."

She understood she wasn't telling him what he was asking. Somehow this relationship seemed private to her.

"I assumed as much." He laughed softly but his laughter was not at her. It seemed he laughed at himself. "How did he die? I might know something about this man."

The sound of his laughter seemed to become part of her soul. Touched a part of her that had been missing since her parents died. She didn't understand how he could know anything. Still... "I lived with him for almost a year. He caught a chill one night when he was out collecting peat for the fire. He never recovered. Nothing I did, none of my prayers saved him." She felt the tears for her lost friend and savior rise to her eyes. Willed them back as she brushed at them with the backs of her hands. "He saved my life. By keeping me with him for that year, I had time to grow, to learn. He taught me a few ways to survive. Learned to snare a rabbit. Prepare the animal to cook." Well, that knowledge got her into a wealth of trouble.

"Go on."

He wiped his bowl clean with a chunk of bread, cooled now. After finishing his meal, he sat back in his chair, his long legs stretched out in front of him. His hands were behind his head.

She smiled at him, contemplating what she saw in front of her. "You have *bonnie* feet." Once again, she blurted the first thought that came to mind. She never thought feet could be beautiful but his were. If his feet were so fine, she supposed everything about him must be beautiful.

He wiggled his toes. Bending over, he lifted one foot seeming to study it, turning his one way then the other. Solemnly, without a hint of humor in his voice, "My toes are hairy."

Laughter bubbled up from deep within, from a place she forgot existed until she met this man. His chuckles joined hers, until tears threatened to fall, until tears did fall.

"I have to stop laughing or I shall surely..."

She waved a hand in the air not wishing to tell these embarrassing thoughts to this man she was just getting to know. Clearing her throat she continued, "The hair is part of what makes them beautiful as well as unique."

"They are not unique. All men have hairy toes." Once again, his voice was grave.

"Not like yours."

She was relieved he didn't pursue the statement she cut short. Seemed content with convincing her that his feet were just like every other man's. She could never tell him she might pee herself because she was laughing so hard. No, never in a million years could she make such a thought a statement.

"You've rendered me speechless. That is a rare ability and you possess it, my dear one."

Dear one?

"Should we return to the topic or are you bored now by my tale of sadness and woe?" In truth, she didn't want to stop talking just yet. Now that she began, the best for her would be to tell as much of her story as she had the inclination to do so.

"Only if you want." He relaxed in his chair again his feet once more stretched out in front of him, "Don't bring up my feet."

"Why?" Shamelessly she grinned at him.

Perhaps he had the same problem with the laughter she had.

"Just know I'll make you rue the day."

She didn't believe he would do anything to harm her. His grin was too wide and charming, infectious as well.

She nodded, looking to the door when she heard noises in the hallway, a man and a woman, laughing and talking. A little cry of what sounded almost of delight followed another.

"It's Kit. He's found his bedmate for the night," Roby said, no expression on his face.

She heard the thud against the wall, Heard, "*Ooo laddie,* you're so big, hard as steel."

"Perhaps you should cover your ears," Roby chuckled, his eyes shimmering with amusement. "'Tis what I would like to be doing with you."

She gasped at his bold statement. "I believe I might want to do something as what they are doing with you too. Just not positive what that might be."

With her lashes lowered, she was unsure of what she should and should not say as the thumping coupled with the cries continued. Heat blossomed on her cheeks. The door to the adjoining room clicked shut. The noises vanished. She inhaled a shaky breath.

When she looked up, she saw his eyes searching her for the truth she hid from him. It seemed he wasn't going to comment further on Kit's behavior in the hallway nor what she just confessed. It was for the best. "I don't know what or how much I should tell you."

"You *ken* I want to learn everything."

"Kit doesn't like me."

"I know."

"You do?" Her eyes opened wide. She was surprised at his admission. Thought he would surely deny the fact or make excuses for his cousin. "This is not meant to *clipe*. I'd never snitch on anyone but..."

He placed her twisting hands in his, holding them until she calmed herself. "I'd like to know what you think, what he's said to you. It won't change anything between Kit and me. We've been best friends since before we could walk. We've shared just about everything two cousins can share."

With a huge breath of air stranded inside her, she began, wishing she never mentioned Kit. "It was nothing really. He told me if I ever hurt you, I'd answer to him. Also, that I would not like the consequences. Don't want to hurt you."

"Well, that tells me he still has my best interest at heart. The important thing here is that he has to learn to trust in you as I do. For so many years it's just been the two of us against the world when necessary. Kit realizes that's all changed now. He might be hurting. There might also be other feelings simmering deep inside."

"I told him I would never do anything to harm you. We both know those words as a lie. So much in my past could rise up to harm you or him even the rest of your family."

"No, we don't know anything of the sort." He reached out to stroke her cheek with the back of his hand. "We don't know anything of the sort," he repeated as if he needed to. "Besides, I'm not afraid of Harry and Horace Finchbottom. The McKenna clan is powerful especially when they join together against a common enemy."

"The Finchbottoms will try to kill you when they discover you've married me. They were my guardians. I didn't have their permission to wed with you. They have the legal power to put the marriage aside."

"Well then what should we do about that?"

His lips met hers. His hands framed her face. Warmth engulfed her.

Softly. Ignited the flames within her. Gentle pressure. Heat surging.

The kiss was over before it even started. "I don't know." Her words wobbled as if they had no substance. Her shoulders lifted in a gesture that left her wondering what exactly he had in mind.

"Why don't you think about it, hmm...?" His lips brushed over hers again. Tantalizing. He drew away. "You are delicious."

In agreement as if she was a ninny, she was bobbing her head. She no longer had any concept of what he was talking about. She would think though. "Alright then. Do you have something in mind?"

Her question went unanswered as he changed the subject.

"What happened after the old man died? What was his name?"

"It was Callum. He never told me his last name. I never asked. Except for my father, he was the kindest man I've ever known. And now you. You are kind too."

"Callum you say. Suppose the name could be a coincidence. Another coincidence."

"I don't understand. How could, well, of course it was a coincidence." Was he referring to his name or their meeting?

"What did you do then? After this man passed on?"

"For a couple of months, I lived in that same home. Callum told me I should go to the McKenna castle. The McKennas would protect me. After I buried him behind his house that is. When I ran out of food, I left again. I rode out on his donkey. I followed his directions. In hindsight maybe I should have stayed where I had a roof over my head. I was afraid the Finchbottoms would find me. There no longer was anyone to protect me. While Callum lived, he shielded me. With him gone I no longer had that protection. I felt as if all my fears were closing in on me."

She watched as his brows drew together, creating deep frown lines. She wanted to reach out to smooth them away. Wanted to see him smile again. He seemed so grave.

"What or who most likely did you need protection from? It wasn't the old man was it then who? Did you still believe the Finchbottoms could find you?"

"Truly, I don't know that I did. I had been gone long enough to hope they stopped looking for me. Was sure they would spend my money. Everything was such a blur. I wandered aimlessly for two days. On the road I met a couple, Thadeus and Tele Tubbles, who told me they would take me to the McKenna castle. I believed they were kind, honest folks. Thadeus told me to call him Tad. When Tad used to stare at me, I felt it was wrong, felt fear slither down my spine. One day he threatened me."

"With what?" She watched his hands fist, saw the muscle tick along his jaw line.

Perhaps it wasn't wise of her to say more. She promised, though, "He knew who I was, knew too that the Finchbottoms were looking for me. Would pay a reward for my return. He told me if I slept with him, he wouldn't tell anyone about me."

She cringed at the thought of sleeping with Tad Tubbles. The act might even be worse than being forced by Harry.

"I see." His breath sucked inward with a low snarl. "I would claw the man's eyes out if I could find him then go for his jugular."

She gulped in air at the sound of his comment as her heart forgot to beat. His words were so fierce. His anger was raw and primitive. "When I saw the covetous gleam in his eyes, I knew he lied. He would keep me and force me until he didn't want me any longer. After that he would sell me back to Harry. Tele, his wife, didn't seem to care what he did or didn't do."

"You were fifteen now? Still practically a child."

"Yes. The men wanting me didn't think so." She looked to the floor then to him, pushed the threatening tears away with the backs of her hands. "Can we stop now? Please?"

He drew in a large breath, his chest rising then falling as he let the air sift slowly out. "Yes, of course, don't want to overtax you. Eventually, I need to learn everything. If I'm going to be able to protect you, that is. Doesn't have to be all tonight."

He poured her more wine then handed her the glass. He sat down with a refill.

Twirling the red liquid in the crystal fascinated her. She did feel a bit light headed as well as warm. She deliberated if the feeling was because of the wine or Roby. He handed her a small berry tart.

"Desert?" she asked biting into the sweet confection. "It's tasty. Almost as delicious as your kisses."

He drank air. "Once more your words unman me. I've never thought of my kisses as being delicious."

Suddenly, she found herself seated on top of his hard thighs. It was a place she liked to be, his hands on her waist. She turned into him, touching his mouth with the very tip of her finger. She inhaled swiftly when he pulled the tip into his mouth, her eyes widening with the pleasure he gave.

"Are we going to bed now?" she asked as he deliberately sipped each one of her fingers into his mouth.

"Not yet. We need to finish the wine. After the bottle is empty, I'll leave so you can put on my shirt to sleep in. What do you say?"

She swallowed hard wondering if she should tell him what she was thinking. "That I..." *That I want you to kiss me and never stop. That I don't want to put the shirt on. That I...* She knew he would take issue with the words popping into her head. She wasn't about to waste time prevaricating.

"That I?" he prompted as he continued his erotic assault along her arm.

When she looked away, hiding what was in her eyes, he gently brought her back to face him. She would be honest. It was the best way to move forward. "That you're wedding me didn't put you in a ghastly place. Kit is right. I will hurt you. My life will come back to haunt us."

"As I told you earlier, I'm not afraid of Harry Finchbottom," he gritted out. "Now, let us continue to dwell on lighter subjects since you are exhausted. You can touch me anywhere it pleases you to do so. Would you like that? I'm not going to take anything you're not willing to give."

Her hand rested on his chest with one of his over the top. Warmth radiated through him into her. His confident words almost made her lose the fear she held inside for so long. Terror was still part of her, lying in wait until the time it would best take her off guard. For the night, she craved to put that aside.

"*Och* and I wish to touch you everywhere." She rested her head against the tip of his chin. "Wish to stroke that part of you that I feel when you press me against your belly."

His hands tightened around her. His groan rumbled up from his lungs. "I would like to kiss every part of you, your breasts, your bellybutton the length of your legs giving major attention to the soft petals that will flower for me when the time is right."

His butter soft words, his highland burr thickening as he spoke warmed her everywhere. Propelled those sensations unique only to Roby, sensations curling into a heavenly fire deep in her core. She wished he would ease those feelings or give her what she *kenned* she was missing.

"Then you should," she told him candidly, focusing on all the places he mentioned. "If you wish that then so do I. I'm a willing *lass* for my *bonnie* husband."

"You are truly a gem, Pippa McKenna. I find your impertinent talk entices me to play with you until you scream my name." His voice turned husky seeming to come from deep in his throat.

"How would you do that? Make me scream your name?" she challenged him hoping he would tell her more, hoping that something like that was possible.

"I'll begin to show you as soon as you finish the wine in your glass. We mustn't rush the loving. It is best when taken *verra* slow. Do you wish to truly become my wife tonight?"

"Yes," she sighed softly. "If I scream, wouldn't that bring Kit rushing into the room? We wouldn't want something like that." She was panting. Just thinking about what he told her stole her breath. Every tiny gasp of air was a gift.

"No, if you scream, he will *ken* why though. He will be happy for the both of us. He will know that we are giving as well as sharing ecstasy."

A rush of fire swept up her body. Quickly, she placed her hands on her smoldering cheeks to cool them. "Ecstasy? Surely that is an exaggeration. What is it you will do that will give such a sweet gift?"

"You blush very prettily. No, no exaggeration."

"People would know what you and I are doing if I scream your name? I don't think I like that."

"Yes, if you yell loud enough. The entire inn will know what we are about. They will know I'm a man's man who can give his lady love the little death."

Little death?

"Then you best not be about such a thing. *Ye* should shake that notion right out of your beautiful head." She tried to convince him as she slanted a stern look his way. "As I've told you before, you are a bad *mon*, Roby McKenna to even think those things, wicked to the core. There is to be no denying that fact."

"You've come to adore this bad, wicked man while you worship even more the things I'm going to do to your luscious body tonight. *Dinna* worry, I'll hush your scream by covering your lips with my mouth while I thrust my tongue deep inside the heated warmth you offer."

"Oh."

He chuckled, the vibrations so close to her ear rushed more heat into her. "I promise you Kit will not storm the room. Even if he hears you cry out my name, he doesn't have a key. He will also be too involved in his own pleasure with a lady love to defer to a tiny shriek coming from my wife."

"I see."

"Do you?"

"No."

"Before the night is over you will."

"Accident down the road!" The yelled words entered into the room.

~ * ~

"The missive said Pippa was found," Harry ground out yet he

smiled.

It was about time. Five long years passed as they searched for her always coming up short. Harry swept his hand down his chest then lower to his crotch. Just thinking of Phillipa caused his rod to harden in anticipation. "Even now my spy is following her travels toward the highlands with the McKenna boy and his cousin. From what was written they, along with Pippa, are headed toward McKenna castle," Harry told his father, thinking he could contain himself, thinking that the lovely Phillipa MacPherson would soon be under his protection and beneath him as he sought fulfillment in her charms.

He would never consider what he meant to Phillipa. He waited five long years. He would only have to wait a day or two now that he was so close. He and his father decided if they were going to succeed with their plans, it would be best to take her before the trio reached McKenna land.

"Good, then our task has been rendered easier since we know where she is," Horace said craftily.

"She doesn't know we are close by. We've the element of surprise on our side. They will walk right into our open arms. I *ken* it will not be easy to get rid of those two popinjays but we've the upper hand." He rubbed his hands together in anticipation of his plans. Finally, everything was coming together.

"Good Lord, but we've been close a number of times. Once she was in the gypsy camp she was protected on all sides. We had to hold back on our strategies," Horace said thoughtfully. "Now all she has are those two men. They shouldn't be a problem."

"I thought that gypsy—what was his name? Aaron Rosmara was going to have her first. I don't believe he did. Seems he was acting the gentleman, planning on waiting until they vowed their love for each other. Ha. Too bad for him. Didn't live long enough to sample what is mine."

"Lord Bigley did our bidding, strung him up for stealing a rabbit. Couldn't have asked for more. Fit into our plans perfectly," Horace said. "What didn't fit was that he allowed Phillipa to leave before we got there."

"When we didn't show up soon enough to claim Phillipa, he was going to hang her too. We just didn't get there soon enough. Glad he didn't succeed. Her inheritance would have gone to that orphanage in Edinburgh. Don't believe she understands that part of the will her father left."

"Somehow the McKenna stepped in. Must have paid the old man off. She went with him willingly from what our informants have told us. Heard in order for him to save her he would have to marry her."

"Do you two suppose he popped her? Took what was meant to be mine? What I claimed five years ago?" Harry asked, thinking he'd kill the McKenna if he took what was rightfully his. No way about it. Roby McKenna would pay with his life. Just thinking about another one possessing her before him sent wave after wave of furry rushing through him, roaring between his ears. That would not do, would never do.

"You *ken* the path home Roby boy and Kit will take," Horace asked as he stroked his chin in thought. "Shouldn't be too difficult to intercept then ambush."

"The fastest one since they've been gone for two years. We're on that road as we speak. We'll meet up with them tonight."

Harry tapped on the roof of their conveyance. The driver stopped. "What is it?"

"All the speed you can get out of those horses. Want to be at the inn soon as possible. Do you understand?"

Horace was panting as he imagined joining with Phillipa MacPherson. Oh, she would be his soon.

The man nodded before he hopped to the top and sent the horses racing down the road.

The carriage took off so fast Harry fell against the opposite side while Horace was pushed backward. Bumped and bruised, he was shaking his head, cursing beneath his breath. *Bampot!* "Gawd almighty," Harry yelled as he settled onto his side of the carriage.

He took a moment to rearrange his gold brocade waistcoat before smoothing his pants and flicking lint from his shoulder.

"You told the man to make haste," Horace said insipidly. "Suppose he took your words at face value. What can you expect from hired help? Hmm...?"

"Good, we'll get to her all the sooner. I, for one, wish we were there as we speak."

Abruptly, they were both thrown against the side of the carriage before rounding another curve tossed to the other side. Harry hit his head hard as he bounced from side to side. He grabbed his arm as wave after wave of agony swept through him. "I think it's broke."

"Broke? Most likely just bruised a bit. You'll recover as soon as you set eyes on your soon to be bride. Bruised and battered a little less than ourselves but we'll reach that inn tonight. We'll be able to *ken* the moment those three make their appearance," Horace said as they hit a pothole thereby tossed so his head banged against the roof. For a moment Harry thought he might faint from the hard impact.

"Bruised and battered," Harry parroted with a snort just as the carriage tilted precariously to one side running on two wheels instead of the usual four.

Suddenly, it banged down touching all four wheels to the road.

The horses whinnied in fear.

Harry held on to the handle on the door to steady himself as he grit his teeth and braced for the next impact. This was the best he could do as the wild ride continued unabated. Once more they rounded a steep corner. The vehicle rolled along what seemed forever on two wheels. Hit another pothole then plummeted to the earth kicking up bushes and grass, all manner of debris flying through the open window as the horses raced forward.

"We're going to die," Horace moaned holding his ribs. "No gel is worth death in order to poke."

The horses raced on. The conveyance bumped along the ground further battering the men inside. The world turned black as Harry finally lost consciousness.

Chapter Three

Roby jumped to his feet at the sound of the hammering on the door coupled with news of an accident. He heard the same announcement at Kit's door. He pulled on his boots, grabbed his pistol tucking it into the back of his trouser before slipping on his shirt.

Hypatia jumped to the table by the door. Her chatter jarred his nerves. It seemed the monkey was making sure everyone knew exactly how she felt about the late-night interruption.

He pulled Pippa to her feet, kissing her quickly on her lush ripe mouth that begged for more than what he had time to give. It seemed his plans for this evening would be hindered. "Stay here and lock the door. Don't let anyone in no matter what they say. Only Kit or me. Hear me?"

He tried to further convey his fear for her with his eyes.

She grimaced and nodded, appearing to understand all he wanted to say to her. "Wish you didn't have to go."

He held the same sentiments. All he worked for today seemed to vanish with the announcement of the accident. "Wanted to share our bed tonight. Suppose there might still be time when I return." He didn't have any illusions that would happen. She would sleep by herself this evening. Ah, but perhaps she would get the rest she needed. Days of travel still loomed in front of them. Her eyes were still shadowed with the exhaustion she dealt with daily.

"I will miss you," she murmured as she walked with him to the door, her hand running the length of his back in silent invitation only he could understand.

He kissed her again, hard and deep promising more when he returned. With regret, he closed the door behind him, turning the key in the lock. Prayed she would stay safe while he was gone.

Nothing is going to happen to her.

The hairs on the nape of his neck bristled a sure sign something sinister was a foot. Danger lurked outside this room. The eerie stillness confirmed that fact. He and Kit would need to take grave care on this night. The storm that threatened never arrived. If he didn't miss his guess, a storm of a different nature would take its place. What exactly it was remained to be seen. When he looked out the window at the end of the hall, the threatening clouds slid across the moon casting ominous shadows below. Once more his gut tightened.

Kit entered the hallway, a grim slant to his mouth, his eyes a smoldering steel gray.

The glint in Kit's eyes told Roby that his cousin had the same apprehensions about this mission, about the dark adventure before them. Something evil lurked down the road they were about to travel. As they entered the main room of the inn, they joined three other men.

"Your horses are saddled and ready. We don't know what we'll find there. A cart for the injured with bandages will follow. The messenger said there were two passengers along with the driver who were injured. Two were unconscious. The driver jumped from the coach before it slid to a stop against a sturdy tree trunk. The driver said the passengers were in a hurry so he did their bidding. Didn't count on the road being so treacherous."

In the telling there was nothing suspicious about the accident. An inner sense told Roby not to believe the obvious. There was something sinister here. It would do to take caution while heeding the voices in his head.

Almost an hour later they came upon the overturned coach. The driver was sitting in the road holding his arm, moaning about the gents and their orders. He should have heeded his instincts. It was dark, the road uneven, he understood the danger even if his passengers had no idea what was ahead of them.

"Wasn't my fault. Just doing what I was told to do," the driver moaned. "Not accountable for these two if you *ken* what I mean. Not goin' to take responsibility here."

Kit along with one of the men from the inn stopped at the driver, checking him over for injuries while Roby and the other two men strode to the overturned coach. The drag marks seemed to go on forever even around the last bend in the road until they stopped with the obvious impact. Still terrified, the horses nickered, pawing the ground while tossing their heads. Roby climbed on top of the carriage to peer inside.

At the sight of the two men, he sucked air. *Speak o' the devil himself. I did not expect this, not so soon.* His instincts about the night as well as the accident were right. He swallowed the lump in his throat as he lowered himself to the bottom of the vehicle. Quickly, he checked the pulse on both men.

He peered out the window on top, "They're both alive. Need help to get them out."

"Thank God," the other men spoke.

"Glad to see we're not taking out the dead to be buried," one said while the others agreed.

"We need to get them out before we can right the carriage. Not even sure if we should, it seems to be broken into splinters in places. It will never be used again. In this condition, doubt it can be repaired."

Roby lowered himself back inside. First, he checked Harry for signs of internal injuries and broken bones. After finishing with the son, he did the same for Horace. It must have been providence that sent them to the Drum and Ox Inn, providence that led them to the accident. He would never have realized Harry was so close on Pippa's heels. Neither of these men would travel anywhere soon. They both had a few weeks of healing before they could embark on a journey. That fact didn't change anything. His spies were sure to follow Pippa wherever he took her.

One of the other men lowered himself through the open window.

"Neither one is hurt badly. A few broken ribs, in this one's case a broken arm. The other guy seems to have a broken leg. I'm supposing the inn keeper sent word for a doctor."

"Believe so."

"Good thing they are both unconscious. Getting them out of here is going to hurt like the very devil itself."

Roby couldn't think of a better punishment for these two after discovering what they had in mind for Pippa. Perhaps it would be better to make sure they were awake for at least part of the enterprise.

The attempt to rescue these two took longer than expected. Both gained consciousness a few times while the men were extricating them from the vehicle. As soon as the men were placed in the wagon to take them back to the inn, Kit and Roby left riding hard for the Drum and Ox. They would have to leave at first light.

For the first few miles they rode in silence. Roby understood he needed to explain a few of Pippa's guarded secrets to his cousin. He just wasn't sure what to explain along with what to leave out. These facts were, after all, Pippa's life. "Do you know either of those two men?" he began hoping there would be little to explain. Going into details was not a priority of his. Although, he'd have to do that if Kit had no idea what types of men these two were.

"Correct me if I'm wrong. The two men in the wagon are Harry and Horace Finchbottom, our neighbors to the north. Didn't they acquire the manor house Clearborne as well as the land after the MacPhersons' accidental death? Wasn't there a daughter involved, one who lived?"

"Pippa is the daughter."

He grimaced as he thought of all the facts he needed to inform Kit about. Pippa would be embarrassed. In any case, he figured it was just a matter of time before Kit learned everything. "Now, I'm not aware of all the explicit facts and details. She's told me as much as she can as quickly as possible under the circumstances. The telling of her story is exhausting. Recalling the things that happened to her because of these two *dobbers* is agonizing. I've told her to take her time."

"I've always believed those two were idiots. I'm guessing nothing good has come from the death of the MacPhersons." Kit looked over his shoulder as if making sure no one was listening or following. "I take it Pippa was left in the control of these two enterprising men who most likely coveted her inheritance."

"Right, on all counts," Roby murmured softly thinking on all the injustices against her during her short life along with all she survived.

Pippa was a fighter, no doubt about that.

"The youngster, Harry, meant to wed her when she was fourteen just to seize the inheritance you just spoke of. He also meant to sire an heir."

"Hardly a youngster. He's our age. Yes, that's what she told me. You don't think she would lie?"

Roby felt a wave of nausea rise to his throat. He never thought he would have to convince his cousin of the misdeeds of others.

Kit seemed to consider for a few strained moments between the cousins. "*Och*, she might lie but not about that. I've a passing acquaintance with Harry. Know a little about his jaunts to Inverness. The women in the taverns avoid him whenever possible. He's a mean son of a bitch," Kit spoke softly yet his voice held a wealth of concern for Pippa.

Perhaps Kit's opinion of his wife was changing for the better. "When he told her he was going to poke his rod inside her that first night they arrived at Clearborne Manor, his words not mine, she packed a small bag of necessities and fled on foot into the hills."

Speaking of this sent a ripple of revulsion through Roby. He could well understand how exhausting speaking of this would be for Pippa. No wonder she could only last a short time with each new telling.

"She was fourteen, you say?"

"Yes."

"*Nay.*" Angrily, Kit waved a hand in the air. "Now you're trying to convince me she's been on her own this whole time. I won't be believing something so impossible." Kit didn't bother to look at him. "She could not have survived all by herself."

"No, you're right. You've an understanding of life in the highlands. For the first year of her exile, she spent her time with Callum."

"Great Grandfather Callum?"

Kit sounded so incredulous Roby found it hard to keep a chuckle behind his lips.

"I believe one and the same since before he passed on, he told her to come to the castle. The McKennas would protect her, Callum told her. The last time I went to visit, I saw his grave. She dug it by herself. Made sure he had a proper burial."

"Does she *ken* he was a shifter?"

Kit seemed taken aback by the information he received along with the possibility if she did have knowledge of Callum's abilities, she would not be a liability to the clan on that front. She would most likely assume it was a trait of the clan Chattan.

"That much I don't know. However, there are bits and pieces of Phillipa MacPherson that I'm beginning to piece together in my memories. I've a strong suspicion I've met her before. I believe I might have been in my cat form. Explains why I felt so attracted toward her, I couldn't say no to the proposal of marriage."

"Such as..." Kit prompted, appearing unmistakably puzzled.

"Do you recall five years ago?" Roby paused unsure if, at the time, he told anyone about the encounter by the loch.

If he did confide in the unique occurrence, it would have been with Kit who he was closest with. He would have never told anyone else, not even his mother and father.

"*Verra* well, we were two and twenty, full of ourselves along with our newfound prowess with women. What does this have to do with Pippa?"

Roby snorted laughing, "Speak for yourself, cousin. I knew my prowess long before then. At two and twenty there was nothing newfound about my convincing way with women."

None of his dalliance meant anything to him though. Every time he bedded a woman, there was some component that was lacking.

"Go on." Kit backed off appearing to understand the semantics involved here.

Arguing would serve no purpose. Information was what was important. In those days as well as the present, they were both overconfident rogues, but they never bedded an unwilling lass, especially not one who was scarcely a woman.

"Don't remember if I told you. One day, I believe it was late summer or early fall, you were busy and could not ride with me. Perhaps you were with one of those women discovering your hearty prowess." Just to tease, he waggled his eyebrows suggestively. "That day I was restless as I felt a need to run. Still, there was something else calling to me. Didn't *ken* what it was, just knew I needed to investigate. I rode north. Found a private spot where I could disrobe then shift."

"Weren't we even then supposed to take great care with that aspect of our characters?" he asked knowing the answer. "Sassenach were roaming the highlands looking for anything they could hold against the highlanders. It would have been trouble from more than one source if you'd been discovered."

The two of them were restless spirits coupled with their inability to conform to the rules set down by the clan. This lack of adherence to the rules was part of the reasons they left the highlands for two years. Not only did they hope to find their mates, they also craved the freedom that was being denied to them.

"*Aye*, all true." Roby drug in a deep breath of air before he continued his story once more. "I ran until I was exhausted, ran until I couldn't run anymore. Not because I was too tired but because there was a girl sitting next to a tree in front of the loch sobbing. As I watched her, she stole my heart in so many ways I cannot begin to count them. Even then, I realized she was special. A unique person I needed to know better. For a fleeting moment, even then, I thought she might be my mate. I dismissed the notion because she was so young."

"You believe the lass was Pippa?"

"Yes and no. I just don't recall that well. I scarcely looked at her. When I sat down beside her, she pushed her face into my fur as if she trusted me implicitly, crying until my fur was damp with her tears. We sat together in that manner for over an hour. I felt her soul seep into mine. She was desperate for comfort so she absorbed it from me into her. I knew I would never forget that moment."

"She was *no* afraid of you?" Kit sounded incredulous, stupefied possibly. "There are not many, a handful at most, who would not be terrified to encounter a huge black panther. Where Pippa is concerned, you're beginning to win me over to her side. Although there is a long way to go before that happens. If she knows we are shifters, she holds too much power in her tiny hands. If and when it does happen, just don't expect me to embrace that monkey of hers. Hypatia doesn't much care for me."

"No, it's one of the conversations I need to have with her. I also need to discover if she knew Great Grandpa Callum was a shifter. So much I crave to tell her about myself."

The right moments would come for them.

"If she knows then she might already be guessing we are able to change our shape, which puts us in great peril. Our families will automatically be put in danger if she has knowledge she can use against us."

"True enough. I've thought on what you said, considered possibilities. Nevertheless, I truly believe she's not going to tell anyone. I *ken* it from the depth of my soul, the inner workings of my heart along with every breath I take. That's not who she is. She would never seek to harm another living soul."

"What about after she no longer needs you?"

"You truly don't trust her. She is my wife, lest you forget. I hold more power over her than any other human. If she chooses to betray me or the clan, as you well know, we have our ways." He was thinking of the Kinnel Stones as well as the departure through them of the last men who betrayed the clan.

"Honestly?" Robby queried hoping the answer was not what he was expecting.

"Honestly no, not yet. She has given me no proof she won't betray you or me, especially me. If and when she does show she cares enough to keep her lips sealed, I'll change my mind about her."

"I would that you change your mind on this fact. We need to stand united until the deal with the Finchbottoms is over and done with."

"I've no idea how I feel about her. I see the way she looks at you. There is love combined with admiration shinning in her eyes. It appears she is besotted with you. That fact alone gives me hope for your future with her. What man could crave more than that? If you trust her, I will also try."

"That day, when I encountered Pippa, as the sun began its downward descent and when I was in my cat form, she wrapped her arms around me. Felt her tiny breast push against my forearm. Even then I felt a stirring for her, which I pushed aside understanding she was too young. She told me she would recognize me if she ever ran across me again. So, she knew I wasn't what I appeared. Way back then there was a connection, a link binding us together through the years. At the time I could not fathom why but it was there."

"You believe that? Then I will too."

"With all my heart and soul."

"Here we are. You *ken* we're going to have to leave the Drum and Ox Inn at the break of dawn. I'll talk to the innkeeper so we can have breakfast on the road. Hot bread fresh from the oven as well as tea would be nice. Not what I was anticipating in the morning. I'll have to send my ladybird home."

"I'll see you at dawn." Roby handed the reins over to the stable lad before racing up the stairs to see if Pippa was all right.

When he stepped inside the room, she was asleep on the bed, one arm thrown over her head. Hypatia was sleeping at the foot of the bed. His white shirt was pulled up to the tops of her thighs. He wanted nothing more than to crawl beneath the covers then take her into his arms. Instead, he grabbed an extra cover before settling on one of the big chairs in front of the fire. His pistol lay on the table nearby. Just as Kit said, this was not how he planned on spending the evening.

~ * ~

The day was a dreary gray when he crawled into bed with Pippa and pulled her into his arms. He kissed her softly on the lips. "Time to wake up, dear one. We've got to get on the road. I'll explain later."

With that said he pulled the warm covers from her. Hypatia jumped to his shoulders, chattering as if saying it was about time.

She cried out as the cold air hit her warm body.

"That was rude." She pushed long tendrils of her glorious chestnut colored hair from her face as she sat up. Those silken strands he meant to bury himself in, twist them through his fingers, feel the softness caress his naked flesh. She stretched, his shirt taunt against her breasts, giving him more view than she probably would like.

"But necessary," he said softly wishing for a different scenario. "Believe me this was not my intention for the morning. How long will it take you to ready yourself?"

Despite the fact Harry and Horace were in no condition to follow them he was in a rush to get as far away from the Drum and Ox Inn as soon as possible.

"Less than ten minutes. Just have a few things to take care of." Sleepily, she pushed hair from her face yet she managed a smile for him.

Closing his eyes, he willed the image of her, the tight hard tips of her breasts pushing against his shirt from his mind as well as what he wanted to do with those hard pink tips. She was right about his character. He was a wicked devil at least where his intentions for her were concerned. "I'll wait for you in the hallway. We'll eat on the road."

She did appear confused yet resigned when he left her on the bed, sleep tussled hair curling around her shoulders. Her trust in him evident in the quick way she went about her business. He stepped outside then relaxed against the opposite wall waiting for her.

Her estimate was wrong. She opened the door about seven minutes after he left. They met Kit outside. The horses were saddled.

Before any questions about the evening were asked or answered, Roby handed her a chunk of bread. Can you sip hot tea and ride? It's in a canteen."

"I'll try."

"Just be careful, it's hot. Don't want you to burn your mouth."

Pippa didn't say anything more. He supposed her reticence was because Kit rode behind them just off to one side within hearing distance. Privacy today was not for them as he well knew there could be others with Harry and Horace, others who might follow them.

Much to his surprise Hypatia chose to ride on Kit's shoulder. It seemed the little monkey had a change of heart where his cousin was concerned.

Spinning gray mist clung desperately to the road they traveled, refusing to leave. The morning chill was all about them. He wrapped the cloak he wore around both of them as she leaned against him. While the morning progressed, the early sun began to eat away at the damp fog. Above them blue sky dotted with clouds threatened to make the day an enjoyable one.

"Why the swift departure?" Pippa finally asked, turning her head slightly.

Her lips were damp, rosy, begging for an early morning kiss. He liked that. He needed to see her face, enjoy the simmering of her green eyes as they assessed him, questioning what they were about and why.

"I'm not sure what to tell you. Don't want to alarm you. Suppose it's something you need to know about."

He risked her fear if he mentioned the Finchbottoms' accident. After all she'd been through because of them, she should *ken* the truth. He should be frank as well as honest about the reasons for their hasty departure.

"Don't hold back, Roby McKenna. You know I will weather any bad news. It is bad news, isn't it?" He felt the deep breath of air rumbling into her lungs.

"You read my eyes too well. Don't believe I can hide anything from you. Yes, the accident last night involved both Finchbottoms. They were injured, not severely. It will take a week or two for them to be travel ready. However, my guess is that they might well proceed sooner."

"They were at the Drum and Ox? They had men following us?"

He felt the moment she realized how close she came to being discovered. How close she came to her life unraveling one more time.

"They might have been on your back trail. It's too soon for us to confront those two. Otherwise, I would have stayed right where we were. Until I feel we are truly man and wife, I don't want to encounter them."

"We are wed," she said stiffly. "At least in my eyes if not yours. There is naught they can do about that fact. Now, I would have it different though. Perhaps we should not marry again. If we didn't, it would make it easier for you."

They both knew what she wasn't saying. As long as they were wed, his life was in danger. While he told Kit a great deal, he did not mention the fact the Finchbottoms would be looking for a means to rid the earth of one Roby McKenna. In any case, whether he mentioned the fact or not, he was sure Kit had the wits to figure it all out by himself.

No help needed.

"I'm not willing to kill anyone. The means to circumvent their nasty intentions is out there. We need to figure it out. That's all. Perhaps if we put more obstacles in their pathway, they won't want to pursue you."

"Very well, we will put our three heads together and create a plan," Pippa said.

"You want to include Kit?"

"He knows who I am now. You would have told him last night when you discovered them, the Finchbottoms. It would be necessary for Kit to understand what we are all up against now. I doubt if he needs to be told all the ways I'm using you."

"*Aye*, he knows. The men were found inside an overturned carriage. The driver told us they wanted to get to the inn fast. They deserved their aches and pains."

"They knew where we were."

"Evidently. Don't believe in coincidence."

"They have spies. I've often thought that they knew when I was with the gypsies. At Callum's I might have been an easy target. There were little things. Nothing I could prove. Yet Horace didn't try to take me away from him. I never entirely understood why."

"Even at his advanced age, Callum would have protected you with his life. You were safe there, much safer than when you traveled with the gypsies. Harry as well as Horace knew that fact. That's why you weren't bothered if they even knew where you were at the time. My guess is that they caught up with you later."

When she turned to look at him, he grinned, thoroughly enchanted by her. It was time to give her something else to contemplate.

"How would you know?"

"Callum McKenna is my great grandfather."

If she knows he could shift, she would start to make more assumptions about him. In time, when she presented the questions to him, he would answer. So far, she kept her knowledge to herself. That fact had to be a good sign.

"Oh."

"Yes."

Truly, he didn't want to spend time on one-word answers. If she didn't ask then he would also assume Callum never showed her his cat. In that case, it would be a while before he gave her information that could harm him along with the rest of his family.

Pippa looked away, stared at her hands for several seconds as they twisted into the fabric of the cloak surrounding them. Kit rode up beside them, hovered while he also watched. Hypatia, still at on his shoulder seemed to have found the man of her dreams. He must have heard part of the conversation and was also waiting for some deep revelation that would give them all the freedom of honesty in the matter of shapeshifters.

She ran her hand along his forearm, her touch gentle, evocative with the many promises still to come inherent in the sensation she so easily evoked. He felt the breath she held in her lungs when she inhaled then slowly relaxing, let it leave her body. "He showed me his cat," her voice was soft. "Callum wasn't the first one I'd ever seen. He told me about his family, about the clan. Your great grandfather trusted me with his life. I, in turn, gave him my loyalty without question."

Roby heard reverence in the tone as he squeezed her waist, hoping her next words would prove that point. "Then you *ken* he was a shifter."

When she studied him, her eyes became dark pools of green. "You are also a shifter. I *ken* that as easily as I breathe. I'd like to see your cat someday. They are all different. If I ever saw you in your cat form, I would always remember what you looked like and recognize you. Your grandfather liked to laze in the sun. He used to tell me he would run free for the rest of his life. If the Sassenach caught him, well then, he would sleep and eat and get fat in their cage, but he wouldn't perform for anyone. Despite his frivolous words, he would not have enjoyed being caged. Neither would you. The two of you must take grave care. The Finchbottoms, if they could prove it, would turn you in without even thinking twice."

His cat prowled in his head searching for the words along with the time to show her who he was. It would be so much more satisfying than merely saying the words. "What if I told you I wasn't a shifter?" He bent close to whisper close to her, intent on her answer. The lavender scent she bathed in last night filled his nostrils. He breathed deeply enjoying the aroma of Pippa. When she turned just enough, he could once again see the crystal clearness of her green eyes.

"I would call you a liar. You are so much like Callum, yet

different. About this, you cannot tell me you aren't what you are. About this, I would always believe what in my heart I know is true."

"You say you would recognize me if you ever saw me. What if I told you that once five years ago, you cried on my shoulder, wrapped your arms around me? If I could have, I would have seen you home safely that day. Perhaps when your cousin arrived at Clearborne, you would have turned to my family and me for help instead of running into the crags of the highlands where there was too much danger for a young woman. I couldn't though. I couldn't shift because I would have been naked. Even then I felt an uncanny link with you." He laughed softly. "Even for you I was not willing to show you all of me. You were too young."

Several seconds passed. It seemed Pippa had to absorb his words. Perhaps he was wrong. Mayhap she wasn't that girl who sobbed her heart out the day her parents died. His gut twisted as he waited for confirmation.

"That was you?"

~ * ~

His confession shocked as well as pleased her. For some time, she thought he might be a shifter. From Callum she knew many of the McKennas were shifters. She also understood not all of them possessed the ability to change form. So much about Roby McKenna was clouded in her mind cloaked in darkness. While he expected her to tell all, he put forth very little about himself. The candid admission lightened her heart as well as telling her he trusted her.

When she looked at Kit, his smile was there but hesitant. Roby's cousin still would not trust her. Would always hold some part of him in reserve. It seemed strange to her. Hypatia trusted him. The little monkey never trusted anyone except her.

"I remember that day as if it were yesterday," she began reverently as she needed to tell him her thoughts along with her tender feelings for the man who helped her grieve.

That day so long ago, she did sob her heart out. Felt the wetness of his fur against her cheek. "The sadness overtook me when I heard the horrible news that I would never see either of my parents again. I walked out the door, kept walking until my feet stumbled to the lake. Going farther was out of the question. After stopping I crumbled to the ground unable to do anything but sob as I recalled all I lost and would never have again."

"That's the way I first saw you. Didn't know what was wrong just knew I wanted to make you stop crying. Even though I didn't understand what caused your pain, my heart bled for you." Gently, he squeezed her hand.

"You helped me in so many ways. You were strong while I was vulnerable. You couldn't speak. Still, I felt as if I heard your thoughts as clearly as if you spoke them." Beneath the cloak, she stroked his arm, turned her face into his broad chest absorbing his warmth into her just as she did that day five years ago. "Tonight, will you shift for me? I want to see you again. I *ken* I will recognize you."

"If an opportunity presents itself, I will. There is still danger in the land." His hand settled on top of hers. He brought it to his lips tenderly kissing the palm before he set it back on his arm. "Know that I will show you the other part of me as soon as possible."

She felt moisture clogging her throat, forced it away. She didn't want to cry. "You think he has people following us now."

"Can't ever be too careful. We will take the little used back trails. Instead of heading directly northeast, we will travel in a more northerly direction then cut east later. We should hit McKenna land in four or five days dependent on the weather cooperating."

She understood there were things he wasn't telling her. Understood she shouldn't ask. "We won't be staying in anymore inns along the route, will we?"

She didn't truly care, just enjoyed the hot bath immensely. As they moved north the streams would undoubtedly grow colder as would any lochs they encountered. A small shiver swept through her.

"No more hot baths for either of us until we reach McKenna castle," he laughed softly his breath tickling her ear.

"You read my mind."

"Most likely because we were of the same thoughts. A man can enjoy hot water over the chilled water we will have to use. While it is good for drinking..." He let his thoughts end on that note.

Kit rode alongside, "I'm going to cut back, get rid of our trail perhaps even go off in another direction to mislead anyone following us. I'll meet back with you in about an hour."

Roby nodded. "An hour." After he left, so very close to her ear, he said, "We will have some privacy so I can continue my wicked ways with you. I cannot let you believe I'm not a bad *mon*, now, can I?"

"I'm looking forward to that. Now, what do you plan on doing that would be so very wicked?"

She was eager to find out, hoped he would kiss her again. Understood sometime soon she should tell him about Aaron Rosmara even though she comprehended he wasn't about to tell her of every woman he took to his bed. The story might be years in the making. In his arms she squirmed. Jealousy was not a pretty thing to feel. Still, she wanted to ask but didn't want to hear what he would have to say.

"How exactly should I be a bad *mon*? Hmm...? Do you have any ideas now?" he asked the question although he didn't hesitate to slip his cold hand beneath her shirt to cup her breast, in the process seeming to enjoy its effect on her. "Is this something you would ask me to do?" Between his thumb and finger, he tenderly pinched the tip.

His hand was so cold she sucked in a bit of air then with the sensation he generated, she gasped. "I like that. What else can you do? The devil inside you wants to do more. I *ken* it."

"Oh, do you truly wish to know? I can do a lot of things."

His lips found a tender secret spot behind her ear, caressed with teeth and tongue. As always, the heat rose around her, grew higher and more intense with each stroke. Beneath the green canopy of the trees, it seemed they were the only living souls. She wanted it all, all he had to give. After that, she wanted to give back tenfold.

He helped her turn so she was straddling him. She felt his hard arousal swell intimately against her core. A tiny rippling sound escaped her lips in expectancy as she twisted against him, seeking something she didn't *ken* but knew only with Roby could she find fulfillment. Her hands rested on the heat of his chest. When she pressed her cheek there, she heard the pounding of his heart felt the rasping of each breath he inhaled.

"Why don't you be a wicked *lass*? Do to my man's body anything that takes your fancy," he murmured placing kisses on all the tender sensitive spots he could find.

She felt her eyes widen, enjoyed a moment of pure speculation as she thought of exploring him, touch manly parts she'd never seen before, listening to his reaction. "You mean that?" Dizzy with delight she waited for the answer.

"Yes. I was hoping for this last night. Unfortunately, we were interrupted in our pursuit of carnal delights."

Her nimble fingers unfastened his shirt in just a few seconds. With her eyes closed, she spread her hands across his chest. Curled her fingers into the soft dark hair she discovered. While she explored down then up, she felt the wall of his chest flex, muscles rippling beneath her fingertips. Just as he did with her, she rolled the hard tip of his male nipples between her thumb and finger. His hands cupped her bottom drawing her closer, so close she thought there was no air between their bodies. He squeezed and stroked her buttocks while she did the same on his chest. She leaned back to view all of him as she traced the line of dark hair to the rim of his trousers then lower to cover his arousal with her hand.

Low in his throat Roby groaned, his voice so husky she barely recognized it. The sound was both exciting and confusing. "Does it hurt when I touch you there?" She was trying to figure out what was happening to him, what he liked as well as what he didn't like.

"Only when you take your hand away."

When Roby groaned again, she was filled with a feminine power she had no idea existed. The sun beat down upon them. Breezes ruffled his hair. With this single caress, she controlled him. Realizing he enjoyed what she did, she pressed her hand against his arousal, moved it up then down. His trousers were in the way. Did she dare unlace them? "What can I do to make it better?"

Her questions were breathless, a soft pant against the soft hair of his chest. While she stimulated him, it seemed she did the same to herself.

Beneath her shirt, he ran one hand up her back, lingering on each bone that made up her spine. Her cry of pleasure was nothing as deep or vibrating as his show of delight. He laughed. Guiding the horse with his knees, with his other hand, he lifted her chin. His eyes smoldered changing color even while she watched from the silver-gray she was used to seeing darken to a very deep pewter.

His lips found hers. She opened for him craving the feelings he created within her when he kissed her their tongues dueling, dancing together in an age-old enchantment.

"Waiting to have you is getting harder by the second," he murmured against her mouth.

"I want you to have me."

"I *ken* it, my dear one. Not now and for the first time, not sitting astride a horse although the thought has promise. Perhaps we shall try it later."

"You can do that?" Her voice squeaked when his roving hand tenderly cupped her breast before moving lower to the juncture of her thighs where she straddled him.

"We could try," he murmured as he continued to stroke the soft petals hidden between her thighs. "You are wet with your passion for me. Your honey pot is overflowing so it seems. My cat is purring and roaming through my head. The fabric is in the way. Should we get rid of the cloth?"

"I like the way that makes me feel almost as much as I adore it when you suck my breasts into your mouth. What else haven't you shown me? I want to know everything."

As he increased the pressure of his finger between her legs she twisted, arching back, moving against him. Continuing to fondle her wetness, he bent low, sucked one breast into his mouth.

"Like this?" he asked.

"Oh, yes, just like that."

"Like this?" he asked again as her trousers came undone and his questing fingers slipped inside.

His palm pressed against her belly but he stroked her. She quivered with her need.

"Don't stop. Please don't stop." She tossed her head back. He sucked harder while one finger delved slowly inside her joined by a second.

"Roby! What is that?"

"Just giving you a taste of what we will enjoy later. Not tonight, with Kit so close but when we can share a bedroom as husband and wife. Instead of my fingers another part of me will be inside you."

She felt the trembling grow, heat rose higher. Noises from the back of her throat rippled forth. She heaved against him. Shuddered against him until tremors took over her. She felt as if everything stopped for seconds and seconds while he continued to stroke and drive his fingers inside her over and over until her body ruled her life. He took her to dizzying heights. Places where she couldn't breathe or think.

"Roby," she cried out again.

Just as he told her she would, he covered her mouth with his absorbing his name into the dark recesses of his mouth. "Roby..."

He stroked her back as he eased his fingers from the intimate part of her he invaded to work his magic. "Hush, my dear one, *ceann daor*. You did well. That was your first climax. Did you like it?"

"Yes." She couldn't move. Her body slumped into his needing his support to stay in a sitting position. "Is this what you were going to do last night?"

"More, we were going to do more. For now, we need to get ourselves fastened. Kit should return anytime."

She found that she had been pressing her hand against his arousal. Was reluctant to let him go. While she touched and stroked him through the fabric of his trousers, she couldn't see him. "I want to see you too."

He laughed, "Tonight when we are alone in the tent, I will let you see all of me. Can you wait?"

"No," she told him petulantly. "But I suppose I have to."

"I hear hoof beats. Must be Kit returning. He'll have news of some kind." He quickly fastened everything he'd undone, finished with his shirt before helping her turn around so once again her back pressed against his chest.

A few minutes later Kit rode beside them. "Two men were shadowing us. They followed the trail I set for them. It should be several days before they find us again if they do. Perhaps if we do keep off the well-known paths, they won't discover our whereabouts."

The next few days they spent were pretty much the same. Kit kept the back trail confusing as they traveled northeast while Roby kept Pippa's spirits alive by teasing her, giving her new things to learn. Kit came to trust her more each day as she gradually revealed more about herself. She still needed to tell Roby about Aaron but didn't know how to broach the subject of another man kissing her. The strange thing was except for that one tiny moment in her life, she felt comfortable telling him everything.

Kit and Roby shared guard duty at night. Each would sleep half the night while the other watched the shadows. She tried to take her turn. Both men refused to allow anything so preposterous. Roby had yet to show her his cat or allow her to see him naked. Pippa realized there was never the opportunity.

They'd been on McKenna land for an entire day. She watched both men as they seemed pleased to be home again and visibly relaxed. If need be, help was close at hand.

"For the first time in ages, I've no words as to how I feel," Kit said grinning. "When we left, I never for a second gave any thought as to what I would be missing."

"You're right. It's good to be home," Kit said.

To Pippa's way of thinking Kit's smile changed his appearance. He didn't seem quite so forbidding but charming in his own way. Hypatia spent all those days riding with Kit, either perched on his shoulder or in front of him.

"Neither did I. All I could think of was seeing new lands, meeting new people. Today, I don't understand what compelled me to leave all this behind. This is the most beautiful land in the world," Roby agreed.

"Perhaps we had to leave it to realize that fact. We did indeed find our fill of adventure. Neither one of us thought our cat would be accepted so readily by the natives in America," Kit studied the landscape, a boyish grin on his handsome face.

Kit would make someone a fine husband. Pippa wondered how long it would be before he found the woman he sought. The whole idea of searching for a soul mate seemed foreign to her when Roby first spoke of it. Now the process seemed right, as it should be for everyone.

The two of them had been so absorbed in her story she failed to ask him about his. While most of his life he lived sheltered and protected, she thought spoiled in much the same manner as her first fourteen years. She wanted him to talk about the Native Americans along with his adventure there.

Later, there would be time. For now, there were too many variables to relax. In the process let their guard down. Talk was so different from the experience. For her, she didn't want adventure. No, she wanted a sheltered safe life where everything was predictable and peaceful. Where men weren't coveting what was hers and plotting ways to take it from her. Now that she involved herself with the McKenna clan, she was so afraid she would have to leave to keep them safe. She didn't want that life again. The one she lived for five years. All the precautions Roby and Kit took on her behalf spoke of the ever-present danger. She vowed then and there, she would not allow Horace or Harry Finchbottom to hurt anyone she loved.

To herself she admitted she was falling in love with Roby McKenna. Adventures were for men. Although one could say she had five years of adventure.

Two evenings later, they dropped Kit off at the manor house where he still lived with his parents, said their goodbyes then headed for McKenna castle. Her nerves seemed to be unraveling the closer they came.

"Are you nervous, *lass*? You're shaking like a leaf with a strong wind blowing on it. Tell me why."

He pulled her close, comforting. Over the last days they had little time for closeness except what they found when Kit left them to see if any danger lurked close by as well as work on the back trail.

"Terrified," she said softly. "I'm about to meet your parents. How else would I feel? They are going to learn how I'm using you. When they hear that bit of news, they will cast me out."

She shivered. Her worst fears could come true in another hour or so because they would be inside the castle. Despite her fears, she understood her leaving was the true and right thing to do. After they wed in the church, she would confront Harry Finchbottom to claim her inheritance.

"They will come to love their new daughter-in-law, my soul mate. So, first thing tomorrow we will have father Damian wed us. Before that happens, I will need to tell you about what occurs afterward."

She felt heat rise to her cheeks. "You've told me about the pain the first time. After the first time you'll never hurt me again."

She insisted since he wouldn't consummate the marriage until he'd been married the correct way, that he tell her about what would happen when they finally did join together.

"Well, I told a little white lie."

"You did?"

"*Aye* and I should have gotten it all over with at once. Instead, I put it off thinking not to scare you."

"You didn't want to scare me then but now it doesn't matter?" she asked wondering what strange being could he be trying to speak and finding himself tongue-tied, an unusual predicament for Roby McKenna. She found his hesitancy endearing. He was such a bold, daring man.

"It matters because if everything goes as I've planned, it will happen tomorrow eve. I'm not looking forward to the telling or the doing but it must be done. I cannot explain to you exactly what will take place because it's different for every woman."

"Seems to me you're speaking in circles. Why don't you just tell me plain and simple all that you know? Get it over with then you'll feel better. I'm sure it's not as bad as you're making it out to be."

She felt the long deep breath of air he inhaled for courage she supposed. Roby didn't strike her as a man who was short on courage. No, he assumed the air of a man in charge, one who never knew a moment of failure. A tiny prickle of misgivings swept through her realizing if he was this nervous, she might truly have something to worry about.

"When I bed you," he cleared his throat, "make love to my wife, you *ken* that when I breach the tiny barrier inside you there will be pain."

"*Aye*, you told me as much the other night while you held me and refused to touch me. I didn't like that, Roby McKenna. You as much as told me that Kit would not care if we made love and that you would take my little cries behind your lips so Kit wouldn't *ken* what we were doing."

"Never mind that. Don't want to argue over what happened or

what didn't happen on our way here. Just be reassured I'm pleased you're a passionate woman and that you want me."

"Thank you, you know I do. Now, get on with it." Frustrated beyond anything she'd known, she punched him on the arm. What is this terrible painful thing you are going to subject me to on our wedding night?" She paused turning to look over her shoulder. He was clearly not wanting to say anything. "I'm a big girl. Just tell me."

"I will claim you."

"Now, that doesn't sound so terrible. Suppose there is more to this claiming than you're saying at the moment."

"There is."

His long drawn-out sigh unnerved her. The expression on his handsome face sent a shiver down her spine.

After what seemed like nearly a minute of waiting. "Well?"

She watched him swallow, his Adam's apple bobbing along his neck. "I unsheathe my claws. You will have ten tiny marks on your shoulders. I'm told it can be very painful for the *lass*, particularly if she is not a shifter herself. I've also been told the more times the man has claimed the woman, the greater the pain."

She did suck in her breath thinking this over as well as everything that he'd told her about shifters. "I'm sure just as every other *lass* married to a shifter, I'll manage the pain just fine if it is necessary. Once it is done, the pain will vanish. Now, thank you for telling me this pertinent piece of information that will only happen once in this life of ours. I would not want to be surprised."

What he said did frighten her. In this instant, she didn't intend to let him know her feelings. She shielded her emotions from him, drawing within herself. Childbirth also involved pain. If she were to have his child, she would have to endure that too. Supposed it was a woman's lot in life.

"I will be brave for both of us," he murmured as they stopped on top of a hill looking across the valley to the McKenna castle, which rose into the air. Mist swirled at its base.

She didn't say what was on her mind. Instead, she stared in awe at the towers of the castle, the dark shape it made against the sky. "It's beautiful."

"That it is. It's going to be your home."

God willing.

She said a silent prayer looking at the castle then the heaven above. It did take God a long time to answer her prayers. In time they were answered in the form of Roby McKenna.

Please, God, don't take away what you just gave me.

~ * ~

"They lost the McKenna. They lost them!" Harry's fist planted itself hard on the oak table in their room in the Drum and Ox Inn. The glass of whiskey sitting there sloshed, spilling over. *Bassa*, he cursed, swearing as he strode from the window to the door.

"You insisted on speed," Horace pointed out mildly his nails drumming a hard staccato on the arm of the chair where he sat. He sighed deeply as he watched his son. "What else could be expected than an accident? Even though the driver was a fool, he could have backed off a bit when he rounded those corners."

"Speed was the only answer. Speed. We had to get to Phillipa as quickly as possible. Roby McKenna is a dangerous man, rumor says. She needs protection from that man. Who better to stand up for her rights than her cousin? If we had a better driver none of this would have happened. She would be mine now not still headed toward McKenna land."

"Well, now we can return home to figure out a new plan of attack. By now they know we are after them. It would take a fool to think this was a coincidence. I'm sure the three of them are safe and sound, secure in the castle. A castle we cannot storm. This is not the dark ages," Horace reminded him pointedly as the nails continued to drum and drum, shattering all semblance of control Harry possessed. "Besides, we don't have the man power to use force. We will have to utilize subterfuge."

"So, you say," Harry bit out as he felt each and every nerve snap.

Bile rose in his throat. This was not his plan. Now that he found Pippa, had her in his grasp after five years of waiting, she slipped away again. She was meant to be his. Five years ago, he should never have waited. He could have taken her that day he told her he would put his rod inside her. Instead, getting the chance, she ran.

"It was foolish thinking that got us into this predicament in the first place. We knew eventually she would return to the highlands. All we needed to do was wait for the right opportunity to nab her. It will happen. In time she will let down her guard, wander too far from her protective suitor. You must learn to be patient. All good things will come to you in time."

"So, you think. Seems after five years there would be no question about my ability for patience. I've been a model of endurance," Harry said as he adjusted his neckcloth for the third time while he postured in front of the mirror.

He would need to purchase a tighter corset. This one just wasn't doing the job it was intended to do. With his padded calves and thighs, he would give the McKenna boy competition in looks as well as form. His shoulders were made broader by the wonderful extras his tailor put in the shoulders of his waistcoat. For a few more minutes he preened, seemingly fascinated by what he saw in the looking glass.

"I know so," Horace said thoughtfully, with his hands in a steeple beneath his sagging chin, "Besides, her ample inheritance is still in our very capable hands. We manage the accounts. Control every groat within. Draining it might be the solution if we were to make sure the coin could not be followed to another location."

"How do you plan on doing that, transferring the coin?"

He swallowed what was left of his whiskey. It wasn't keeping his pain at bay as the doctor told him it would. Perhaps he should have another. After all, he deserved it. The accident had been agony for him, excruciatingly so.

"Let me worry about that. You concentrate on the girl. If you can catch her in the village or just out on a ride, it would make matters simpler," Horace went on to say. "She's a flighty little thing. Doesn't sit still for long. If it weren't for the watchful gypsies, we would have had her sooner."

"What if she marries Roby McKenna? What then? Can you answer that question? You seem to have an answer for everything that turns up."

Harry didn't want the woman for a wife if she was no longer a virgin. If that was the case, he'd just take what was rightfully his. Once he had what he sought, she was useless to him. Even though he suggested it when he first approached the girl, he didn't have the stomach to force a woman. She didn't know that. Perhaps he'd been premature in his threat, as they appeared to have had the opposite result.

"He won't wed the girl. She would have to be his soul mate in order for him to take such drastic measures, whatever that means to be a soul mate. The McKennas don't wed just any *lass*. Don't understand their way or the rumors surrounding them. You don't have to worry about Phillipa becoming another man's wife." Horace spoke as if he knew everything about the strange clan. He couldn't possibly be so sure of what he spouted.

"What if, just saying what if, she is McKenna's mate? He would marry her as fast as he could. Wouldn't he?" Harry asked, snapping his finger in the air as he was growing more concerned if something like that would happen, his circumstances would become more precarious.

He would go to any length to protect what he thought was his while maintaining his lifestyle, one he didn't want to change. Including finding some way to make Roby McKenna impotent.

Horace was scratching his head as his brows knit together in concentration, irritating Harry even further. His father never failed to aggravate him. Horace was not a man of action as he was always content to sit back and see how circumstances transpired. He was a weak man.

Harry wanted answers not theories. If Horace didn't have them, he didn't know who would, certainly not the aged butler who they continued to pay, or the cook who never served a meal that was either burned or overcooked. The chief chef at the manor even served bread that was still doughy. They didn't have competent help, not one person who stayed on after Horace's brother and his wife died was competent.

Finally, Horace said, "You've probably thought about everything. In these matters it might not be wise to cross the McKennas. No, I do believe you might need to do without the girl. You're going to have to decide what is more important, bedding the *lass* or gaining the considerable coin that was left to her. I will figure something out, a way in which the funds cannot be retrieved by Phillipa."

"It was more than coin. The MacPhersons owned holdings in Edinburgh as well as Inverness. She won't be able to maintain either of those properties without the money left to her or the wise council of a man. We won't be able to live in them without her consent. After what has happened to her these last years, she's unlikely to give her permission," Harry pointed out. "We're damned either way."

"A fact that is entirely your responsibility. If you had left her alone..."

"You don't think I've considered that?" Harry asked, feeling thoroughly beaten at the moment. He needed to replace that feeling with the anger he should exhibit.

"They also have two ships that carry goods to and from the colonies. Someone has to manage the cargos as well as the shipping schedule. A mere female has not the mental capacity to oversee such extensive holdings. We could offer our services while we continue to skim off the top. She will never know what we are up to. A fine plan, a fine plan indeed."

"McKenna will take over if they are wed. He will see what we are doing faster than you can put that monocle up to your eye."

It was something else that annoyed Harry about his father. That damn monocle.

"Do you suppose Phillipa has any idea the extent of her families holding?" Horace asked seeming to think of all the possibilities. "Without her permission once she is wed or comes of age, we will no longer have control of anything. If she chooses to keep us as advisors, we can of course continue what we do best."

"We'll be paupers," Harry moaned.

"No, we will not be poor, just not as rich as we would have been if we had control of the MacPherson fortune. Come now, we don't know what has happened yet. Let's not think the worst until it becomes necessary."

Harry was thinking the worst. He was thinking about the races and having the groats to bet whenever he wished. He was thinking of the gaming halls where he lost more often than won. While he wasn't addicted to gambling, he did enjoy the occasional trifling with lady luck. He was also thinking of his two mistresses ensconced in nice homes in Inverness as well as Edinburgh. He didn't want to give up his creature comforts, his way of life he'd grown used to over the last five years.

Damn Phillipa MacPherson for reappearing when everything was going so very well.

Chapter Four

When Roby and Pippa finally walked into the great hall in the castle, the room was quiet. A few guards along with two servants were about. Quickly, he requested baths and food to be sent to his rooms along with the room he intended to put Pippa in for the night. Roby didn't expect his parents to be anywhere except in their tower rooms. He didn't want to see them yet. It was late. All he wanted was to tuck Pippa into his sister's room just down the hallway from his. Tomorrow night they would sleep together. Tonight, he didn't trust himself with her innocence if she slept curled up next to him.

Over the last week they grew closer as well as more intimate with each other. Despite her complaints to the contrary, he wanted their true wedding night to be their first time together as man and wife. If they slept together tonight without benefit of Kit as chaperone, he wouldn't have the willpower to leave her untouched. No, this was the best solution, the only answer to his burgeoning need for his soul mate.

"Come on, I'll show you where you're going to sleep tonight."

Roby tugged on Pippa's hand urging her up the long flight of steps toward the south tower where his rooms were located.

She stopped midstride, as it appeared she guessed his intentions. "I'm not going to sleep with you? That's the only place I'll be sleeping in this huge castle. What if I wake up and start sleepwalking? I'll get lost. You can't be meaning to...to leave me alone in this strange place," her soft voice squeaked. "I won't do it, Roby McKenna."

"You don't sleepwalk." He wanted to laugh at her antics.

Although, he was also pleased she didn't want to be away from him. He was tempted to give in to her wishes, wishes he felt too. Steeling himself against his soft heartedness that seemed to be robbing him of common sense, "It's only for one night. You'll be just down the hallway from me."

"Just so you understand, I'm not agreeing to this arrangement, Roby McKenna. Want you to know that. Don't like what you're making me do, against my will. What if Harry or Horace, sneak into the castle and find me? What then? They'll just waltz right on out of here with me in tow. You'll forever be regretting that, now, won't you?"

She was jabbing her finger at his chest with each word as she tried to make the point.

Hypatia chattered as if she was also angry with him. While Pippa held the monkey in her arms, the animal mimicked Pippa's jabbing motion.

He couldn't help the grin erupting. "The guards won't let them inside the walls let alone the castle itself. You have a lock on the door. Use it."

His amusement grew, his pleasure even more. It would be nice to sleep with Pippa. He'd grown used to having her body curled next to his at night as well as by day while they rode. He found he was already missing the closeness.

"Without you next to me I won't be able to sleep one wink," she told him indignantly, "I'll have red eyes tomorrow and be too exhausted to mate with you when you do decide it's the right time. Just because you're a man." She walked in front of him and was once again poking him with her sharp little finger. "Doesn't mean you get to make all the decisions. I, too, have a say in what is going to happen in my life. You cannot think to dictate everything."

He did laugh then, amused as well as flattered by her complaints. She enthralled him, fascinated and intrigued. He knew spending the rest of his life with Pippa would never be boring, "That's where you're wrong, my *ceann daor*. Because I am a man is the reason I make all the decisions, the important ones at least. You will have your say in some less important matters. It's my job to protect you, to fulfill your needs. So, I must have final say."

"You're a beast, a cruel monster. If that be what you're thinking for the rest of our lives, I might just not be willing to wed you tomorrow. I do not have to agree to the marriage. Have not believed this wedding is necessary as you think or the right thing to do. Thought the first one was good enough. You'll have me at the altar but I won't say I do. Just deal with that, Roby McKenna."

"Ah, so, you do not forget we are husband and wife already. I do have the say. I'll make sure the good father does not ask for your permission. There are ways around that stubborn little head of yours."

A surprising anger with her words grew in Roby, simmering, blinding him to the reality of what she told him. Be damned but she would say what was necessary to bind them eternally. He didn't understand why she thought that ridiculous ceremony by the hangman was sufficient to tie them together through perpetuity.

"You *dinna* seem to believe that we are wed in God's name beneath the moonlit sky."

"I do, Pippa. This is a formality to appease my parents as well as the clan. We need to be married by a priest from the clan Chattan. It is the only way we'll have a real marriage in the clan's eyes as well as mine. The ceremony is an important ritual we cannot overlook. You cannot seek to deny us our future by your stubborn notions that you must get your way in all things."

"Then..."

With his thumbs he brushed moisture from her eyes. Her pain was his, her sadness too, "Trust me in this, Pippa. I *ken* what is essential, what must be done to insure our future."

Tenderly, his lips smoothed across hers moistening the tender warm flesh beneath. He held her close for a solemn moment before stepping away from her. If he deepened the contact, he would be lost. "Come, you will sleep alone tonight and wake refreshed in the morning, ready to see the day end as my wife."

"You *dinna ken* that your mother and father might have something different to say?" she asked. "We are legally wed. There be no reason to sleep apart."

Silently, she followed him, her delicate hand held in his. When they reached Crissie's suite of rooms where Pippa would stay the night, he pushed the door open. "Only this one evening, Pippa. After that, I promise you we will rarely if ever be separated. I will stick so close to you, you will grow tired of me and wish for time by yourself."

"That will never happen," she whispered softly as she leaned into him again.

He understood she didn't want to be alone tonight. Neither did he. The exact words he wanted to hear, he wasn't certain about.

"Now, first look down the hall. The door straight ahead is mine. If you need anything, don't be afraid to come to me. Second," his hand resting tenderly at the small of her back massaging gentle circles of reassurance with his thumb, he ushered her inside, "Crissie will not mind if you use anything she has left here. If it is here, it means she no longer wants or needs it. She is a little taller than you however..." He couldn't think of anything more to say. "In any case, I will see you in the morning. Sleep well, my *ceann daor.*"

After another slow leisurely kiss, which was not truly a kiss he'd like to share with her at this moment, he left. Heard the lock click. He wondered if he did the right thing leaving her alone in this huge place. She looked so forlorn, a lost waif in a home where he was the only person she knew. No, he wouldn't back down now. If he returned to the room, he'd frighten her to death.

Reluctantly, he closed the distance to his rooms, opened the door and found it the same as when he left. If anything changed, he couldn't tell. For several seconds, he leaned against the heavy oak door with his eyes closed, inhaling the familiar scents, hearing the normalcy of the castle. Here someone was always awake.

After a few seconds, he pushed away from the door, disrobing as he walked to the bath he'd had brought to his room. He let the clothing lie where it fell, bent on a thorough soaking in the steaming water before he found his bed for the rest of the night. Setting his head on the rim of the tub, he leisurely washed while he was thinking it would have been nice to share the bath with his wife. Tomorrow. Then he reminded himself he was the reason she was down the hall instead of with him. He soaked until the water became tepid. Once he was dried, he left the towel where it fell. For the first time since he met and wed Pippa, he slept naked.

Without her cuddled next to him, without the heat of her small body warming him, he found it impossible to sleep. She belonged next to him. He missed the small sounds she made while she slept.

He needed her.

Wanted her.

Craved her.

Foolishly, he sent her away for the night. Well, curse it all. He had a mind to walk to her rooms to make sure she slept with him. Groaning, he closed his eyes. He turned to one side then the other. Thumped his pillow trying to make it the right shape.

Cursed his stupidity.

I dinna ken what I was thinking.

When he heard his door open, he reached for his pistol, which wasn't by his bed.

"Doaty!"

You're an idiot, Roby McKenna. Scrambled to find his pistol. While the door to his bedchamber opened, he held the pistol still peering into the darkness, searching for the intruder. Holding his breath, he watched and waited. An apparition in voluminous white moved in an ethereal manner toward him, closed the door then held still. Hypatia jumped from her arms, swinging from one piece of furniture to another until she perched on top of a wing chair near the fire.

Speak o' the devil.

The breath he held slipped out slowly. When he inhaled, he could speak, "I should never have expected you to stay where you were put, Pippa McKenna. Perhaps I yearned for you to defy my wishes, which weren't actually my wishes. So, you are here. What do you plan?"

"No, I was afraid," her whispered words floated through the room, jerked his body into instant excitement. "I'm not used to sleeping by myself any more. In any case, I never want to be deserted again, at least not by you."

She tempted and aroused him like no other woman could. His body clenched in anticipation of the possibilities this night held, "I told you there was nothing to fear." He almost stood and walked to her then realized he was naked. Perhaps it was time for her to see her husband fully aroused and needing her.

"Can I come in?" She stepped forward without waiting for an answer. Even in the darkness he could see the way her body trembled.

"That nightgown has enough material to cover three of you." Laughter bubbled up. "You enthrall me."

"It was the only one in the armoire so I put it on. You told me to use whatever I needed." She moved closer. Her hands were clasped together in front of her. "You didn't answer my question. Can I come in?"

She waited by the closed door, shifting from one foot to the other. "Of course, yes."

Without revealing anything save his naked chest, he moved the covers to one side to make room for her. He didn't know if she was ready for this. Now that the time was here, not that there would be nothing between them save air, he didn't know if she would be ready, if she would understand. While she was bold beyond his wildest imagination, he didn't think she comprehended what went on between a man and a woman when they made love.

"I was lying here regretting the fact you were not with me. Over the last week, it seems I've become used to your sweet curvaceous body lying next to me as well as all that warmth you generate."

He resigned himself to the now inevitable outcome of this evening. Unless she told him no, she would be his wife in every way. They would consummate this marriage tonight.

When she settled in next to him, he wrapped his arms around her, pulling her close, inhaled the sweet scent of lemon and spice that floated to his nostrils. She must have bathed with the soap Crissie would have left. The scent was nice. Lavender suited her better.

"Do you think it will be easier to sleep? I've grown so used to you beside me, I knew I would never fall asleep without you," she murmured as her head settled onto his chest, her hand a bit lower.

"Probably not," he said gritting his teeth, telling himself he needed patience even as he ran a hand along her arm, pushing the sleeve away so he could feel bare skin beneath.

He was only a man. *With a man's desires.* Withstanding her charms another night was an impossible feat for him now that she lay once again in his arms. At this time, he didn't understand his determination to have a true wedding night, one that would occur after the clan Chattan wedding he intended. Would it make joining with her any sweeter? *Most assuredly no.* She was so dear to him, so very important that he didn't think he could live without her by his side in every way.

What did it matter?

Obviously, Pippa wanted the wedding night now or she would not have come to the room. She must comprehend why he set her aside for this one evening, at least a little part of the reason if not all of it. Just about anything she wanted he would move every obstacle to give it to her.

"We need to get rid of this thing," his words whispered close to her ear had the desired effect. He felt her body tremble, shudder as she moved closer to him if that was possible.

"It's called a nightdress. I would like to know the feel of you against me."

She slid her arms along his chest then across his collarbone to bury her face against him sending a tempest of heat pulsing through him as her lips touched upon him then stroked again then again. Her fingers found his nape then the back of his head as they played with his hair, toying with the length, massaging his scalp. She touched him, stroked him, moved lower then hesitated returning upward.

Desperate to feel the length of her tight against him, he fumbled with the buttons on the gown. He never felt so inept and clumsy in his life. Eventually, his trembling finger finished their chore. The fabric fell open, freeing her to whatever he wished to do. His hands on her legs, he pushed the fabric up her length, touching and caressing her as he traveled the route that would rid him of this outrageous hindrance to his objectives.

"A man would have never contrived such a blasphemous creation to hinder his lovemaking. All your nightdresses should be burned," he mumbled as he finally divested her of the horrible article of clothing.

He groaned as he felt her entire body pressed against his for the first time, lush full breasts next to his hard chest, wide hips against his narrow ones, flat belly pushing on his swollen member, thigh to thigh, toes running the length of his lower leg.

"I'm sure they did not. It was most likely a woman who wanted surcease from her husband's amorous attentions for one night who contrived the gown. It would not be my wish though."

Her voice sounded like a sultry dark purr against his neck. Warmth generated more heat as her tender moist lips continued to wreak havoc to his man's body, pleasing her ardent assessment.

"You are hot and curved in all the right places."

His hands bracketed her face while he studied her, searched her eyes. Her features were shadowed yet he was positive she was smiling, delighted with her small victory over his orders for the night. Soon, he would hear her cry out his name. Shortly, he would feel the heat of her secret depths yet to be entertained by the steel length of him.

"You are hard all over. Your body compliments those parts of me that are soft. I *ken* the tiny fact as surely as my heart pounds at the same tempo as yours. We beat as one. Did you know that? Can you feel them beat together? It seems I've waited for this moment for an eternity. Now it is justly here."

"Dearling, you are mine tonight and for always. Don't ever forget that fact."

His lips touched down upon hers, lightly at first. Sweeping his tongue along the softness of her full bottom lip, he took one second to memorize the taste and feel of her. Kisses were placed on her closed eyelids, the tip of her nose before he returned to her lips. He lingered there, stroked, caressed before he touched the heated underside of her lip, swept his caress across her teeth only to delve even farther inside the depth of her.

She moved against him, breasts touching him, inviting and dancing with his body until he thought for a certainty he could last no more than a moment longer. Surely, he would explode if he didn't slow the pace she unknowingly set that would drive him to take her before he could be positive she was ready for him. Her fingers stroked his chin, along his jaw. She rose up, her body sliding along his, placing tender kisses on the lobe of his ear, behind it. She touched him, teased and taunted him until he groaned with the pent-up desire he held in check for so long. He wanted to bury himself entirely in the magic of her slick hot center. Yet more than any of that, he yearned to bring her to the deepest, heated pleasure she'd ever know.

Ecstasy.

Delicious delight.

Petite mort.

When she arched her back, her belly pressed against the most sensitive part of him, he throbbed and pulsed. Scents of lemon and oranges wrapped around him. He took the moment to caress the tightened tip of her breast with his tongue, curving it evocatively around each one before sucking one then the other deep into his mouth. He delighted in the tiny mews of enchantment undulating from within her depths.

She bewitched him.

"You are the man I've been waiting for, the man of my dreams, Roby McKenna, you bad *mon.* I want you to show me every wicked thing you know about pleasure, touch me as you've touched no other. After this night I hope you won't remember any other woman who came before me."

"You enchant me. Enthrall me."

His breath was shallow, desperate for more air but more than that desperate to learn the essence of Pippa, his wife, his moonlit love. This was what dreams were made from. The primal dance they played was something from beyond their past, would continue into their future as he understood this knowledge would follow them through time as they encountered each other in another life then another.

Forever his.

He pulled her up to kiss her again and again. While his body cried out for release, he craved to make these moments last until neither one could hold back an instant longer. His kisses covered her face along her neck, trailed across her collarbone to return to her warm moist lips to explore and play the game she evoked.

This is what heaven is made of.

She ran her hands down his sides then behind him to curl around his buttocks. Squeezing then exploring, touching all of him there, even running her fingertips down the backs of his thighs for as far as she could reach. She stroked then caressed, rose higher to touch him intimately. What more could a man want from his woman?

"You are so hard..." she murmured licking his nipples, biting gently. "Except here," she squeezed.

He nearly jumped from his skin. Had not expected her to touch him there.

With all the power he could will to his loins, he held himself in check. His rod pulsed and begged for that which he was denying himself. He tangled his hands in the silken strands of her dark hair as she moved lower placing delicate kisses on him, his bellybutton, lower to evocative spots then lower still. She sipped and nibbled with her sharp little teeth down the length of one leg, lingering on one foot then the other before following the same pattern up the other leg. She nibbled daintily, laved with her hot tongue on either side of his rod, ignoring the pulse of his greatest need.

"Are *ye* trying to kill me, *lass*?" he asked as he pulled her up to lie sprawled on his chest.

"Your feet are still *verra bonnie*," she said softly her whisper floating across him, beguiling, luring, "But not as *bonnie* as other parts of you. Do you *ken* what I'm saying?"

"What parts are more *bonnie*?"

Truly, he didn't know if he could take much more of her exquisite investigations, the curious examination her daring words. He willed himself to do so.

"This part."

Her tiny, hot hand closed around him, squeezed and caressed until his growl he tried to hold back burst from deep inside. "I would like to kiss you there. Is that something that is allowed?" The low sultry quality of her voice aroused him even more.

Tempted.

Beguiled.

"Don't hold back. Everything is allowed."

When her lips closed over the tip, when she sucked him deeper into her mouth, he was sure he would lose his seed, in the moment embarrass himself, in the process terrify her. He wound his fingers through her hair, urging her on until he could withstand the suggestive, haunting caresses no longer.

She lifted her head to look at him and question when he would have her stop. "I please you?"

"*Verra* much. Now it is my turn to please you until you can do naught but twist and coil tightly as you beg for more of the same. I want you frantic with your need before I enter you, before we join together. Do you *ken* what it is I'm saying?" His voice was measured, throaty, holding promises to be sustained.

He followed the same pattern as she did as he discovered every sensitive, subtle part of her. His hungry kisses behind her knees, then to the tips of her dainty toes, left her panting and jerking at his hair. When he closed his mouth over the soft petals between her legs, she cried out, tiny sounds, imploring sounds, all surged and undulated from her as her body followed the same rhythmic pattern he planned. When he pressed his lips and tongue against the tiny pearl that would give her the greatest pleasure, he nibbled, bit lightly before laving with his tongue as he felt her nearly unravel from her skin. Beside herself with the need he generated, she cleaved to him. Her fingernails bit into his shoulders just as his would when he claimed her.

Above and below him the small world they were encompassed in whirled, spinning around him until he was too mindless in the throes of such divine ecstasy he wondered if either of them could endure. He'd never before believed the tales of seeing past lives in the subconscious when a shifter made love with his mate.

He did now.

She was in Edinburgh castle, tiptoeing into his room, sneaking past chamber doors. He surprised her, leaping out, scaring her for a second. She was in his arms, laughing, running her hands beneath the fabric of his shirt. He kissed her and kissed her. She looked the same except her hair was pitch black with a hint of blue, her eyes dark, deep sapphire blue.

He saw her in a field of heather as he walked toward her. She was spinning on her toes, her skirt flying around her knees. When she recognized him, she flung out her arms running to him smiling a kittenish grin. She was startling in her purity, the innocence he saw in her eyes. He swept her into his arms twirling and twirling in circles as she laughed, kissing him on the neck. His visions went on and on as he laved her most intimate parts with his tongue, nibbled with his teeth.

His glory, the splendor met no more boundaries when she twisted and arched beneath his hard body, giving more of herself than he would have asked for. This was what making love was about. He never experienced this before.

He rose above her then. With his knees he spread her legs farther apart. His mouth met hers again, sucking and nibbling while his fingers danced on her breasts, played with the tiny knot between her thighs, trailed lovingly over her softness.

"Please..." Her voice rocked him to his core.

"Are you ready, *lass*, a bit of pain before the pleasure? I will try to ease the way."

"Please, Roby, please."

This was the worst part of taking her, a virgin. He did not want to give her pain, only the rawest passion and ecstasy as possible. Clenching his teeth he touched her with his rod, slowly eased himself inside her slick heat. The rush of her cream surrounded and heated him. She was small, so very tiny, delicate and dainty. He was her antithesis.

He knew he would hurt her. Understood there was no choice if he was to go forward with the mating. Pushing in farther he touched the delicate shield guarding the essence of her womanhood.

"Only once," he reminded her. His wish for no pain was powerful but it would be to no avail. "After this you will feel nothing but joy."

With a powerful thrust he breeched her maidenhead. She cried out, writhing not in pleasure but in agony as she tried to buck him off. "Roby?"

He heard the torment as well as accusation in her voice. Saw the tears in her eyes as one slowly slid down her cheek to pool on the pillow beneath her.

Using all of his will, he remained motionless inside her as he tried to absorb the worst of her pain into him. "Hush, it will soon be done with. The pain of your first time will vanish."

He placed tender loving kisses along her lips. Tried patiently to wait until she responded to him again, until he felt the arch of her hips against his belly. The moment the pain vanished, he knew. She touched his face with her hands, her eyes opened while her hips rocked gently against his.

"You are mine," she murmured softly. "Make love to me. Empty your seed inside me."

"With pleasure, my *ceann daor*. With the greatest pleasure."

His thrusts now were fast and deep. He held her hips in his hands as she urged him on with her cries of fulfillment. Her tremors began as miniature spasms rippling along his length urging him deeper insides until they grew with their intensity. Tiny nails bit into his shoulders as if she claimed him. Still, he thrust harder and faster. The tempest inside the two of them matched each other. A wealth of hungry raw passion and need spurred him on.

"Roby...Roby...Roby..." she cried out his name over and over again as her body responded to his.

He drove and drove until he called out her name then fell against her. His kisses on her lips were gentle now, soft meant only to soothe and calm. He held her close taking all her emotions inside, binding her to him with his gentleness.

"How do you feel?" he asked as he braced himself on his forearms and pushed damp tendrils of hair from her face.

"As if I've run all the way from Inverness."

She laughed then, stroking his face with soft fingertips.

"You have sharp little claws, my tiny kitten. Was that your attempt to claim me?" he whispered.

"Did it work?"

"*Aye,* it did and very well."

"You're still inside me." The awe in her voice surprised and pleased him. "Does that mean we can do it again? I didn't think..."

"We can. As many times as you like."

He bent to kiss her chastely. Instead, he deepened the kiss enticing her, coaxing her once more. It seemed he was unable to stop the ever-rising heat within. "But perhaps we should get some sleep. Tomorrow will be a busy day for us."

He heard the outer door to his chambers open. He was only vaguely aware of the sound as he was so immersed in Pippa and what she was feeling. He didn't want to even imagine someone would invade this sanctuary of his.

"Roby! You're home and you didn't even stop by to tell us and give us a hug," Wynnie McKenna said as she stepped into his bedchamber all smiles with arms outstretched for a welcome home hug.

What the devil was happening? He sought to bring the covers over their heads. Couldn't. He peered harder at the light in a useless attempt to see through the shadows. The candlelight blurred her face. He recognized another figure behind her.

"Mother..." He raised a fraction of an inch from Pippa as he brought covers around her as quickly as possible. "You shouldn't be here."

Hypatia must have felt the same. She landed on Wynnie's head, pulling at her hair, chattering angrily. Wynnie ducked then swatted at the animal sending the monkey flying through the air. Hypatia caught herself. Now, instead of attacking she sat on place high above voicing her anger.

"Hypatia, no!"

Pippa was too late with her verbal command.

Roby's mother was staring at the animal then back to the bed. For a moment at least she appeared speechless.

It seemed his mother saw Pippa beneath him. "What are you doing? What is that animal doing here?"

She had the nerve to sound indignant, *nay* furious. This was an invasion into his inner sanctum. Since he turned sixteen his mother never came here unannounced.

But then again, he had been gone for a long time. He didn't have a quick answer that would appease her tender sensibilities. This was his room, his wife she was intruding on. He thought an apology would be offered. Didn't know how to explain Hypatia who was clearly frightened and angry.

"I told her she shouldn't barge in on you that she should wait until the morning hours to greet her long lost son," Connal said from somewhere behind her.

With a shrug of his broad shoulders, a wicked smile gathering on his face, "I've found she seldom listens or takes my advice when she's set on a course. Now she's embarrassed someone. Been attacked by a wee animal."

Robby groaned and Pippa whimpered.

"I asked you what are you doing in bed with a woman? Thought we agreed you would bed your doxies somewhere beside your bedchamber."

Wynnie was standing with her hands fisted on her hips, a harsh expression on her face. It looked as if she recovered from her fright as she was also trying to put her hair into place.

Of course, she knows what I'm doing in bed with a woman.

"We did," he agreed trying for a pleasant tone still waiting for an apology though he was sure he wouldn't get one until he explained himself.

At the moment he felt many things, pleasant would not be one of them.

"You get her out of here this instant."

She marched toward them appearing as if he didn't take care of the troubling matter, she might indeed yank Pippa from the bed despite her lack of clothing.

He saw his father's hand snake out to stop her but he was too late.

"I'm naked, mother, and so is Pippa. You need to leave."

"Not until..." It seemed she mulled over his words.

When he had time to look at Pippa, she was peering over the coverlet, only her wide green eyes showing her absolute fear.

It seemed to Roby his mother realized how inappropriate her demands were as Connal finally caught up to her. He brought her back against his chest. "Be silent now. We'll leave these two alone."

"She needs to go. As soon as we depart then we wish to see you in the north tower."

"No, there will be no meeting tonight." He heaved in a long deep breath. "Wynnie, Connal I want you to meet Pippa McKenna, my wife. I will not be seeing anyone besides Pippa tonight. I'd like both of you to get out of this room. Now. We will, however, see you in the north tower tomorrow morning after we rise. Whenever that may be. We've traveled for over a week now, slept on the forest floor and both of us are in desperate need of sleep."

~ * ~

"I'm sorry for the unannounced invasion as well as the insinuations," Roby said after his mother and father apologized more than twice before returning, he supposed to the north tower. "They can be overbearing when they think they are right," Roby said, tenderly stroking Pippa's flushed cheek with the back of his hand then smoothed his warm hand down her back.

"*Ye* can stroke all you like, Roby Mckenna. It's going to be a long time before I'm calm if that's what your efforts are trying to accomplish."

She found she could not draw in enough air to compensate for the minutes she couldn't inhale a miniscule drop. Could not breathe to keep her heart beating. Despite what she told him, she did find Roby's caresses comforting.

"If it's any consolation my father will keep her away from my suite of rooms for the night as well as the morning. We should relax and enjoy the rest of our wedding night. Since we began it early, I intend to wickedly have you more than once. Have to live up to my reputation."

Resting her head on his chest, she wanted to do just that. "I can try to relax. I lied. Holding me does help."

"Good then we should have a glass of wine as well as the food that I had brought to the room earlier. I keep a few bottles in another part of the suite. I'll be right back."

Her breath caught in the back of her throat. This time, this exquisite moment, she would remember forever. She was about to see him naked, all of him, every gorgeous male part revealed just for her. He rose from the bed. Didn't turn around. A ripple of disappointment washed through her. Still, she studied and enjoyed the back view, his taut buttocks, the play of his muscles across his back as he walked, the width of his shoulders tapering to a slim waist and narrow hips. With breath held, she watched as he returned.

"You are just as magnificent as I thought you would be."

Actually, he was more magnificent than her imagination. She had no words to describe his physique. She decided she would have to think about the right words. Starting with his feet a depiction she dubbed them with earlier already fit, *bonnie* feet.

Moving up his legs, his legs. She swallowed hard drinking in the sight. Hard, that was the best word. His muscles flexed with each step. She could have never imagined such handsome legs. His thighs were broad, well-muscled to do everything a man should do.

Such as making love to his wife. Speaking of making love, his sex wasn't the same right now. Unlike every other part of him it wasn't stiff, unyielding in what she assumed would be anticipation.

Deciding she should wait to describe it to a more appropriate time, she lifted her eyes to his belly. Flat. His belly was flat and solid just as the rest of him. There were lines across his stomach just like the washboards used in the scullery.

Amazing.

Truly, her body was nothing like this.

She found she was responding to the sight of his exquisite male form.

His chest was just as appealing as his feet, broad and hairy, soft hair, curling hair, hair she liked to wind her fingers around. The tiny male nipples on his chest fit him perfectly, not too big or too small.

He was flawless.

Perfect in every way.

His neck was broad. At the moment dark stubble covered his jaw. She liked the way the stubble rasped against her skin when he kissed her. Everything else, all the other parts of him, she'd seen before. Tonight, his smile was broader, wider. Spoke of male satisfaction while his silver-grey eyes shimmered in a language of confidence and arrogance that was exclusively Roby McKenna.

Now all she craved was to see his cat. He handed her a glass of wine before sitting down beside her.

"Like what you saw?"

"You are beyond a doubt the most perfect man in the world."

He chuckled softly, "And you, my little kitten, are also perfect. You fit me, all your soft curves blend and mold themselves with my hard planes. We are made for each other, a flawless fit."

"I'll never be a cat as you are."

Her soft sigh was wistful. Spoke of things she could not change. "It would have been fun to be able to shift, to run with you among the heather."

He was a silent for several seconds, seeming to ponder all that happened to them over the course of the days they passed together. "My little kitten, your flesh is just as silken as it would have been in a cat form. When I stroke you, you arch and purr begging for more. Your voice, when you hum softly sounds like a low purr. You are my one and only tiny kitten, given to me so I can pleasure you. See even now you are purring as I stroke your back. You twist beneath my hand, arch and coil in hopes of more attention."

"You are just being nice. Your gentleness is one of the things that has drawn me to you," she hummed in the back of her throat giving to him all that he spoke of.

"Truthful," he said as he figured out a way for her to agree. "Shall we talk about our marriage tomorrow?"

"I told you, *nay*."

She persisted in this course despite comprehending he would have his way. He gave her few choices. In this case, she was determined to garner a few of her wishes.

"If I agree to this second wedding, can we wait a day or two before the ceremony?" She held her breath in anticipation of his forthcoming answer. She held the air inside her lungs longer than she thought possible before he finally spoke. Just didn't know if he would bargain with her about something he felt so strongly about.

"Why? Why do you want to wait? I would know." He was twirling a strand of hair around his finger, bringing the length to his nostrils. Seeming to think on what she told him. "I *ken* no reason for this. The sooner we are truly wed in the ways of the clan the better."

Perhaps she had a chance here with him. She would be honest even though this honesty humbled her, knowing it was selfish to ask for these things, "Traditions," she spoke softly. "It's all about tradition."

"You've lost me," he said sitting against the headboard before pulling her against him.

He held her tight, his hands spanning her waist. Even that tiny contact generated thoughts she needed to put to the back of her head until they finished this conversation.

"If we are going to have a proper wedding as you see it, mayhap I'd like a proper wedding the way I see it. There are things a lass wants when she dreams of her wedding day."

She was keeping her hopes up. What little he said encouraged her. Little girls always have dreams about their weddings. She was no different. When she was standing on the gallows expecting to die, there were no dreams left for her.

Now she had them.

It seemed she also found the perfect man. Since it seemed logical now, she wanted to experience everything.

"So." He was stroking her arm, trailing a fingertip from her wrist to her shoulder generating a host of sensations none of which were compatible with talking. "What do you deem proper?" he asked, his voice soft. "I would like to make you happy. What will it take?"

"Not a lot," she murmured, trying to distance herself from the sensual coaxing he was about, refusing to give in to his sweet wheedling until they settled this to both their satisfaction. She didn't intend to lose all her powers of thought.

"Truly, not a lot doesn't tell me anything I can do for you, Perhaps you should trying be more explicit."

Nerves taking over her to watch him carefully, she plucked at the covers, folding the fabric between her fingers. She didn't intend to appear ungrateful. "I..." she began as she tried to figure out where exactly to start. Catching her bottom lip between her teeth, she tried to concentrate.

"I'm not going to bite," he told her tenderly, taking her chin between his fingers, turning her to face him more directly.

His thumb ran across her jaw.

She cleared her throat. "A wedding dress would be nice. Conversely, that would take more than a day. You did say that Horace and Harry would not be able to journey for at least a week. Can we have that time? A week?" Truly, she didn't believe that was too much to ask for. "They cannot possibly arrive soon enough to disrupt anything even if they were planning on coming to McKenna castle, which I sincerely doubt."

He didn't speak. Instead, she watched him draw into his lungs several deep breaths of air. The motion didn't bode well for her. "*Aye*, you deserve a dress. You are even smaller than my mother. Neither she nor Crissie would have anything appropriate to lend you. I would not want to see you marry me in your trousers and shirt. So, I suppose you have a valid point."

"It would not be seemly to do so as it would also serve to remind me of the gallows. I *dinna* wish to have that awful night in my head ever again, especially not on my wedding day."

If possible, she would put that dark evening in the deepest recesses of her mind never to think on it again. A new wedding would give her other happier places for her mind to travel.

In his arms he turned her, once more pulling her to rest against him. Her head rested on his chest "What else would you like mayhap a wedding feast? Some flowers?" His hands relaxed possessively on her belly while he absentmindedly stroked her.

"The eve before and if possible one after the wedding." Tears stung her eyes. Over the last five years she'd not thought to have anything like this. "Am I asking too much?"

"*Nay, lass*, you've every right to wish for everything a normal bride and groom request. I'm impatient to have all the necessities taken care of, that is all. If we do this, don't be surprised, we find more barriers to sleeping together. Mother will insist we wait until after the vows are said even while she is enjoying planning our wedding. She was unable to do so for Crissie."

"I cannot possibly sleep alone in that big room. The place terrifies me. Without placing guards at our doors, they cannot keep us apart. Can they?" She inhaled quickly thinking there had to be some way to counter his mother's not so good intentions. "What does it matter if we sleep together or not since we are already wed?"

"Mother would tell you that waiting will enhance the wedding night. She might be right even though I don't see how anything could be better than what we had together a few hours ago. We do have enough relatives for guard duty if she chose to go that route. Father might stop her though. One could only hope," Roby chuckled. His laugher next to her ear sent vibrations against her back.

"I would also like it if you could wear your kilt and sporran as well as your knee-high socks, ruffled shirt, velvet jacket. I understand it's against the law, but no one but the family needs to know. There would not be many guests."

"I would like that too," the sound of his voice grew husky, his kisses along her shoulder, tender.

"Will you ask your parents if they approve?" she asked as she twisted to look at him.

"I will do that." He moved her so she sat astride his hips.

She knew what he wanted again. Except she didn't, not now, not until they settled one more thing between them. "No, not yet, Roby. Please. This has to wait a few more minutes."

"You are tired? So soon?" He laughed brushing a palm across the tips of her breasts before settling a quick kiss on her forehead. "Did not think you had so little stamina."

"No, not tired, just wishing to see more of you." She stroked his chest with fingers that wanted to explore all of him. This needed to come first before any more lovemaking.

"Don't think there is more of me to see than you've already perused to what should be proficiency in the scrutinizing department."

He continued wheedling, sweet-talking until she arched against him, scarcely able to withstand his ardent devotion to her breasts then her lips. When he moved even lower, she understood if she was to truly get what she wanted, she would have to make sure he understood completely.

"Roby, stop. I want to see your cat. Show him to me. Please," she murmured as she bent to kiss his lips, touching the bottom gently with her tongue, eliciting a deep groan. "I wish to know if you're the one I saw five years ago."

"We will send for the dressmaker in the village as soon as we are up and about, before we interview with mother and father in the morning. How much of our story do want to tell them?" His voice was soft as he purposely changed the subject meaning to tease her.

Pippa had the clear feeling he knew what he wanted to say. Roby wasn't truly seeking input from her. He was a man. He would do what he thought best. "Eventually, they should be told the truth of our meeting. I'm not sure tomorrow is the right moment."

"Actually, I was thinking the same. We need not tell them about the way we wed in front of the gallows to save you from swinging or exactly how short the ceremony was. Obviously, we need to tell them the marriage was in haste. Why, is the biggest question hanging over our heads?"

She cringed at the mention of her swinging. She'd come perilously close, too close. "I suppose we could mention something about fate stepping in, having a hand."

"Fate," he mused softly his eyes twinkling with amusement. "What better way to describe what happened between us? When it comes to the interview, you need to let me talk. Mother will ask you direct questions. Whenever possible you need to defer to me."

Five years on her own made her stronger than she expected. "I won't comply to you, Roby McKenna." She wanted to poke him in the chest to emphasize the point she tried to make with him. "If she asks me directly, I intend to give her an honest answer."

"No, I don't suppose you will defer. You must, however, realize I've a much better idea what to tell as well as what shouldn't be mentioned where my parents are concerned," he told her tenderly running his long fingers through her hair.

Once again, she leaned into him, a soft hum forming.

"You're purring again," he told her.

"No lying. I won't stand for it. They will either like me the way I am or not." She felt far too defensive when it came to speaking of her most recent past.

"They will love you."

"You've no idea."

"Would you like to see my cat or let me slip inside you? You're after all ready for me. I can feel your dampness as well as your heat against my thigh where you are pressed."

"To see your cat, of course. If I allow you liberties right now, well then, it will be morning before we come up for air. I *ken* that fact just as you do also." She realized she wanted both, couldn't have both. One or the other would have to wait.

"I was afraid you'd say that." With a low groan he set her aside. He stood beside the bed in front of her. "I'd much rather make love to you."

"I understand," she murmured refusing to give in on this issue. "I will only ask this one time."

Avidly curious, she watched him, allowing her gaze to travel his long muscular length down then up. "Are you as magnificent as a cat as you are a man?" His gaze seemed to be centered on her lips as she moistened them. Her nerves spun as she realized the beat of her heart sped faster with expectation. Eagerness to see him took hold.

The transformation took little time. One moment he stood in front of her as a man the next instant he was a huge black panther. The very one she remembered from five years before. She forgot to breathe as she watched, unable to rip her gaze from him. Swallowing hard she reached out to him only to draw her hand back.

He sat, stared at her. Seemed to grin. Rubbed his head against her arm as if he wanted her to stroke his head. She did so, reveling in the softness of his fur. He had the ability to crush her between his jaws.

"You are a pussy cat, aren't you? Gentle, so very gentle."

Pippa ran a finger across the top of his eye following the path of a scar. "How did you get this, gentle creature," she said softly then ran her hand the length of his back.

Somehow, someway she didn't understand, she felt as much of a connection with the cat as she did for Roby, the man. She set her head against his, drinking in the connection they shared. This was something she never expected, never thought would happen to anyone let alone her. She wished she could understand exactly what he was thinking.

The power between them was loaded with energy. The strength seemed to suck the air from the room. The bond was undeniable. Who would have thought one moonlit night would change her life forever as well as make it so much better? When she stepped on to the gallows and the hood was placed over her head, she believed she was about to breathe her last.

Roby changed all that

She continued to stroke him as his purr grew stronger sounding more content with each pass of her hand along his spine. Beneath her fingers, he twisted and rounded his back. Tears welled in her eyes remembering the solace he gave her while she mourned the loss of her parents. Recalled how he let her cry against him until he was soaked through with the tears she shed on that horrible day. She would have never guessed they would once again be united.

More than fate brought them together twice, more than destiny written in the stars. Yet, she understood it could not have been coincidence. It wasn't. To what purpose were they bound eternally?

What was it?

She thought then perhaps now would be a proper time to tell him about Aaron and the few kisses they shared. He could roar and wake whoever was in the castle or he could listen quietly. *Or he could change back and confront her.* She pressed her hand along his back before sliding her questing fingers across his chest. "Cats are not supposed to like to have their belly rubbed. What about you, Roby McKenna, sleek panther? Do you like your belly stroked?"

Immediately, he jumped on the bed then rolled over, leaving his underside vulnerable. It seemed he craved her attention, even as a cat. His eyes, she was certain, were saying caress away while his grin told her he would make sure when he was back in his other form that he would with his body give attention to every part of her. She did so, laughing at his antics, his deep dark purrs rumbling up from what seemed to be his belly. She found him fascinating.

"It's time to speak of something I've neglected to tell you about my time in the gypsy camp."

She caressed a spot between his ears, ran a finger along the inside of his ear until it twitched. He set his chin on her shoulder.

He sat back. His eyebrows seemed to arch upward in inquisitive expectation. She grinned at him as she watched different emotions flit across his cat visage. It was so very interesting that he could not speak, could not assume command. Yet, if he so wished to, he could swiftly change to his human.

"I see by the way your brows are sloped upward you want me to continue my story. I only tell it now because you cannot speak your outrage. Well, you are not the first man I've kissed."

Her eyes grew cloudy with tears as she thought on the young man whose life was taken from him way too soon. Had it only been a month ago that they sat in front of the campfire and laughed? She had thought to make light of the kiss. Though, speaking of it brought more horrible memories to mind. A tear slipped down her cheek.

He cocked his head a bit sideways.

She let out a slow breath of air, listened to the wind sigh softly through the open window near the bed. A horse whickered. Another one answered. Somewhere far distant a dog barked. She wiped the evidence of her tear from her face. Aaron deserved more than a solitary tear. He did get more though. She sobbed for more than a day when they took him away while she sat in the stench of small dark enclosure they tossed her into.

Dragging in a long shaky breath, she began, "His name was Aaron. He was only a year older than me. He kissed me on the mouth."

Slowly, she brought her hand up to run across her bottom lip. I remember thinking it felt nice then wondered if that was all there was. I pondered that question for a while. I didn't have the answer until a man named Roby McKenna taught me there was so much more to a kiss than simple contact of mouth on mouth."

Her lightly whispered words seemed to cloud the air. She heard him purr, felt the pulsations too. It didn't seem to her that her tale made him angry.

Aaron was a boy not a man. Therein lay the difference. He wasn't inexperienced at all. She *kenned* he was not so experienced as Roby. She supposed there was good and bad about that fact.

"He died. Lord Bigley caught both of us with that rabbit roasting on a spit over the fire. He was hung the following morning. For some reason I'll never understand, I was saved. I sat in that foul smelling stench so long I wished I died alongside Aaron. If I had, Aaron would have been by my side standing on the gallows. I would not have been so terrified of dying."

Holding back the pain was no longer possible. Sobs wracked her body as she remembered and thought of other times, long ago moments that shaped her. If she'd had the ability to change form, she might have gotten away from the men who surrounded their little campfire that night. Might have been able to help Aaron fend those men off until they could make their escape.

It was not to be.

"I do so wish I could change form." Her breath was burdened with wistfulness, dreams that would never come true. She would have to take solace in the fact the man she was coming to love possessed that amazing ability. "I wonder," she spoke out loud as she continued to stroke his long back, "if in any of our other times together, I could also shift."

Silence wrapped around her as she waited for what? For Roby to shift back? For an answer to an impossible question? He seemed so content, purring while she gave all her attention to him, arching against her hand as if it was the best of all feelings. Gently nudging her hand when she stopped. "I'm hoping your mother and father will not judge me harshly. They could you know, when they find out what I did, what you did to save me. Will it matter if you believe I'm your mate?"

Startling her he leapt from the bed. Before she could gasp for a breath of air in surprise, he was a man again, tall lean and so very hard. He pulled her into his arms. "They will not judge you at all. I won't allow it. You're my wife. They will have nothing but love for you as will the rest of my family."

"Truly...?"

He placed a finger to her lips as he shook his head, his eyes sending messages. "Hush. Truly nothing. If you're thinking about Kit and his reaction to you in the beginning, well then think again. Kit has come around. He cares about you because I do as well as what will happen to both of us. He will help everyone understand what we mean to each other."

"Does he?" She wasn't as positive about this as Roby seemed to think. "What about Brady and Crissie? What will they believe when they find out who and what I actually am? A thief meant for the gallows. Can I ever go back to a normal life?" She had too many questions, ones that no one could answer. Roby only held promises to events and people he could not control.

"All we can do is forge ahead, make the best of everyday. Now, it is getting late, we should continue with our wedding night. Don't you think? There are so many ways to make love. I would enjoy exploring a few more before the sun rises."

He set her astride his hips once again. She felt his arousal intimately pulse against her. Felt the strong lean muscles of his thighs press alongside hers as he pushed her legs wider. He kissed her softly, so very gently as if he wanted to take all her pain away. They did make love then again until morning sunshine woke them.

She found herself curled into his arms. When he rose, he pulled the covers from her. "Come, let's not waste time. I've ordered a bath for you. A modiste will be here early after lunch. I will be back in an hour then we'll have our interview with my parents. There is a tray of breakfast foods along with a hot pot of tea."

He was dressing while he spoke. When he finished, he left. She smelled the fresh baked bread nearby on a table. Saw the hot steaming water. Wanted both the food and the bath at the same time. After grabbing a piece of bread slathered with butter, she settled into the water, soaking up the steam along with the ambiance.

Roby didn't say anything about Aaron. She was sure he agreed to extend the wedding to the end of the week. He never actually told her what he decided. Too many things sidetracked them. A dressmaker would come to make her wedding dress he told her before he walked out the door.

She had only the dreaded interview with his parents in her immediate future.

~ * ~

"What kind of explanation do you think Roby will have this morning?" Wynnie asked Connal as they were eating their breakfast in their rooms in the north tower. "He cannot possibly think we will believe he is well and truly married to that woman. He wouldn't do such a thing. Not without his family to be with him."

Connal sat back judging his wife's irritation with their youngest son as one of frustration coupled with disbelief along with an unwillingness to accept what was right in front of her nose. He understood his Wynnie wanted the best for their son. Understood too she didn't believe he was wed. This was passing strange. She would need to get to the bottom of his lies. Connal knew he didn't lie. Roby wouldn't say something to that effect just to keep a willing *lass* in his bed for the night. Together they came to an agreement a long time ago that the boys would not entertain women in the south tower. What Connal craved to hear was exactly how this all came about. It could be a grand story. Well worth the time it would take to tell.

"I believe him," Connal said softly with a grim smile.

He did not bring his children up to lie. Raking his hands through his hair, he thought carefully as to what he meant to say. "I too want to learn the details. However, you should trust your son to do the right things. After the two of you decided he needed more discretion in his life, I don't think for one second he would defy you. Especially not on his first night back after being out of the country for two years."

"Then she is his wife?" Wynnie tossed a pillow at him before she plopped down on the sofa close to the fireplace. "He truly married someone without our knowledge and acceptance. He did so in haste. What could have been so important that he couldn't wait to return home?"

He laughed as he deftly caught the airborne object. "Come here, wife," He patted his knee as she walked to him. "I'd like to hold you, soothe away some of those self-induced fears of yours. We need to be pleased with his choice, show our unity to him. What I saw of her, she is a beautiful *lass*."

She huffed as she leaned into him, her soft rounded breasts pushing against the hard planes of his chest just as he liked. "We are going to be denied planning a wedding for yet one more of our offspring. That is simply not right, not right at all. I have three children. Each and every one of them defied convention and married without the family nearby."

"You are disappointed though I'm sure when the first grandbaby comes you will forgive all assumed transgressions. We can still give them a celebratory feast tonight, perhaps a wedding breakfast on the morrow if we act quickly. I'm sure they will not be pleased."

She hit him on the shoulder before poking him several times to send her point home. "These are events that cannot be given back. Piffle, one feast or even two are just not enough to satisfy me. First Brady demanded an instant wedding. We caved in because there simply was no other choice."

"Much like ours," he mused thoughtfully thinking of that night. "Do you recall the events leading up to our hasty marriage? I'll never forget it. All I wanted to do was make everything right for you. You were so terrified. At first, I thought it was me who frightened you. Later, I came to realize the truth. As for satisfaction, we both will have to make do with their choices."

"That I was terrified of all men until you showed me how much I could always trust you." Her long sigh ruffled the collar of his shirt. "Then, then," she went on waving a hand in exasperation. "Our children are going to put more gray hairs on my head. Crissie was increasing with no wedding vows said as well as no groom insight. He didn't even show up until after the baby was born. When they finally did wed, they didn't bother to invite us. It was another hasty wedding."

"We could not stop what happened. In the end they settled their differences. They wed. We would not have been able to travel to Ireland in time for the wedding. It seemed they were not about to wait."

"Their reasons for not wedding sooner were many. It took them two babies and more than two years to say their vows along with a great deal of heartache. Crissie as well as their second child nearly perished because of his recklessness. I'm still not certain I've forgiven the man."

"True, should we get back to Roby and Pippa? They are the children who are frustrating us at the moment as well as causing us to go gray before our time," he asked as his hands found their way up Wynnie's ribcage to her soft breasts.

He cupped them in his hands as they filled them to perfection. He wished he knew if they had time for a bit of pleasure before the upcoming interview with his youngest son.

She batted his hands away in a feeble attempt to restrain him. "You just stop that, Connal McKenna. You had plenty of that last night to satisfy you for the rest of the day. We need to talk about Roby and Pippa. We need to demand a true wedding when they come here to see us in order to discuss the nature of their relationship. If they ever come to see us."

He smoothed a finger across Wynnie's eyebrows before caressing her cheek with the back of his hand. "What is there to talk about? We have to wait until they come see us to hear their story. And, my dear wife, my eternal love, I can never get enough of you to satisfy me for the whole day. A quick dalliance would not take too many seconds. If my guess is right, you are ready for me now. Should I discover the truth?"

She tried to ignore his advances. He was not about to allow her that. "They could not be wed for very long." She protested. "I'm sure of that, since he was not wed when he landed on Scottish soil. So, he met a doxy then in the process of bedding her decided she was his soul mate? You cannot believe that kind of story. Can you?" she asked.

"Seems to me to be a tale worth hearing. I recall that night you ran into me. We married the same night. I *kenned* you were my mate almost the moment I caught you off your horse and you claimed me by running your nails across my cheek in the process drawing blood. There was no question in my mind."

"That was different." She crossed her arms over her breasts to ward off his wandering hands.

"How so?" It took no effort for him to take her hands and wrap them around his neck.

"Stop that." Wynnie pulled at the top of her gown to cover her while he did the opposite. He chuckled as he knew who would win this battle of wills. "You *dinna* want to have me naked when those two finally decide to get out of bed and come see us."

"They will knock first."

"If it takes too long for you to open the door, they will know what we were about."

"Most likely."

Chapter Five

All the way down the stairs, Roby whistled, his joy this morning seeming contagious as he passed servants and friends. They all smiled back. He sent for the modiste with instructions that an entire trousseau was to be made up along with a wedding dress to incorporate the McKenna dress plaid. Roby wanted to see her in dresses. While he liked to watch her adorable backside in trousers, he didn't want anyone else to see her curves, at least not to that extent.

He decided that five days would be long enough to take care of all the details for the wedding. If the modiste thought the gown would take longer, well then he would hire more seamstresses to make sure the sewing of the dress was accomplished in record time. After speaking with the cook and arranging for the celebration on the eve of the wedding along with the wedding breakfast after the ceremony, he strode straight to the church to speak with the good father. It was to be a clan wedding including the Celtic words that would bind them through time.

Roby understood the importance of explaining some of the clan's rituals to Pippa. If he didn't, it would frighten her immeasurably. He would hold on to her during the chanting. Wouldn't let her fall. He didn't truly understand what someone like Pippa who was not a shifter went through during the ceremony as well as the claiming which wouldn't happen until their real wedding night. Brady's wife, Lilly, never spoke of it except perhaps to Brady. Their clan wedding had been done in private. So, perhaps there was little to speak of. He should ride out to Brady's home and ask a few questions.

Her eyes lit early this morning when he showed her his cat. The way she looked at him instilled a sense of pride in his abilities as a shifter.

A man couldn't want more than what she gave him when she showed him how much she cared for both of his male forms. The fact she wasn't in the least bit frightened, was surprising yet it wasn't.

When she told him about her first kisses with a boy named Aaron, he pushed thoughts of jealousy aside reminding himself she had a life before him, as did he before her. As he thought on all the women he bedded before Pippa, along with the life he led, he had no reason to feel jealous of a single kiss. He had his share of bed playmates.

Strangely, he did feel jealousy coupled with a sharp tinge of pain that it had taken him so long to realize she was his mate. He should have known the day she held him while he was in his cat when her parents died. If that had been the case, she would have never found herself standing on the gallows waiting to die.

Ah, now in a very few minutes they had the interview with his parents to endure or look forward to. He wasn't at all positive what the outcome would be. They would have to accept Pippa as his wife. In this his parents had no choice. If they didn't do so immediately, time would have to work in their advantage. They would have to find a means to convince Connal and Wynnie of their truths. He didn't expect there to be too much trouble though. His parents were reasonable people, at least most of the time they were judicious and thoughtful. He could think of a few instances, when he was younger, he thought them anything but evenhanded. So many times, his mother would jump to the wrong conclusion before hearing all the facts. If the situation was dire enough, at times she would mete out the punishment then listen later.

After all the two of them allowed Walker Endicott to take his sister and child with him without benefit of marriage. He recalled his own anger at the time. If Crissie had been his child, he would have never allowed such a travesty of disrespect to take place. The man would have wed her or he would have taken him north and lost him in the wild crags of the highlands. Perhaps he might have sent him through the Kinnel Stones never to return. That would have been a fitting punishment.

This situation wasn't anything the same.

He sent a message to his parent's suite of rooms telling them they would arrive shortly then he strode up the steps to the south tower and

Pippa. She would balk. He would have to reassure. When he entered, she was sipping tea in one of the large brocaded chairs by the fireplace. A smile formed when she saw him step through the door.

A penny for your thoughts.

"I wondered when you would be back. I'm not looking forward to meeting your mother again. Anyone tell you she can be highhanded? Maybe we should take Hypatia with us for protection," she spoke softly as she stared at her fiddling hands. A hint of desperation clouded her green eyes and there seemed to be more gold flecks around the edges. It was possible the flecks appeared more dominant when she was nervous.

He chuckled at the thought of the little monkey, the way she'd come to their defense last night. It was probably another something they would have to defend. "I had a few errands to run." He sat down on the chair next to hers, picking up her hand in his as he did so, massaging the wrist gently with his thumb. "I did hurry but there were a lot of people to speak with. All took time. The wedding ceremony will take place in five days. Is that enough time for you?"

"Yes, of course. Errands such as...?" With her eyes she questioned. He could almost see the wheels turning in her head.

He grinned as he touched her lips with his finger, journeyed across the soft fullness, hesitated before beginning to speak. "I talked to father Damian. Saw the cook about the celebration the evening before the wedding as well as the breakfast after the ceremony. They are all eager to do their best for us. Perhaps you could give them a list of foods you adore."

"Thank you." For a moment, she looked down, seemed to be staring at their joined fingers.

"You will have the celebratory feet washing?" His soft chuckle produced an answering smile. "I would not want to bed you if your feet were dirty. Subsequently, there is the chance for the next bride to be picked when she finds the hidden ring in the dirty wash water."

She let her lashes lower, her endearing smile widening then speaking softly. "Yes. I believe I would like everything that goes with a wedding including wearing white heather in my hair."

"You've turned unusually quiet. Are you still nervous about

meeting my parents?" His mother truly put fear in her eyes when she barged into his bedchamber last evening. "Do not fear them. They are actually quite nice once you get to know them and see past their bluster. They will listen to our story without judgment. I promise."

"I cannot help but fear the unknown. Cannot help but wonder what my parents would have said at our hasty marriage. Probably they would think the same things as your parents. They would also question the authenticity of the union." She stole a wavering breath from the air before closing her eyes for another moment.

He wanted nothing more than to drag her into his arms and reassure every doubt of hers from her head. Even when he understood the fear would not go away until she actually met these people she believed were monsters.

"My parents will know I haven't lied."

"They will hate me."

"They will come to love you," he said softly. *As I love you.*

The unspoken thought caught his breath, took him totally unaware. The sensation of deep love coursed through him. He supposed it was natural for a shifter to love his mate. The sentiment seemed to go with the idea. He wondered if she felt the same about him.

He wanted to hear words of love flow from her lips.

"I will keep that thought in the forefront of my mind. What about you, Roby McKenna? Will you come to love me?" she asked even as he knew the identical emotions were surging inside.

It was too soon for him to voice his sentiments, too soon to tell her what he just now realized. She wanted his love but once again he wondered if she loved him as well.

"Are you ready to go?" Roby stood while ignoring her question. Saw the frown lines mar her tiny face. He held out his hand. "I would get this over with. First thing, we should explain that we want another wedding here with our family surrounding us. Mother will be pleased."

She placed her hand in his. Her fingers were cold, chilled from the worry over meeting his parents. He supposed if he was going to be introduced to her parents for the first time, he would feel shaky as well. When she stood, he pulled her into his arms. He held her close for the longest time, resting his chin on the top of her head. His hands ran the length of her back, stopping at her bottom to tug her against his straining arousal. He wanted her to understand this wasn't his choice of events at this moment either.

"It will all be fine." He brushed a gentle kiss on her lips, lingering for a few seconds as he thought about foregoing the meeting. In its place he could take her to bed. He pulled away, tenderly touching the length of her jaw. "Shall we?"

She settled her hand at his elbow. He placed his on top of hers. Then with a long breath of air, he began the journey to his parent's room. For some reason this march felt like a walk of doom.

When they knocked, his father called out for them to enter. As he pushed the door open, he felt Pippa's resistance. Against him her petite frame stiffened. Yet with a barely concealed trembling, she stepped inside. There was nothing more he could do to ease her fears. He only prayed that when they left, she would feel better.

"Good morning," Connal met them, picking up Pippa's hand in his, he kissed the back. "I hope you had a good night's sleep." He winked at her.

His father had the audacity to wink at his wife? Roby watched as heat swept the length of her. When he looked at her, a beautiful shade of pink stained her cheeks. He wondered if his father planned the not-so-subtle last statement to unnerve both of them.

"I slept well, thank you," she murmured softly looking away for a second before boldly meeting his gaze.

At that instant he was satisfied.

"As did I," Roby laughed, proud of Pippa for not backing down. "Do you not care about my sleep."

"At the moment, no," his father said laughing while he ushered Pippa to a comfortable place to sit. "Come in, we've tea along with bread and cheese if you are hungry. Cook sent up some lemon tarts, which are delightful as well as lavender cakes with sweet icing. This could be a long morning so please help yourselves."

"Tea would be fine," Pippa murmured softly as Roby followed her taking a possessive place near her. She sat as he walked behind and stood, his hands rested protectively on her shoulders. He hoped his presence would give her some much-needed confidence. Beneath his hands her body still trembled.

"Now," Wynnie began while she was pouring the tea and setting a few treats on each saucer. "How did the two of you meet?" She was staring at Pippa, but Roby's squeeze to her shoulders told her he wanted to answer. In her present condition, he didn't believe she would object. It was just like his mother to start with the most difficult questions. Perhaps he could skirt the truth without actually telling a lie.

"We met just west of Glasgow, an isolated place. Not too many people live there. The moon was huge that night. Pippa was in need of some much-needed assistance so Kit and I decided to help her. I'm heartily glad we made that decision. As you can see that one choice has changed my life forever."

"How so? What kind of help?" Wynnie leaned forward as she set the cup on the saucer. She was glaring at him as if she knew he did not tell everything. "It seems you helped out considerably more than Kit. Did you have to wed her? Was her father chasing you out a window?"

He felt the sting of his mother's words, the insinuation that was more a statement. His reputation with the ladies was not a good one, but he'd never fled a woman's bedroom with the threat of marriage riding on his freedom. The women he was amorous with were widows or certain barmaids he'd been attracted to since his youth.

"None of your suggestions, mother. Let's just say, the only way out of the predicament she found herself in, though no fault of her own or mine, was marriage. I volunteered."

He hoped that would be enough information. He could hardly mention the part about the gallows and the hood over her head.

"I see," Wynnie murmured, her eyes focused entirely on Pippa as if she stared at her long enough, she would actually see the truth.

"I don't," Connal said. "Can you be a bit more explicit? What exactly was the circumstance?"

Short of telling his father what he wasn't ready to confess, he had to tell him the topic was closed. "No. No, I cannot be more exact. The circumstance is between Pippa and myself."

"You intend to keep secrets," Connal said clearly appearing displeased with his answer.

"In this I do. Now, we can also tell you that we would like a real wedding. I would just as soon dispose of how we met. You should understand Pippa is my soul mate. We have an unquestionable bond. I would have father Damian wed us in the way of the clan."

"You would. Has he agreed?" Wynnie asked, she stared at Pippa who was still obviously distressed.

"Spoke with him this morning. Talked to the cook to arrange two celebratory feasts, one before as well as one after. He's in agreement. Sent for the modiste who should be here after the midday meal." Roby enjoyed the ever-changing expression on both parent's faces. He knew now they would accept his decision to remain quiet about their meeting.

"You have everything taken care of then," Wynnie said her voice still held a hint of disapproval. "I don't understand the need for two weddings although I'm pleased."

"I don't have a ring as of yet. I'll take care of that tomorrow." Roby wanted to tug Pippa into his arms then tell her she'd won over his mother even though he didn't believe for a moment all the questions would end.

"What about you, Pippa? Do you want all this?" Connal asked seeming concerned at her silence.

She cleared her throat taking several seconds longer than necessary to answer. She looked to Roby before her gaze turned back to his father. Her fingers continued to pluck at the fabric of her trousers. "I asked him to wait for a few days. He wanted to marry tomorrow, well, today. At first, I didn't want the second wedding. I thought better of it."

"You want what he can give you," Wynnie changed tactics it seemed trying to elicit more information.

"I do. If you are asking If I'm using your son, well, then you should know that I am. I haven't lied to him nor will I lie to the two of you. I need him as well as his family if I'm to survive." She paused then for several seconds. Once more, she looked to Roby as if seeking advice. "He does gain some advantages with the wedding."

For a few seconds Roby looked everywhere but at his father and mother. There would be more questions, many more. Well, it couldn't be helped. She brought this up. Perhaps it was best to get as much of the truth out of the way as soon as possible. This was, however, sooner than he wished.

"How so?" Connal asked as he settled himself into his chair stretching his long legs out in front of him, appearing content now just to listen.

To Roby, it didn't seem his father was overly concerned about her confession. Roby squeezed her shoulders hoping she would understand his need to answer. "Pippa comes into her inheritance when she turns twenty-one. Since I married her, I now control her estate."

"Who's controlling the funds now?" Wynnie asked clearly displeased by the direction of the conversation. "I know there is more the two of you are not telling. I get the feeling there might also be danger to you, Roby. So, out with it."

Roby whished the interview was done. Nevertheless, they were a long way from finished. "As soon as I can visit Clearborne Manor and thereby take over the running of the estate, I will be in charge. Pippa will have one-hundred percent say in what happens."

"You will have to visit the advocate for my parents. They have all the necessary documents," Pippa told him with a shaky breath of air. "If all the paperwork is in order, then..." she swallowed the lump forming in her throat seeming to wonder if she was saying too much.

He interrupted her. "Not until after I have the second marriage license," Roby said, determined now to make sure everything was in order by the time the Finchbottoms returned to the highlands. When they did, there would be nothing for them to claim. He understood he would have to move quickly.

"That all seems well and good. Why do you have to wait until after your second wedding?" Connal asked, sitting upright now, appearing to lose some of the nonchalance of a few seconds previous. "And how is she using you? It appears to me and from what you've said, you are faring very well from your marriage to Phillipa MacPherson."

"So, you *ken* who she is."

"Yes as well as a few other things," Connal spoke softly, his brows

124

narrowed. "There is much you haven't told us."

Pippa held up her hand to stop Roby. He didn't want her to tell them what he knew she was going to say. "As you guessed there is more to the story. My cousin along with his father has been in control of my inheritance these last five years while I've been gone. They won't want to give it up easily."

"No, I would think not," Connal said seeming to understand they might go to great lengths to maintain what they deem as theirs. Thoughtfully tapping his chin, "The Finchbottoms...seem to recall hearing about them moving themselves into the manor after your parents' untimely death."

Pippa turned ashen as she fought for air. Her hands clasped so tightly the knuckles turned white. He pressed his hands on her shoulders. "Correct. Pippa believes they might do anything to keep what they want. The younger one, Harry, intended to wed her, threatened her as well. Didn't see a reason to wait until she came of age."

"Five years ago?" One of Connal's eyebrows arched in conjecture, as it appeared he mulled over all that had been said. "She was gone all that time. No one knew where she was. At least no one spoke of it. Phillipa survived. She must have had substantial help."

"We will have to make sure none of what you're alluding to occurs," Wynnie told them ignoring her husband's speculations. "Now, a plan needs to be set in motion to insure Phillipa's future, beyond the wedding."

She turned to Pippa, a wide grin on her face. "Do you know the name of the barrister who controls your family's estate?" she asked then, "These Finchbottoms, how are they related to you? They are obviously not highlanders."

Pippa didn't answer right away. She gave it some thought as if she was reaching into the depth of her memories. When she looked at Roby, he nodded his approval. "McPhee, Cameron McPhee. His office is in Inverness. I don't know where though. Horace and Harry are distantly related to my mother. They lived in Dorchester before they moved into the manor or so they say."

"Good," Connal said, "I didn't expect you to remember his name.

It's nice to understand their relationship to you is slim to not at all. How old were you when you left Clearborne Manor?"

"Fourteen."

"We heard rumors concerning your sudden disappearance. The Finchbottoms tried to make light of the fact you seemed to have vanished into thin air. People did search for you. It was presumed you were dead. So, they settled into your home with no one to gainsay them."

"Obviously, she is no longer in seclusion," Roby said blandly. "Pippa intends to claim all that is rightfully hers."

"Clearly she is not," Connal agreed with a soft chuckle along with another wink directed at Pippa. "I will send Alistair into Inverness to locate the man, your family's barrister. He must be found soon and brought here before the Finchbottoms can sink their hands into more of your money. They've had ample time to divert the money elsewhere. Although they cannot assume the land holdings, deeds and tittles as easily. Those will still be in your name only because nobody was found."

"Is it that easy?" Pippa asked. "They will try to kill Roby to get to me. I know they will."

"That will not be so very easy to do," Roby said, realizing his family was behind him.

Now, they would accept the fact Pippa was his mate. They were already banning forces as well as making plans to secure her future, which until now had been severely jeopardized.

"Shall we plan a wedding?" Wynnie asked, a delightful smile now replaced the furrowed brows. "I shall like very much to be a part of this."

"I've started the plans in motion. You may help if you like. The modiste should be here soon," Roby said looking from his mother to Pippa who was once more backing away from his mother.

"I understand we got off to a rocky start. If it's all right with you, Pippa, could I come along with you for the fitting and to select a gown? I didn't get to do that at my daughter's wedding." Her voice sounded wistful with a touch of pleading.

Pippa pushed back against the chair, her shoulders tightening. It was clear to Roby his mother's presence was the last thing Pippa wanted to agree to. Yet, he sensed how much her agreement would mean to

Wynnie.

"Please say yes. I didn't get a chance to even attend my daughter's wedding let alone help with the gown." She reiterated the facts. "You are my daughter now, you *ken.*"

Pippa turned to look at him, her green eyes shimmering with what he thought looked like dread. She closed them for a second before looking at Wynnie and nodding her head. "I would like your help along with advice. I've been away for so long I've no fashion sense whatsoever. Mayhap we can get to know each other better by sharing this time. My mother along with my father died five years ago, you know."

"We know. Their deaths were a terrible tragedy. While I cannot replace your mother, I can be your friend. You're a McKenna now. You have the support of the entire clan. The clan wedding will bind you to clan Chattan even more. Together we will make sure your wedding is everything you dreamed of having for yourself."

"I would like a friend here at the castle. Who but the mother of my husband would make a better one?" she spoke softly touching her hand on top of Roby's.

Roby allowed a slow breath of air to leave his lungs. This was what he wanted for them. She would be happy here. So would he. Pippa now had his mother's approval. She would learn soon enough Wynnie was all bluster when it concerned her children. That night when she found them in bed together, she'd been a mother bear defending a cub that needed no defense, at least until Hypatia attacked her.

"What did happen over the last five years? Where did you go?" Connal asked appearing to want more of her story.

"Until great grandfather died, she lived with him," Roby said, his thumb moving in gentle circles on top of her hand.

Of course, they would want to know everything. "After his death, for a short time she was with Thadeus Tubbs and his wife then she lived with a tribe of gypsies. That's how she managed to survive all that time. She was never truly on her own."

"Callum?"

"Yes, he was truly," Pippa paused, "wonderful to me. He wanted me to come to you. It seems I got lost on my way here."

~ * ~

Five days later Pippa was escorted to the church by Wynnie and Brenna Stuart, Roby's aunt. Hypatia was to come later with Kit who she seemed to adore. As she rounded the corner of the gardens redolent with the scent of rosses, a tiny gasp of surprise rippled from her when she caught site of Roby. He stood in front of the huge wooden door to the church with Kit and Brady by his side. Connal walked up to her, lending her his arm so he could escort her to his waiting son.

"Are you ready to wed my son, *lass*?" he asked, his smile wide. "I *ken* he is more than eager to begin his new life with you."

"As I am with him." She had her fears though, too many to count on one hand. Harry and Horace were still a threatening force in their lives despite what the McKennas thought of their own prowess.

She tugged into her lungs a wealth of rose scented air, knowing that despite the intimidations this was her destiny, to be with Roby. Fate decreed they meet on that moonlit night now a fortnight gone by. It had also commanded that they meet on that long ago day five years in the past. She prayed everything would turn out as they planned. "Yes, I wish my mother and father could see me. I am ready though," she paused looking into Connal's eyes, which showed her his sincerity.

Connal patted her arm, seeming to understand her sentiments. Last evening the celebrating carried on into the *wee* hours of the morning. The *lass* who found the ring after the traditional foot washing had a lad she said she loved. She hoped she would soon be his wife along with the fact the discovery would spur him into making a proposal.

The skirt of Pippa's gown was made from the McKenna dress plaid. She wore a small sash fashioned from the MacPherson plaid to show the uniting of the two clans. The corsage was a dark green, the neck lined with tiny seed pearls and lace.

Roby stood with his hands clasped behind his back rocking slightly on his heels. The sight of him stole her breath as he was clad in his kilt and sporran. Her gaze traveled the length of him taking in first his knee-high socks then farther up to rest on the fine lawn of his ruffled shirt.

The green velvet jacket he wore fit his broad shoulders. When he grinned at her, she was positive he was thinking of the night to come. Despite her very real nerves stretching to a breaking point, she couldn't help but grin back.

Wynnie did keep them separated at night but only for the last two days. Pippa was certain the woman was correct about the wedding night. The fact they weren't allowed to sleep together before would make the wedding night different if not better. Just thinking about his naked body flush against hers sent her heart thundering.

He would claim her tonight. He told her he didn't want to wait. She wasn't entirely prepared for so many unknowns. He explained to her it might be painful. That didn't bother her as she knew he would do his best to keep the pain minimal.

What worried her was the ceremony inside the church. He was unable to tell her much of anything only reiterating that it was different for every woman. None of the women he approached wished to speak of the ceremony.

While they walked in the direction of the church, flower petals were thrown at the path in front of them. Rose petals coated the ground. This was what she wanted, dreamed of since she was young. Oh, not just the rose petals but everything that went with them. Connal squeezed her hand as they stepped forward. When she stood in front of Roby, her father-in-law kissed her on the forehead before he sat down.

Quietly, they both spoke their vows. The priest conducted the joining ceremony then they were led along with the witnesses into the church. This was where the clan Chattan would make her one with them. What would happen here was unknown. While she wouldn't become a shifter, she believed she would see much of her past life.

It could be a harrowing experience for one who was unaware of the traditions of the eternal joining of two people. She breathed in deeply while her hand tightened on Roby's arm. Strengthening his hold, it seemed to Pippa he was trying to give encouragement.

"You will be fine. I won't leave your side," he murmured as he bent low so only she could hear his words. "This will be for solely the two of us to know. As with the others what happens now, we are the only ones who will *ken*."

"Still, I'm terrified," she said as she walked beside this man who she loved more than she ever could have imagined. They had been together such a short time. Still, she felt as if she'd known him her entire life. What was between them was life changing.

In front of the altar they stopped, her small hand within his larger one shook. She felt a breeze filter through a door or a window, ruffling her hair. Nevertheless, it seemed strange. Was it happening already? She tried to draw in a full breath. It settled on top of her lungs not seeming to go further.

She faced Roby, her hands held tightly in his. When he placed both hands around her waist pulling her close, she was surprised then not surprised. He told her he would support her. She thought the words were theoretical not actual, not realizing she might not be able to stand on her own. A shudder undulated through her. His fingers tightened. She closed her eyes for a moment before focusing on the silver shimmer of his eyes.

When the priest began to chant words she didn't entirely understand, she closed her eyes again, to no avail, listening trying to concentrate on the words that were being spoken in the traditional marriage of two members of the clan. The floor along with the walls spun around her, slowly at first then increasing in speed until it all became a blur of constant motion.

As did Roby.

She caught her breath in her throat. Held it for as long as she could. He pulled her flush against him as her knees threatened to buckle.

I will support you.

Her mind reeled as the slight breeze turned harsher, blowing against her face, whipping at her hair. Strands fell loose, touching her face as well as her neck. The priest's voice grew louder, ringing uncomfortably in her ears. A huge black panther loomed up in front of her. His forelegs rested on her shoulders. She felt his heartbeat as if it was her own. It was Roby. Her head fell against his chest. For a moment only, she closed her eyes again opening them when she sensed there was more she needed to see. Some unseen force insisted she keep them open.

Bile rose in her throat, a tightening of her belly left her winded, panting for air, unable to think beyond the shadows and lights that played around her. The panther vanished as suddenly as it appeared. In its place was another cat. She knew then that once in another life she'd been able to shift. Here, she wasn't a black panther but she was a panther. He stood in a field of heather and watched her as she ran in her cat form. When she wasn't looking, she didn't realize he followed, he ran beside her.

Those scenes vanished to be replaced with a slender beam of light that surrounded the two of them as he held her in his arms, filled her soul with happiness she didn't know except when her parents lived. He lifted her off the ground, turned in a circle as he gently kissed her. She didn't know if this was real or imagined.

At this moment, her mother and father were standing in front of her. She filled her lungs with air as she tried desperately to reach out to them, to touch them. They were too far away.

"We are proud you," her father told her. "You survived when all the elements seemed to be against you. Fate helped. We're sorry we couldn't be there for you."

"We love you, Phillipa. Don't ever forget that," her mother said as both forms began to fade into a different light.

"I love you too," she whispered with bleak despair into the nothingness that was left for her to see.

Slowly, the spinning began to slow. The whirling in her ears became nothing but chattering of birds from outside the church. Her head rested on the warmth of Roby's chest. She heard his slow even breaths along with the strong, steady beat of his heart. Tears stung her eyes. Once again, her knees threatened to buckle or perhaps he'd been supporting her through this entire ordeal. Now he swept her into his arms.

A cheer resonated throughout the small church. She allowed him to carry her down the center aisle all the way to the main dining hall where the feasting would begin. When she gazed into his eyes, she saw the concern etched in the dark gray depths. He tried to smile, his lips quivering.

When he finally set her down in a chair, tender concern written on his face, she reached out to touch his jaw. Lightly as well as in awe of everything that took place this day, she trailed her finger along his chin.

"I *dinna* think I can stand for a while. Do you mind?"

"You will tell me all about what happened? Your experiences?" he asked as he hailed a servant who was carrying a tray filled with goblets of wine. He picked up two then handed one to her. "Drink slowly. You'll feel better in time for the wedding night, I pray."

He smoothed his thumb across her lips a twinkle in his eyes. She was sure she knew what he was thinking.

She wanted it too.

She nodded as she drank deep, the warmth filling her insides her gaze focused on him. The wine was delicious. "I..." she had no words at the moment to descried all she felt and thought she'd seen. Yet she knew he would persist. He deserved to hear from her lips what happened to her.

"I?" he chuckled softly as he still observed her with more concern than was necessary.

"In a while, I promise you will be apprised of everything that happened when the priest was chanting. Did you see anything?"

She was so very curious about his part in the images dancing around her. Curiosity drove her to wonder if he saw the same things she did.

Roby lifted his shoulders that were encased in the green jacket, the ruffles shivering as he did so. "I saw you, your pale face. Watched as you slowly lost the ability to stand. I held you upright while the priest chanted. I saw only you, Pippa."

"You kept me from falling?" she asked her voice weak with the overwhelming fatigue she felt.

"Yes, I felt your warmth, the beat of your heart, the breaths you inhaled throughout the ordeal. It was as if you were part of what happened to me. Understood you were as much a part of the ceremony as I was. Truly, you didn't see anything?"

The thought he saw and felt nothing unnerved her, shook her.

"Congratulations to the bride and groom."

Kit stood in front of them, a goblet of wine held high. Hypatia sat on his shoulder, chattering nonsensical sounds. She appeared happy. Kit was grinning foolishly. Then laughingly, "I'm glad I was of help with the introduction of the two of you. If it wasn't for me..." He left the thought hang in the air as the celebration of their joining grew louder.

"Thank you," she murmured holding her own goblet high before drinking again.

If he'd had his way, she would have died that night. He had to have no interest in her though. He wasn't her mate. Roby was.

"Thank you, Kit. That means a lot to us," Roby said.

"I will leave the two of you alone to pursue what husbands and wives do at marriage feasts," he chuckled grinning widely.

"It's the afterward I'm looking forward to. The feast is for the others," Roby winked at Pippa, while his questing hand grew bold.

Somehow, she found the energy to punch his arm.

Platters of food were served, placed on the tables. More wine was brought out as the musicians began tuning their instruments. Friends of Roby's wandered by offering blessings to their union. She leaned into him, soaking up his warmth, her hands holding on to his arm as if he could give her strength.

Pippa smiled and nodded as she moved slightly away from him. She picked at the huge plate of food Roby placed in front of her. When he poured her the third goblet of wine, she pushed it aside thinking to leave it until later. She didn't want him to find her asleep, her head on the table. *Nay*, she wanted everything, including the wedding night she'd been looking forward to since they first decided they would have this day.

He would claim her.

She sucked in a shaky breath of air, her nerves shattering.

Fiddles and bagpipes played lively tunes. The attendees danced and ate. Much of the village was now in attendance. Everyone had been invited to share in the celebration of the laird's son and his new wife. If there was any trouble brewing beyond the walls of the castle, no one knew of it. The Finchbottoms were out there somewhere, plotting. For the first time since they decided on this second wedding, Pippa had misgivings. Perhaps this had not been prudent. What if those two plotted his demise or her demise? She couldn't live with that.

"When can we retire to our rooms?" she asked as she rested her head against his chest. He played with the strand of her hair that came loose during the ceremony. She felt the soft rumble of his laugher.

Beneath the table he placed her hand on his straining erection. She felt him stiffen even though his grin was obvious.

"Well," he began a tender smile twitching at the corners of his mouth, "We must dance at least once. I do believe you will owe my father as well as Kit one dance, perhaps not a lively jig but something a bit slower. Not positive you've the stamina for too much. So, depending on how you be feeling, it might be a little while before you are up to dancing."

"I would tell you that we should just do it. Though you would have to hold me, prop me up in your arms all the while praying I don't step so often on your *bonnie* feet. Would not want to mar them."

With every second that passed she was feeling stronger, more and more eager to spend the night alone with her husband. The wine might have helped or the bits of meat and cheese Roby fed her. Even now he was holding a strawberry in front of her lips insisting she eat. Slowly, he ran the berry across her bottom lip, teasing her, enticing her. She didn't need coaxing to want him as much as he seemed to want her.

"Nothing of any value should be just done. Our dances together will hold a wealth of meaning, our first as husband and wife. What do you think? Are you ready?"

He bent to touch her ear with his lips. He was cajoling her, tasting her so she would be ready when they reached his room, no their rooms this evening.

What he was doing was working. If he kept it up, she would never be able to dance with him. Already she felt the languorous heat he was generating within every part of her. "If you ever want me sturdy enough to dance with you, you should be advised that you need to stop the tender wheedling of your *bonnie* lips."

"I thought my feet were *bonnie*," he murmured as he wrapped an arm around her shoulders, his hand resting on a spot where with a slight change in the position of his hand he would touch the tip of her breast one that was puckering from his tempting activities.

"More than one part of you is *bonnie*, Roby McKenna, as well you know," she spoke indignantly as she desperately held onto his hand. "You should *nay* be fishing for compliments when you don't need them. You know just how handsome you are."

He let his head fall back as he roared with laughter. "You are feeling better, my *ceann daor*. Are you not? We should dance then retire for the night so we can pursue more tempting engagements."

He kissed her soundly on the lips. The kiss was short but so sweet and appealing she wanted to wind her hands in his hair then pull him close for more of the same. After that she wanted to show him everything he taught her about kissing. "I'm not wheedling anything. Come, let's dance and see how your legs are holding up." He stood, extending his hand for her to take.

"You should go slow with me. I'm not feeling at all normal yet."

"Whatever you want or need."

His arms surrounded her. He led her through the dance. By the time the tune stopped playing she was breathless. Kit was beside her bowing deeply, offering to dance with her. One after another of Roby's friends danced with her until exhaustion claimed her and she had to beg off.

She sat down at her place beside her husband. One of his large hands claimed hers. She downed the wine she set aside earlier, ate some of the food on her plate. When she looked at him, she saw the desire in his eyes.

She felt the same.

"Good girl, you will be needing nourishment to make it through the rest of the night. Eat up. Mother will have made sure there is more food and wine in the bridal chamber. We have all night, just the two of us. No intrusions. I believe Kit volunteered to take your little monkey off our hands. It is a bit disconcerting to know she watches us."

"What naughty things have you planned?"

She was beginning to look forward to those same mischievous things he initiated her into the previous nights. The ache for him deep in her core began to pulse in anticipation. Little butterflies seemed to dance and flit about deep inside her belly.

"Plan on keeping my wife guessing."

His large hand encircled her waist just beneath her breast. He was definitely tempting her, teasing with his body with subtle gestures meant to entice and enchant. Meant to set a tempest brewing. Now that she understood what would come after the playing, she was more than eager to experience everything with him.

"You are a rogue and far too self-assured for your own good. As I've said before, you are a verra wicked *mon*, Roby McKenna."

She tapped his hand with hers. He brought his idle hand to encompass hers. It did surround hers. He held so much power. He could hurt her if he wanted. She knew how gentle he could be.

"You love it though don't you, Pippa?" His mouth settled on hers for another soul-shattering kiss, this one longer than the last. In Pippa's mind not long enough. Deep in the back of her throat she moaned softly, wishing, hoping he would claim fatigue so they could leave the feasting to the others.

"Perhaps the two of you should find the bridal chamber," Riley, Kit's younger brother sat down beside Pippa, his grin broad as he flashed even white teeth. "You seem to be wanting more privacy than you can get here."

"What do you *ken* about such things," Roby jested knowing full well where the ladies were concerned Riley followed in his brother's footsteps.

To the ladies he was dashing, as well as a sweet-talking rouge.

Riley laughed then with a nod toward the steps and a wink at Pippa he left, sauntering away, his strides long and purposeful. He reached a *bonnie lass*, bowed deeply before sweeping her into his arms. The man would most likely take one of these lasses to bed this evening.

"More than the women in the village are ready for," Roby chuckled as he watched his best friend's little brother sweetly seduce a willing maid. "I'm thinking he is right though. I want my wife. I want her alone in the privacy where I can do anything I please with her femininely charms."

"As I please," she corrected him. "I have plans for you too. You wouldn't want to disappoint a *lass* now, would you? One who has been waiting for two long nights to have her husband to herself?" she asked as she tossed down the last of her wine before shooting him a wicked glance, at least she hoped it had the desired effect.

"What is it you would do with this man?" he asked, his grin wide, his white teeth flashing as he spoke. "My curious mind is plotting so many different scenarios I can scarcely wait to discover what you have in mind."

"First, there is this." She leaned toward him, touching his ear with her tongue, giving him some of his own coaxing that could never be construed as subtle. "I would take off your socks so I can look at your *bonnie* feet."

"The thought of a woman looking at my feet should not get me rigid as steel but it does or perhaps it's the way your lips feel on my ear. Which is it, I wonder? Mayhap the truth will come out tonight. You should touch me to understand just how stiff I am," he said as his thumb caressed her breast in enticing circles. She squirmed. "What is second?"

"Ah, the second." She brought his hand to her lips then kissed the palm, tracing the lines she found there with her tongue. His groan brought her head up with a smile. "Do you like that? It's not the second though. My naughty mind thinks I should press tender alarming kisses up your mighty legs until I reach the most delicate of all your *bonnie* places."

He wrenched air into his lungs. "What place would that be. I'd like to hear the name on your lips."

The heat from her blush swept through her entire body. He laughed showing his flawless white teeth. She decided she was not going to play his game now that she began one of her making.

"You will have to use your agile imagination, Roby McKenna. It is not at all appropriate that you ask such a thing of a lady as well you *ken*. Now thirdly..."

One dark eyebrow rose in a perfect arch, "There is a thirdly?" He traced her eyebrows.

"Oh, so very much more. If you wish to wait to hear then I will be more than willing to put off the verbal seduction of my husband. For now, do you want to leave thirdly in your manly imaginative brain or do you want me to tell you what I've planned?" She was hoping to dance this tune with him a while longer as she was enjoying his strained features.

On the other hand...

He leaned forward. It was becoming obviously clear he decided he could play her game also. "Thirdly, I will caress you in all your secret places, stroke and nibble until you beg for me to bring you that sweet release, I *ken* you are craving, Pippa McKenna. The one that makes your body as well as your mind soar to dizzying heights." It seemed he took over the verbal seduction.

She sucked in air that didn't have any place to travel. She coughed. He tapped her on the back. Her goblet of wine he held out to her. Pippa drank, letting the liquid slide down her heated throat.

He held out his hand as he stood. She accepted. He held both hands high in a salute to the people of the village, to the clan Chattan who celebrated their joining. It appeared that in his mind it was time to change the scenery to something more secluded.

Connal stood in front of them blocking their departure. "Not yet. There is something that must be decided before you leave."

"Now?" Roby asked, sounding incredulous as well as angry. "Can't it wait until morning?

"As you know the gates are down. No one could enter the castle. Now, yes now, we have visitors. It is up to the two of you to decide if they should be allowed inside. No one else can make that decision for you."

With a rush of air, a soft curse, "Speak o' the devil. It must be the Finchbottoms come to celebrate our wedding."

Pippa swayed on her feet. Roby's arm pulled her close. "*Nay*, it cannot be. I don't feel well."

"Don't faint on me now, *lass*. It was only a matter of time before they showed up here. While I *ken* you *dinna* want to let them in, it's always best to keep your enemies close."

"The two of you are surrounded by friends," Connal reminded them. "Nothing will happen tonight or any time soon. The clan will protect you along with your wife forever."

"I don't want to see them. Not today, not ever."

Her breath fell from her lungs in short sharp breaths. Panic consumed her as she felt moisture bead on her forehead.

"While I deem it would be for the best if you stood by my side for this meeting, I will understand if you want to go up to our room where you can wait for me. You've had a trying day. I would not see you more exhausted."

His hand around her waist, reassured. The width of his stance along with the confidence he assumed did wonders for easing her mind. She could not stop thinking about how his life could be in danger from these two horrid men. "You're not alone, Pippa. You don't have to do anything necessary to survive nor do you have to run. Clan Chattan will stand beside you. I will protect you."

She didn't want the end of the statement to be "with my life."

For several seconds, it seemed to Pippa she failed to think, couldn't feel. The air around her was stagnant the air chilling her to the bone. "I will stand by your side."

"Good, you have nothing to fear. We will meet them in your office," Roby was staring at Connal. I assume you will be there with us. I'll ask Kit, if he's still celebrating, to stand by my side."

"Do you want Alistair?"

"*Nay*, not today. This is a show of force but we don't want to overwhelm the Finchbottoms anymore than necessary. I'll get Kit and meet you in the north tower."

"Why not overwhelm?" Roby asked. "They deserve to be so overwhelmed they are afraid of their shadows."

"Not tonight, trust me in this," Connal said turning to leave the room and prepare for the upcoming meeting.

Roby guided Pippa through revelers toward Kit. Told him what was happening. Wynnie joined them as they made their way to the meeting place. Wynnie had ale brought to the room along with some of the delicacies from the feast that had yet to be eaten.

"I'm sorry, *lass*. There should have been only joy today. We will deal with this mess then proceed to the first step of your plan. Perhaps I shall examine your *bonnie wee* feet. I'm certain they are *bonnier* than mine." His whispers close to her ear gave her more hope than she dared have. What would these two men think to gain by invading her space?

They should have gone home.

As if Roby read her mind, he spoke again. "They have no home to go to. I took the liberty to send some of the clan, servants as well as men who are more adept at fighting to Clearborne Manor. Some were to clean the others to make sure when Harry and Horace arrived, they would find themselves unwelcome. In short, they are homeless. I assume they will be begging for our mercy along with some other plans to give them the upper hand. They won't find it here."

"Clearborne?"

"It is yours."

"Ours," she murmured. "You would like to live there?" The thought surprised as well as pleased her.

~ * ~

When Harry and Horace Finchbottom entered the office of Connal McKenna, the laird sat behind his desk, a pleasant smile on his face, Roby sat on one edge, his powerful leg braced on the floor the other one swinging idly. Kit stood nearby. Pippa sat in a large dark blue brocaded chair. She appeared to be staring at her hands. Perhaps it was her feet or the Persian rug.

Harry felt an instant tightening of his gut, the sour feeling he'd felt since they found Clearborne Manor occupied by McKennas. This was a staged scene, one to show the power of the McKennas, one to illustrate their weakness. He studied the three men and the implacable glare on all of their faces, the smiles that didn't reach their eyes. He always found it easy to intimidate as well as blackmail a lady. These men would not be so easy. They would not fall into his plans. However, as he watched the way Roby McKenna looked at Phillipa, a new plan began to form. It was apparent to any observant person the man was besotted with the woman.

There was still hope.

"What is it you want? I assume since you were so insistent on a hearing tonight of all nights you do want something from the McKennas." Connal rose when he began speaking. Now, with his hands in front of him, he braced his weight on the desk. "What is it?"

"We've no place to stay since you commandeered our home," Horace said as he stepped forward his arms out in supplication. "You had no right to do such a thing. We are legal guardians to Phillipa MacPherson. We control her as well as all her lands until she comes of age, for two more years. There is naught you can do about that. So," he paused in thought, "hand over what is rightfully ours."

Roby didn't bother to stand. Harry heard the well-intended insolence in the man's voice as he spoke. "It's not your home, never was your home and never will be. It's my wife's home, always has and always will be. Since we are now wed, we will live at Clearborne. There is no place there for either of you. Find someone else to mooch from."

Harry grimaced. The words were all too true. Still, he felt as if the wind had been sucked from his gut. He puffed out his chest trying to bluff once again. "Well, we'll just see how long she is your wife. There are ways around this wife business."

"I've been her guardian since her parents died in that horrible accident five years ago. Had control since she was fourteen," Horace said. "She was intended to wed my son. The papers are in order."

"She feared for her life, for her wellbeing when you and your father came to stay at the manor. It is why she left without telling anyone, why she put her very life in danger." Roby spoke softly but his words held a dark threat that didn't go unnoticed by either man.

Harry stepped back. "Horace is her guardian," he reiterated. "My father will decide what happens to Phillipa."

"Only by default," Roby said as he watched them with hooded eyes along with narrowed brow. Then he cleared his throat, "Her parents failed to name one. So, you made assumptions that were not true. Connal McKenna was intended to be her guardian. It was a verbal agreement between the two men."

Harry puffed up his chest as he waved his hands in the air as if that would help make the point. "We're her closest relatives so the duty went to us. We, my father and I, stepped up to the formidable task of bringing up a young lady. It wasn't easy." Then he added, "You cannot marry her without our permission. Not until she's twenty-one."

"Pippa has been wed to me twice, once over two weeks ago by a man who will remain nameless and today by the Holy Father who resides here in McKenna castle. The legality of our marriage cannot be disputed. You arrived too late to protest or stop anything that was put into motion. No one would have allowed such a thing in any case. The marriage has been consummated more than once. So, it cannot be annulled. Pippa might already carry the next heir to Clearborne Manor."

Horace continued to babble meaningless words. "We will take her home with us. You will tell your men to leave Clearborne. There is no room for them there. I will listen to no differing arguments," Harry blustered, his belly shaking with his obvious agitation.

He knew he should withdraw for the time being. Stealth was a much better tactic to use in this case. When he stepped forward in order to reach Phillipa, Roby stood, his hands fisted at his sides, Kit too.

Pippa, still sitting in the chair seemed to have lost all the color in her face. She said nothing as she stared vacant-eyed at the men. Roby moved to stand behind her, his hands placed on her shoulders, massaging muscles.

I will have what I want, Clearborne manner along with Pippa no matter what I have to do to get it.

"No." The pause following gave emphasis of the harshness of Roby's voice. "No, you won't. Pippa is my wife. We will live at Clearborne, raise our children there as well. Nothing you believe you possess is rightfully yours. I've already set the wheels in motion to save whatever funds are left from the Clearborne estate. I've seen the counsel to the MacPhersons. Much will have to be paid back if the two of you are to avoid prison. If you think to see to my demise, be forewarned there is a will. One that names my father then Brady as heirs. If that is not enough the line continues through the Stuarts, first naming Alistair then Houston and so on. Do you get the drift of it?"

Harry drew in a sharp breath, surprised by the revelation of reprisals along with the will that would make it infinitely impossible to gain access to Phillipa's fortune. His eyes narrowed at Roby McKenna. He knew in that instant he hated that man, despised him enough to see to his demise if it wasn't so foolhardy. He also knew the McKennas won this round. They would not be victorious on the next. He would find a way, some way if not to gain the fortune but to see revenge done.

"You owe us a place to stay tonight," Horace stepped into the conversation, his brows furrowed in obvious anger. His intrusion was an apparent attempt to stop his son's tongue from wagging any farther.

"We owe you nothing," Roby said as he readjusted his stance

behind his wife his fingers squeezing lightly where they touched. "As far as I'm concerned, a bed of dirt and pine needles would be fitting."

When he finally had Pippa as his own, conceived an heir with her, Harry would see to an accident, one where he couldn't be blamed just as his father saw to the accident that took her parent's lives. Now that he thought about Roby's words, he was sure Roby was bluffing. He would have to act quickly.

She was still a skinny little thing. Not much for a man to hold on to. He would have to make do with her lack of feminine charms while keeping a mistress on the side. He hoped he would have the heir sooner than later. He didn't know how long he could stand to bed her. With a heavy sigh, a woman was a woman if one closed their eyes and didn't overthink the situation. A man could still find a small amount of pleasure.

"You may stay the night in the east tower. There will be other guests in residence for the night also. If you set one foot outside that area, you will be escorted outside the castle gate to fend for yourself. Is that clear?" Connal said, his voice soft yet still held the promise of harsh retribution if his order was defied.

"Perfectly," Horace said.

Chapter Six

At the door to their rooms, Roby swept Pippa into his arms to carry her over the threshold into the suite they would share for a few more days before they left for Clearborne Manor. Her slender form was still shaking from the encounter with her ex-guardians. He needed to change the pallor that encapsulated her skin to a rosy bloom.

He thought of her three steps to seducing him and grinned.

Harry and Horace were nuisances he didn't want to think about tonight of all nights. If he never saw them again, the meeting would be too soon. Looking at Pippa's face he understood that wouldn't be possible until he undid the memory of their visit. All her little and very endearing flirtatious comments would have to wait until she was more herself, until she could put the untimely visit of the Finchbottoms on their wedding night from her head.

It was up to him to accomplish that feat.

While he saw no threat in either of these bumbling men, he knew Pippa did. To her they were still powerful as well as a threat to her happiness. He would have to discover some way to ease her mind before she did something stupid that would be difficult to correct. He realized she might consider herself the pawn in their evil game. She wasn't now that she had him along with the rest of the clan to protect her. He would make sure she understood she no longer needed to take care of herself as well as the fact he was more than capable of thwarting any nonsense that came their way via the bumbling Finchbottoms.

She needed to trust him though. Needed to do as he said. Doing so might be difficult since she'd been on her own for so many years. Gaining a promise of obedience would please him as well as ease his fears that she might do something foolish on her own. He couldn't very well have her trying to protect him when it was his job to keep her safe and well.

He wasn't at all sure she could give all her trust to him, at least not yet. Pippa had little trust in anyone. She would in time.

"Penny for your thoughts?" he asked after shutting the door with his foot then setting her down on a comfortable sofa where he meant to have a bit of conversation with his wife. If she would open up to him about her fears, he would feel saner.

"I don't like those men," she sighed softly as she spoke, her lashes lowered, casting shadows across her cheekbones. Her shoulders quivered slightly as she spoke "They mean you harm. I cannot let that happen."

There it was, what he feared. She could not take control. In the process do something foolhardy. He could not allow her to put herself in any kind of danger. "Neither do I like them. Rest assured they will do neither of us any harm. I won't allow it," he spoke as he walked back to the door to turn the lock. "You are to do nothing that I would consider foolish. You are not to risk your life in any way for me. You should also know there are numerous men guarding the passages in the castle." Still, he didn't want to take chances where Pippa's safety was concerned especially when enemies lurked within the castle walls. It would not be too difficult, if the Finchbottoms put their heads together to find a way from the east tower to his suite of rooms in the south tower.

"You don't trust those two to stay put as ordered, do you?" she said as she nervously arranged and rearranged the fabric of her gown. She didn't look up. Didn't acknowledge his presence for the longest time. "I don't either. Nothing about them inspires trust." She continued to stare at her gown then she finally lifted her head so he could see into her eyes. "They want you dead and out of the way. I won't allow that to happen."

Once more those words sent fear for her straight to his gut. His nerves stretched to a snapping point. "You're right. I don't trust those two. Not as far as I can toss a caber," he laughed softly, belying his fear as he slipped from the velvet jacket he wore, flipping it over a chair.

His fear was for her not for him. Wished to think of other things. He wanted to slowly disrobe his wife. Longed to linger over every soft secret spot of hers where he knew fires within were easily ignited to an inferno.

That would wait until later.

They had vital, important things to discuss. "They will not succeed in any of their wayward if not evil plans for you or me. But, my dear one, you have to trust me. You cannot try to do anything on your own to thwart whatever plans they might be hatching."

"How far would that be?" she smiled, the sight as well as her words catching him off guard.

His heart fluttered softly within his chest praying this was a good symbol she was forgetting the Finchbottoms. A sign that perhaps the earlier encounter did not affect her as much as he previously thought. It was what he wanted, longed for. "Farther then most men around these parts. Alistair can still beat me. He's the brawniest. If Houston still lived at the castle, he took after his father in brawn and can toss it even farther than Alistair. I have better technique, however." He preened in front of her for a few seconds, watching the light in her eyes begin to sparkle at his arrogance.

"So, you're saying you look the best when you toss that huge stick of wood." She did laugh then, her smile giving him even more reason to believe the wedding night would be as delightful as he planned.

"Stick of wood?" One dark brow rose in question.

"Would it be alright for me to tell you I agree?"

He was heartily glad of the sound of her laughter, as he loved the deep sultry noise her voice made when she spoke and yes laughed too. With very little effort, she caused everything inside him to harden.

He wanted fulfillment now.

"What do you think? You're the only opinion that matters to me."

He unfastened his shirt allowing the fine lawn fabric to hang free, showing his chest. Yet he didn't fling the ruffled shirt to the side. It was too soon. He didn't take it off as he was thinking of the first, second and third steps she spoke of when she described his seduction. Without further thought, he strode to the table where Wynnie had the servants bring wine and ale. He poured a goblet for each of them.

"Oh, and you want me to stroke your ego so it grows even larger?"

She blushed. The red color rose on her face. To his delight, instead of withdrawing because of her embarrassment, she became even bolder. "I'd rather stroke your chest until I hear you growl deep in the back of your throat, a sure sign of your pleasure. Then I could move on to a different part of you."

"My *bonnie feet*?

"*Nay*, I believe you know. Or have you forgotten?"

"Perhaps you should tell me so I don't have to keep guessing."

The red intensified while the color spread down her neck continuing along the tops of her breasts. "*Ye ken* what I be speakin' of."

He roared with laughter. "What are you thinking about my person that grows larger? I need for you to tell me. Say the word, Pippa. Any one of them will do."

He sat down beside her taking her hand in his, leading it to the spot he spoke of even though he didn't believe her thoughts went in that direction, at least not the first time she said them.

Truly, he thought she'd be more worried about Harry and Horace. He was heartily thrilled she didn't seem to dwell on those two miserable souls and what they might want to still steal from her. If she could put the Finchbottoms aside perhaps before they became lost in each other's arms, she might enlighten him to the events of their wedding that he missed out on. He craved her, the knowledge of what happened to her so he could understand all she experienced.

"Are you hungry. Neither of us ate much at the feast. I for one need sustenance for the night to come." He piled one plate high with a sample of all the food on the platter starting with the sweets then ending with the meats and cheeses.

"I don't know if my stomach will stop rumbling. Don't *ken* if it's sounding obnoxious because I'm worried about the Finchbottoms or if I'm actually hungry."

With a tiny lift to her shoulders, she stared half-heartedly at the plate of food he set in front of her.

"You're in need of nourishment." He winked at her as he let one finger trail across the top of her gown while he touched soft white flesh. With the sound of her slight sigh, he removed his touch. She needed sustenance, as did he. This was not the time for seduction. Those moments would come later. "We've all night to play. Let's eat now."

For a few minutes they ate in silence. He watched her for any more signs the appearance of her late guardians still upset her. He was more than ready for the rest of his life with this little lady. He was more than ready to act out the first, second and third steps of his seduction.

"How long will we stay here?" She asked him as the plate of food he gave her seemed to be vanishing. "I, well, I'd like to see my home again. I was surprised you wanted to live there."

He thought for a moment. "I'm not the heir of McKenna property. Brady is. I would have to find my way eventually. Thought you would like to live in the only real home you've ever known. We can go whenever you like."

"I do, I..." She swallowed the strawberry she'd been chewing. "I want that. It's just that..."

For a moment she appeared lost in her thoughts. He understood she was probably once more thinking about Harry and Horace residing in her home.

He sat back, spreading his arms along the back of the sofa where they sat. One hand rested lightly on her shoulder. "It's just that you're afraid Harry and Horace will find some way to stop us. Don't be. I'm not going to let anything bad happen to either of us."

"I *dinna* want to be the cause of your death." She spoke with a softness that also held a wealth of fear. "I should have never wed you. If I could take it back, I would."

There it was again, her desire to put herself in the path of the Finchbottoms in order to save him. The thought frustrated him, angered him too. She was too tiny, too vulnerable to even think of putting herself in a spot where she thought to protect him. Yet, he could not come up with the words to convince her.

"Come, no more thoughts of those two reprobates and withdrawing from a marriage that is supposed to be. One that was written in the stars. Tell me what happened in the church. What did you see?" he asked as he traced the line of her jaw, his vision of them in bed clear while he tried for patience.

He was sure that was not what she'd seen. It was what he saw though as she leaned her meager weight against him, felt her breasts push against his chest, her belly against his groin.

For a few seconds she closed her eyes. When she opened them, she stared straight at him, at his mouth. Slowly, she moistened her lips, her pink tongue gliding between the two. His body jerked.

"You saw my mouth?" he asked grinning as once again his body responded to her unhurried coaxing. Perhaps it wasn't deliberate.

"No," she said touching his moist lip with a finger tracing the fullness as she looked at him a wistful expression on her face, "No, I didn't see your mouth. Your lips are soft, wet," she paused thoughtfully. "The world spun so fast everything was a blur. Nausea enveloped me. Thought I would lose the meager contents of my stomach. Thought it was a good thing I had not eaten. Wind whistled harshly around me. Tore at me. At least I thought it did but when it was all over not one strand of my hair was out of place."

"One strand," he corrected her. "Now it is." He pulled a few pins from her hair, letting soft, silken strands fall around her shoulders then lower to her waist. "In the church there was no wind. Nothing spun, at least not for me. All was normal." His fingers sifted through her hair, brought a strand to his nose. Her female sent filled him.

"I *ken* it. I saw you as your cat. Your huge paws rested on my shoulders for a moment while I looked into your eyes. You grinned at me then you vanished as if you were never there. I wanted you to stay. Missed you when you left. Other things began to happen."

He wondered what the chanting would create, what images a woman would see. No one who experienced the ceremony spoke of it in a public forum. He supposed that was true and good. It seemed so very private between the two of them. Wondered too if it was her imagination playing havoc with what truly happened. "I never turned into my cat form."

"You think I'm lying." She visibly bristled, her green eyes flashing the golden sparks rimming the green. "You think I'm making this all up or I'm imagining what I wanted to see. Well, Roby McKenna, I *dinna* think I'll be talkin' to you any longer about what I saw or didn't see if you're not going to believe what I'm tellin' you. 'Tis a waste of my time."

"You don't lie, Pippa. I *ken* that about you. Truly, I do." Roby spoke from the heart. He clasped her hand in his, threaded his fingers through hers before he brought her hand to his lips to kiss the back. This fact was something he knew from the moment he saw her standing so forlorn on the gallows, her face covered by the black hood. That night a wealth of visions swept through his mind. He saw so much he didn't understand. Now he did. Perhaps that was why he said yes to wedding her. At the time he didn't understand what he saw. Now, he was beginning to comprehend.

"What is it you be thinkin'?" she asked defiantly, challenging him, jerking at her hand to get away from him. He wouldn't let it go. Instead, he wound his fingers tighter, kissing her hand once more tugging her closer. He wouldn't let her escape.

Never.

She was his.

"It all seems so real to you. I know it transpired just as you told me. I only wish I could have been more a part of what occurred. I'm in the dark." With a huge expulsion of pent-up air, he finished his thoughts. "It's not your imagination then? You saw my cat during the wedding. The wind howled as the floor whirled around your feet. If you think on what you said, it is a great deal to absorb for a man who has never..." he paused again thinking that he had seen a vision. She was his vision.

She fiddled with the strands of hair he pulled free. "I don't know. Why would I imagine something like that, the whirling walls, your cat form, my cat form..." she looked at him a startled expression in her eyes.

"Your cat?" He was quick to jump on those two words. "Are you sure it was not me in another time?"

"No, the second cat I saw wasn't you. Until now I forgot. In another life I was a panther too, not a black one but the normal type, the kind of panther where you can see the spots. I know it wasn't you." She brushed more hair from her face, her eyes imploring him to shed some detail on this new revelation.

"You are unique. I'm sure there was nothing normal about you in a different life, in any life." He watched her wishing she were a cat, not for him but for her sake. She wanted to be able to change form so badly. He wondered if perhaps she wasn't a cat too? Her parents would have figured it out, taught her if either one of them were able to change form. But they weren't. At least to his knowledge they never showed themselves as shifters. There were no rumors of the possibility.

"I always believed that a shifter would always be able to do that in any life, change form. Do you think you just don't know how to alter yourself into a cat?" he asked, clearly puzzled by her revelation. "I might be able to teach you."

"How can it be? My parents were not shifters." She blinked at him several times as if attempting to understand what he was trying to tell her. "Doesn't at least one parent have to be?"

"I don't know. Would you like to try sometime?" he asked, his heart in his throat, his grin widening as he wanted nothing more than to encourage her to break free from her preconceived idea. "Do you want to try?"

"Try what?" her voice wavered as if she was just as unsure of herself as he was. "I *dinna ken* that's something possible for me to learn."

"Shifting. I'll teach you." He wanted that more than anything. How the devil did one teach another to shift? "If you can't though, I don't want you to be disappointed. If you say yes, it will be just between the two of us. Our secret."

"Not right now. Yes, if we try and I cannot change form I will be disappointed. Perhaps we should not even try something like that."

"I thought you were more courageous than that," he whispered close to her ear, felt the shudder of longing pass from her into him as her body flushed with heat.

He breathed in her sweet scent inhaling all that he could before slowly letting his breath dissolve in front of him. He didn't want to spend time on their wedding night playing with something that might not even exist.

"I don't know. I've only been brave when there was no other choice," she sighed as she lifted her chin so he could place tender kisses along the soft, snowy column.

He touched the rapidly beating pulse at the base of her neck with his tongue, sipping the beat of her heart.

"It seems to me most of your life there has been no choice for you. From here on out, I'll be brave for you. Is that alright with you?"

His lips floated and lingered, coaxed her body to respond with passion discovering each evocative area. He explored secret spots that only he knew about, traveled along silken flesh that left him in urgent need of so much more. She had no idea how easily she flooded him with heat.

Her fingers wound into his hair, pulling him closer as she arched against him twisting her body, to come in contact with his. She was sweetly scented, eager for the coupling she knew so well, just as eager as he was. He realized he wanted to put into action her three steps then teach her more. Perhaps later in the night he would have the control necessary for her to begin with his feet then kiss her way to his groin. Just thinking about her soft moist lips on his person sent searing heat to his loins and a snarl to his throat. His hands tightened on her arms, ran the length down then back lingering on each vertebra while she writhed in his arms.

He kneeled on the floor in front of her. Spread her legs with his big body. Pushed the skirt of her wedding dress to the tops of her thighs Took her slippers from her feet, lovingly massaged the arches as well as the toes. He kissed the bottom of each one. "'Tis a good thing your feet were washed last night. I might not be kissing them."

"I'm—I'm supposed to do that to you," she blurted as her voice wavered softly telling him just how much she craved him. "You need to stop that, Roby McKenna."

"Next time," he chuckled as his lips sipped and followed the path of his fingers as they made their way along her legs to her inner thigh. He continued the blatant seduction wishing to go as slowly as possible, needing her to cry out his name, twist and coil delightfully with her need before he found solace in the sweet velvet of her sheathe.

She tugged on his hair. "*Nay*, there won't be a next time because you'll already be naked. I want to undress you. Want to do all those things I spoke of when I was embarrassed and afraid someone would be listening to what I said. Didn't want anyone to overhear. I was brave then."

She tried to close her legs. His lips found more secret tender and so very sensitive places, hot places, slick with moisture places to attend to before he could willingly give her permission to seduce him.

He heard the undulating loss of breath, as he knew he would give in to her wishes. He didn't know how he could be more aroused than he was now, but he understood he would have to restrain himself while he let his wife play attendance on his body. It forever pleased him, this passion of hers. "What would you have me do?"

"Change places with me," she panted, her breath along with her words short sweet bursts.

He did. He sat in the chair while she knelt in front of him. Her hands rested provocatively on his knees. He couldn't still the groan rumbling from deep inside his man's body as he tensed and tightened in anticipation of this blatant seduction of hers. Dragging compulsory air into his lungs was nearly impossible as she slowly slid one of his stockings to his ankle before taking care of his shoe. Her gentle fingers stroked the arch of his foot, found the bones running along the top as she traced to the tip of each toe.

"Pippa..." his voice was a low rumble of need.

"Do you like this?" She kissed his foot, tickled the arch with her nails then found her way, playing with her fingers back to his knee where she repeated the process with her lips and teeth. If she didn't finish this soon, he was going to jump out of his skin.

"Jesus, Pippa, don't stop. Whatever you do, don't stop."

His breaths were shallow and fast. He did jerk when she repeated her antics on the other leg stopping at his knees, not venturing higher where he wanted her moist, hot lips to find their intended target. The tempest within him brewed.

"I'm skipping step two or perhaps I've just reevaluated." She moved upward, her hands pushing his unfastened shirt off his shoulders while she flicked a nipple with her fingernail. The journey continued over his upper body while he found the chance to unfasten the bodice of her dress, slipping it downward until it pooled around her knees.

Catching her under her arms, he pulled her up so his mouth found hers. His lips folded across hers, touched and licked, bit and sucked every soft tender spot he could find until he heard her tiny cries echoing through her mouth into his. Her breath became his. Now she wore only her chemise, her nipples tight buds begging for him to play.

"No, Robby, not yet."

She caught the hem of her chemise with her hands before lifting the fabric over her head. Her ever-questing hands slipped beneath his kilt then her head disappeared beneath the tartan. She found his most tender and sensitive male places, nipped with her small white teeth, soothed with her tongue moving always higher until her mouth closed around him, the soft then the hard. She moved between his balls and his rod. He tore at the fastening of his kilt before he lifted her to straddle him. She was climaxing before he impaled her with his penis.

His claws appeared, dipped into her shoulder until ten small drops of blood appeared. He claimed her. She cried out. He spilled his seed within her. The moment shattered his soul.

Pippa lay on top of him, her breathing ragged, her breasts pushing on his chest. Against him he felt the hammering of her heart in tune with his. When he could finally inhale good air, he picked her up and carried her to the bed. He pulled the covers back before setting her on the bed.

Stepping back, he watched his wife, who sat on the bed her legs curled beneath her while her breasts beckoned to him with each subtle movement of her body. She ran her tongue across her lips.

Little minx.

"More wine?"

Roby didn't wait for an answer. He brought her a full goblet.

"Should we do that again?" she asked as she drank deeply.

"Only if I'm the seducer."

He settled on the bed, his back against the headboard ready for round two of his wedding night.

~ * ~

Two days later Roby and Pippa stared up the long drive to Clearborne Manor. Looking at her childhood home for the first time in five years sent tiny tremors of longing and happiness through her. Tears

154

formed in her eyes as she remembered and noted the changes. The trees lining the drive were larger, the grass longer, the hedges ragged and overgrown. To Pippa it was obvious that the Finchbottoms didn't take good care of the home they thought to inherit.

She supposed that was just the kind of people Harry and Horace were. Lazy. They would take care of their needs before turning their attention to anything else.

"I will guarantee you my men will see to the cleanup of the grounds before they leave. Of course, they are not all going back to McKenna castle. Some will stay to serve us."

"The house? You don't think it is this bad?"

"No, last time I was here the main rooms were all cleaned and polished, the banister shiny with the scent of lemon oil. I'm sure the master chamber will be ready for our use. If we have anything like our wedding night..."

Pippa felt the heat of embarrassment rise to her cheeks. "I was so..."

"So exactly like I love you, Pippa McKenna. You beguile me." He pulled her onto his horse so she rode in front of him. "If there weren't a wealth of people who might come out to watch, I'd make love to you here and now."

"Wicked *mon*."

"On this horse," he added, his grin wicked.

"No."

"Roby McKenna stop that," she batted at hands that were roaming. "Someone will see what you are about."

"Let them." He pushed the long braid away from her neck kissing the nape softly. "I can hardly wait to check out the bed. You know, all the way here I missed this. Should have insisted we ride together. We could have tried something I've never done before."

"If you insisted on that, we would not be here yet. I for one would rather make love on a bed than inside a tent on the cold ground." Her indignant words caused him to chuckle while exploring more of her.

He found her lips, caressed with his tongue, tempted her to open, challenged as he bit gently. "What about under the stars with the silver of the moon glow shining on your naked body."

"You might enjoy that but I wouldn't care one way or the other. It seems I would just be cold." She pushed at his hands until he let them settle on her hips rather than teasing the undersides of her breasts.

"I would keep you hot."

"So you say."

"Anywhere I am making love to you pleases me."

He chuckled next to her ear, goose bumps sprinting across her arms. The sensations he generated left her breathless and while she didn't want to admit it to him, hot.

She shivered from escalating desire, "Perhaps we should check out the bed in the master chamber before you embarrass me in front of the staff. I would not be able to live that down."

He urged his horse down the drive, hers following behind. When they reached the front of the house, Kelly rushed from the stables to take their horses. "Welcome home," he announced to the pair. "When you get a chance, you should come check out the stables. It's spruced up just fine now. Although, when I first arrived, it was a bit worn down. Thought it would take weeks to fix it up to standard but you sent along enough help we got it done, most of it anyway."

"We will, perhaps tonight or tomorrow morning." Pippa slipped from his arms to land gently feet first on the ground. Roby followed handing the reins to the groom.

Hand in hand they walked up the steps leading to a large front porch. The door to Clearborne swung open.

"Greetings." Bessy curtsied, smiling at them. "I truly do hope the two of you find this to your liking. We've put in long hours so your home would be ready for you. Everything in the west wing is livable. We are working on the east wing now."

"I'm sure we will love all that you've accomplished," Roby said. "If there is anything that needs more attention, I'll let you know."

"Will you like a tour?" Bessy asked.

"I will show Roby around."

Pippa felt the warmth of the home surround her. More than anything she wanted to show him where she'd grown up, where they would bring their children into this world. Her parent's room would be theirs now. The thought left her with bittersweet longing.

The tour took far longer than it should have. It seemed Roby wanted to make love to her in every room. If she wasn't quick on her feet, he would catch her then toss her skirts. As they made their way through the manor, the chase and catch routine became a game that Roby won more often than he lost.

In this game Pippa didn't mind losing. She laughed and flirted outrageously as she egged him on.

By the time they found their way to the drawing room before dinner Pippa was exhausted. She sat on a large gold brocaded chair that she decided needed replacing first thing. He sat opposite, a silly grin on his face. She was sure she knew what he was thinking.

"*Och,* seems my bride has lost her courage." He poured her a cup of hot tea and a glass of brandy for himself. "Still, I could find a means to sit there with you. We could pursue other strategies that would be infinitely delightful."

She didn't miss the challenge in the tenor of his voice. "No, just too tired for another dalliance," she told him smiling as she sipped the tea letting it warm her all the way through. "You've worn me out, Roby McKenna. You wicked *mon.* All I want to do is go to bed." She held up both hands. "To sleep. Do you think Hypatia is getting along with Kit?" She didn't want to admit to the fact she felt a bit jealous how her monkey took so quickly to Kit.

"If I have my way, by the end of the week we will have made love in every room in this house. After that we can start in the stables, the loft as well as all the out buildings. Do you have a gazebo? We've made a good start in this pursuit of exploration. When we finish, we can decide where we like the best."

"Do you ever think of anything else?" she laughed as he screwed up his face thinking.

"Not when I'm looking at you. All I want to do is get you out of your clothing then do other wickedly naughty things with your naked body."

She felt the same as he did, having no objections to his wanton need to make love at every opportunity. "Will we ever stop wanting each other so much?"

She thought of her mother and father. Wondered if their love had been so grand.

"Lord, I hope not," he said as he sat down beside her in the opposite chair.

Picking at the fabric on her chair, all the worn places she wondered who in their right mind would pick out such a horrendous color. Struck suddenly by the thought of how much repairing the damaged house needed, she asked, "How much money do we have?"

"Are you asking if they spent it all?" He reached out, stopped her from tugging the worn spots on the chair. "Enough to replace the fabric on the chairs and a lot more. You are a wealthy woman without need of any of my money."

"They didn't siphon off everything then?" While she didn't want the task of managing money, she wanted to understand their position.

"No, actually most of the fortune is intact. It seems Mr. McPhee did a wonderful job protecting what is rightfully yours. The man is a genius where it comes to finances."

"How?"

"It appears he had every confidence you would return to claim your inheritance. He took steps to protect all you own. So, he wasn't exactly truthful as to your real value. He managed to put funds into investments the Finchbottoms knew nothing about. Even if they'd known they would not have been able to touch them."

"By lying."

"If one wants to call it that. Your parents picked a marvelously honest man. After reviewing all the facts as well as going to the scene of the accident, he said he was sure their deaths were not an accident. When Harry and Horace showed up all bluster and arrogance claiming to be your guardians, he made some quick financial maneuvers, which appeared to have been instigated for you by your father. While your father set up a trust fund for you, it did not have much in it. McPhee transferred over half of the MacPherson investments into your trust then made sure no one except you could touch the wealth stored there. He made sure not to tell the Finchbottoms about said trust fund. It was also made available to you on your eighteenth birthday.

"I could have come home." Disappointment flooded through her. She missed so much yet if she had come home, she might never have met Roby.

"Yes, we both know it would not have been wise for you to do so. Horace was still claiming to be your guardian. He had power over your livelihood. He might have found a means to force you to wed Harry. In doing so you would have undone all that McPhee worked diligently to do in your behalf. The fact you almost died was not well done of you. However, everything else including our chance meeting worked out for the best."

Her stomach rolled at the thought of Harry touching her. His hot wet mouth slobbering on her. "I might have killed him if he tried to," she swallowed hard, "If he tried to..." There was no way she could say the words.

"He did not and he will not. I will kill him if he touches you. You have my solemn promise."

A tiny bubble of what felt like hysteria erupted. "Let's speak of more pleasant things."

"You have a townhouse in Inverness as well as Edinburgh. Did you know that your father gave yearly donations to an orphanage in Inverness? No, I don't suppose you would know something like that or why."

"He did?" she was wondering the same question as Roby. The fact seemed elusive to her. "Do you know the name of the orphanage?"

"No, but it is located near the castle and a woman by the name of Mother Theresa runs it. Has been in charge for nearly thirty years. I should like to visit the place, ask a few pertinent questions."

Nearly two hours later after they ate, Roby decided to check out the gardens. Hand in hand they walked along an overgrown pathway to the gazebo, which was set back from the house. While a person could see the upper floor of the manor from the gazebo, she remembered that the inside of the structure could not be seen from the manor.

"Tomorrow we'll make love here. You do seem tired." He pulled her onto his lap, her head on his chest. Absentmindedly, she stroked his shoulder.

"I am tired and I'd rather be sure there is no one about to see us before we make love."

"There is no one. I would hear them." He smoothed across her eyebrows with a fingertip.

"You would?"

"I would."

"When can we go to Callum's cabin? You said you sent men to clean it up. I would like to put flowers on his grave. Would tell him all that happened to me, to us. I think he would be pleased."

He wrapped his arms around her. Her ear next to him, she heard the sound of his heart. It beat steady and true.

"Whenever you like?"

"I would go before autumn when it is still warm to take walks in the hills. I felt so free when I lived there with your great grandfather." He took her in, fed and clothed her until he died. She even thought he might have loved her as a grandchild. "I think he knew something about me. Don't *ken* what it was though."

"We can take a belated honeymoon there," he whispered along her neck. "Shall we walk?" His large callused hand wrapped around her small one. This security he gave her was something she never felt before meeting him.

"We will have to or you will get distracted with other ways to make love to me. You've next to no patience."

"I've a better idea." He trailed a hot finger along her nose.

"What is that?" She didn't believe Roby would think any idea was better than making love.

"I can teach you to shift."

She sat up, blinked a few times. "I don't know. I can't. What makes you think...?" She felt winded, confused at the thought.

"Come on, what have you got to lose?"

"All my hopes and dreams since I met you."

Both her hands pressed against his chest. If she tried then couldn't...her breath caught in the back of her throat. This was something she wanted with all her heart.

"If you are a shifter? What then?" he asked taking both hands in his before bringing them to his lips. He brushed his lips gently across her knuckles before looking into her eyes seeming to hold her protectively.

She heard the footsteps, stiffened. Roby turned to look down the garden path. "Kit? Didn't expect you so soon."

Hypatia leapt from Kit's shoulder to land in her outstretched arms. "You love sick girl. You have abandoned me for this wicked *mon*. I hope you are happy with yourself."

The little monkey held her face between her hands. She placed a huge kiss on her mouth.

Pippa laughed, "Is this what Kit has taught you?"

Kit looked aside for a moment. His grin brought Hypatia back to his arms. "I *dinna* teach that monkey anything. She watches me when I'm..."

To Pippa's amusement a slight tint of color painted Kit's cheeks. "When you are...?

It appeared he wasn't going to answer. "Seems Harry and Horace took off right behind the two of you. They are nearby. I'm sure of it. I've more men. They're scouring the land around the manor. Lord knows there are a lot of places to hide. Take care. You should get Pippa back to the house."

She nodded agreeing with Kit. "You know I'm tired. We can do the other, you know, later. Whether she could shift or not was between Roby and her. This was private. Perhaps it would have been better to try while they were alone behind a locked door.

"I'll meet you on the front porch." Kit turned on a heel before striding ahead of them.

"Those two won't give up." She could not stop the shudder from tearing along her spine nor could she stop the fear from ripping through her.

"Of course they will because we'll outlast them. Their resources are now severely limited. They've little money as well as nowhere to stay that is free of charge. Everything they treasured has been removed from their grasping hands." He stopped, turning her before taking hold of her shoulders, pointing out once more, "They have no shelter that we know of, no money nor a means to feed themselves."

"I can tell myself that one hundred times but... That means they are desperate. Desperate men do desperate things." He pulled her close his big hand cupping her head to him. She wanted to believe Roby. Nothing in her personal experience lent herself to that notion.

"Go to bed. I'll be up as soon as I take a look around." On the porch, he kissed her quickly. "Promise this won't take long. If we do find them, I'll send word with Bessy."

She found herself nodding, watching him as he strode to meet Kit. They rounded the house. She didn't see him again. Pippa couldn't help but wonder what she would do if something happened to him.

When she reached the bedroom, a fire blazed in the grate casting an orange-red glow throughout the room. Warm shadows back lit by the glow of the fire danced in the space. She poured herself a cup of tea. On another chair that needed to be replaced, she curled up as she decided to watch the flames while she waited.

How is he going to teach me to shift?

Did one just think about turning into a huge cat then it would happen as if by magic? She'd never believed in magic. As she rested her head on the side of the chair, Pippa tried to remember exactly what she'd looked like during the ceremony, deciding she would have to envision that persona if she was going to be successful.

Pippa must have fallen asleep. The next thing she knew Bessy was sobbing hysterically that Roby had been hurt and Kit was bringing him up to the room. She was standing in front of her wringing her hands, tears sliding down her ample cheeks. Her dark brown eyes shimmered with the moisture.

Jerking to a sitting position, Pippa was instantly awake. "Roby's been hurt?" her heart settled in her throat. "How bad?"

"Not bad at all." It was Kit's voice she heard from the hallway. "Bessy, stop scaring Pippa. Roby just got a little bump on his head. That's all. Nothing to worry over. We just can't let him go to sleep. She probably has ideas to keep him awake."

When she saw him, he was standing, held up by two men who

ushered him to the bed.

"You should get him undressed," Kit said. "Don't let him fall asleep for a while. He was out for a few minutes. Talk to him. Do whatever newlyweds do." Kit winked at her.

She didn't think making love in his condition could possibly be wise or prudent. "Who did this?" Pippa asked the question she already knew the answer to.

"Father and son Finchbottom are responsible," Kit told her while Roby groaned. "The men took us by surprise."

"You promised me they were idiots. That you could handle them. Look at you."

She found herself pointing a finger at him. Her anger rose notch by notch as he slowly started grinning at her.

He lifted his shoulders as the smile grew another notch. "We did. Kit did. Well, the men didn't get away. We did more damage to them."

"So much for handling them."

She felt the urge to stomp her foot before she realized this would just keep happening to them until she was no longer the catalyst causing the trauma. Roby wouldn't be safe until she was gone. She had to leave.

He held out his hand, "Come to bed with me, *ceann daor*. I can think of a million ways to stay awake for a couple of hours."

"I'm too tired," she told him petulantly turning her back on his arrogance.

She heard Kit's laughter as he sauntered from the bedchamber.

"Pour me a brandy then you can sit by me. Promise I'll behave myself," he spoke softly as he patted the spot next to him.

The tone of his voice told her he wasn't going to do as he promised. It was just a ploy to assuage her anger. "You never behave yourself, Roby McKenna," but she did as he suggested. "I'll stay here if you tell me what happened."

"The long story or the abbreviated one?"

He wrapped an arm around her shoulder then pulled her close. Her head rested on his chest. He traced a slow gentle path up her arm.

"If you plan on staying awake for a few hours then it must be the long version," she told him shivering with the desire he generated.

163

He trailed his finger along the top of her corsage. "There really isn't a long version. It all happened so fast. One minute I was walking into the stables, the next I was hit from behind with a steel pipe. It was a good thing the man missed his mark. Hit my back instead of my head. Bessy cleaned me up before Kit's men brought me up here."

"The Finchbottoms?"

"Possibly behind this but not the perpetrator. Kit was two steps behind me along with two others. They didn't get away. If the price is right, it's possible they'll give us Harry and Horace as the culprits."

"I see," she said softly as she snuggled against him.

As soon as she could, she would leave for Inverness. Pippa knew she couldn't continue to put his life at risk. The rest of the evening was bittersweet. She had trouble holding back the tears. Leaving Roby was the last thing she wanted for herself. She saw no other choice for her future. More than anything she didn't want to be the reason for his death. By marriage her inheritance was his. She hoped the trust fund Mr. McPhee arranged was still hers. In time he would forget about her even though she knew she would never forget Roby McKenna.

~ * ~

"Our men didn't kill McKenna, probably didn't even scare him as we hoped," Horace said as he tossed back a shot of whiskey. "Mores the pity. Could have hoped for a bit of fear."

"That man *doesnae* fear easily."

The tavern where they were staying was dark, smelling of unwashed bodies and stale beer. The alehouse was situated in the worst part of town. They took a room upstairs because it was cheap, all they could afford. The whores were cheap, which also suited Horace just fine. He never believed he should have to pay for the use of a whore's body. At the moment Harry was enjoying one in the other room. Horace could hear the grunts and shrieks of delight. He rubbed his crotch, thinking it would be his turn with the little red-headed harlot next. Hell, he was just going to join them even though Harry rarely liked to share. Wanted the woman all to himself.

When they got the MacPherson's whore back, they would share simply because they both knew in sharing, they would humiliate her more. A threesome, yes, a threesome would be just fine with him. He was getting harder by the second just thinking about the girl beneath him. Revenge eventually would be sweet. Patience was the key to what he sought even though he was realistic enough to know they lost the money. He poured another glass of whiskey then strode to the window overlooking the slums of Edinburgh.

It made no difference to him when the man they hired to kill Roby McKenna was caught. Made no difference if the man implicated them. McKenna would know who was behind the accident without anyone telling him so. He would also seek some manner of restitution. It would be up to them to make sure they were out of Scotland by then.

Next, when McKenna was out of the picture, they planned to terrorize Phillipa. She would be an easier target. Once left unprotected by Roby she would definitely become easy prey. It would do McKenna good to feel some fear when it came to his wife, the woman who should have been Harry's wife. He had some perfect plans in his head.

The knock on the door surprised him. For a moment, he feared it might be McKenna or his friend, Kit Stuart. He sucked in a deep breath of air debating whether to open the door. His heart fluttered as he debated.

"Horace Finchbottom it's just me, Mary. I'm off work now. Do you want to come downstairs for a pint or two or would you like to visit me in my room? There's some games we didn't play the other night."

"Is there a choice in that?" he asked as he strode to the door. Mary had lovely kettledrums, large big breasts, ones that overflowed his hands tipped with dark pink buds of deliciousness. They puckered up beautifully to greet his tongue. She always shrieked with delight when he bit. Outside in the hallway Horace pulled her into his arms, his hand finding its way down the bodice of Mary's dress. He squeezed before pulling her breast out to suckle the nipple. He bit while she squirmed and twisted, her body coiling against his.

"Oooh, Horace. Oooh, lovey! You should wait until you get to my room. Someone might see us." She tossed her head back just as her hand slipped beneath his trousers. She fit his rod into her hand and squeezed.

"Can't wait that long." He unfastened his trousers then pulling up Mary's skirts he impaled her on the length of him. He shouted out his pleasure.

All the while he was thinking about Pippa.

Chapter Seven

Pippa spent the days trying to lose track of her ardent husband who seemed to be always at her side. The nights were spent making love. So far, the father and son duo had not made another attempt to seek out either of them. She was beginning to think they went their separate ways, in the ensuing time forgot about the revenge they planned. Perhaps she didn't need to leave to protect the man she loved.

This Sunday morning the sun shone brilliantly against a cerulean sky. A few clouds could be seen fluttering high, well above the horizon. Pippa felt a sudden urge to picnic with Roby. He would find a nice private spot near the creek that meandered through the rocky hills. She wondered if he'd ever grow tired of her. So far, the topic of her shifting had not come up again. He must be waiting for her to say something. She avoided the matter, as it seemed he did too. She was afraid to try, terrified to fail. This all meant so much to her.

Roby told her he'd be gone most of the morning, visiting some of their crofters. Kit had tagged along she supposed for company as well as protection. Hypatia still seemed to like Kit the best. She now rode in front of him wherever he went.

He seemed loath to leave saying they couldn't be sure it was safe until they discovered where exactly Harry and Horace were living. This day would have been a good time to make her escape except she lost the urge. Two months had passed since the attack on Roby. Nothing else happened. They both supposed the danger was over. At least she prayed daily it was.

She draped her long braid over her shoulder as she started down the steps of the porch. Sun shine beat down on her, heating her. A soft barely-there breeze ruffled the tiny hairs that slipped loose from the braid. Summer scents, flowers and fresh highland air tickled her senses. She pushed the strands behind her ears as she walked to the stables to see her horse.

The surprise had come on that day she first visited the stable. The horse her father gave her when she turned thirteen was still there. The bay mare recognized her, whinnied as if delighted to see her. Today, she brought her pieces of apple.

Once inside, the stable was dark and cooler than the air outside. She ran her hand along the mare's nose as she held her hand out for her horse to nibble on the sweet offerings. Pippa couldn't help herself, she laughed delighted with the sensations.

"We'll go for a ride later when Roby returns. It will be cooler then. Would you like that, a ride through the heather?"

She rested her head against her horse's head. Breathing in deeply of the stable scents.

"You won't be going anywhere with McKenna. Not today. Maybe not ever."

The voice behind her was harsh, threatening. Her heart fluttered to her throat, beating hard and fast, furiously so.

Startled by the fact Harry was here, she turned, felt the sudden drain of color from her face. "Harry?" Then she saw Horace. He stood on the other side of her. "What are you doing here? Roby won't like it."

"Your husband isn't here. Can't rescue you this time. No, Phillipa, you're all mine for as long as I want. I mean to enjoy every moment as well as leave you thinking about the next time I get you alone. Maybe I'll let Horace enjoy your charms too," Harry said his grin wide, his eyes narrowed on her breasts as if he undressed her in his head.

"Yes, it's us. Thought you were rid of us, didn't you?" Horace sneered then tossed his head back and laughed. "Won't ever be rid of us because we're going to haunt you. We'll keep turning up when you least expect us. All we needed was a bit of patience."

She backed up, moving her head from side to side, searching for a place to run as the two men slowly closed in on her. She felt prickles slither along her spine to settle in her stomach churning there.

"You're not going to get away from me this time. You got nowhere to run," Harry said sniggering. "Why don't you take your dress off for me. I want to see you, see what has McKenna coming back for more every night."

"No." The one word sounded calmer than she felt.

"Oh, but I think you will." Harry ran his finger along her lips then down her neck. He stepped closer, pressing his lower body against hers. He held her hips with both hands.

Pippa felt him hard against her belly. She swallowed the huge lump of revulsion in her throat, knowing and wishing Roby would walk inside the stable. "Wh-what are you going to do? You need to leave now. Go before it's too late." She tried to be bold to assume control of a situation she had no control over. "Roby will kill you if you touch me."

They were right. There was nowhere for her to flee. Her back was against the stall door. Horace stood on one side Harry in front of her, holding her still. Their stench nearly suffocated her.

Harry tightened his hands that held on to her, pushed her face down into a pile of straw. While she twisted and struggled to get away, he held her head in the straw until she couldn't breathe. She squirmed trying to fight them off which only caused more bits of straw and dirt to burn her lungs, scrape her mouth raw while embedding into her face and hands. Horace held her head while Harry clawed at her dress, ripping away one piece at a time until she was naked.

"What do you think, Horace? Can you enjoy that little body as much as Mary?" Harry asked laughing as he placed a foot on the small of her back holding her still.

"Think I can still get a mouth full. Maybe they taste like peaches and cream. I could enjoy that," Horace said. "How about you?"

"Just knowing Roby will be blazing mad when he finds out, I'll enjoy her. We can make sure we both have her."

"Yeah, tonight?"

"Maybe."

No!

Still, she fought.

He pressed harder with his foot. "Hold still."

Her lungs burned. She closed her eyes as she held blistering air in her lungs, scorching as her body fought her mind trying to stay calm.

Harry bent closer to her. His knee was pressed hard against her back. Ropes were wound around her ankles and wrists and tied securely. Then she was tugged back, her chemise used as a gag.

"I like that," Harry laughed. "All trussed up and waiting for us to do whatever we please. Should we, or shouldn't we?"

"I could use a drink first," Horace said as he trailed his finger down her spine, squeezed her buttocks. "We need to put her some place safe. Somewhere no one but us will know to look for her."

"Where only we know," Harry agreed as he, too, ran a hand along her back then dipped lower to caress her hips.

She moaned and jerked. Harry laughed, still bent on tormenting. "We could take you now. Roby won't have any idea."

Harry tossed her over one shoulder. His hand lay on the small of her back as he made his way up the ladder to the loft above. He tossed her down. Raw wood off the loft floor met her. She bruised her shoulder and hip on the fall. Terror coursed through her. She tried to swallow, to moisten her parched throat. She couldn't.

Both Horace and Harry stood over her. Staring at her. Grinning.

"She's a tiny little mite. Gots nothing I'm interested in except McKenna's jealousy. How about you?" Harry asked his father. "It might be fun to watch you take her. I could get hard, maybe. Otherwise, there's nothing she has I want."

"Be more fun to let Roby watch you take her. We can just keep her up here, until we can get to McKenna. He won't know if we've had her or not. Her word, will be all he has."

"I do still value my life," Harry said to his father adding a long slow output of air. "Not going to risk any more McKenna wrath. No telling what he'll do to us after this if he catches up to us."

"Won't catch us," Horace laughed sounding delighted with his thoughts and what they'd done. "Let's get out of here."

Harry bent close to her, pushing her hair aside. "Don't' forget, when you least expect us, we'll show up. Just when you're feeling safe, just when you think we've gone, we'll show up. Who knows what we'll do? Keep in mind, I will have you, you little bitch. Sooner or later, you'll spread your legs for me. Want you to feel the terror every moment of every day."

She heard the two men grunting as they climbed down the ladder. Heard the footsteps then the horses as they left. When there were no more sounds, she heaved a small sigh of relief. Pippa tried to slow her breathing, tried to keep the hysteria from welling up inside until it overcame every part of her. She was shivering, shuddering with the terror as well as the cold. The dirt and straw still clogged her throat.

How long would Roby be gone? He told her he'd be home in time to do something with her.

What did that mean?

She pushed up enough to try and see if there was anything she could use to tear the ropes apart, a sharp edge, a knife, anything. The way they trussed her up with her hands behind her back tied to her feet, she couldn't move, could barely breathe.

Her world whirled and coiled in ever-spiraling circles as she passed in and out of consciousness feeling dragged ever downward, a heavy weight descending on her chest suffocating her. Light from the sun dimmed more. The air took on a decided nightly chill. She choked back the bile threatening.

Prayers she hadn't said since she stood on the gallows waiting to die passed her lips. God saved her then. No, Roby saved her. She wasn't sure at least for her God existed any longer. If he did, he must have abandoned her five years ago when the Finchbottoms arrived changing her world forever. She admonished herself for thinking blasphemy.

From outside a cow mooed, horses nickered, a pig squealed. She longed to hear the steady beat of horse hooves. Instead, she heard nothing but the sighing of the wind surrounded by the usual barnyard sounds. Shivers passed in undulating waves through her body each one growing stronger than the last until every breath of air she inhaled was a gasp fraught with pain. Her teeth chattered, louder and louder. With her tongue she pushed at the gag.

Nothing.

Even if Roby came home this instant would he think to look for her up here? In the loft? Would he search for her? Because of the horses Roby and Kit, would have to come to the stables. They would take care of their mounts. Surely, he would see the trail of torn clothing left on the floor one slipper here the other dropped near the ladder.

Unless the ripped clothing had been picked up. No, Harry would want to rub his nemesis' nose in the fact that he got to her. That he wasn't the bumbling idiot Roby called him. That he was one step ahead of the arrogant Roby McKenna. She paid the price now for Harry's hatred and greed as she had since she was fourteen.

She managed to push herself to the edge despite the pieces of hay digging into her skin. Scratches covered her naked flesh. She tasted blood. Never again would she take anything for granted.

Roby, please come home. I dinna ken if I can survive much longer.

She willed strength into her heart. Closed her eyes and tried not to feel the pain or the terror. Pushed the hysteria to the farthest part of her brain. More images swirled in her head. She saw her cat then Roby's. Memories of his sweet kisses filled her. His touch, his caress, the way he held her tenderly. A sob caught in her throat. Tears slipped from her eyes. She tried to fight them back.

Pippa didn't dare cry. Her cries would turn to sobs that might choke her. The loft faded in and out of her sight. She thought she might be losing consciousness. No, she had to stay awake. Had to make some noise when he arrived. Had to let him know where she was. He would return home.

Darkness began to invade the loft. The sun must be setting. Rain began to fall. The sound of the drops hitting the roof had a soothing effect until she remembered the dour events she was caught in.

Her hands and feet were numb, cold, freezing. She tried to move her toes and fingers. Pain ebbed and flowed as blood attempted to circulate. She caught a fevered breath of stale air. Then it seemed nothing registered in her brain. It was as numb as her limbs. She floated above herself, looking down on her silently still body.

Move something.

Fingers or toes.

She couldn't.

He was too late. She was going to die here today or tonight in this cold forbidding loft at the hands of her guardian and his son. It must be night now because she couldn't breathe couldn't catch a small gasp of air. Her heart rate slowed. She could no longer feel.

At least she'd known love. Met a man who cared for her.

The loud voice woke her. Startled, she shook with the fear it was Harry and Horace returned to do more revolting things to her. Shudders once more flooded her giving rise instantly to panic. She groaned wishing she was still unconscious.

"Is this Pippa's dress?" Kit was asking Roby.

The voice floated up from the floor below her. They asked questions she could answer. Just climb the ladder. Yes, it was her dress, her shoes. Cold settled bone-deep hours ago. When she tried to move, none of her body parts worked. What little air was left in her lungs fluttered out as in a silent sigh.

She tried to make noises. No one would hear the tiny grunts.

Suddenly Hypatia was chattering. Pippa saw her silhouette at the edge of the loft. Thank God for the little one.

"It is," Roby's voice sounded just as cold as her body. "What the devil happened to her, to Pippa?"

They didn't seem to pay attention to Hypatia.

Please don't leave, please listen to her. She's telling you wear I am.

Silently she begged.

"Stay calm."

It was Kit's voice she heard. Her heart began to thunder in her chest. Surely, someone would hear the beating of it. The sound was so loud. "She's alright. We just have to find her."

The yell of pain crying out from below her sent a shiver through her. Roby felt her pain as well as her fear.

Hypatia leapt from her perch. Must have landed on Kit. "Stop that!"

"I'll look outside," Roby said as she heard booted steps leaving the stable. "Pippa! Where the devil are you?" His voice faded just as her hopes began to vanish. For a few more seconds there was only silence. It seemed her monkey decided to obey.

Then...

Kit was below calling out her name. She heard things being moved then shoved aside. Heard the hay he kicked with his feet swish along with the hoarse cursing.

"Where are you, Pippa?" he murmured.

Once more she tried to make sounds. Managed a few grunts from beneath the gag as she twisted and turned her body. He paused for a few seconds making no noises. She prayed he listened. She wriggled and squirmed even more while the tiny noises she was making grew louder.

Hypatia was back on the ledge. Pointing to the floor below then pointing to her. The noises she made louder. She was angry, jumping up and down then swinging herself onto the ladder before returning to the edge of the loft.

"The devil, you're in the loft, aren't you? Hypatia you're a god send."

She inhaled the moist dark air in a gulp as the sound of his boots clamoring up the ladder filled her ears with relief.

"Pippa, dear God. What did they do to you?"

A few seconds later, his shirt covered her nakedness. She was thankful yet embarrassed. She would have had Roby find her.

"Roby! Roby, she's up here in the loft. Kit bent over her, untied her gag. "Are you alright? What happened?"

"They," she swallowed, couldn't speak. She tried shaking her head but the insides pounded. Her eyes closed as she tried to ward off the encroaching pain.

"Harry and Horace?" he asked as he pulled the knife he wore in his boot and began to saw on the rope binding her legs.

"Pippa!"

It was Roby's voice she heard now. He was bending over her, pushing her hair from her eyes, his own filled with moisture. "I was so afraid." His eyes seemed to speak to her giving her encouragement.

"I'll leave the two of you," Kit said as he started down the ladder. "I'll wait for you below."

Roby finished with the rope binding her ankles together before going to work on her hands. She understood he was filled with questions. As soon as he finished with the binding on her hands, he pulled her into his arms. His warmth soothed, calmed her.

"You'll feel as if needles are pricking you. Just be patient. Back to normal you'll be feeling in no time," he whispered into her ear as he slipped the sleeves of Kit's shirt onto her arms before buttoning the front. He was kissing her forehead, nose, as well as her eyelids. "I was so afraid for you. When..." He stopped then as if he understood her fears.

"They didn't," she spoke so softly he leaned down closer. "This was all they did."

"They didn't?"

"Rape me..." Tears slid down her cheeks. "No."

He wiped the moisture away with his calloused fingertips. "I'm so sorry, so sorry I wasn't here for you. I should have left more guards. Should have taken you with me. I will in the future. Until those two are gone from this world, I won't leave your side."

"It doesn't matter. They would have found me alone sometime. They want to hurt you through me. Harry despises you for all you took away from him."

She was still shaking, the words coming out brokenly in a soft whisper. She felt so weak she didn't think she could walk, looked at the ladder and knew she couldn't go down it without falling.

"I won't let him hurt you again."

She rested against his chest absorbing his warmth and strength into her. "You can't stay by my side all the time. Just like today you had work to do, people to see."

"As I said, I can leave guards with you. Keep you protected. They won't be able to get at you again. I should have taken more care. Was careless."

"That sounds like a prison to me."

She was more positive than ever the only recourse for her was to leave. Harry said he'd be back. He had plans. She had to make sure Roby wasn't hurt because of her.

"Let's just worry about getting you down from here, hmm... Can you walk down on your own?"

She was shaking her head. Her legs still felt weak and wobbly. "No, I *dinna* think so."

"I'm going to have to put you over my shoulder. Is that alright?" He sounded apologetic. "Although I would rather carry you in my arms, close to my heart. It will only be less than a minute."

She almost laughed, hysteria once more consuming her. "It was how I got up here, over Harry's shoulder. At least it's you this time carrying me."

"You must be getting better. Seems you can see a bit of humor." Gently, he hefted her over his shoulder.

Kit was at the bottom helping them. "I ordered a bath for her. She's going to need some tender care. I covered her with my shirt as soon as I saw her. I knew you would want to be alone with her for a few minutes."

"They are dead men," Roby growled through his teeth.

"I'll help," Kit said with genuine sincerity. "They can't be allowed to get away with this."

Roby readjusted Pippa in his arms then spoke as he strode to the house and the waiting bath. "Men like that should not be allowed to breathe air."

Upstairs in the room, he set her gently on the bed. Quickly, he removed Kit's shirt then Pippa's stockings.

Pippa reached out to stroke his cheek. "You came for me. I was never happier than when I heard your voice. For a while I didn't think I would live to see you again. Thought they would return for me before you could find me."

One more time Roby picked her up. He set her in the steaming water. Tenderly he soaped a cloth and washed her. She sighed softly, the air in her lungs leaving slowly. How did he *ken* she needed to cleanse herself of Harry's touch, the scent of him?

"You are cut all over. What did they do? *Nay*, don't think about what happened. You can tell me later. Does the soap and water sting?"

She nodded her head, this time gazing into the steel gray of his eyes. "The pain will pass. They pushed me into the hay. Held my head down. I couldn't breathe without inhaling bits of the hay as well as the dirt on the floor."

She was shocked by his curses. His fists tightened on the cloth he held. "I'll get you a glass of wine. You must be hungry."

~ * ~

The sight of Pippa bound and gagged, naked except for her stockings lying on the floor in the stable loft would be seared in his memory throughout eternity. The bile rising to his throat was not easy to push down when he needed to comfort Pippa. All he wanted was to hold her and vanquish the demons in her head. She looked so fragile and terrified. Her eyes wide with the horror she was feeling.

Guilt drowned him, sucked him in over his head. She could have died and with a bit more foresight, he could have prevented this from happening. He should not have left her alone at the house. He made too many mistakes. This one could have killed her. If she could shift, she might have been able to fend them off. She would have been stronger than the men, quicker too.

In that he failed her. He should have insisted she learn instead of allowing her to wallow in her fear. While there were no guarantees she could change form, he was nearly certain she was a shifter who had never learned. For some reason her parents chose not to teach her. Perhaps it was because of the difficulties they were all having with the Sassenach along with the rumors the English wanted to cage them while showing them as anomalies, freaks of nature.

When he finally freed her from the bindings and she was once more in his arms under his protection and now an even more watchful eye, he could breathe again. Now she sat in steaming water attempting to reassure him that she was fine. He would never be fine until he rid the earth of the Finchbottoms. They might not realize it yet but they were dead men taking their last breaths. Best they enjoy the air while it lasted.

When the water grew chilly, he held the bath towel out for her, helping her to stand. By the fireplace, he combed her wet hair. She sipped the wine he poured for her, ate the cheese Bessy brought on a platter along with a few lemon tarts and fresh baked bread slathered with sweet butter.

Pippa appeared stronger. She was resilient, tougher than she looked. Her color was slowly returning to her cheeks. Still, she shivered. He brought her one of her neck-to-floor nightgowns. She slipped it over her head without removing the towel until the gown hit the floor. He fastened the gown to her neck, running his hands along her arms in an effort to warm her. He was afraid if he touched her, it would bring back memories he wished forgotten.

Yet he wanted to make love to her, chase away the demons if that was possible. She reached out to touch him, her eyes imploring something he didn't understand. He wouldn't touch her unless she asked.

Nay, she wouldn't.

She seemed to be slipping away from him, her eyes glazed over, her lips thinned. He didn't know why. This was different than when he found her in the loft. To Roby it seemed she purposely pushed him away, distanced herself. A shudder of terror undulated through him. His gut turned sour. Suddenly, he was sure she meant to leave him.

That thought terrified him. Had from that first night when she tried to slip away from him dressed in just his shirt and trousers. He convinced her to stay but he was never truly sure what designs were sketched in her head.

The smile on her face was hesitant, her sucked in breath of air wavered. When she reached out her arms to him, he pulled her close, kissing her deeply. She responded as if it was the last time they would kiss. Her kiss tasted of fevered desperation. He couldn't wait to get her to their bed as he needed to bind her completely and so thoroughly to him she wouldn't think of doing anything so foolish as heading out on her own.

Pippa was his. She wasn't going to leave him.

"Will you make love to me?" she queried softly her voice whisper thin strained as if she could scarcely say the words.

"Yes."

Without pausing to consider anything save her request, her gown was off and she was beneath him on the rug in front of the fireplace. Her breasts were bathed in the warm orange glow from the flames. His hands were slow as he tenderly journeyed over her softness, her feminine curves. He teased and caressed savoring every part of her as she responded lovingly to him. When they finished, he tenderly placed her on the bed with her glass of wine and the tray of food between them. He wanted to laugh with sheer pleasure when her stomach grumbled eagerly anticipating the feast in front of them.

"When we're through eating, I want to start teaching you how to change into your cat. If you could have done that today, you would not have been so helpless. In your cat form you could have saved yourself. Might have even given them a few scars to remember you by."

"I'm afraid." She settled her hand on his arm, her green eyes dark with worry.

She felt so fragile to him. So very tiny.

"I know you are." His voice was deep and husky. "There is nothing to be afraid of. I'm certain this is something you will be able to accomplish. I'm positive."

"What if I can't? If I'm not?" Now her eyes were huge pools of green, the tiny flecks of gold shimmered with unshed moisture.

"If you are not able to change form we will deal with the fact. I will make sure Harry cannot ever again get to you or hurt you. Will you promise you won't do something foolish? I see the wheels spinning around in your head. You think to keep me safe by leaving. I'm not in danger. Promise you that." He told her knowing that even if he rendered a promise here in this hour, anything could change.

"I *dinna ken* if I can do that? I don't want him to hurt you. If that happened, I could not live with myself." With the backs of her hands, she wiped glimmering moisture from her eyes.

"You know I can take care of myself. Together we are stronger than apart." Pippa still thought to protect him. He didn't know how to change her mind or how to convince her she need not put herself at risk to keep him safe. He'd never been more frustrated.

"Not if he finds a way to surprise you," she argued. "Like last time. You do *ken* he could have killed you."

In many ways her argument was valid. Harry's men surprised him the other day when he knocked him out for a few seconds. Harry no longer had the groats to hire men to suit his purposes. If Kit hadn't been there his injuries might have been worse. Regarding his own life, he didn't intend to take anything for granted as long as the two Finchbottoms lived. His arrogance caused him to make a mistake. It wouldn't happen a second time.

"We *ken* what he's about now. I've men looking for the two of them both in Inverness and Edinburgh. I added guards to the house along with the outbuildings. Once they find them, they've orders to put them on any ship bound for Australia or New Zealand."

"They could come back," she argued her breath sharp with fear.

"True, but it's a long trip. Takes almost a year in good weather to get to the country. Would take almost another year to return. I don't see the two of them coming back especially since the orders include different ships as well as different countries. The two would be left to fend for themselves."

"I'd rather see them dead," she bit out her fists tightening around her goblet. "I despise them. Since they came into it, my life has been horrific."

He found he was holding his breath as he watched her. "As would I see them permanently snuffed from this world. We cannot entirely take the law into our hands. We can see to sending them away without much reprisal if any." He thought once more, an idea sparking to life. "Perhaps a stint in the British Navy might prove just the thing to rid our lives of these two."

The plan was good, much better than booking them passage on a vessel bound someplace far away. This way they would have to work for their meals. If they slacked off, they would be disciplined. He would make sure they would be bound to two different ships. It might be just punishment, a living hell for these two. Bringing them to the Kinnel Stones was another option. He would think on it.

What could be better?

Satisfied with the plan he could set in motion, Roby knew he would hold her until she slept. He needed to speak with Kit, hoped his cousin would still be awake waiting for him. She surprised him though as he watched her down the end of her wine. If he guessed correctly, she was up to something. Well, he would just have to wait and see.

Her breasts rose with the air she inhaled. Her smile was weak and hesitant but it was real. Breathlessly she began in a soft voice, "Should we start now?"

"Start?

"Teach me to shift."

"I'd forgotten," he told her a slow grin of satisfaction along with hope for their future creeping into his heart. "Tonight, what better time than the present? If you cannot, I *ken* your disappointment. We will deal with it, but if you can..."

"Why didn't my parents teach me? Why didn't they ever let me know they, too, had the ability? When I attempt to consider the fact from every side, it simply doesn't make sense."

"I cannot answer those questions. Now, you are already naked. Perfect condition for you to change form. Although disrobing you again would have been pleasant."

"What if I've clothing on? How would shifting have helped today? I was fully dressed." She sounded disgruntled as well as confused.

Unable to help himself, he laughed, "One does not have to disrobe before they change shape. If you don't have the time to undress, your clothing will be ripped to shreds. Of course, that makes it difficult when you want to be a human female again."

"Or male."

"True enough," he laughed again delighted with her questions.

"I see," she said softly her eyes lowering as if she was thinking about his words.

He knew she understood. "So, I've never really thought about how to change form. I just think about my cat body, the way it looks along with how I feel when I'm in it and then my body makes adjustments. It has always seemed so simple. With a little time, it will also be simple for you."

"I've done that and nothing happens. I've imagined myself as I saw my cat." Her breaths were rapid as she watched him. "I close my eyes and think and try truly hard to make the change. Nothing."

"Perhaps you are trying too hard. Don't make it so difficult nothing can happen."

"I..." she moistened her lips shaking her head. "I don't know what else to do."

He felt the first stirrings of his cat form, sensed the sinew and muscles as it grew to larger proportions. His arms and legs changed shape as did his face. The sensations stole his breath, caused his heart to stop for a second. Curious energy pulsed around and through him while he utilized his mind to continue the process. This would all be new to Pippa. It seemed so easy. Yet he understood he grew up with his father and siblings doing this very thing, teasing and taunting each other, challenging themselves to be the quickest and the best. Swiftly, he changed back as he thought of his human form. He realized he didn't have to truly see his male human form as he did his cat.

"What if I change to a panther and I can't get back?" Pippa's voice wavered squeaking as she shivered with the same terror he saw in her eyes. "What if I *dinna ken* how to do that? I could stay as a cat forever. I don't want that, Roby. I couldn't bear something like that to happen."

"That won't happen to you. I promise," he said with all the confidence he could muster for now.

He'd never heard of such a thing occurring. Never thought anyone else ever feared not being able to become human again after shifting. Justly, he believed her fear to be irrational.

He couldn't tell her that.

Patience.

"How do you know? How can you be so sure?" With her seeming anger, color rose on her cheeks. It was better than fear and panic.

Shrugging while adding a grin to the wicked combination of sensual expressions he flashed at her, "I just know. It will be easier for you to change to a form you are used to being in. All you will have to do to change to human is think about yourself."

"That's what you think."

"It's what I know. You will have no trouble changing back to human. I promise. Trust me in this. Let's work on deciphering your cat. Let her prowl around in your head. Remember what you saw during our wedding."

She looked away for several seconds, wringing her hands her

breasts swaying beckoning to him. Perhaps they should put this off for a few minutes.

"I don't... I just don't... I'm afraid to take a chance."

He willed himself to control his solid arousal which was growing firmer and thicker by the second. "Do you trust me, *lass*? If you have trouble, I'll walk you through. Don't be afraid of a challenge. I've not heard of a single case where a body got stuck in their cat and couldn't get out." He was attempting not to laugh. She wouldn't appreciate laughter. Not his Pippa, she would believe he was laughing at her but he wasn't. It was the image he thought humorous.

"Yes, they'd be in their cat and wouldn't be able to speak. Would have no way of telling anyone that they weren't truly a panther."

She sounded as if she was struggling to convince herself not to attempt the feat. He didn't truly understand the vacillation.

To Roby, Pippa's ire seemed to grow with each second that passed. He didn't want to continue the argument. She was terrified. He would accept the fact and put off the challenge until she felt truly ready. There simply was no other word to describe what he was seeing in her eyes. This might be better left to another day.

"If you don't want to try right now, we'll wait. It's fine with me if you never do give it a stab. Except for the fact it would present an advantage if you were ever attacked again." His gut soured at the idea she could be so vulnerable. "I need..." The devil but this wasn't about him or his needs.

He watched her struggle with a breath of air, her breasts moving provocatively as she did so. He gasped for a breath as his mind shimmied with newfound ideas concerning Pippa's breasts.

"Alright then. I do trust you. I will do this if you promise to make sure nothing will happen to me." She closed her eyes running her tongue along her full bottom lip swollen slightly from their earlier kisses.

Once again, he struggled with ideas other than watching his wife shift to a panther. Yet he wanted to see her, devour the way she would look in her cat form. In her other life she wasn't black. She said, just normal. There wasn't a single thing normal about Pippa.

She was amazing.

An enchantress.

"You said to think how I appeared when...during the ceremony when I saw myself."

Her eyes were still closed. She straightened her shoulders. Lifted her chin in the air. Her breathing appeared to be nonexistent. She was as stiff as a tree trunk, unbendable.

"You're too rigid, my *ceann daor*. Relax," he murmured as he sat in front of her, stroking her arms. "Use your imagination. Loosen your body. Think about running in the heather as a cat. Try to remember what it was like before. You said you saw the two of us racing in the crags, along the river. I know the perfect place we can go. We'll be alone. We can play all you want. Think about running with me."

She shivered. To Roby it seemed her body was shuddering, shaking so thoroughly she would never succeed. He didn't know what to do for her. Still, she strained, her muscles too taunt. She caught her lip beneath her tiny white teeth as her body shook and shivered.

"Relax, *ceann daor*. Think of the beautiful spots you have on your skin. I see them forming on your shoulders, rippling down your beautiful breasts. Relax. Breathe. Breathe deeply. Now breathe again. This will work. Breathe deeply, breathe with me."

In a giant spasm she changed.

"You did it!" He laughed switching forms then sitting on his haunches to gaze at his wife. Her tail swished back and forth. She grinned at him. He nuzzled her with his nose.

Her eyes widened as she walked around him as if checking him out, searching for possible flaws. She licked the scar above his eye. Sat back and looked at him as if asking 'what do we do now?'

She strutted around the bedchamber. When she stood beside him, he heard the soft purr emanating from her. Lord, but he was proud of her. She conquered her fears. She was safer now than she'd been a few hours ago.

It was time to prove his point.

He changed back to his human. "Now it is time," he told her watching her carefully.

In less than a second, she was Pippa again.

She stood in front of him, grinning. Breathless, "I did it. Didn't I? I changed into my other form. I can do it. Really do it. I'm babbling, aren't I?" She wrapped her arms around him, kissing him, running her tongue along his mouth, begging for him to open for her. He toyed with her for a few seconds, then did her bidding, allowing her to stroke the inside of his mouth, to caress and investigate wherever she wanted.

His moan of arousal rumbled from deep in his chest. He cupped her buttock before dragging her belly against him. She wriggled and twisted. He groaned, jerking her closer before falling on the bed. She lay on top of him, her legs straddling his. It was several minutes later before they lay sated with a fine sheen of moisture on their skin wrapped in each other's arms.

"I did it," she murmured nuzzling against his chest, running her finger through his hair, teasing him to full arousal once more.

"You did. Would you like to do it again?" He laughed when her small fingers closed around him. "I didn't mean that."

Her deep throated laughter was haunting magic. "Of course you did. You were just waiting for me to decide what I wanted. I did, Roby McKenna. I want you. Later we can change. Right now, I just want you to love me."

At this moment, that was what he craved. He could never get enough of her. Would never be fully sated, not when she lay naked in his arms more than willing to explore his man's body while allowing him the same liberties.

"When can we go run?" she asked as her hand followed the path of his hair past his navel to his groin. She cupped him. Stimulated him to a fine breaking point. He shuddered as he stopped her hand. He sat up pulling her with him. After pouring more wine, he handed her cheese and bread.

"Tomorrow, if the weather suits," he told her as he watched her eat. "I was very proud of you."

"Should I practice?" She nibbled on the cheese her smile wide as she focused on his mouth before roaming lower.

"If you like." He laughed then finished off his wine. "You realize, you cannot shift anytime the mood suits. It is dangerous. We must always

185

take precautions. We will play together once. After that, we will not shift unless there is very real and present danger. Do you understand?"

Pippa nodded, her smile turning downward in a tiny pout of disappointment. "That's all I want right now is to practice this new found skill." She leaned against the backboard, closing her eyes. "Why didn't my parents teach me? Why didn't I ever see them change form? Surely it couldn't have been that they were not shifters."

Roby let his breath out slowly. "I don't understand either. It isn't normal for shifters to abandon their children in the way your parents deserted you. I too would like to have answers, but I *dinna ken* where to look? It isn't as if you can ask them."

~ * ~

When Roby entered the drawing room, Kit looked up from the papers he'd been going through. "These are some of the financial records left by the MacPhersons. They are worth the time to sort through and may give us an idea about several puzzling things you've brought up. It seems the Finchbottoms were never able to open the safe. Truly, they didn't know what a gold mine Pippa's inheritance was."

One eyebrow arched skyward in conjecture. "Pippa is a rich lady?"

"By marrying Pippa you've added substantially to your already vast holdings. You, my cousin, are a *verra* rich man."

"Such as?" His brows drew together as he poured a brandy before sitting down across from him. "What's puzzling?"

"First, it could be a coincidence. Might not have anything to do with what happened to Pippa today. I found a dead cat in the stable. I buried it before either of you could see it." Kit waited for a reaction as he watched his cousin's expression change.

Roby sipped the brandy. "What kind of cat?"

"Does it matter? It was mutilated," he paused in thought carefully considering more repercussions. "Suppose it does make a difference. "A calico, probably doesn't mean anything. The Finchbottoms couldn't possibly *ken* we are a family of shifters or to what form we change." Kit was watching for some sign from Roby. His face remained serene, composed as if he too was thinking.

"It has been a rumor for years that we are of the clan Chattan. They might not know but they certainly have the ingenuity to guess. If mutilating a cat and leaving it for us to find would terrify Pippa, I wouldn't put the feat above them."

"Guessing, yes, and if it turned out they were right all the better. They wouldn't *ken* that we are black panthers in our other form hence the plain cat. Pure black cats are more difficult to find. Something else you should know about if you don't already."

Kit continued shuffling through the papers in front of him. Specifically, he was searching for the documents from the orphanage that Pippa's parents donated money to each year. He knew Roby would want to verify this particular fact.

"Pippa can shift," Roby spoke blandly as he sat forward. "She did so just before I left her upstairs sleeping."

"Truly? That does make things more interesting now, doesn't it? Even more curious when you see the document I'm looking at."

"Indeed, my friend. Her parents could not or they didn't want Pippa to know. What do you think?"

It was apparent to Kit that Roby was searching for answers. Kit handed the document he was looking for to Roby. He read it, whistled through his teeth before handing it back.

"Could it be a forgery?" Roby asked.

Kit lifted his shoulder slightly, shrugging off the question. "Anything can be. The Finchbottoms might have had an illegal document drawn up in order to prove she wasn't the heir even though she is named as sole heir in the will. This particular piece of paper was in the safe. As I said earlier, I don't believe they were able to access these papers."

"If they had such a document made up, why didn't they use it?" Roby asked as he drummed his fingers on the arm of his chair. "Doesn't make sense none of it does. I'm going to get to the bottom of this puzzle."

"Harry and Horace are living in Edinburgh. Our men found them at the Angel and Devil tavern."

"You don't say?" Roby said looking pleased. "Couldn't have

picked out a seedier place to stay. Glad we know which direction to look for them. I take they aren't back there yet."

"*Nay*, it would take at least two days of vigorous travel most likely more. I believe for now they are more intent on frightening Pippa. They must have a place nearby."

"Find it," Roby ordered.

Chapter Eight

Pippa and Roby rode north well past any villages, past hunting lodges into the most barren landscape in Scotland. They wound their way through the rugged hills as well as over them until they reached a river flowing over jagged rocks lined with huge stones along with some small jutted trees. During their travel they saw no one. The scent was of heather and gorse.

He felt good about that. For his purposes, it would not do to have witnesses. No, he needed absolute privacy to accomplish what he meant to do. Teach his peace-loving wife how to fight. Perhaps fleeing in the face of adversity would be the best procedure. Yes, he believed it would be however, what if running wasn't plausible?

Too many factors to consider. The possibilities haunted him, kept him awake at night.

Roby liked to watch the expressions flitting across Pippa's face while she rode, the devil take him he wanted her again. Her enjoyment glimmered in the clearness of the deep green of her eyes along with the wide smile on her lips. He needed her to forget that day she was attacked. She should learn some fighting techniques in case anything like that happened again.

While they were keeping a watchful eye on the Finchbottoms, the two men were successful too often in eluding his men to give Roby the peace of mind he craved. The fact bothered Roby more than he wanted to admit. He couldn't tell Pippa. If he did, she might leave to protect him. He couldn't allow that to happen. Kit promised to follow him here with two of his men as an added precaution.

The day was perfect for the excursion he planned. Sunshine

littered the air with its heat, the warmth touching on his skin. Thoughts of basking in the sun with Pippa in their cat forms gave him reason for a deep throaty growl of delight. No threat of rain hovered to drench the enjoyment he planned. No clouds to block the heat from the sun. Bessy packed a basket of food complete with two bottles of wine, one for this afternoon as well as one for the evening dinner.

They would shift and play then they would spend the night at Callum's lodge. He sent men to clean the place several weeks ago. It was ready for an extended stay, which he meant to do with his wife as soon as Harry and Horace were safely tucked away in the British Navy. It would end up being their honeymoon. Privacy would not be needed by then.

For now, he was content to ride alongside Pippa so he could watch her. She rode her little bay mare. He pointed out a hawk, hovering on currents of air while the bird searched for prey. A herd of elk grazed in a nearby field of heather and clover. A rabbit darted across the road.

She almost died because of a rabbit. He tried to push the memory of Pippa standing on the gallows to the farthest recesses of his mind. Robby didn't think he would ever forget her slim body shaking as she waited for the noose to slip over her head. With all that was going on anything that threatened her, threatened him. His body tightened when he recalled the night in the stables, the way he found her then the dead cat.

He managed to keep the information about the cat from Pippa although he had to stop himself a few times from bringing it up. Her tender heart would be more concerned for the cat than for herself or the implications. For some unbeknownst reason, Hypatia abandoned Kit the night Pippa was attacked. Now she rode in front of Pippa.

"When will we be there?" she asked as she rode up alongside him, grinning as she pushed wayward locks of hair from her face.

"You aren't excited, are you?"

"What gave you that idea? Of course, I'm enthusiastic and nervous, a bit overwrought also. Not sure I want to learn anything about fighting or hurting someone else."

No, she wouldn't be but he was determined for her to learn.

He was tempted to pull her from her horse so he could ride with her as he did when they first met. He didn't think the monkey would like to share. She'd been so possessive. That week held delights as none other than he could think of as he began to learn about his new bride along with just how tempting she was. "I would say before the sun sets this afternoon."

"You are such a tease. I'm famished and if we don't arrive shortly, I'm going to stop so we can eat."

He laughed then and decided having her sitting on his lap and between his legs was exactly what he craved. He wanted to feel her heat. Needed to feel the soft curves of her body pressed again his hardness. Her position in front of him would give him accesses to all of her, every tiny succulent spot she possessed. They had not made love since last night. He craved her now, at least the closeness of her body.

With a quick calculated move on his part coupled with a soft voice of protest on hers, she was sitting astride him. Her core pressed tightly against his hard length. The sensations were heavenly, erotic in the extreme.

For a moment Hypatia chattered in disapproval then seemed content to ride by herself on Pippa's saddle.

"Roby McKenna, you put me back on my horse." She thumped him on the chest.

He laughed, delighted. "My thoughts of you are way too delicious to even contemplate something like that."

She emitted a little harrumph of displeasure as she wiggled her tiny yet curvaceous form closer.

He nuzzled her nape, pushing loose hair away for better access, heard the sigh of contentment while he felt the shiver of gratification. The scent of Pippa filled his nostrils. "No, don't believe I want to do that now that I've got you exactly where I want you."

His hand slipped beneath her skirt to journey and explore the length of her leg. He stopped behind her knee, caressed slowly. She spread her legs wider encouraging his ardent endeavors. He found her heat and the slickness waiting for him. She was all heat and passion. Her desire for him overflowed.

"Naughty," he whispered against her ear, nipping and licking while she arched against him, rotating her body closer, begging for more twisting and squirming ever closer. She panted with her frantic need. "You want me as much as I want you don't you little darling? The devil but I don't think I can wait even a few more minutes."

"You're a *verra* wicked *mon*, Roby McKenna, to seduce a girl when she has no means or desire to say no. I *dinna* want you to stop."

He didn't want to stop either.

As they rode, he continued the path he began, caressing and teasing soft swollen parts, hard tipped buds at the tips of her breasts. With gentle fingers, he explored all of her, visiting every tempting part of her. She would be ready and desperate with her need by the time they reached the waterfall where he was headed. He touched as many sensitive erotic spots he could reach. Found the swollen knub of her delight. Pleasured her until she had no control.

Tiny sounds of ecstasy rippled from her lips.

Her body coiled against his, begging him. She arched her back giving him better access to the soft rounded globes he loved so well.

"Roby!" she suddenly cried out his name as she found her pleasure in his arms. The feel of her climaxing against him sent his body to a point of hardened steel as he continued to entice the magic between them. When her body shuddered its last, she relaxed into him. Her body sated, his arousal full and hard. He wasn't about to allow her respite. His fingers found the tight buds, once again pinching her beautiful breasts, tugging until they were even harder, until she writhed once more pleading for more, so much more.

"I want to taste you, all of you," he told her as he sent first one then a second finger inside her. "Do you think you can climax again before we reach the place I'm headed for?"

"Roby..." she moaned softly. "*Ye* cannot mean to continue with this. I can scarcely breathe. We need a bed."

"But I can. To do what I plan one doesn't need a mattress. A bed of sweet grass is more than sufficient." He laughed, totally enthralled by her response.

Soon they would reach the falls. Soon he would be inside her. Shortly, she would find her pleasure again. It was only a few minutes later when he stopped. He set her on the ground then dismounted behind her.

Sweeping her into his arms, he carried her to a grassy spot. Sun shone on the ground. Soft breezes wafted through the leaves above them. He could think of no better place than this one to make love to his wife.

Her hands fumbled with the laces on his trousers. By the time she had them undone, they were both lying on the grass. He was on top of her, between her long slender legs. The loving was quick and anxious. He came inside her with a single thrust. They both reached their limit in seconds. Once again, she cried out his name as his seed exploded inside her.

"The devil what you do to me."

He was sated for the time being. She was exhausted.

In his arms, she rested her head on his chest. They were both still fully clothed. It would be time soon to disrobe and shift. He planned on satisfying her at least one more time before they got on with the lessons he wasn't truly looking forward to. For her there was danger. She had no experience.

"Are you going to feed me, Roby McKenna? A girl cannot survive on solely your love making although it is a wondrous thought. Someone once told me, I need nourishment if I'm going to continue in this vein. Hear my stomach? *'Tis* growling in displeasure."

"*Aye*, my *bonnie* wife, I'm going to feed you and love you again. After that we'll shift and play in our other form. We can race across the heather here where no one will see. We can climb the mountains and stand on top while we let the wind sift against our fur. When we wed, I never thought to have a wife as a shifter. This is a heaven I never expected."

"Are you happy then?" she asked stroking his jaw with her fingertip. "Are you glad you saved me from the hangman's noose?" She shuddered at her reminder of what almost ended her life.

"*Verra*," he said gruffly, his voice hoarse with emotions as he tasted and kissed the nape of her neck while her body quivered her need for him, not food. "We best eat or I'll have you in another way than beneath me again and again. It seems I can never get enough of you. Just looking at you, I want you."

"Nor can I fill myself with your body enough times to satisfy my hunger," she spoke softly.

At least another thirty minutes passed before they settled down to eat. When they finally finished, Roby was ready to teach her how to spar, how to use her claws to protect and defend as well as to use against another. For him and his siblings it seemed to come naturally. Where Pippa was concerned, he couldn't be sure. She didn't have anyone to play or fight with as she grew. She was an only child. He would have to tell her to keep her claws sheathed.

"Are you ready?" He held out his hand to help her rise. Lord, but she was beautiful, her flesh white and silken, her breasts swaying slightly as she stood. He clenched his teeth. He inhaled a deep breath willing himself to have strength of determination where she was concerned. It would not do to tumble her to the ground again when he had another important purpose.

"I want to run with you," she said her voice soft yet determined. "I don't wish to learn how to fight. I want to know again how it feels when I shift."

"When we play don't be alarmed if I'm more aggressive than you are used to. I won't hurt you. Just keep your claws covered. We will indulge in a little rough play before we run. If I get too rough, unsheathe your claws for a second and let me know your displeasure. I've only had Brady along with the cousins to spar with. Don't want to hurt you."

"I *dinna* think you would."

"Yet, even in your cat form you will be smaller and weaker. I need to understand your strength and the power you possess. You have only one way to show me."

"With my claws."

"Yes."

Shifting came easier to Pippa this time. He thought perhaps in private she had practiced. He nudged her with his head. She stumbled back a few strides, a curious look on her cat face. He nodded to her hoping to encourage her to push back at him. She didn't. Instead, she sat, glaring at him as if wondering if he lost his mind. Well, she told him she didn't want to fight. There wasn't anything aggressive about Pippa. He would have to figure out a way to make her fight.

Perhaps he had.

This time he plowed into her with his shoulder. She staggered, falling on her shoulder. She let out a small yowl of fury as well as pain. He did hurt her. He would have to check her shoulder later. If perhaps he got her angry, she would realize what was expected of her and she would retaliate. Slowly, she stood. He wanted her to attack. Craved for her to not just defend herself but take the offense.

He shifted to human. "Pippa," he began trying for the patience he understood he was going to need, "You are supposed to defend yourself. If I hit you with my body, you need to do the same to me. Knock me over. Use your paws. Pretend I'm Harry. Clout me in the face. Should we give this sparing another stab?" He was hopeful even though he had his doubts this would come to fruition.

He changed again. When he was pure cat, she nudged him in the shoulder with her head. The push was one of affection. Clearly, she didn't see him as Harry or Horace. He rose on his hind legs pushing on her shoulders. Once again, she stumbled backward. He blocked her on the side. She fell again. Putting her head on her front paws she appeared defeated before they barely began. He sensed she wasn't about to move.

He was going to get dizzy changing back and forth. "Hit me, Pippa. Do it now while I'm like this. Give me a good solid push on my chest. Fight me. Show me how strong you are."

She shook her head. With her eyes she was telling him an absolute and resounding no. Roby drug in a ragged breath as he repeated the procedure hoping she would eventually figure out what he wanted. All he accomplished was to knock her around. It was something he didn't want to do. He wasn't sure how to explain to her that defending herself was right and good. It was what she needed to do if she was to survive a conflict with either or both the Finchbottoms.

Suddenly, she changed to human. "I cannot do this, Roby McKenna. I will not hit you or push you. It is not right of you to ask such a horrible thing of me. I *dinna* want to hurt you." Tears ran down her cheeks. "I will have to settle for running away. It is, after all what I do best. Can we race the wind now?"

He nodded giving his consent to running even though for some reason his gut told him no. It was never wise to go against the sixth sense all cats seemed to have. Danger hung on the breezes floating around them. The scent of heather wafted through the same air. Nothing stirred in any direction for miles around them. He reassured himself it was safe. Told himself Kit was close by in case it wasn't. Still, once again it seemed he took a chance he should not.

She ran now while he watched her muscles play as she quickly covered a short amount of distance. In her cat form she was also beautiful. She stopped on top of a hill. Probably not the wisest thing to do. Anyone could see her, could see a panther in the highlands where they didn't belong.

Pippa was magnificent. He ran after her, catching up to her on top of the hill. The panoramic view was beautiful. Purple and white heather dotted the mountains. A heard of elk grazed nearby. He motioned for her to follow as he made his way to more protected places. They ran along the river, jumping from rock to rock. He wanted to roar his pleasure.

So far it was a beautiful day.

Nothing on the horizon threatened.

When they reached another secluded spot on the river, he stopped then stretched out on a sun-warmed rock. She sat down beside him. He nuzzled her neck just as he would like to do if he was human. She purred softly as she stretched out beside him. He wished he could understand what she was thinking. In any form he didn't believe that was possible.

They must have fallen asleep. When he woke, the sun was descending. He needed to get her back to the clearing where they stopped. Where their clothing was spread on the ground around the blanket. They spent too long in their cat and asleep.

It was not well done of him. He knew better.

The last thing he wanted was to put her in danger. The thought of someone coming upon them curdled his stomach. He nudged her until she woke and stretched. He tossed his head in the direction of their horses.

She nodded her understanding.

He caught human scent on the wind. Terror for her spilled through him. Quickly he shifted.

"Shift now Pippa. Now!"

She did as he said and just in time. Without hesitation, he pushed her against a rock, covering her nakedness with his body. It would not be enough. He knew it. She would realize the fact soon. His heart raced as he searched the remnants of his mind for some way out of this.

"What have we got here? A naked couple dallying in the wilds. It's a bit surprising. Don't see horses or clothing."

When Roby looked over his shoulder, he saw two Sassenach soldiers. Patrolling this area of the highlands had two expectations. One was finding Jacobites who might be hiding and the other catching shifters. He would have to do something to create a diversion. His mind seemed blank.

"We're doing no harm," Roby said as he turned keeping Pippa covered to the best of his ability. The thought of these men ogling her ate at him.

Guilt swamped him. This was entirely his fault, his doing.

Fear for her flooded his veins.

"We could use some of what you're enjoying," one said as he tried to see behind Roby. "Seems the small gal is a pretty little thing. You'll share."

"She's my wife. You'll not be enjoying her."

Not as long as he lived and breathed. This might be a time when she needed to run. For a short distance she would be faster than the horse. If she could find someplace to hide, he could attack at least one of the soldiers. In his cat form perhaps render the horses useless. It might be their only chance, yet he didn't want to take it unless there was no alternative. Presently, it seemed no choices existed.

He would never let either of these two bloody Englishman touch her. The devil but he once again made a foolish decision. He allowed the enjoyment of the day muddle his senses. He would never forgive himself. It seemed where Pippa was concerned, he lost all reasonable intelligence.

Turning, he whispered, "When I tell you, shift. I want you run as fast as you can until you find a place to hide. I'll come for you. Do you understand, Pippa?"

He watched her signal with her head that she did indeed comprehend what he wanted. Next to him he felt the frantic breaths she inhaled.

That didn't mean she'd do it. The devil but this wasn't the time for her to learn to fight.

"Whose to stop us? You?" one of the soldiers sneered his contemp. "You're only a bloody Scotsman. We can do what we want with your woman. You can watch the fun. Of course, you could show us your true colors. Been thinking perhaps the two of you are shifters believing you could gain a little privacy way up here in the north. In that case, we'll be having even more fun when we watch the two of you in separate cages, confined. You'll wish you never sought your freedom out here."

"Just newlyweds," Roby paused, thoughtfully rubbing his hand along his jaw. "What's a shifter? Never heard tell of such a thing."

"Quick, aren't you? Well, let's just see what you do and you don't know." He dismounted striding toward them. "Going to get a sample of the little lady standing behind you. You're going to watch. Grab him."

"No!" Roby's fists tightened at his side. "You're not going to touch my wife. I'll see you rot in hell before that can happen," he grit out, fury over this rising as he waited on the balls of his feet. He meant to leave this to the last minute, hoping the other man would also dismount, giving Pippa a better chance of getting away.

Kit could show up at any time. Damn him for being late and giving us too much privacy.

"Maybe I'll go first," the other soldier said as he too left his horse. "Should we see who gets her first? We could toss a coin."

"I'm the officer in command so, I'll make the decision. You just keep an eye on the naked husband." He strode forward, unlacing his trousers, the bulge in his crotch growing with each step.

In a whisper, "Shift now, Pippa."

He changed form even while he felt Pippa standing behind him do the same. He let out an ear-splitting roar before he leapt on the first soldier tumbling him to the ground. Killing an English soldier was not an option even though he felt the rage engulf him.

A shot rang out. He heard Pippa roar while he prayed she was running. From the corner of his eye, he watched her leap on the second soldier, knocking the pistol from his hand.

Now she chose to stand and fight? She should have run for her life.

Hypatia landed on the head of the soldier Pippa knocked to the ground. The little monkey covered the man's eyes. He batted at her. Adeptly, she leapt around him keeping his hands busy.

With a mighty jump she landed on top one of the horses, terrifying the beast. The horse reared up. When its hooves hit the ground, they landed on top of the soldier Pippa sent to the ground. Hypatia jumped away. The cry of pain resounded in the tiny glen. The fight was nearly over before it began. Pippa could take care of herself.

Roby sliced the chest of the first soldier, doing his best to incapacitate not kill. He smelled shifter on the wind. Caught the scent of Kit. When he moved off the soldier, Kit was standing on the ground appearing more than willing to lend a hand if needed. It seemed all they required at this point was corroboration and clothing.

"Don't let me get in the way," Kit murmured, watching. "This has made my day." He walked toward a crevice that was large enough for Pippa to hide behind then left her to dress there. "I'll watch this one for you, Pippa. It might be wise now to get dressed while they both seem to be unconscious. I think from fright. No other reason as far as I can see."

Pippa followed Kit's instructions. Too bad she didn't follow his. He needed to make sure she paid attention to his commands. Still, he was proud of her. He never thought she would be able to fight. A sigh of pleasure sifted through him as he realized she didn't want to hurt him, not that she could unless she left her claws out.

When Pippa returned dressed, he followed suit only he didn't go behind the rock.

"Why did you wait so long?" Roby asked Kit. "Thought you'd never show yourself."

He realized how true that was. When he told Pippa to shift, he'd never been so terrified. Everything pooled out of his control. It was not a heady thought.

"Seemed the two of you had everything under control," Kit shrugged a self-satisfied smile on his smug countenance. "She's a real scrapper. Didn't need my intervention."

"Would have been fortuitous if we didn't need to shift. If a third party, male, arrived none of this would have happened."

"I didn't get here that soon. Left too much distance between the two of you. Privacy, you *ken*. What did you do? Take a nap?"

Roby felt the rise of heat sting his cheeks. Kit tossed his head back laughing. "Brought your horses too. Wouldn't want you two to have to walk back. What should we do with these two?"

"Leave them here without a stitch of clothing. Don't have reason to grant concessions to men who would take advantage of a helpless woman."

The sting of that truth filled Roby with more guilt. This in truth had all been his fault. He had no one else to blame. If he hadn't been stupid, he wouldn't have needed Kit's intervention.

Pippa was standing beside him mute, her face pale as ash. He pulled her into his arms, rubbing her back. She was quaking and shivering. He wanted to yell at her for not following his commands as well as praise her for the job well done. She defended him. Without her he might have met a far different end.

"I guess when it comes to defending your husband you don't need any practice," Roby said softly his voice cracking with the surging emotions that rushed through him.

"I couldn't let anything happen to you," she murmured. "You are my life."

He understood more completely how true her words were. He'd done nothing to prove to her he could keep both of them safe. The devil but he had a huge job in front of him. At the next sign of danger, she might truly bolt.

~ * ~

She'd never been so terrified in her entire life than when she thought Roby was going to die at the hands of the soldiers. Not even when Harry stripped and tied her or when she waited for the hangman. Pippa wrapped her arms around her as she tried to warm herself. It didn't seem to work. Chills swept through her so strong she didn't think she'd be able to stand. She felt herself sway. Stiffened her knees.

Roby and Kit were talking, discussing something. She couldn't seem to comprehend anything they said. Snippets of words filtered through the haze surrounding her brain. Her body started to weave, her knees trembling until she stood no longer.

"Pippa!"

Out of the fog that was her mind, she heard her name. Heard Roby calling out to her. She wanted to open her eyes. Cold filled her from the inside out freezing every part of her. His hands were on her shoulders, her face. She tried to look at him.

"What happened? I thought you were fine." He searched her body, running his fingers along her arms and legs as well. "I don't see any blood. Don't feel anything broken."

"I believe she just fainted from sheer terror or perhaps exhaustion," Kit said. "A great deal happened here none of which she is used to experiencing. She fought for her man, saved him from a fate that is too difficult to contemplate."

His voice sounded so very far away. Roby carried her now, handed her over to Kit. Once more she was in his arms, sitting in front of him. He pulled her close, closer still. She was beginning to warm. She heard her heart pound. Felt each breath of air as it burned her lungs.

"I'm such a fool," he murmured close to her, his mouth brushing across her ear. "One would think I'd get smarter with age. I promise you nothing like this will ever happen again."

The heat from his body began to slowly warm her. The chills seemed to dissipate as they rode. He told her they would stay the night at Callum's hunting lodge. The same place she lived when she first ran from Harry's threats.

"We'll visit his grave. Leave some flowers. You can tell me everything about your time there."

His gut churned when he looked at her. He couldn't help but pull her close then closer still. He never wanted to let her go. Hypatia was now perched on his shoulder chatting away, clearly displeased with what just transpired. Seeming to need confirmation that Pippa was alright.

Keeping his little family close as well as safe became paramount in his head. When he thought on all Pippa endured, fear flooded him, engulfed all that he was.

Kit rode beside them, silent as the gloaming began to descend. His cousin watched them with hooded eyes. Roby knew his best friend searched for his mate. It was time to settle. The woman was somewhere in the world but where?

Seeming to be satisfied with Pippa's recovery, Hypatia switched to Kit's shoulders. She jumped so suddenly Kit swore. "The devil take you, you damn monkey." Yet he reached up and stroked her tenderly.

The little animal chattered, pointing an accusing finger at Kit before placing a kiss on his lips. Roby laughed. Pippa smiled. It was the first since they settled on the sunny rock for an ill-fated nap earlier in the day. He tried not to remember. Couldn't help recalling the sight of the soldiers, the way their eyes widened when they realized Pippa was naked and vulnerable. Drool oozed from one's thick lips.

He squeezed her tighter. Needing her. This mess they were in needed to come to an end.

"Will we go home to Clearborne Manor tomorrow?" she asked, her fingers playing with the fastening to his shirt.

"No, not until there is some resolution. Harry and Horace need to be dealt with. At the moment they are nearby. At least I have reason to believe they are. We have support here. Mac and a few more of our most trusted men should arrive at the lodge. Could be there already."

"Mac with the red hair and sparkling green eyes?" she asked tenderly touching his jaw.

"Should I be jealous?" He grinned at her. Mac was old enough to be her father.

"*Aye*, he's a *verra bonnie* man. A girl could get lost in his dreamy eyes. Those tiny gold specks that sparkle when he's amused at something."

"It's not nice to tease your husband. You're a naughty girl, Pippa McKenna. If I didn't know you so well, I might believe you."

He delighted in the way she snuggled her bottom against him. She would recover nicely from the ordeal. Pippa had an uncanny way of bouncing back.

"I would never think to tease my husband."

She laughed at him squirming closer again knowingly arousing him to an instant hard.

"Why, Mrs. McKenna, is that all you think about? Making love with this poor man's body?"

She would neither deny or question the fact that he insinuated she was wanting him. There would be time later to fulfill both their needs. He caressed her belly. The thought of her increasing generated a heated smile. It would not be too much longer before she told him. Shifters were able to tell almost to the moment conception happened to their mate.

"It is what you want. What you think about," she told him, demurely lowering her gold tipped lashes. "Is it so bad that I might want the same as you?"

Yes, it was what he thought about almost every moment of every day. No, it was not bad at all that she thought along the same lines. He wondered if he'd ever grow tired of dreaming about her soft curves as well as how she felt against the hard planes of his body.

Wisely, Kit rode ahead. His intuitive side always seemed prevalent. Of course, they were obvious in their desire. It did not take much for another man to realize his intentions were anything but carnal in nature.

"I admit to the thinking, Pippa. You enchant and puzzle me. I long to understand you but more than anything I want to be inside your heat. I wish to feel your sultry core kiss my rod when you receive pleasure."

The devil but it was the truth. If Kit wasn't close by, if they hadn't just made one of the most foolish mistakes of his life, he would turn her around and impale himself inside her. He would ride slow, let the even pace of the horse tempt and arouse then he would gallop. He could hear his name on her lips.

Thank goodness they were almost back to the lodge. He pointed. Straight ahead was Callum's place. Smoke curled from the chimney.

"It looks just the same," she sighed resting against his chest. "I always felt as if the house was as much mine as his."

"You loved my great grandfather?" Roby knew the answer just by the way she always spoke of him.

"I did. Who do you suppose is there?" she asked as she leaned forward to get a better view.

Roby chuckled, "Unless they are sitting on the porch, you're not going to be able to tell. My guess is that the troops rallied their forces. Father and mother have most likely taken up residence along with some of the men. Connal spoke of an escape to be alone, just the two of them."

"So," she paused, "your father is just like you or perhaps it is the other way around, you've taken on the proclivities of your father. All he wants is to spend the days along with the nights making love to his wife.

"I hope you never grow tired of me." Her breath whispered from her damp lips in a soft, wistful sigh.

"I don't see how I could," Roby said with intense sincerity as they stopped the horse in front of the lodge. "We are here, sweet one."

He let her gently down then followed. One of Connal's men was beside them taking the reins.

With his hand at the small of Pippa's back he walked inside. Kit sat on a large chair, Hypatia perched on his shoulder, chattering happily to Connal. The little monkey took an instant liking to Roby's father when they were at the castle. Hypatia sniffed Kit's whiskey, shaking her head while pointing a finger at the man.

Kit laughed. "You *dinna* like the way whiskey smells?"

More noises and pointing from the little monkey caused everyone to laugh at the antics as well as what they thought she tried to tell Kit.

"She doesn't want me to drink. Thinks it's bad for my health," Kit said solemnly.

As he spoke the words Hypatia nodded her head in seeming agreement then leapt onto his shoulder.

Hypatia let out a screech of delight when she saw her mistress. She dropped to the floor. In seconds she was happily ensconced in Pippa's arms.

"Does she ever leave the two of you alone?" Wynnie asked with a raised eyebrow. "Seems there are places that might have..." Wynnie grimaced. "I just think sometimes it might be awkward with another...with an animal in the bedroom."

"Think my dear wife is trying to say it might be difficult to make love to her husband if she knew Hypatia was watching," Connal drew his wife onto his lap then kissed her soundly.

"Hypatia went with Kit when we wanted some time to ourselves. But then Kit is one of her favorite men next to Roby. I believe Hypatia is in love with him. She would most likely give me up if she thought Kit wanted her full time."

"*Nay*, she will always be yours. Hypatia is loyal," Kit murmured stroking the little monkey's back.

Roby stood, holding his hand out to Pippa. "I ordered a bath for you when we arrived. Would you like to go up now? I'll walk with you but I've got to speak with Connal and Mac."

"A conversation you don't want me to be privy to I suppose," she spoke softly. "I would like a bath. Would like to wash some of the events of today from me. If the memories could wash away so easily, I'd be more than pleased. Yes, have your conversations." She turned to Wynnie. "Could you come visit in about a half hour? Bring a bottle of wine with you?"

"I'd like that, a little girl talk when our men are plotting and planning," Wynnie smiled and laughed.

"I'll take you upstairs. We are in Callum's room until we leave since my parents' visit was unplanned, spur of the moment one might say. The things we needed were sent ahead and taken to the room."

When they reached the door, Roby drew her inside. With the door shut behind him he framed her face with his hands. Kissed her deeply.

"Roby..."

"This has to last until after dinner," he told her softly. "I cannot wait to hold you in my arms again."

She pushed from his arms before skipping away to put distance between them. "You are lying. I can see it in your eyes. What is so important I cannot hear. What is it that has you lying to me?"

"It is none of your concern, Pippa," his voice was harsh.

Her nerves stretched tight. She would get to the bottom of this. He would tell her or Wynnie would know. It seemed Connal must have learned it was more prudent to inform his wife than not to do so. Roby would need to learn the same thing.

"If it's about your intentions toward my guardian, then it is my concern." She held the breath of air she inhaled inside her lungs until she burned.

"Probably so, but I don't want to worry you. We also need to speak of what happened today with the Sassenach. There could be repercussion when the men return to their unit. If we have any luck on our side, father will know their commander. He's friends with most in this part of the highlands. He's made it his business to remain on their good side."

"Both of those issues concern me."

She remained steadfast even though she understood he would never relent.

"You wanted a bath to wash away the Sassenach stench," he reminded her. "The water grows cold."

"I did. Promise me you'll tell me what's been decided."

Her fluttering heart would send her to her knees any minute now if she didn't get ahold of herself. Mayhap Roby was right, at least about the attack by the British soldiers.

"I can promise you that."

He kissed her again.

When she caught her breath, the door was closing softly behind him. Wynnie would be up any minute now. She stripped. The bath was hot and heavenly. She soaped and soaped, scrubbed until she finally felt clean.

It had not been luck today that saved her.

Roby did so.

He taught her so many things.

She rinsed then towel dried herself and her hair in front of the warmth of the fire. She dressed in a gown brought from Clearborne Manor. Two full glasses of wine sat on a small table. Flames flickered and glowed. Pippa opened the door to let Wynnie know she could come in.

"You ready to talk?" Wynnie asked as she stepped through into the room.

"Your husband and son are up to something. I'm hoping you can tell me just what that might be."

She held one glass out for Wynnie, who set a tray of delicacies created by their cook on the table.

"I cannot tell you everything. If I did so, it would betray a trust. So," she paused long enough to bite into a piece of lemon cake. "They have your best interest planned," again she paused to take a bite. "As they see it."

"Men..." As much as Pippa loved Roby he frustrated her, overwhelmingly so. "At times he doesn't give me credit for a brain."

She lifted her arms for Hypatia who grabbed a blueberry tart before launching herself into Pippa's arms.

"Men, they do that. They want us to follow all their orders without asking our opinion. It's for our best interest they say. It's to protect us."

"That is certainly true of Roby. He says all he wants is to make me happy." She set Hypatia on one of the chairs.

"If you comply with all his wishes, you will make Roby a happy man," Wynnie said softly. "I won't speak ill of my son. What I will say is he is just like his father in how he treats his woman. Gentle as a kitten, protective as the black panther he is. At times he will want to do everything for you."

"At times? It seems like all the time."

"You should give him that opportunity, don't you think?" Wynnie said her gaze on the fireplace, the flames as they danced with each other.

"I try but don't succeed. He can bring me to anger in a blink of a second."

He could bring her to other delightful things in about the same time. She thought on his words about making love on his horse while it was galloping across the heather.

Her insides tightened, ached where he would bury himself.

Her sigh was heavy and needy.

"Connal does the same to me," Wynnie said. "I've had more practice. Since he sent my father through the Kinnel Stones years and years ago, we've had few difficulties. The biggest arguments came over bringing up the children. He does *nay* believe in discipline. Would allow them to do as they please."

"I do suppose practice in dealing with a man would help. Aaron never challenged me. He let me do as I pleased."

"Aaron?"

"A gypsy boy I thought myself in love with. I wasn't. He was just the first boy who ever kissed me. Now I *ken* that wasn't a real kiss."

"Where is he now?" Wynnie sounded concerned.

She needed to be. "Dead. Hung because we killed and ate a rabbit. We didn't tell you about that. Roby didn't think it prudent at the time to tell you he saved me from the gallows by agreeing to wed me. That was why he insisted on a second marriage. He didn't *ken* if the first was legal and binding. That was also why I was loath to marry in the church. I was afraid of committing myself so thoroughly to a man I scarcely knew."

Wynnie poured a second glass of wine. "Connal knew there were things the two of you weren't saying."

"Anyone would know by looking at my face. Roby says I don't lie well." She remembered that first interrogation the morning after Wynnie stormed into Roby's room to welcome him home to find her in bed with her son. "You thought I was his whore."

"A big mistake which I hope you have forgiven me for making." She leaned forward touching her hand. "I think you are making Roby a happy man. I've never seen him so. I wish now that Kit would find his mate."

"He wishes that too."

At the mention of Kit, Hypatia set up a happy chatter where she sat on the hearth soaking up the heat. She leapt off the chair then out the door.

"Poor, poor girl. Hypatia is in love with that man. I'm just glad she doesn't love Roby," Pippa laughed before sobering, her smile thinning as she recalled how she met the animal. "I found her in a small village. A man was beating her. Aaron helped me rescue her. He paid the man every coin he had with him." A small chuckle coupled with a look of chagrin followed. "For the longest time I thought Hypatia was a boy just because she wore little trousers. Funny, once I put her in a dress, she was much more pleasant. I felt obligated to change her name from Plato to Hypatia."

Wynnie looked in the direction Hypatia went. "We should go downstairs. I've a feeling it's time to discover a few truths about our men's intentions.

~ * ~

Harry and Horace rolled on the ground laughing. Harry laughed so hard he peed his pants. "The c-cats," he chortled.

"The cats," Horace echoed as he held his jiggling belly. "I would have loved to see the look in their eyes when they caught sight of the two of them dangling from the rafters.

"It was fortuitous that we ran into those two British soldiers," Harry said as he recalled the condition the men were in, butt naked. At the thought he giggled like a schoolgirl.

"Butt naked," Horace said echoing Harry's thoughts. "Ready to spill the tale. Seems they got caught by a pair of shifters."

Harry sobered, second thoughts about their plans assailing him. Perhaps a change would be necessary. "Didn't know Phillipa was a shifter. Not good, no, we need to skedaddle out of the territory. After the McKenna's find those two cats they're going to be after us but good."

"You're right of course. We've got nothing left for us here. We can't try to fight the McKenna clan."

"They're too powerful. Those soldiers' tale is not going to be believed. Hear the commander of their unit is a friend of Roby's old man. He's not going to listen to them. If he gets wind of what they were trying to do to Pippa, they might end up on the whipping post," Harry said, scratching his chin as he tried to piece together a plan of sorts.

"Wouldn't want to be wearing their shoes," Horace said as he stood.

He looked around the small hut.

"No, wouldn't want that either," Harry agreed with him. "Nothing here for us. Need to get back to Edinburgh then move on to London. Got some connections left in England. We've got just enough to make our way."

"My sister owes me," Horace mumbled.

"Good idea. Your sister, Aunty Miss Prim and Proper, we'll check out her and her husband," Harry said. "We can stay with her until we get back on our feet. Just hope the McKennas don't figure out what we're doing."

"They won't. They'll never guess we're giving up on the MacPherson lass. She was never related to us anyway," Horace said giggling again.

"It was lies all lies. No familial ties. Wasted five years though. Once we're in London we can engineer another accident and claim another guardianship."

Chapter Nine

"Wynnie and Pippa are inside?" Connal asked while he leaned against one of the posts on the porch, his arms crossed in front of him, his stare hard as if he wanted to understand everything between, he and Pippa in that instance. Roby told him nearly everything, just left out the part about the hangman.

The only person who knew was Kit.

He wasn't going to say anything.

Connal appeared relaxed and unconcerned but beneath the bland façade Roby knew his father sensed the tension emanating from him. Roby felt helpless, a pawn in a game he was unwilling to play any longer.

"Yes, I hope Wynnie didn't frighten Pippa half to death when she showed up in your bedroom. Pippa is in a fragile state. Delicate right now."

Roby ran both hands through his hair, concern for her overpowering every sense he possessed. He needed to understand how she was feeling.

"She is stronger than you give her credit," Kit said hiding a smile that threatened to get out. "No one, man or woman, can survive the ordeals she's been through and not come out stronger."

"You wouldn't know," Roby said realizing he was in love with Pippa.

Never thought he'd love a woman, even his mate. Before now he never knew what love was or how it felt. The emotion staggered him, left him breathless so in need of air he gasped. With the realization came an overpowering joy.

Kit didn't answer. He looked wistful at odds with his usual teasing self. He walked to the porch railing. Leaning against it he stared into the distance. His cousin was multifaceted, different in some ways. He was a thinker more interested in philosophy. Perhaps that was why he never took anything at face value. Why he always questioned.

"I would know more than you believe. Much we haven't spoken of. Perhaps it is time to share. The sharing would have to be up to my wife. Wynnie survived more than any woman should have to. With the events, she became stronger, more resilient." His father seemed to challenge him while he looked toward the house and upward to the second floor. "Pippa, now that's a woman I wouldn't want to cross. I didn't even see her attack the Sassenach and I understand the hidden strength she possesses."

"She did well," Roby acknowledged even though he didn't want Pippa to start thinking she could challenge men and win. She surprised him with her fierceness. "That was one time. It's not going to happen again."

"Maybe not, hopefully not," Connal agreed as he seemed to be studying him. "Time will tell. One never really knows what the future will bring. She may be faced with other battles during her lifetime."

"Are you going to tell her about the dead cats?" Kit asked as he turned seeming to join the conversation once more. "You should."

"No."

Roby didn't hesitate in his answer waving his hand in the air thoroughly disgusted with the idea. He never intended to give Pippa all the information. He needed to protect her with all the male senses he possessed. "Knowing would only terrify her more."

He didn't tell her about the first one, he wasn't going to tell her about the black and calico cats that were found hanging from the loft in these stable.

"She deserves to know," Kit said pushing Roby to a point he disliked. In ways he agreed, but in more ways he disagreed.

"Don't anyone tell her. It's up to me what she learns and what she doesn't," he said his harsh voice tolerating no interference.

Always the one to pursue a topic that should be put to rest, Kit persevered. "Perhaps if she understands everything, she won't be so frightened when something else bad happens and we both *ken* it will. For all we know the Finchbottoms are not done with Pippa. Now we have the Sassenach to contend with."

"Do you think the Finchbottoms might have discovered exactly what the two of you look like in your other form? The soldiers might have told them," Connal questioned with obvious challenge in his voice that couldn't be ignored.

"Likely," Roby said softly as the front door opened.

His gaze shifted even while he wondered what the women heard discussed. He might have no option but to explain the appearance of the cats.

Wynnie stood in front of Pippa. "What cats?"

Connal cleared his throat his steely gaze fastening on Roby. Roby shuffled his feet, shifting positions as he sought a means to avoid the topic.

He could think of nothing.

"Can't keep anything secret around here," Kit said with a soft laugh sounding pleased the truth would come out.

"Nothing," Roby said turning away while heat stung his cheeks.

The devil but he didn't have anything to be embarrassed about. There was no guilt for him in keeping the truth from her.

"Don't you nothing me, Roby McKenna. What cats were the three of you talking about? Why don't you want to tell me? We heard nearly everything that was being said." Pippa stepped around Wynnie with her hands on her hips challenging him for an answer he didn't want to give.

"Didn't strike you for a coward," his father said curtly. "You or me? I want Wynnie to know everything. It never serves a good purpose to keep secrets from those we love, especially our women folk."

Pippa looked from one man to the other, crystal green of her eyes shimmering in the late afternoon sun. Her scent caught on the breeze. She was angry. Didn't take a mind reader to see. He stuffed his hands through his hair.

"Don't care for secrets either," he mumbled caught on the defense, a position he never liked. "This case it's necessary."

"Caught in a trap, a cat trap," Kit laughed then.

He sobered a bit when Hypatia chose that moment to jump on him, pointing an accusing finger his way. "Think I'll go see what your new cook is fixing for dinner."

He whistled as he walked away with the little monkey in his arms.

"You just want to warm her up for after dinner," Roby pointed out feeling the levity for the first time.

Kit stopped at the door in order to give one last parting shot. He placed his hands over his heart. "You know me all too well but only because one moonlit night you happened upon your woman."

"The cats," Pippa reminded him.

To Roby it seemed Pippa wasn't going to forget her question. He knew that tone of voice. He drug in air that didn't reach his lungs. Sought courage that didn't want to exist. Her lips thinned. He wanted to sleep with her tonight. Craved holding her in his arms. He realized he wasn't going to be here tonight. Even if he didn't satisfy her avid curiosity, he would not be anywhere near her bed. Pippa didn't know that fact either. His father nodded with encouragement that didn't settle in the pit of his stomach.

Roby cleared his throat then a second time. "Cats, you want to know about them."

He wiped sweat from his forehead. Couldn't reach the drops of moisture slithering down his back. Couldn't do anything about his shaking fingers. This was something he wanted to shelter Pippa from knowing. He could only imagine her reaction.

"Roby McKenna, if you don't infuriate me more than I can bear." Her voice changed tone, frustration as clear as the anger.

He stood then reached for her hand. His fingers closed around hers. "If the rest of you will excuse us. I want some privacy if I'm going to have to tell Pippa about the—cats."

To him, she still felt fragile.

Delicate.

He didn't want her to worry.

When he truly looked at her, he saw her pouncing on the soldier, watched as she thought out the situation and leapt on the horse creating more havoc and panic within the glade where the soldiers found them.

Perhaps he was wrong about her. Maybe she could handle all the unpleasantness of the present about the death threats the cats represented.

He drew her into the house then up the steps to the master chamber. After the door shut behind them, he tugged her into his arms. A second passed then another while he held her so tightly, he could scarcely breathe. He pushed a hand beneath her hair to clasp her neck. "It's all such a ridiculous waste. We will put an end to it. You don't have to be frightened."

"You are not going to kiss me and in the process make me forget what you are supposed to be telling me. You will not." She struggled against his greater strength. A tear slid down her cheek.

He didn't want her to cry. He would tell her, would have to let her become a part of this. "I am going to kiss you. I promise you I won't forget your question. It's been a devil of a long time since I kissed you," he murmured as his lips found hers. He parted hers, delved inside, groaned with frustration as well as the burgeoning heat of his passion as she responded.

She melted into him. He knew the moment he could forego her question and take her to the bed.

He promised though. His hands trembled.

He did swing her into his arms.

He did carry her to one of the chairs sitting in front of the fire. Not the bed. She didn't push entirely away from him. When she gazed into his eyes, hers spoke of the promise he gave her. Her mind would be spinning with scenario after scenario, each new one probably worse than the one before.

He cleared his throat.

"Cats," she reminded him a fingernail on his chin to give emphasis to her word.

"Cats," he wanted to groan, needed to divert. Couldn't. Wanted a moment more before he spoke the words. There were no more seconds he could gain. "A couple of days ago Kit found a dead cat in the stable. It was a calico."

"It was supposed to be me?"

"No. Yes, maybe it was. The threat could have been for me. There is no way of telling. At that time, we were just aware of your hidden talents. We were the only ones who knew."

"Since we didn't know I could shift then." She placed one of her fragile, delicate fingertips on his lips. Traced it as he felt the sudden rise of shivers in response.

Everyone was right. She was not what she seemed on first inspection. The news didn't terrify her, didn't send her into a fit of vapors. Perhaps he needed to rethink exactly who his wife was.

"True. It's my opinion Harry wanted to threaten me. Rumors told the story of the McKenna's being shifters. They turned into cats. Harry would have no idea I change to a black panther. It's pretty simple. He found a cat, poor cat, killed it then left it for me to find.

"Go on." Her fingers wound around his neck before they found their way into his hair. "I garner this is not the end of the cat story."

He stared at her, thinking of other things he would like to do with this small amount of time he had with her. "If you are trying to seduce, me it's working. But then you *ken* it's not too difficult to coax me into wanting to make love to you."

"That was one cat," she told him.

"Today, we found two dead cats hanging in the stable." His hands rose on her ribcage, his thumbs rubbing against hardened peaks, tempting and teasing. He reciprocated Pippa's seduction.

"Two?"

"Aye, one black and one a tabby."

His lips found the frantic pulse at the base of her neck. Pippa kneaded his back. His heart drummed. He heard its wild flight.

He watched as her eyes crossed. Focused on the frantic beat of her pulse at the base of her neck. Understood her fear. He experienced it also. Perhaps this was passion.

"I see."

Needing to understand more, "What exactly do you see?" He drove his fingers into her hair, forced her head back until he could see her face.

"I can't let you go without me, Roby. I know you are planning on leaving, searching for the men who did this."

"I'm not going anywhere."

"Yes, you are." She ran her hands along his chest. "Don't lie to me. You do not have to sneak away in the middle of the night while I sleep."

"Pippa..."

He couldn't keep the truth from her. She guessed what he was about.

She didn't wait for his kiss. Instead, she stood, gazing at him. She turned from him, walking to the window, seeming to search the grounds. "For starters someone who doesn't like me or us was here while we were taking no precautions as to our secrets. Second, either those soldiers had time to kill two cats and place them where we could find them or my distant relatives did."

She paused for breath sucking in air. He didn't want her to faint again. She appeared stronger than before. He didn't think there was enough time for either of those scenarios to happen. Didn't want to believe someone else was plotting against them. Who knew both were shifters? Who knew only he was a black panther? The list was too short.

He saw the slight trembling of her shoulders before she stiffened. "My intuition is with Harry and Horace. They've been making inquiries in Edinburgh. All is based on guesses stimulated by rumors. Besides those we trust, no one save the Sassenach soldiers know you are not black. As you surmised, there was very little time. Luck in meeting with the soldiers as well as finding too different cats, well, the feat would have been difficult not impossible."

"What are you going to do?" she asked surprising him. He was sure she had a pretty good idea. "Perhaps the Finchbottoms saw us while we were running. They might have had time. We did nap."

He didn't like the reminder of his foolish behavior. "Kit has word Harry and Horace are staying in a small hut about ten miles from here. I want to see them on a British Naval ship fighting for the British. Connal, Kit and I are going to hunt them down then make sure it happens. We'll follow them all the way to Edinburgh if necessary."

"I can come with you."

It was a statement not a question. Her determined stance told Roby there would be another argument. She must have forgotten she was supposed to obey.

She wasn't going to win this one. He couldn't allow such a notion.

Roby bristled even though he half expected the request. In too many ways to count, he wanted her beside him just to know she was breathing, her heart beating as well. If she did go with him, he would always be looking over his shoulder to make sure nothing was happening to her detriment. He would not be able to focus on the task at hand.

He didn't like the fact he hesitated. "No. You're to stay here with Wynnie and the rest of the men. It shouldn't take *verra* long to find those two then take them to Edinburgh for their departure from Scotland. We will return as soon as we've accomplished this."

"You will have to take them to Edinburgh," she repeated, as she seemed to be thinking to herself. "That will take a week or more from here." She moved from the window where she'd been standing for the duration. She sat on his lap; his face framed between her hands. "You have to take me." She ran a finger along his jaw, moistened her lips as she moved slightly on his crotch.

Her actions blatant.

"*Ye* cannot seduce me to get your way, *lass*. Best you understand that fact now before you get in over your head."

He took her hands, kissed the palm of each, ran his tongue along the fine lines he found there. She gasped for air as he continued his onslaught of her senses, trailing his tongue, scraping with his teeth along the inside of her wrist, lightly nipping, enticing.

If he had his way and he would, he meant to leave her wanting him. If she wanted to play sexual games, he would win. The pulse point at the base of her neck beckoned. He obliged. Followed by the tiny sounds she made that he loved to hear.

She let her head fall back. "Do you mean to seduce me then leave?" she murmured softly.

"*Aye*, that way you'll be hot and slick ready for me when I return. I want you to think about this, about me touching you where you like it best."

"You are a mean, wicked *mon*, Roby McKenna. I will follow you if you leave me."

The tone prominent in her voice told Roby she meant every word.

"*Nay*, I'll have you locked into the bedroom. You cannot."

His heart raced at the thought of her following along behind him, alone with no protection. She would be easy, vulnerable prey to anyone you might encounter.

"There are windows."

"You're provoking me to do something that I won't like."

The devil if she pushed this, he would have to tie her as well as lock the door. He would also have to bar the window. Wynnie would never stop her if she chose to leave. This was not a situation to bear. He would do whatever was necessary to stop her.

"What is that?" She challenged him, determination at the forefront. "Something you wouldn't like? I would escape anything to follow you, to be there when you put those two away from my life forever. You cannot keep me here against my will."

Beside himself, he was shaking his head frustrated beyond anything he endured before. "If you persist in this foolishness, I will tie you to the bed. You won't like it. I won't like it. If I cannot get your promise to stay put, you will force me to take desperate measures." At this point he was sure he was left with no option except to secure her somehow in this room.

"You wouldn't dare," she said as he set her aside.

At the window he peered downward. She would hurt herself if she chose to jump. It was the second story. She wasn't a cat with nine lives. He tugged in a ragged breath before he finally turned to her. "Where your life is concerned, Pippa. I would dare anything, risk any displeasure you might conjure."

"When are you leaving?"

He didn't appreciate the tenor of her voice or what she wasn't saying. "As soon as we've settled this to my satisfaction."

He didn't think the settlement would come via words or promises. Actions that wouldn't please her or him would have to be taken.

The emotions on her face changed dramatically. She was flushed, color spotting her cheeks as well as the delicate swell of her breasts all peaches and cream, female to her core, fragile. She turned to run from him. By the time she reached the door he was upon her.

"*Nay*, Pippa." His hand by her head held the door shut. "You are not running. If you do, I'll find you and drag you home. Your destiny will not be with me despite the time you will make me waste. There is no discussion in this matter."

She turned, her back pressed against the door. Her breasts heaved. He smiled. She made the decision for him. He wasn't going to ask for the promise he understood by looking at her eyes she would break.

No promises or broken vows only the truth he would create.

When he took hold of her arm to lead her to the bed, she struggled against him. "Don't Roby. Don't do this to me. You will regret it. I." She moistened her lips, "I will promise."

"Promise what?" He asked knowing it was too late for promises. Too much had been said between them. She was used to doing as she pleased.

"To stay here."

"Little liar."

"*Nay*." The one word was desperation coupled with the obvious lie. "Roby, *nay*. You cannot mean to do this to me."

"I would do anything to know you are safe. Now, you leave me no choice," his voice was soft tenuous as he thought of binding her to the bed, a hated notion.

Tenderly, he ran his hand along her jawline then down the column of her slender neck to the pulse point. "By pushing this too hard, you've set all I must do in motion. By blatantly defying my wishes, you've left me no plausible option. I'll leave word with Wynnie that she should untie you in an hour. That should be long enough. I would want you to... hell, I don't want to do this to you."

"Then don't," she grit out behind clenched teeth. "Don't tie me. Trust my word to you."

Trust was not something he could do at this moment. She said too many things to the contrary. "I cannot. You would follow. Follow even with the promise still fresh on your lips."

"You could give permission for me to ride beside you, so I would be able to witness Harry and Horace boarding a naval vessel. That would be the best choice. It would make both of us happy. You wouldn't have to do something you don't want to do. By all that's holy, if you don't give in on this as soon as Wynnie unties me, I'll head for Edinburgh by myself. I promise you that now."

His gut churned, tripped over itself as he didn't doubt for a moment what she threatened she would carry out. His men wouldn't dare to physically hold her back. He didn't know what to do with her. He knew the man to leave her in protection of was Mackenzie Bruce. He was solid. Would never sway when threatened with her womanly charms. "I cannot in good conscious take you. 'Tis too dangerous for a female."

"For a shifter?" She dared bring that up.

Perhaps he should have never taught her how to change her form. His chest burned with fury. Her obstinacy might well be the death of her. At this moment, he felt sure he could throttle her himself. It would be best if he left before he did something besides tying her that he could not take back.

"*Aye*, too dangerous for a female in any form, human or cat. As I've said before, I will not take chances with your life nor will I allow you to do so."

His voice was harsher than he intended. Perhaps it needed to be. He never commanded her to do or not do anything before this. "At least this one time you could obey your husband. You did vow before God to do just that."

"That is unfair of you, Roby McKenna. Don't bring the husband lecture coupled with well-meaning vows into our argument. I would obey you if your wishes were logical, if I didn't disagree with you. You *ken* it is not the same."

Her breath was ragged puffs, tiny bits of air that couldn't possibly fill her lungs.

"Don't bring an argument such as this into the conversation then. You, my dear one, are not going with me. If I live and breathe, you are not going to Edinburgh by yourself."

"I am," she shouted at him, her small fists clenched at her sides while her shoulders shook with the emotion of the moment. "If you are gone, you cannot stop me!"

He marched from the room. She didn't follow. Thank goodness for small favors. He didn't want his father or mother to see what he intended. Wynnie would eventually discover her, would free her and perhaps by then some shadow of sense would have filled her head. If she ran while he was finding the rope to bind her, he would go after her and bring her back. She could not get far in the few minutes this was going to take. The others wouldn't like the delay nor would they appreciate him taking all the horses, but whatever he had to do he would. By taking all the horses they could move more quickly. Reaching Edinburgh might take only a week. He could be back sooner.

When he returned, she was the picture of docility as she sat by the fire sipping a glass of red wine. What the devil was she pretending now? The ensuing skirmish between them was slight. She was so small against his power. He wished this event would put the fear of men in her. With a sigh of distress, he realized she fought men all her life. With him her battles were not always lost. He allowed her wins whenever possible whether the fight was physical or a battle of wills.

This win was his. Why the devil did he feel so damn guilty?

By the time her hands were tied to the bedpost, she had spilled some of the wine on the bodice of her dress. Her skirts were hiked to her knees, very pretty, delicate knees. Where her breasts nearly spilled from the corsage because of their tussle, they were rounded globes baring a slight flush from the exertion. He wanted to taste them, suck them into his mouth, as well as hear her tiny sounds of delight she would make. Ah, tied as she was, she would be angry, too angry to melt for him.

"I'll get even with you, Roby McKenna. Don't doubt that I will." Her eyes shone with the fire and passion he so loved. "I'll find a way out of here. I promise you again. I'm going to Edinburgh without you since you're leaving me behind."

She would battle him time and again. Drive him to distraction while she fought for supremacy. "I don't doubt it for one second. Indeed, I will enjoy whatever you place at my feet. Right now, all that matters to me is that you will remain safe and secure while I am gone. The need to worry about you is not something I want to concern myself with when we are facing whatever devilry the Finchbottoms toss our way. I need a clear head."

"I won't be here when you return," she promised again seeming more determined to assert her will.

He turned to leave. Thought better of it. Kneeling beside the bed, he pushed flyaway hair from her face. He kissed her tenderly then harder seeking as much raw hungry passion from his wife that he could generate.

She didn't disappoint.

No, she melted.

"When I come back, I will bring you something."

He wanted to leave her with curiosity brimming. Right now, he didn't know just what he'd bring her, but he'd think of something.

"I won't be here."

This time her spoken words were soft, defeated in tenor. Almost as if by saying them she could make them come true.

Just wishes.

Nothing more.

He didn't doubt for a second she meant what she said. Shy of walking to the city there would be no way for her to leave the lodge. His men, especially Mac, would make do for the days it took for him to get to Edinburg and home. If need be, they would follow her as well as keep her whereabouts known to him.

"When I left here the first time, I walked. If you think I won't do that again, you better think on it one more time."

"You rode with Tad Tubbles and his wife if I recall your story correctly. You weren't' walking. You've no idea."

She turned her head away from him.

Her words shot ice through his veins. Quickly, he strode back to her, whipping off his neckcloth. "You're older and wiser now, Pippa, a beautiful woman. You know the ways of men who have wickedness in their hearts. The devil, Pippa, but you almost died because you made a foolish mistake. You don't believe that could happen again? I'm sorry for this also. When I return and you are healthy and whole, I'll make it up to you."

With lead weighing down his heart, Roby gagged her.

~ * ~

It wasn't until the following morning that Wynnie looked in on her. Pippa was bleary-eyed from lack of sleep. Just as the time when Harry tied her, her hands were numb. Her fingers lost their feeling hours ago. Humiliation flooded her. Most of the night was spent thinking of ways to get even with Roby. He could only do this to her because of brute strength. She was helpless against the power he possessed. Her mind was just as agile as his. She would not have gotten in his way.

What time wasn't spent thinking of ways to get even, she spent swearing silently at her husband, cursing him to the devil as well. In the *wee* hours of the morning, she finally drifted off to sleep only to wake up with the rumbling of her stomach. Yesterday, they had little to eat of the picnic that was packed for them. Because she was tied, she missed dinner and now, it seemed, she would miss breakfast as well. That wasn't the worst of her problems. She had to relieve herself. If she couldn't get untied soon, she would be even more embarrassed.

Someone has to miss me.

The knock on the door reassured her mind. The footsteps leaving sent her into a spiraling depression, a tailspin of hopelessness. Wynnie would return. She had to do so. Because of the gag she could not cry out to whoever was behind the door.

No.

It can't be. No, Wynnie must miss her. She would peek inside the room. What if Wynnie thought she went with Roby? By the time Roby returned she would have starved to death. Her death would serve him right. One more time she struggled with the bonds tearing her wrists. One more time she tried everything possible to allow her wrists to slip through the bindings. They were just too secure. She pushed against the headboard, hoping the noise would bring Wynnie back.

What to do?

She pushed on the gag with her tongue. Pounded the soft mattress with her heels. Scooted backward to try thumping her head on the backboard.

"Dear God..." Wynnie spoke softly, her voice quiet. "What has happened here?"

Pippa froze, held still as she looked at Wynnie's wide eyes. She didn't even hear the door swing open. Wynnie walked to her, bent over, brushed hair from her face.

"What happened to you?" she grimaced while she began fumbling with the bindings. "I'm going to have to get a knife. I'll be right back."

Your son, Roby McKenna, happened to me, the bastard.

When Wynnie returned only a few minutes later, she sawed through the thick rope along with the gag. "You've been this way since they left yesterday afternoon?"

Pippa nodded rubbing at her wrists, her tongue so dry she couldn't swallow. "Water," she croaked out.

"There is no water. Wine will have to do for the moment."

Wynnie handed her the glass of wine left from last night that Roby never drank.

The wine disappeared quickly. After that Pippa saw to other immediate needs. When she was back in the room, Wynnie sat, waiting for her. "Your son has a lot to account for," she grit out. "Right now, I'm going to get myself something to eat. Then I'm going to change my clothes."

"Why did he tie you?" Wynnie's voice was gentle but all-knowing as well.

"To keep me from following him when I couldn't get him to agree to taking me."

She wasn't going to lie. She sat down in a huff and poured herself more wine uncaring if it was in the middle of the morning. "Told him I'd jump out the window if he locked the door."

"Perhaps in the future if you mean to disobey my son, you will learn to not be so forthright in your intentions," Wynnie said with a half-smile followed by a soft chuckle. "There are ways around our domineering men folk. You should be wiser if you wish to disobey. Eventually, they forgive."

"You will have to teach me some other time. As soon as I eat, I will follow him all the way to the docks at Edinburg."

Determined to see this through she watched Wynnie grin. Suddenly, she had second thoughts. Inverness was closer. Perhaps she should use this time to visit the orphanage her parents donated money to, where the certificate noting her birth was issued, not to the MacPhersons but to Jillian Masson.

"I've rethought this. I'm going to Inverness. Makes more sense to me since the trip won't take so long. I can visit the orphanage where I was supposedly adopted."

"You will persist in this foolishness. If you leave right now, you won't arrive until tomorrow afternoon at the earliest and that's if there are no problems. *Nay* it will take you longer. I forgot the men took all of the horses so they could move faster."

"The devil," Pippa murmured understanding he would indeed go to any length to keep her here. "I'm never going to forgive that man. I will do as I see fit despite the obstacles he's put in the way."

"You will. Now shall I fetch you some food while you change your clothes. It's a long walk to Inverness."

"You're not going to tell the McKenna men what I intend?" she queried watching Wynnie for a reaction other than a smile.

"I made a promise to Connal. I will speak of your plans to the men. I'm presuming they will not hold you back. Someone will walk with you, however if my guess is correct, they will do nothing to help you unless the situation becomes life threatening nor will they physically put a hand on you to stop you. I'm also sure there will also be a man who will keep Roby informed of your whereabouts."

"I see."

"You don't. Truly you've no idea how much Roby loves you. If you are as smart a woman as I *ken* you are, you will remain at the lodge. You can wait for Roby. He will do all humanly possible for you. All he wishes right now is for your safety. Do not be so bull headed that you put yourself in danger."

"Enough to tie me and not tell anyone." She drug air into her lungs, coughed. "Yes, I would like food but I'll come downstairs. You don't need to wait on me. After that I'm heading for Inverness. Nothing you say can deter me."

"They follow the trail to Edinburg."

"I ken it. I could not walk that far."

"Why Inverness?"

"Decided to see if I could locate my birthmother."

"Wish you luck, Pippa. If that is what you want, I won't stand in your way. I'll make sure Mac Bruce will be with you." Wynnie left.

Quickly, Pippa washed from the basin of water in the room then dressed. She found the trousers and shirt Kit bought her that first night she spent with Roby. If need be, she would walk. If Wynnie spoke the truth and there were no horses, she'd have no choice.

If she succeeded or not, the Finchbottoms might miss the sailing. She had second and third thoughts about the prudence of this venture. Her decision wavered from moment to moment. She remembered the look in his eyes as he left the room.

Resigned.

He believed when she was free, she would follow him. The man took all the horses.

Foolish stupidity on her part. She still wanted to believe she held a small amount of independence despite the fact he stacked everything against her. Wanted to think that all the time she spent on her own taught her something.

Fool, you weren't on your own except a small portion of the years. Most of it you spent with the gypsies. They took care of you, saw that you were fed and clothed. It wasn't until you were truly by yourself that you got into trouble.

I was with Aaron.

See you weren't truly by yourself.

I want to prove to Roby I can do this.

Fools die. Or they are captured. He only wants to keep you safe.

I'm going.

What if he fails in his mission? Harry could still find you, take advantage of you.

With that last thought, more determined than ever, she ate then marched out the door. Pippa checked the stables just to make sure there were no horses.

Cursed.

She started walking toward Inverness.

A man caught up to her from behind. He cleared his throat. "Mam, now I'm not supposed to give aide of any sort. You should *ken* though you're not going in the right direction. If I'm guessing right, Roby is going to want to catch up to you, not ride west to find you after he gets back. The way I see this one is that I'm lending aide to Roby not you."

Pippa sucked air. "You wouldn't lie to me?" she asked beginning to realize more thoroughly she was inept in more ways than just her size. Before it never mattered what direction she traveled.

"*Nay*. I don't lie." He pointed in the directions she was walking. "By the way, I'm Mac. Won't let anything bad happen to you. Promised your man."

He was truly going to follow her. The devil.

A few minutes later she passed the lodge all the while hoping if she traveled in the wrong direction the man trudging behind her would catch up to her and say something. She could use someone to talk to right now. Roby probably told Mac to keep her feeling lonely.

Sunshine stung her face. She needed a bonnet. Her feet hurt as a callous began to rub against her boot. She gritted her teeth against quitting as the sun rose higher in the sky. What little breeze wafted through the loose ends of her hair served to heat her further. She limped.

I'm not going to give up.

Sweat trickled down her face to her neck then between her breasts. From the nape of her neck more moisture slithered down her back. Her leg muscles began to ache and cramp. When she turned, she no longer saw the lodge.

You should go back.

Quitting will serve no purpose.

You are a stubborn fool, Pippa McKenna.

Determined to have my way.

She trudged on for what seemed another eternity before stopping. Wiping damp hair from her face, she called herself all kinds of a fool. Roby had thought she would give up. She wasn't about to do anything of the sort.

"Mam...

McKenna's man, Mac, was beside her. Most likely to give some type of advice.

"It's getting late."

"What?"

She could see that. Pippa didn't understand what he implied. She pushed the damp, tangled mass of her hair from her face. Puffed upward to get rid of the few dry stands that tickled and annoyed.

"We should be turning back to the lodge. It's going to be dark soon." He pointed to the horizon. "Didn't think you would walk this far. Worried about the storm coming our way."

Over the last few hours, she didn't notice the towering clouds growing higher and higher. Now they were dark masses that reached to the top of the sky. A trickle of fear whipped through her growing bolder as the meaning of the clouds became more apparent.

"You can go back," she said stubbornly refusing to acknowledge the very real threat hovering in front of her. 'I'm going to Inverness."

"Just to teach your man a lesson?" he queried, his voice soft with the hint of amusement.

"No, to find out who my parents were if it's possible."

The devil but she wasn't going backward, only forward from this point on.

"*Nay*, Mam, I cannot. Got to keep a wary eye on you, protect you so your husband has a wife to come home to. Seems at the moment the only way I can achieve that is to convince you to return to the lodge. The storm is going to hit. We'll need shelter."

Far in the distance a jagged blue-white light lit the sky followed by a low rumble echoing across the crags. Pippa flinched wishing she was anywhere but here. "You're right of course. We need to find cover before the storm hits. Are there any crofter's huts or out buildings close by? Even if they are falling apart, they might keep some of the rain off."

"There is no cover out here. We'll be soaked through to our skin if we don't get hit by lightning and die. The McKenna would never forgive me if something like that happened."

"I'm going on." Despite her fear she kept moving, one step in front of the other. "Not going to die because of a little storm."

"The way I see it, I'm damned if I do, damned if I don't. Wasn't supposed to put a hand on you."

"What are you...?"

Her words were cut off when he boldly picked her up, giving her no choice but to comply with his wishes.

"Put me down this instant." Squirming in Mac's powerful arms, she found herself unable to dislodge herself from his grip. He nearly dropped her. Righted her as he recovered.

"If I have to, Mrs. McKenna, I'm going to carry you all the way just to keep you safe. It would be faster, more efficient as well if you agreed to come along with no more protest," he gritted out. "We're too far to go back so maybe we'll get lucky and find some hovel to take refuge inside."

He looked hopeful. She almost caved. Perhaps if she could convince him she would do just that, he would set her on her feet. She could proceed to Inverness without further hindrance. Instead, she shoved hard, landing on her backside. Pain shot up her back. She froze for a few seconds as she allowed the pain to simmer while she gained a breath of air. Quickly, she scrambled to her feet, racing away from Mac and into the tempest.

You were truly born yesterday if you think such a ridiculous notion has merit. He will not give up. He will come after you.

It was just a thought.

A ridiculous one at best.

I ken it.

His strides were long, taking the ground twice as fast. She heard the pounding of his feet behind her. He throttled her. Once more she lay on the ground, panting hard. Closing her eyes, she wished for shelter.

"I'll walk," she whispered disgusted with herself and her easy capitulation.

These men they were all the same, using brute strength to get what they wanted. If she refused, he would pick her up again. On her hands and knees, she stared through the loose strands of her hair. She pointed. "You were wrong, Mac. There's a hut right in front of us."

"Speak 'o the devil," he muttered. "We best get moving then."

"Should we take shelter. After that discuss the merits of walking back to the lodge?"

"Glad to see there is shelter ahead. If we're not going to get caught in the brunt of the storm, we're going to have to run. Let's just hope no one is occupying the hut. If someone is, we should send a tiny prayer to the heaven above he'll let us inside." He held her hand as he increased the pace. Fine drops of rain splattered them as well as the ground.

She stumbled slightly. For the first minutes she was able to keep up. Gasping for air and bent over at the waist she heaved mammoth gulps of air. He looked to the sky then back to her.

"It's not much farther. I'm going to have to carry you. Is that all right?

"This time you ask."

He wasn't breathing hard.

Darn him.

He smiled at her. "This time I ask because I'm sure you want the same thing I do, a roof over our heads when the blue-white lightning brightens the sky and the rain drops are as big as golf balls. We can only hope there is no hail. The tempest is coming upon us fast and furious."

With Pippa cradled in his arms, Mac ran and ran. The dark clouds chased them sending gales of in front of them just to taunt, keeping their pace slow. What seemed like hours passed when only a few minutes ticked by. Guilt flooded her. Because of her ridiculous and foolish decision, this man was paying a high price.

When the first real smattering of drops hit, they stood by the hut. Mac set her down carefully as if she was made of fine china. When the deluge was dropping buckets on them, he was knocking on the door crying out if anyone was at home.

Only silence greeted them.

"Looks like we're here by ourselves. Lucky for us, the storm waited to do its worst until we found shelter."

Inside it was dark. Wind whistled around the eaves. Thankfully, there didn't seem to be any leaks.

She watched as he set peat in the fireplace then lit the fire. She walked closer holding out her hands to warm herself. Her shirt plastered against her. She shivered.

"Too bad I didn't think to pack a knapsack with food along with a blanket."

This had truly been one of her more foolish ventures. She understood it happened because she was reacting to Roby's orders instead of thinking for herself.

"Mrs. McKenna, the other Mrs. McKenna thought of it for you, for us. She told me she didn't think you would give up easily. Told me you were a good hearted but stubborn *lass*. She made sure we wouldn't starve."

Pippa stood. Her arms wrapped around her shivering bone deep as the chill seeped farther into her. Roby was going to be furious with her. "You have food and blankets?"

"Surely, I do indeed." He set another piece of peat on the fire before taking off the backpack she never noticed.

While she wouldn't forgive Roby for tying her to the bed, he'd been right about her attempt to follow him. If she'd been alone...a sob in the form of a shuddered gasp escaped her lips. She sunk onto the blanket Mac spread in front of the fire. She might have eluded the hangman's noose because of Roby. Tonight, she might have died. Didn't because Roby had the foresight to make sure Mac was there for her.

"You should probably change into something dry. Seems there's a bedroom over there. I'll just keep my back turned," Mac told her as he handed her the dress Wynnie packed for her. "You can hang your shirt and trousers up near the fire so they'll dry by morning."

They reached Inverness two days later. Pippa made inquiries about the orphanage. Once they stood in front of it, Pippa felt her heart thunder. While she didn't know if she would discover any truths about her past, she remained hopeful.

"You don't have to come inside with me."

His green eyes flashed. "You truly think I would stay with you all this way only to abandon you at the orphanage? Then my name isn't Mackenzie Bruce. I was charged with keeping you safe. I'm not going to leave you in a foreign place."

"You make the orphanage sound like a different country."

"Don't know what anyone inside that building is about now do we?" Mac stepped forward to open the door for her. When she walked inside, he held his hand protectively at the small of her back.

Mac walked by her side into the structure. It was dank and gloomy. She wondered if she'd been born here. Questioned, too, if her mother left her in a basket with a note attached. The thought she was unwanted didn't sit well with her. She reminded herself her adoptive parents had loved her. She was well taken care of.

You don't even ken if you were adopted.

I was.

You're pig headed.

From the shadows a woman appeared. She was small her hair dark brown with blond highlights. Her eyes highlighting her features simmered a deep, dark blue. As she walked her hips swayed slightly, her strides long. She wore a dark blue dress.

She smiled at them, "Can I help you?"

"I don't know. I'm looking for something."

Mac touched her on the shoulder. "I'll come back in an hour. I'm going to find lodging for the night."

"I understand what you are about. You will also send word to Roby where I am."

He grimaced before smiling brightly. "Of course. Did you truly think anything different? You should know we will stay at the McKenna townhouse. I'm not truly searching for a place for us to stay, just giving you privacy."

"Roby had this all planned out, didn't he?"

"He understands his woman."

It would only be a matter of a week or so, if that, before Roby would be here. She inhaled a deep breath of air, trying for the courage a confrontation with her husband would need. She never strictly lied to him. Told him all along she would go to Edinburg. Just because she changed her mind, didn't mean anything.

Pippa watched Mac stride form the building. She turned to the woman as she rummaged through the only small bag she brought with her. She held out the certificate claiming her birth to Miss Jillian Masson.

"Can you tell me anything about this?" Her voice shook as she spoke, her hands trembling with curiosity as well as fear. In the present, she wasn't all that sure she wanted to know the truth. Didn't want to dismiss her parents from her thoughts. They loved her with all their hearts until she was fourteen.

When the lady saw the document, she clasped her hand to her throat before staggering back a step. Staring at the certificate, she sank onto a chair. She wiped tears from her cheeks with the backs of her hands.

After several minutes she looked up, "I'm Jillian Masson. That means you are the MacPherson's daughter?"

~ * ~

Roby, Connal and Kit rode quickly. With the extra horses they were able to double the distance they covered. When they reached the small cottage where Harry and Horace were rumored to be staying, it was vacant. Signs that the men were there once remained. It seemed they evacuated the premises quickly.

Roby shuffled through the litter on the floor. In the bedroom Connal tossed through the linens that were still on the beds. Rotting food sat on the counter tops in the kitchen where Kit searched.

"Nothing," Roby said as he met the others in the main room.

His body tensed with the realization the two men might be slipping away from him. He kicked at a basket of peat then sat down his head between his hands.

"They can't just vanish. We'll find them," Roby muttered thinking about Pippa, the things she endured because of these two.

"My guess would be they continued to Edinburgh. That's where they have rooms," Connal said. "They have no funds to speak of. Will have to work. To eat."

"It will take another couple of days maybe more to get there," Roby said wishing this had gone as planned.

He needed to get home to Pippa. Needed to see her as well as make sure she didn't set off on her own. So far none of his men caught up to them bringing news. With the speed they were traveling, he doubted anyone would. By the time they returned to Callum's lodge, she could be anywhere. He had no way of knowing.

Mac would be with her. That was the only part of this he felt good about. Perhaps he wouldn't go back to the lodge. He was so certain she wouldn't be there. To save time he should go on to Inverness after he secured sailing vessels for the Finchbottoms.

"The hearth is still warm. They aren't very far in front of us. I'm suspecting they knew when to admit they weren't going to achieve their goals and leave," Connal pointed out.

"On to Edinburgh. We've got another couple of hours of light. With any luck we'll find them camped out along the road," Kit said.

Half-heartedly Roby listened to the chatter. He was ready to leave. His worries were real. Deep in his heart he knew Pippa would leave. Wynnie would not have found her yet. He hoped he would have until morning. Every little bit of time he gained by tying her to the bed, worked in his favor. She would be on foot. Mac was told to do everything he could to slow her down.

If anyone could, Mac would keep her out of trouble.

She might still be cursing him to the devil. He chuckled softly, looking forward to the reunion. Her passion would be simmering over the top, boiling. He thought of her three steps to seduction. He would use each one to bring her back to his terms. Thinking about her lips on him, the feel of her hands as they journeyed across all the most sensitive parts of him, he hardened instantly. He would do the same with her body until she wept for him, her softness ready for his sword.

"Best we start out." He stood striding to the door and the horses hoping his arousal wasn't noticeable.

Once again, they rode, quickly changing horses without stopping. The sun slowly dipped behind the hills shedding little light on the surroundings. In the distance a small fire lit the side of the road. Roby knew it had to be his prey.

"Finchbottoms," Roby muttered.

They dismounted, leaving the horses tethered. Silently, they made their way to the camp. Horace was leaning against a boulder, his feet stretched out in front of him drinking whiskey. Harry sat across from his father in a similar position as they bemoaned their fate.

"We could try to find another heiress," Horace said.

"I could marry one," Harry said. "Rather have my mistress. Don't have to give her anything I don't want. She doesn't make demands on my time."

Harry's words were slurred. Horace's too.

"We take them now?" Kit asked with a soft chuckle. "Not going to be much fun in that. They're drunk. They can't stand up let alone give us a good fight. I'm in need of a good fight or a good tumble. Doubt if I'll get either tonight."

"What better time than this," Connal said. "All we have to do is walk into their camp."

The skirmish lasted less than a few minutes. Harry and Horace were trussed up, ready to move on to Edinburgh as soon as the morning light filtered through the clouds. Their fate awaited them.

The Finchbottoms were breathing hard and red faced. Roby watched with fascination as they sputtered their outrage.

"You've got no right here to do this," Harry blustered spittle flying. "I'm an Englishman."

"Sassenach," Kit said, his tone demeaning.

"While you've the right to terrorize a young woman with dead cats as well as threats of rape?" Roby asked his voice whiskey smooth, contemptuous. He wasn't about to forget the words that sent Pippa running into the highlands to escape certain rape at the tender age of fourteen. "You've no rights here."

"What are you going to do with us? You can't keep us tied up forever," Horace sputtered some more as he squirmed against his bindings. "Where are you going to take us?"

"Where we can see justice is done," Connal said as he sat back against the same rock where Horace sat earlier. His powerful legs were stretched out in front of him. "It's what you deserve."

The two men were tied across the clearing from each other. The beans for their dinner simmering in a pot on the fire looked good. Roby dished himself a plate of food while he sat back watching Kit and Connal do the same.

"You can't eat our food," Harry said as if he had a say in what was happening around his campfire.

"Watch us," Kit laughed as he swallowed the beans. "Very good, filling too. You can go hungry tonight. It will make tomorrow's dinner appear even tastier."

"What kind of justice?" Horace asked seeming to ignore the fact the McKenna's were eating his food. "I would ask that you..." He fell off, his words seeming to rethink everything.

"Should we let them discover later when we reach the city?" Kit asked with a deceptive chuckle. "Or should we tell them now? What do you think will be more fun?"

"They'll be afraid all the way to the city if we tell them. That might not be the kindest approach to their destiny," Connal said with a wicked half-smile painting his face, his steel gray eyes twinkling with unremarked humor.

"They'll die of curiosity if we don't give them a clue or two," Roby said, a smile matching his father's, forming on his lips as he thought about the dead cats along with the verbal threats.

They deserved to be terrified after what they put Pippa through. They had no concern for her, sought only their greedy ends.

"You'll be pleased. Your new accommodations are all arranged, bought and paid for. Won't cost either of you a penny, money you don't possess." Kit dropped to his haunches in front of Harry, looking him up then down very slowly, his gaze resting at his crotch. "Won't be purchasing any whores for a long, *verra* long time. No carnal delights for the two of you."

"Meals will all be free as will room and board," Connal added as he finished the last of his beans wiping the plate clean with a slice of bread.

"No travel expenses," Roby said beginning to enjoy the conversation. He liked the terror on their faces. Well, the expressions weren't quite on the level of horror. Once they understood their plight it would be. "You'll see the world. What more can a man ask for?" He waved his spoon at the pair.

"What the devil are the three of you talking about? I'm not going to some Sassenach prison," Harry said indignantly. "I've committed no crime. You can't just haul us around as if we were naught but a sack of grain."

"No, you're not. A prison might be better than what we've in store for you. One can't see the world from a prison, now, can they? Already spoke to the people who will arrange your new duties," Connal said his voice thick with burgeoning anger.

A tone Roby knew full well from his younger days. "It pays to have friends in the highlands. As to crimes you might or might not have committed that is debatable. I suppose the killing of animals isn't your only crime. Siphoning funds from a helpless young woman definitely is a crime worthy of punishment. Don't you think? Leaving a young woman trussed up and naked is also a crime."

"The two of you are English so you understand what goes on in their prisons," Kit said with a false grimace. "Rats, whippings, torture of the worst sort, yes this is a better fate. At least you will have a chance, a small chance at survival. If you can survive, you will do well."

"You got to tell us where you're taking us," Harry said beginning to appear more concerned about his fate than the lack of his dinner. "You got to give us some of our food. I'm starving."

"Or what?" Roby asked. Perhaps he was wrong about Horace's concern over his dinner that he wasn't going to eat.

Kit tipped the whiskey bottle up taking a long drink before wiping his mouth with the back of his hand. "Don't have to do anything. You'll get enough to eat in a few days when you reach your final destination. Won't starve before then. Of course, it will be some time before food is presented to you, or should I say gruel. Enough begging and whining, I've heard too much simpering for grown men. Rations in your new environment aren't always palatable."

"While your stomach is grumbling, I want you to think of the fourteen-year-old girl you terrorized into running away. She didn't have food. She was on her own. A young woman, a very young woman helpless to defend herself from the likes of you or anyone she might meet on the road," Roby grit out as he recalled much of Pippa's story.

She made light of the pitfalls though, accepted what came with her decision to leave as well as what might have happened to her if she stayed.

"I've decided to take pity on you," Connal said as he looked from Roby to Kit, "unless either of you don't want them to know their fate. Speak up now if that's the case. I for one want them to have time before here and there to ponder the consequences of their actions."

"I'll do the honors," Roby said softly, enjoying the pained expressions on the Finchbottoms' faces. "If that's alright."

He spared a look at his father. It's because of their evil plans against my wife they are in this predicament of their making. They need to understand there is no turning back for them. No amount of begging or pleading will change my mind.

Connal waved his hand in the air as he grinned. "Go ahead. You're the second half of the wronged party. Pippa is your mate. In the identical circumstances I would want the same."

Roby hunkered down in front of Harry. He watched him for several seconds before he began. "We've bargained for your place on the British ship, the Flying Eagle. Your captain is one of the most ruthless captains in the British navy, brooks no disobedience or shirking of duties. His men have to respond on time and with courtesy or they feel the cat 'o nine tails, might even find themselves keel hauled. I think you're going to enjoy the journey. The Flying Eagle is headed to India. Might see a tiger or two. Doubt if anyone there would take kindly to cat killing. Who knows, you might turn out a better man. If you survive."

Roby stood then walked to the other side of the fire. He stood looking down on Horace, contempt in his gaze. "Now for your fate, dear Horace, you will serve your duty on the Calypso with a similar captain. Your vessel is on its way to Australia. You might see a kangaroo or a wallaby if you're lucky. Would you like that? What fine outstanding Englishmen you two are to volunteer for duty. The two ships wait in the harbor for the arrival of their new sailors."

"You can't do that to English citizens," Harry blustered, spittle flying from his lips. "Shanghaiing is illegal. I protest."

"Protest as much as you like. Doesn't change your

circumstances," Kit said his grin flashing even white teeth.

"Oh, this is very legal. All the documents have been signed. By what the papers say, both of you volunteered. Were eager. Nothing dark or unsavory about this deed," Connal said his voice mimicking sweetness as if he spoke to a child. "My dear friend, Captain Davidson saw to the documents himself. I witnessed your signature."

"I didn't sign anything." Horace protested to no avail. "This is just a threat. You wouldn't do such a thing. As you said earlier you just want to scare us. It worked so now you can tell us what you are really doing."

"You *ken* the truth."

"*Nay*, it's not legal." Harry's face flushed with his anger.

"You will have to prove that. Your word against Roby's and mine. From the bottom of the hold to swabbing decks. If you're adventurous, look out for pirates from the crow's nest. The sightings will not change the fact the documents were signed with your given names. The same ones the two of you used to rob Pippa of her rightful inheritance."

"You'll regret this," Harry sputtered struggling against his bindings. "I demand you untie us. Demand justice. I'll see you rot in hell."

"I doubt that I'll regret anything. You've signed on for the next thirty years if you survive that long. Short of escape, you won't see landfall for a very long time. You see sailors like you are not allowed shore leave. No dallying with a willing whore at every port. Oh, I don't doubt after a time, you will be allowed to leave. What good would it do you? It's not as if you've a home to come back to in Scotland or England. If you jump ship, they'll hunt you down and toss you in the brig where you might think you are rotting in hell. No, you won't be returning here until your stooped and your beard is white and reaches your knees."

They were both sputtering and cursing the McKennas to hell and back. Roby didn't think either one of them stopped all the way to the city. When he watched the men brought on board their separate ships in chains and in protest, he felt a surge of relief.

Now he had to find Pippa in the aftermath of the heated meeting to contend with her needs. Convincing her of her foolishness might be a fiasco. She might never admit she couldn't do as a man does.

First things first, spend the night in his townhouse then find out where Pippa was. His gut told him she was on her way to the city even while he prayed she was safe with Wynnie at Callum's lodge. Tomorrow, he would have to search the road for her. Still, one way or the other he prayed he would find her before anything bad could happen to her.

She did have Mac for protection.

Chapter Ten

The lady Pippa handed the document to stared at her from her sitting position. Her lips thinned as her deep blue eyes clouded for a moment. She swayed. Silence lingered longer than usual, as she seemed to think. Her breathing slowed, eventually evening out to almost normal.

Slowly and in a *verra* soft voice, she spoke, "I'm Jillian Masson. You've given me quite a start. I'm not certain what I should be thinking."

"You?" Pippa didn't know what to say. Her breath caught in her throat. A few moments later, "You are?" Pippa swallowed her fear along with her curiosity. "Are you my mother?"

Pippa had not meant to blurt out the words. She was so overwhelmed with the knowledge she was sitting with the woman who might have given birth to her.

The woman who didn't want her.

Nothing like getting straight to the point without any preliminaries.

"I don't know. I gave birth to a baby girl nineteen years ago. Almost twenty. Could that be you? You've got your father's eyes, the gold flecks even now shimmering in the light around the green of a forest. Your hair is not his or mine. He has red hair you know. Yet there are hints of red mingled with the brown, a lot of red."

"I think I might be your daughter. Do you know the adoptive parents?"

Pippa wanted to reach out to her, touch her as a daughter would want to touch her parent. She faltered. There were too many unanswered questions. Too much to talk about in such a short time.

Why did you give me up? Did you not love me?

At her question, Jillian was shaking her head. "It's possible. Anything is possible. You've got the same eyes as your father if he is your father," she repeated as if she was still in a daze of confusion ticking off past years from her memories. "I loved those green eyes flecked with gold. The gold always glistened with heat when he was passionate about something."

"I've so many questions if you are my real mother. Not that I wasn't loved. I was until both mother and father died in an accident."

"Ask the questions, maybe together we can figure this out. I didn't want to give you up. Need for you to understand that. I wasn't wed to the father. I had to leave, go home to London. When I returned..."

"Did you love my father?"

Pippa was sure now this woman was her mother. Her eyes were like her father's. Her hair was a reddish brown, a bit of both her mother and father. Both her adoptive parents had black hair, blue-black. Neither had green eyes. Neither could shift which is why they never thought to talk to her about her abilities.

"Oh, Pippa, with all my heart I loved him. Still do. I believed he was my soul mate, an eternal love. He told me as much. In the end I lost him though. Could not hang on to his love. I've not seen him these last twenty years even though I've searched."

"How? If the two of you loved each other, why would he leave you? Were you pregnant then? Were the two of you married? No, you said you weren't."

There was so much unsaid. She wished to learn everything all at once.

"I *dinna ken* if Mac loved me. He never said as much. Yes, the last time I saw him I carried a babe within my womb. It was too soon to know. I guessed but I couldn't tell him until I was certain."

Mac? Lots of Scottish lads were named Mac.

"You never saw him again. What happened?"

She closed her eyes, sighing softly. "My parents called me back to England. Father is an earl. He didn't want me to stay in the highlands. There were rumors that reached him about a man and myself. I thought Mac would be here for me, would wait for me. I told him I would come back. Promised him. He tried to talk me out of going." She let out a long slow breath of air. "I intended to return. Evidently, he didn't believe I would. He had duties and obligations of his own."

"Why didn't he search for you?"

"I lied to him. Never told him I was English. Never told him my surname. He would not have known where to look. I returned to Inverness as soon as I could scrape together enough money to travel. By then the trail was gone. I was alone, about to give birth. I found the orphanage by accident. The lady who ran it then was old and very kind. She called in a midwife when it was my time. You were so tiny, precious. Giving you up was the hardest thing I ever did. They made me promise not to seek you out."

"I see." Pippa spoke softly as she tried to understand the pain her birth mother was going through. "Have you continued your search for the man you love?"

"Everyday. I've looked and questioned people for the last nineteen years. When is your birthday?"

"August twenty-first I've been told. It was mother who told me."

Jillian's eyes filled with tears again. She pushed the moisture away with her thumbs. "It is the same day my baby girl was born."

"Did you name her?"

"No, the MacPhersons were waiting for a baby. They tried for years and were never able to conceive. She had a name picked out. I would have named you Daisy. I love daisies."

"Daisy…" Pippa mulled over the name for a few seconds while she smiled at her. "I'm Pippa McKenna now. Phillipa, it's what my parents named me. I would have liked to be called Daisy."

Jillian smiled gently, a motherly smile. "Come, shall we walk in the gardens. It's one of the gifts that have come from the MacPherson donations. The older children like to work in the garden while the little ones often play. We have lots of flowers and in the summer, we grow our own vegetables."

"You've been here since you gave birth?" Pippa asked, thinking this was a fine place to live with all the children around.

"I have. The MacPhersons also made sure I had a job here. I

believe in the end they owned this small plot of land. You own it now since their deaths."

"I do? Truly, I've no idea what my wealth entails."

She told Jillian her story and why she had to runaway speaking briefly of the Finchbottoms. Left out the part about the gallows although she might have to say more when it came to the meeting of her husband.

"You're wed now. I hope you will allow me to remain at the orphanage. It's the only place I've known. I would not like to be tossed out since I've nowhere to go, nowhere else to live." She looked hopeful.

"I would never do that."

Pippa felt outrage that Jillian felt the need to ask such a question. She had thoughts to deed the orphanage over to her mother. She would have to tell Roby and see if he would agree with her.

"Thank you kindly. I appreciate you."

"I might have spoken too soon. In the end, whether you stay or are forced to leave is ultimately up to my husband. Though he is not the kind of man who would turn a woman onto the streets."

Nay, he might tie her to a bed to keep her from doing as she pleased.

"I will pray that he will look kindly on me. Who was the man with you? In the shadows of the entrance, he looked vaguely familiar."

Pippa laughed softly, a smile forming as she thought on all the poor man had to endure. "My protector, poor man. Roby assigned him the job of following me if I decided to leave Callum's lodge and head for Inverness. We had to walk the entire way. He found shelter for us during a storm, brought food and water so I wouldn't starve. Even carried a change of clothing for me."

"Why walk? A woman of means, you must have had horses, perhaps a carriage to make the travel more pleasant."

"*Nay,* Roby didn't want me to go. Thought if he took all the horses, I would stay where he left me. Told me it was too dangerous for a woman. I took issue with that statement. Not used to being told what to do. I've been on my own for what seems longer than not."

"You left," she said chuckling softly. "Reminds me a bit of me, sometimes too stubborn to keep from doing something foolish. Mac always told me I often reacted before I thought about the consequences. One time he threatened to tie me up to the bed so I wouldn't get myself into trouble." Her eyes grew wistful. "Truly, I wish I could see him one more time in this life. The man still owns my heart and soul. Always will."

"Is that all you wish for? Just to see him? If it were me, I'd be wishing and praying for a whole lot more," Pippa said knowing if it was Roby, she would wish for at least one more time to be held in his arms.

"*Nay*, not all, but I don't dare be too greedy. If I got all my wishes, I'd wish for him to find me and wed me. I'd hope that he never found anyone else to love." Her long sigh escaped with a gentle whisper. "I'd wish for a child such as you."

"What did you say my father's last name was? Did you say?" Pippa asked, thinking the McKennas might help her find the man she loved.

"I call him Mac."

Each time she mentioned the name, Mac, butterflies fluttered in the pit of Pippa's stomach. "Mac with red hair and green eyes," Pippa prompted thinking of another Mac she knew. Another Mac who might be the right age. "Does this man have a last name?" she asked again wishing Jillian would be more forthcoming.

"*Aye*," Jillian laughed, "Of course, he does. His full name is Mackenzie Bruce. I suppose there might be a hint of gray in his brilliant red hair by now. He was ten years older than me at the time. I was only seventeen."

The sound of her lover's last name gave her heart a flutter. She gasped as she tried to force air into her lungs. "I'm thinking you might be getting your wish sooner than you expected. I'll introduce you to my protector as soon as he returns for me." Pippa felt the burgeoning smile all the way to the tips of her toes.

"You know him? He's your protector?"

"*Aye*, and a *bonnie lad* he is too."

Outside in the garden, the air was brisk even though the sun shared its rays with the earth. Flowers danced in rows within the finely tended beds. She breathed in deeply the scent of roses along with the jasmine climbing trellises. This was her mother. Now she was sure she would

246

confirm Mac as her father as soon as he returned. The day couldn't get brighter. She planned on staying here until Roby arrived. She wanted as much time with her mother as possible. Craved the time to learn about her father and how Jillian fell in love with him. Wondered which one of her parents was the shifter. It had to be Mac. He was part of the McKenna clan.

It was a love match.

Jillian was Mac's soul mate.

They would be reunited.

Roby would be pleased to learn he picked out her father to be her protector. Who better than a father to make sure his daughter arrived at her location safely? In this case, he should not be so terribly angry with her.

"I fell in love with Mac the first time I looked at him." Jillian recalled her eyes turning dreamy. "He challenged and surprised me in too many ways to count. I suppose he wanted me as much as I did him. You're the obvious result of how easily he coaxed me into his arms as well as his bed. The only part I regret is that I had to give you up."

They sat down on a bench surrounded by clusters of daisies. *Her namesake.* A robin strutted on the lawn searching for worms. Above in a tree a nest of baby birds squawked nosily to their mother yelling for food. Humming birds found the brilliant red flowers they liked to feed on while they hovered, wings beating rapidly.

"I almost died," Pippa told her mother.

"Harry Finchbottom?"

"*Nay*, I killed a rabbit on Lord Bigley's property. Supposedly, the killing of one of his animals was a crime, hanging the penalty. Roby volunteered to marry me in order to keep me from the end game one finds on the gallows."

"I'm sorry, so sorry..."

"Don't be. It's probably the best thing that happened to me. He'll arrive here in a day or two, all manly bluster, furious that I would dare defy his orders. He will forgive me though."

"You think it will be that easy?"

"I will give him whatever he wants. I'll forgive him his manly blustering, ordering me around without a thought to my feelings."

She laughed softly thinking about her husband. He was easy to divert. Wynnie said the same about Connal. It would just take creative thinking on her part.

"There you are. I was told you were walking in the garden."

Mac appeared striding down the path, his powerful limbs eating up the distance between them until he reached the bench where they sat.

He stopped, running his hand along his jaw his gaze roaming the length of Jillian then back up to focus on her eyes. "I've the feeling I know you *lass*. Do I?"

Jillian laughed softly as she stood. "You do indeed, Mac Bruce. I'm sorely distressed that you *dinna* recognize me. It has been scarcely twenty years."

"Should I recognize you? I feel it in my soul that I do know you." It was then his breath seemed to catch. "Jillian? Jillian, is that really you? I believed you to be dead."

"I came back to Inverness and searched, in the end couldn't find you anywhere." Tears flooded her eyes. "When you weren't where I expected you to be, I didn't know where to look. It was as if you vanished from the face of the earth." Her tears turned to an emotional sob then another and another.

"I waited for you."

He stepped toward her, his voice gruff. One arm wrapped around her then another. "I could only wait so long, you *ken*. I didn't think you were coming back. I knew your father wasn't happy with us. Don't cry. Please, Jilly don't cry."

"C-can't s-stop."

Gently his hand cupped her head, pressing her against his chest.

It seemed to Pippa he wanted to put the past where it belonged. They should be alone with each other. Yet, she felt protective of the woman who gave her life.

"*Nay*, Mac, the two of you need to speak of the past and what you want for your future before you seduce my mother into your bed. Obviously, you were able to work your charms on her before. I'm heartily glad you did, but the two of you should have a chaperone until you know what you want."

"I *dinna* need a chaperone to help me figure out what I want. It's the same thing I wanted twenty years ago when I lost her. Jillian will be my wife."

A significant pause followed before Mac turned his gaze away from Jillian and on to her. "Mother?"

"Jillian is my mother. She gave me up for adoption when she couldn't find you. You couldn't find her. Rubbish. You must not have tried too hard. She was here all the time."

"She wanted me to raise another man's bastard?"

His fury simmered beneath his skin, flushing it with heat above his short-cropped beard.

"Your bastard," Jillian said softly as she placed her hands over her heart. "Pippa is our child, yours and mine. I never cheated on you. To this day I've never had relations with another man. For all these years I've prayed and wished for this day. Now it is here and you dare accuse me of..."

He sputtered seeming to struggle for words while his green-eyed gaze shifted from Pippa to Jillian then back. Pippa watched them together. Their love shone in their eyes. She was in the way. They needed time together, time alone. He did just say he wanted to marry her.

"I'm your father?" His words sounded incredulous yet eager to learn the truth. The next pause coupled with the look in his eyes gave her reason to panic. "Then I should tan your backside for your stupidity of a few days ago. If I had known, I would have defied Roby, stopped you from ever starting this ridiculous journey."

Oh my, she never thought about that. She'd not been accountable to an adult for the last five years. Callum never told her what she could or could not do. Neither did the gypsies. Now she stood in front of a furious father, a father who just learned he possessed a daughter.

A daughter who disobeyed her husband.

Her mind raced, frantic to come up with a plausible answer. "You wouldn't dare. Roby would..."

"Not say a thing." He finished for her his voice tight with emotions. "When he finally catches up to you, he will probably want to do the same which is why I'll leave the punishment up to him."

"He won't."

A heavy sigh followed, his eyes narrowing in conjecture. "No more than I would. You do need to become more prudent in your actions. You're too much like your mother. It wouldn't do for you to defy your husband. Whatever you do, don't shift again. The first time was nearly the death of you."

"You are the shifter in my life. I wondered if it was my mother or father."

She looked to Jillian who was shaking her head.

"*Nay*, I cannot."

"He told you."

"While I kept things from Mac, I believe he was honest with me."

"So much more makes sense to me now. No wonder my mother and father never taught me. Never spoke of it. They most likely didn't know anything about the irregularity, thought the presence of shifters in the highlands was gossip or old wives' tales."

"If you don't mind, I would like to be alone with Jillian," Mac said as his tender gaze focused on her mother. "We've a great deal of catching up to do. After that there is the present to speak of."

Pippa stiffened at her father's words. She felt protective toward her mother who seemed ill prepared for this encounter. "What are your intentions? I believe I've the right to ask. Jillian is vulnerable. Her heart belongs to you as well you *ken*. Without any effort on your part, you can crush her, make her life hell. I will have your word that you won't do anything to hurt her. You will not make love to her until you make her your wife or at least promise her you will do so."

Mac tossed his head back, laughing. "I promise. There hasn't been a day in my life I haven't thought on what I would do when I finally saw Jillian again. Strange, there has never been any doubt in my mind that she would someday come to me. Even though there were moments I thought she might be dead. I never truly believed it." He held out his hand to her. "We will walk and talk. I intend to steal a kiss if you're willing."

A blush settled on her cheeks.

She reached out. He twined his fingers between hers. They walked talking, love for the big man shining in Jillian's eyes. Pippa wanted to know what they were saying. Instead, she thought about Roby, wondered how many days it would be before they were reunited.

She plucked a handful of daisies. Thinking of Jillian...

He loves her. He loves her not.

Her heart light she strode into the orphanage, searched for an empty room. When she found one, she made herself comfortable before wandering back to the main room. There weren't many children residing here. She wondered how successful Jillian was in placing the lonely children in permanent homes. Wondered too how they found their way to the home.

She wanted to play a larger role here. Needed to find children on the streets who needed a home. Find women who were in dire straits, pregnant with no help who could live here. This was a large home. The building could be used for more than just the children. It could be used to help out abused women.

In the kitchen she made a pot of tea, found some milk and lemons. When Mac and Jillian located her in the kitchen, they were still holding hands, still smiling as well as laughing.

Still in love with love.

New beginnings.

"Well?" Along with her cup of tea she lifted an eyebrow in speculation. When they stood beside her with apparently nothing to say, she cleared her throat. "Well?"

"We are handfasted," Mac said softly a wealth of tenderness directed to Jillian then he held up his free hand as if he meant to hold her comment behind her lips. "We will wed in the church as soon as possible. I cannot wait a moment longer to call her my own."

"At the McKenna church." She put this out for them. "You only want to get into her bed. It's why you handfasted. I won't be denying that it is probably about time, long past time. The two of you have waited what must seem like a lifetime to be together. You'll receive no judgment from me. Although you must *ken* the wedding night will be all the sweeter for remaining celibate." She remembered her coupling with Roby before their wedding. It changed nothing about their wedding night.

"My daughter lecturing me," Mac said sporting a huge grin, he didn't make any attempt to hide. "Unless Jillian insists, I won't be waiting for the wedding night to make love to my soul mate. We've been together before. There is no reason I can see to torture ourselves."

"Together before a wedding," Pippa pointed out.

"I could not resist her charms. Now she is even more beautiful." He brought her hand to his lips. Kissed the back. "I'll make no promises to anyone save Jillian."

"Don't forget, I will continue to look out for her welfare. If you think to take advantage of Jillian, you will have to answer to me."

Jillian's cheeks turned pink, the shade attractive on her. She was embarrassed. Mac tenderly ran his knuckles along her blush.

"The blooming color on your cheeks is *verra* pretty."

"What do you say, Jillian? Did my brute of a father give you a choice or did he kiss you until you melted in his arms and couldn't say no to his wicked suggestion of handfasting?"

Not giving Jillian a chance to answer, Mac cut into the seeming rant before Pippa could get started. "I find it difficult to listen to my daughter speaking of melting in a man's arms when he kisses you. I will not ask how you know because I *ken* it. You're a married lady. Nonetheless, it's quite disconcerting. I'd rather not know anything about how Roby McKenna makes you feel when he kisses you. It's not seemly for a father to hear his daughter speaking in such a manner."

Pippa felt the rise of color on her cheeks that must match her mother's. A change of subject was definitely in order. "Jillian wants to run the orphanage. Are you going to stay here with her or return to continue work as one of Connal's men?"

Despite her apparent embarrassment, Pippa continued to challenge.

"We haven't spoken of any of this. We've no' had the time," Mac grunted as he looked at the woman who stole his heart more than twenty years ago, a woman who bore him a beautiful vibrant daughter, a woman who still held his heart in the palm of her hands. "I would do whatever Jillian wishes."

"I spoke of the orphanage before I saw you, before you returned to me and we handfasted. I would go wherever you go. Perhaps I can help you find someone else to run the orphanage. It's very dear to my heart. I've lived here for twenty years."

"We'll work together. I found a room upstairs. I want to stay at the orphanage. Don't want to return to the McKenna townhouse." She turned to Mac. "Do you have knowledge of my trust or money that might be available to me? I'd like something other than these trousers and shirt to wear. I do have a dress but..."

"Sorry, lass, you'll have to wait until Roby arrives. I would not dare presume too much even though you are my daughter."

She wanted to look her best when she encountered her husband. Seducing him to forget she defied him was first and foremost on her mind. "I understand." Pippa couldn't hide her disappointment.

"I will buy you a couple of gowns," Jillian smiled seeming to understand why she wanted something to wear. "I'm sure Mac could too if he was so inclined. It's nonsense what he says. He owes you an entire wardrobe of gowns."

"You have the funds?"

"Of course, we can go shopping together. I for one have the need of a gown suitable to be wed in."

~ * ~

As it turned out, Pippa was in soapy dishwater up to her elbows when Roby chose to pop into the orphanage. Strands of hair fell from her chignon. The apron she wore hid all her curves. Sweat beaded on her forehead.

To Roby, she never looked lovelier. Of course, he missed her, missed holding her in his arms, hearing the sweet music of her passionate surrender. Now, that he knew she was safe, he could forgive her. A continuing argument was not in his plans. Perhaps though, he should make her plead her case.

She didn't hear him walk into the kitchen. It pleased him. She didn't turn as he strode on silent feet toward her. He tried to keep his smile behind his teeth. His pleasure at seeing her was undeniable. His delight with the fact she was unharmed from her little escapade left him breathless as well as wanting to shake her until her teeth rattled. Eventually, they would reach that stage in their reunion. Ultimately, he would make his wishes clear to her. In the end, he understood she would continue to do as she pleased.

Stepping up behind her, his lips swept across the nape of her neck. With a startled gasp she jumped. "Hush, it's only me, Pippa. Your husband come to claim you a second time. You defied me, walking all the way here. Poor Mac, he didn't have any choice but to follow you. His feet must be riddled with callouses. You owe him a pair of boots." His hands settled on the saucy curve of her hips.

"You scared the breath out of me." She tried to turn but he kept her where she was as he proceeded to coax and heat her passions until he could sense her response sharp and potent. Before he would allow her to turn to him, he needed her soft and compliant, melting liquid heat.

"If it scared some sense into you, I'm heartily glad."

His hands settled on her waist, pressed against her slightly swollen tummy. She carried his child. Had been for over a month, possibly closer to two. She would begin to round even more soon. He could scarcely wait to see her huge with his child. He was sure of the fact. Shifters knew those things, could feel the life growing in its mate's womb. She didn't tell him. He wondered if she knew.

"You're wicked, a *verra* wicked *mon*, Roby McKenna. You should be ashamed of yourself sneaking up on a lass this way. Scaring her until she *verra* nearly jumped out of her skin."

He nipped her ear, traced the lobe with his tongue while he massaged her belly, thinking of his *bairn*. The shivering of her small form against his created the smile he previously tried to hide. "Where is your room?"

The devil but he stayed away two days. Stayed away so he wouldn't be tempted to do something foolish when he saw her. In the interim he calmed down. His nerves and temper that had been stretched to their snapping point settled now.

He was in control of his emotions, at least where her behavior was concerned.

Their troubles were over.

She had no reason to run off on her own.

"They are gone. Settled nicely on separate ships," he murmured stroking the lobe with his tongue, teasing her passion. "The Finchbottoms, you know your guardians, the reason behind your disobedience," he finished as his hands rose to perch beneath her breasts. He caught the rapid beat of her heart in his palm. His fingers itched to explore higher.

He held back.

He wanted the total rise of her passion until she was frantic.

She squirmed pushing her little, curvaceous bottom against his hard arousal. She would feel it, want him inside her. In a few seconds, she would be totally in his web. "Such a passionate little minx. You want me now, don't you?"

"Why are you doing this?" Once more she tried to turn in his arms. "I'm not going to mel...the devil, Roby."

"I think you know why." His teeth nipped down her neck unfastened the top of her dress before biting tender enticing kisses across the back of her shoulders. "Should we explore steps one and two?"

He needed her to be so desperate for him, she wouldn't discover the words to make excuses for her insubordination.

"Roby, *nay*, the children."

"I don't see any. Do they generally spend time in the kitchen? I don't think so. What I think is that they are all on the third floor with their teacher. Hmmm...any other excuses to keep my hands from their master's intended exploration? When we reach the very last step, I will put you on the table, wrap your legs around my shoulders. You can guess the next step."

She quivered.

He grinned thoroughly aroused by the way her body responded to his words. "You want that don't you? You know what will happen after your long, slender legs are wrapped around me. Tell me, Pippa. I want to hear you say the words. There's a naughty girl. You can do it. Talk to me, Pippa."

Tiny cries simpered from her. "Roby..." His name on her lips was an aphrodisiac.

"What will happen after that? Tell me, Pippa, and it will be yours."

In his arms he felt the shuddering of her satisfaction, felt her body soar higher and higher until she was crying out her pleasure. He didn't even make it to the first step and she climaxed in his arms. The knowledge and the feelings so exquisite it left him panting with his need.

"Pippa? Who is that and why are you making such strange sounds? Is that big man hurting you?" Roby looked down.

The little boy's voice behind him sent a chill that coursed along his spine. Pippa nearly wilted in his arms, her knees buckling. He was very glad they had not yet made it to the last step or any of the other ones. "I'm sorry, dear one. I'll take care of this."

He passed a palm over one of her nipples still veiled by her dress. She arched. He grinned.

"You've got to keep me on my feet. Without you holding me up, I don't think I can stand." Her whimpers of pleasure inflamed him. She was such a delightful little package. She was his.

"You're coming home with me. I'll have no argument from you. In this case you will do as I say."

"*Nay.*"

"*Aye,* I'm your husband."

"Pippa?"

The little voice was there again, haunting him. He didn't know how but he'd forgotten about the boy who was now insistently tugging on his trousers. He hoped the little boy wouldn't notice the hard evidence of his blatant arousal. He had to be too young to *ken* what he might be seeing. The boy was practically eye level to his groin. Roby groaned.

"I'm fine. Why are you down here in the kitchen? Don't you need to be with your teacher on the third floor?" Pippa asked, the remnants of her voice whispered softly against him.

"She sent me for a snack. Said it was on the table. Why were you going to put her on the table with her legs around your shoulders?"

The boy sounded way to curious for his good or his age. The answer to the question was damning.

A deep, low growl rumbled up from the pit of his stomach. He wasn't getting an answer to that question for at least ten years. "Just get the snack, young man. Pretend you didn't hear or see anything. Pippa and I are leaving."

He waited several torturous seconds. "Is he gone?"

"I think so. I'm not leaving with you." She found her voice. Defiant that was the only way he could describe the tone and tenor.

"If I have to toss you over my shoulder and carry you out. I will. Don't you think it would be wiser as well as more prudent if you don't give me a reason to remember your last disobedience?" His hands wound around her waist. "What's it going to be? Willing or not willing?"

She stiffened. He understood she was deciding. Her wishes were the same as his. She wanted him inside her now not when she damn well thought she could make him wait. Not when she thought he would forget what she did.

She tucked her top lip under her teeth. He squeezed.

"The carriage is waiting."

"I..."

"I?"

"Willing but I'm sleeping here tonight."

"That's a discussion for later that I'm not eager to waste time on at the moment. Right now, I've other things on my mind, as do you. Step one. All the way to the townhouse I want you thinking about step one. Want you thinking about me underneath this dress, caressing every sweet, swollen slick spot you possess. Bringing you to another climax with my words."

"Roby, stop."

She was panting. There was no other way to describe the short spurts of air she was trying to suck into her lungs.

"*Nay*, you're going to climax again, aren't you? Why should I stop? Can't think of one good reason to end this here and now. Want to see your face when you reach those dizzying heights that make me grin with pleasure." The devil but he was tormenting himself.

Her breasts were rising and falling, the tops painted with a sweet rosy blush. She lowered her lashes. Noticed his arousal beneath his trousers. He didn't dare let her touch him. He understood explicitly that touching him was on her mind. Her very first as well as her only thought.

"No, Pippa, not here. I was wrong. The children..." His pulse thundered as he enticed her to fulfillment, he did the same to himself.

Perhaps this coaxing talk wasn't such a good idea.

She was sweeping her tongue along her moist swollen mouth. "I could touch you, stick my hand inside your..."

He covered her mouth with his, silencing the words that could make the trip home even more uncomfortable than it was going to be now. "Don't you dare," he whispered, the words catching deep in the back of his throat as she placed her hand on him. "The devil you're very naughty, Pippa McKenna." His rumble of pleasure was low and deep. His voice husky "Don't ever change."

"I like to please you," she whispered slanting him a flirtatious grin as he took both her hands in his to stop her from further investigation of his manly parts.

"Let's go." He tugged her with him.

"I need to leave a note. Jillian..."

"All right, make it quick. Just tell her you left with me to go to the townhouse." He rocked back and forth on his heels before he jammed his hands through his hair. This was his doing. He created a sexual monster in his wife. He couldn't be more pleased. He would deal with her disobedience after they were both sated.

Perhaps by tomorrow morning.

The note writing was taking far too long. "Pippa, now. If you *ken* what's good for you. Now!"

"Just a moment," she breathed softly. "A few more words."

"I swear you're doing this on purpose." He strode to her, his hands clenching and unclenching. Quickly, he scooped her into his arms. The note fluttered to the ground, the pen plopped splattering ink on the floor.

They sat in the carriage. The time to the townhouse would take at least ten more minutes. He drew her onto his lap, one hand on her ankle. "Think we'll start with step one right now. Can't think of a better time. With your slippers off, I'll carry you to the bed after we finish on the table. By then we will have traveled through all the steps. We can begin anew."

"The servants," she said as she tilted her head back so he could reach her neck more easily.

"The devil with the servants. They need to get used to seeing me with you in a compromising position. You are my wife. You're mine, Pippa. Don't ever forget that fact." He was surprised when she pushed away from the trail of his lips down her neck.

"Don't you ever forget you're mine, Roby McKenna."

He laughed then he laughed again. "What will you do if I forget?" He was *verra* pleased with her statement. Jealousy suited her.

"Cut it off."

His laughter clogged his throat choking him. He imagined the knife as well as the sight of her wielding the weapon. "Don't worry. I'll never stray."

"You better not. If you do, you're the one who needs to worry."

"That's not because of your threat."

"Why then?"

He liked the way her smile reached her eyes. The golden flecks shimmered hot and potent. Enjoyed the jealousy.

"Are you probing for blatant flattery?"

He was ready willing and able to tell her whatever she might want to hear because it would all be true.

She tilted her head down. When she looked at him again, "Maybe. Maybe I want to hear how you feel about me."

"Words, my dear one, only words. I think I should show you *verra* slowly how I feel."

He squeezed her ankle, traced the soul of her foot with a fingertip. She twisted. A little mew of pleasure escaped her as she tossed her head back. Her body squirmed. Her breasts pushed against his chest. "Are you going to climax again?" he asked, as it seemed her eyes got that far away look, the slightly dazed one when her body was about to send her to that point of no return. "I'd like to see that. How many times can I bring you to that pinnacle of delight before we reach the townhouse, I wonder?"

"No, I won't. I'm not going to let you. Ohh...Roby!"

He found a well-known sensitive spot. That little place on her ankle always seemed to create sensations within her that left her crying with her need. Not as much though as he moved higher on her leg. Behind her knee always created a twist as well as a squirm. He meant to prolong this until they reached home. If she found her pleasure again, it made no difference to him. When it was his turn, she would be slick and swollen, soft and ready for him.

He would have her in his arms all night. All they would stop for would be food and drink. He would make sure there was plenty in the room. Two bottles of wine might be enough to last the night. In the morning, late in the morning, he would set her down for the lecture she knew was coming. Because, if possible, he meant to keep her awake the entire night. He still wanted to make love to her on the table. He would have to lock the doors to the dining room or perhaps excuse all the servants for the night. It would be nice to have her to himself as well as the house for twelve hours.

"Are you going to keep denying what you feel? What I make you feel? You know I'm the only one." He was laughing at the expression on her face.

She hit him, punched him with a closed fist on his chest. He obliged her by grunting. "You're cruel, Roby McKenna? I've never denied anything."

"For giving you pleasure?" This time he kept his grin behind his teeth.

"*Nay,* for teasing me so."

"It's so much fun," he laughed as he continued to coax and wheedle her to undeniable pleasures.

He counted three more repeats of the culmination of her ecstasy before they reached the townhouse. Inside, true to his word he carried her to the kitchen table where he proceeded to thoroughly make love to her. He pleasured her with his lips and tongue then his rod deep inside the velvet core he loved to feel surrounding him.

"Mine, only mine," he murmured. "I discovered you on a beautiful moonlit night. I'll never forget."

"One moonlit night," she murmured as he carried her upstairs. He set her on her feet.

"Shall we start from the beginning?"

"I'm exhausted, Roby McKenna. You can just...just..."

"Just what?"

"I want to eat."

He poured her a glass of wine. Touched the rim with his. "Drink up. Eat your fill."

Turning her so her back was to him, he unfastened what was left on her dress.

"I thought we were going to eat."

"You are. I'm going to undress my wife then I'm going to feed her."

His lips lingered on each bone down her back as he pushed the dress from her shoulders. The fabric pooled on the floor by her feet. When he was finished, "I don't want to stop looking at you."

"You're wearing too much," she told him as she reached for him.

He stepped away. "Not so fast." He chuckled watching her frown lines become more obvious. He fed her a piece of cheese let it slide across her lip before he set it inside her open mouth.

"What?" She ran her tongue across her lips. "Are you going to keep your trousers on? Not fair, you *ken*?"

She postured for him. Turned so he saw only her backside and a pouting nipple. He touched her lips with a plump blueberry, followed the path her tongue travelled with the berry. She shuddered, her body once again quivering her delight.

When he stepped in front of her, he ran his palm across the tight bud puckered enchantingly just for him. He stripped. Allowed her to see him. Several hours passed before they came out from beneath the covers to eat and drink again.

With a glass of wine perched on his belly and sated from the lovemaking, "When were you going to tell me?" He stared pointedly at her stomach as if that gesture would give her the clue she needed.

"Tell you what? That you're a wicked *mon*? I've done that. I've done that time and again. Still, you don't change."

He laughed enjoying the blank look she presented him with. "That you are carrying my child."

"I'm what?" Truly she did appear confused.

"You're increasing."

He grinned, pleased with himself as well as the fact he would be a father. To a shifter he hoped. Most likely since they both were shifters.

"How do you know? Are you just guessing?" She punched him in the chest.

"You haven't had your woman's time since that moonlit night when we met. Besides, shifters can sense it when his seed takes root inside his soul mate."

Her cheeks colored. Her breasts turned a creamy shade of pink. She turned her head away. "I haven't."

He pulled her closer. "You've no need for embarrassment. I'm your husband. Now that you carry our child, there is more need for you to take care with your person." He didn't see how carrying a child and taking care of that was more important than Pippa caring for herself.

In his mind the two concepts were inseparable.

"Are your pleased?"

"More than you can ever know. I will always blame all my happiness, yours too I hope, on one moonlit night in June. I love you, Phillipa McKenna."

"I thought you would never say the words. I love you, too, more than I can say."

She lifted her glass in salute, "To Roby's moonlit night."

"To Pippa's moonlit night."

Coming Soon by the Author
at
Rogue Phoenix Press

Made For Houston
Sweet McKenna Book Five

Chapter One

Scotland 1750

Houston, Dr. Stuart, stepped back slanting a look at the little freckle faced, red headed boy sitting on his table. The boy wore a pained look on that cherubic face of his. He was barely five. It was the third time in a month that Mrs. MacKay sat nearby, shaking her head. The boy was a little hellion except when he was asleep. At least that was what his mother continued to tell him.

"I've warned him a hundred times he was going to fall out of that tree. I tell him not to walk along the top of the fence. He's not supposed to go in the shed with the cows or the field with the bull. Does he listen to me? No. He thinks he can fly. Last time it was a concussion, the time before that a sprained ankle. Now he's got a broken arm. What next?" She threw up her hands in desperation as she stared at the boy.

"I believe he has no fear and that I'll see him more as he grows older. For now, though, he'll be limited in what he can do." Houston had a difficult time stopping the laughter that bubbled deep in his belly. His brother, Kit, was just like this boy. He didn't fear anything. In his life his brothers Kit and Riley along with his cousins, Roby and Brady, got into more scrapes than he could count. They defied all rules of common sense.

"Don't know if anything will stop that boy. I tell him time and again not to push the limits. It's almost as if I'm puttin' ideas into his head by warning him not to do something." She was pointedly shaking one finger at him. "Well, you can't be climbin' the trees for a while. Swingin' on them as if you was bein' a monkey."

"Make him keep the splint on his arm. He needs to rest the bone and muscle to assist the healing. You're absolutely right, he can't be using it to act like a little monkey. This is going to take some time to mend. You can give him willow bark tea to ease the pain but nothing stronger."

Dr. Houston helped the boy down from the table before patting him on his head. He shuffled to the cabinet where he kept medicine, handing her the willow bark. "Bring him back in two days. At that time, I'll rework the splint, check to make sure the arm is recovering properly. He'll most likely have it in tatters by then. Remember, rest and time are the most important factors for him to get back to normal."

Houston watched the woman with her child leave his office. Wondered if he would ever have a wife, family too. He sat down on a chair as he stretched his leg out in front of him. His foot ached. It always did when there was a change in the weather. He figured they were in for snow soon if it wasn't falling already. When he peered outside, the sky was gray darkening as the seconds ticked by. Lights from the buildings cast an eerie glow on the surroundings.

He thought on the day, five years ago when his toes were crushed in a steel trap. In his cat form he'd been racing across a deserted part of the highlands. Agony tripped across his body, swirling through his veins to trigger all his nerves. His roar reverberated through the valley. As his cat he couldn't spring the trap. Too many English soldier roamed the area for him to shift back to human. He had to take the risk. There was no other choice. He could hardly stay pinned to this spot while praying some kind soul would chance upon him. Houston wasn't sure if his prayers had been answered when a young girl found him. He recalled how soft and gentle her voice was, almost a whisper in the air.

She sprung the trap. When she touched his mangled foot, he felt a surge of protectiveness swamp him. Nerve endings burned. Her caress, gentle as it was eased some of the pain. She brought out a vial of lavender oil, rubbed the essence on his paw.

After he limped back to his clothes where he could dress, he thought of that moment. With tenderness, she rubbed his head. Told him all would be better. Her last words to him were to make sure the bones were set properly.

They had not been set correctly. At least he didn't think so. Believed to this very day if they had been he would be able to walk without a limp. At the time he knew nothing about doctoring. Apparently, the bone-setter didn't either.

Ah, Mrs. Mackay had four children, a fifth one on the way. He tried to explain to her that she should stop having children. Too many could cost her her life or that of a child. She laughed telling him he should talk to her husband about that. How to approach a man to tell him he should only have sex with his wife at certain times of the month or that he should take his great rod from her body before he ejaculated?

It wasn't a conversation he would relish. Knew for the sake of her health, he should do so.

Actually, he felt it was a conversation he should initiate with Mr. McKay.

Pondering on that thought further, maybe he would do just that. He knew her husband loved her. Wouldn't want to see anything happen to her. She told him paying attention to her cycle wouldn't work because she wasn't regular.

Oh, he closed his eyes for a moment thinking. Perhaps it was time to move on with his career. He received an invitation to study with one of the finest surgeons of his time in Edinburgh. His earlier apprenticeship taught him a great deal. He was more than just a bone-setter. He was a surgeon. He knew things. Understood how a human body worked. Never believed in bloodletting. Never thought it would cure a disease. What he did know was that people died when they lost too much blood.

Maybe for a short time he'd go to Edinburgh then he thought to be close to his family as well as his extended family, the McKenna's. His mother, Brenna McKenna, wed his father Alistair Stuart. Both he and Kit had the raven black hair and silver blue eyes of the McKenna clan. His littlest brother, Riley, received the red hair and green eyes from their father. Riley's mischievous temperament fit the color of his hair perfectly.

More often than not he found himself homesick, wishing to be back in the highlands. He wasn't cut out for living in the city nor was he meant to live away from his clan. He missed the births as well as the marriages. He knew Crissie had two children, Brady and Lilly two babes as well. He was the oldest.

Yes, it was time to think about selling his practice so he could move home. When he first arrived here, it had been an adventure the land almost as wild and untamed as his homeland. He couldn't remember the last time he shifted. With a long-drawn-out sigh, he realized it might be much longer before he was able to do so. Even in the lowlands there were Sassenach patrols. Now with his schooling and apprenticeship in Edinburgh coupled with the year he spent here, he'd been away for a long time, too long.

Houston wandered upstairs to his living quarters. It was three o'clock, almost time to close up shop unless there was an emergency or Sara Jane's baby decided to arrive early. If that happened, he would be gone most of the night, possibly into the morning hours. He flexed the toes on his bad foot, reminded himself he should not walk with a limp. He needed to do better.

A groan emanated from his belly at the sound of his office door being opened. It had been three days since the simpering Marie Hughes came to him with some imaginary complaint. Her family was the wealthiest family in the small town of Selkirk, Scotland. For some reason she decided she saw more in him than he wanted any woman to see, any woman except his mate. She wasn't his mate. He groaned again, his belly coiling. If he was to find his special woman, he would have to get out of Selkirk. Although Roby found his mate in the most remarkable manner, at the end of the hangman's noose. How he realized that fact from the tales he heard via letter was beyond him.

Making his way downstairs, he cursed the change in weather. The snow had not started yet but it would in minutes. If it did before he could give Marie a diagnosis, he would be obliged to walk her home. She would have thought of that, planned for that very scenario.

When he opened the door and saw her, she appeared suspiciously healthy. Her welcoming smile was coy, deliberate. Her head must be whirling as she sought symptoms for some imaginary illness. Just last week she had a strange ringing in her ears. Said she felt dizzy. Pretended to faint while she was sitting on his table.

That wasn't well thought out by her. She should have waited then fainted when she stood. He would have caught her in his arms. The devil but he was glad she did not. Today he wondered what she would come up with. What fake illness assailed her? Her dark brown eyes gazed at him, trailed up then down his body as she took stock of him, lingering in strategic places meant to seduce him. Unable to help his disgust, he shuddered. He didn't know why she was putting her hopes on him. He wasn't rich. Hell, but there were dozens of wealthy young men in surrounding towns she could set her hooks on.

Why him?

The rush of air that passed his lips was meant to remind him that he was a professional. It didn't matter that he was the most eligible bachelor in this small out-of-the-way town. He was the only doctor. Marie wasn't the only unmarried lady who sought ways to come meet him. He had to admit she was the prettiest as well as the most imaginative.

"Well, hello Houston," she greeted him with the slight lisp she affected for reasons he couldn't understand. Her smile was brilliant though, her eyes brilliant.

"Marie," he returned pleasantly. "What can I do for you today?" It wasn't worth getting into another argument. Miss Hughes was a much more appropriate way to address her. He just didn't have the energy. It wouldn't get him anywhere if he tried.

She nodded, walking by him to sit on the table. He wasn't going to examine her even though he was sure it was exactly what she wanted. She leaned back placing her hands behind her for support. Her small sassy breasts pushed upward on display for him.

"Do you have to be so formal?" she asked, lowering her dark lashes so they fanned out across her ivory cheekbones. She opened them while she waited for an answer. "I much prefer a bit of casualness."

"I assume you're here with some sickness you want cured." His words held a wealth of sarcasm. As always, the tone slipped past Marie. "We should go about the business of curing you. What ails you this time?"

"Well, I've been having headaches." She looked straight at him as she narrowed her eyes feigning the pain that would go along with what she claimed. "Very bad headaches. They happen most every day. I have to take to my bed when they occur."

"Do you have one now?" he asked wondering what excuse she would give him as he knew she wasn't in pain. She just didn't know how to pretend the agony she was trying for. "I won't give you laudanum. Willow bark tea is the best. The taste is bitter. However, with enough honey the taste is palatable. The tea will help without any lasting effects. I've some lavender oil you can massage on your temples that might also help."

"The stuff is horrible," she told him grimacing. "I've still got the willow bark you gave me last time. I'm might try the lavender oil though. It smells divine."

"You didn't use it?" he quarried trying not to smirk at the look of utter distaste on her face. Then I won't be needing to give you anything else." He extended a hand to help her down.

She slid from the table with a tiny puff of air as if she was exasperated with him. "My family is having a get together, well, a small celebration Saturday night if you'd like to come, I'd love to see you there. We could dance. It will be ever so much fun."

"Thank you," he told her, hesitating while knowing he would never attend. Interesting though, before his accident he would have attended just to mingle, to meet new people. He didn't care any longer. That wasn't entirely true. It was just he didn't like small talk or flirting girls. "That's actually quite nice of you to ask," he told her as he tried to think of a polite way to say no.

"Then you'll be there?" she smiled. This time it wasn't coy or affected just sincere. "I'll look forward to a dance or two."

He marveled at the nice change. "Maybe. Sara Jane's baby is due anytime. You know I don't dance." That was something else he missed, dancing. He thought it had been a longtime since he held a woman in his arms. The strange thing was he didn't have one inclination to hold Marie Hughes.

"Well, that doesn't make a wit of difference to me." She stared at his foot then back to his face. "We can stroll through the gardens, hand in hand. You can kiss me if you like. I believe I would like that."

"That's a bit premature, don't you think? Besides it's winter. The weather will be far too cold for a late-night stroll." He was thinking that was a blatant invitation only a cad would take advantage of. He also didn't have one inclination to feel Marie's lips beneath his.

His foot wasn't diseased yet she always had such a look of distaste when the shape of his maligned foot was brought to attention. He wondered what she would think if he did take more notice of her or if she actually saw his foot. He didn't want to find out. She would have to hunt up some other poor man to finagle into marriage vows.

It wasn't going to be him.

On top of his disability if she knew he was a shifter, she'd most likely faint dead away.

The door banged open, shaking the walls along with the glass vials that were on the shelves around the room, startling both of them. He jumped at the sound, his mind reacting to the pending emergency. His heart thundered. He was thinking ahead.

"Stick!" Marie cried out stepping back. "What are you doing here? Barging in like that?"

Stick ignored Marie and bent his attention toward him. "You've got to come, Doc. Got to come now!"

Stick stood in the doorway. He was a young man, tall and skinny, blinding red hair. He was known around town as someone who didn't have all his wits about him. Stick was nice enough. Sometimes he didn't make a great deal of sense. This time there was no question about what he wanted.

Holding her elbow, Houston saw Marie to the door. When he peered outside, there was still enough light left for her to walk home in safety. Snow wasn't falling, might not for the next five minutes or more. She would be fine. Her coat was warm. He felt as if he dodged something. Next, he felt as if he was about to meet his destiny head on. He suddenly remembered the young girl who helped him so long ago.

"Got to come, Doc. He's hurt real bad, somethin' terrible. Hurry!"

"Who's hurt?" Houston had his medical bag in hand as he strode toward Stick, his mind whirling with possibilities. "Who did you say?" Houston asked again. This time he pulled his hat from the coat stand.

Stick was backing out the doorway, turning toward the frozen rutted road. Houston slipped his coat on and followed the gangly young man to an old wagon sitting across from his office. A young woman stood in front of the mule drawn wagon. She was wringing her hands, the saddest look on her face he'd ever seen. Despite the despair, she was beautiful, ethereal in the fading afternoon light. Her golden blond hair was braided down her back, the tip brushing across her slim waist. Because of the brewing storm, the day was too dark to see the color of her eyes. His gut clenched when he saw the ribbons of tears sliding down her cheeks.

"It's Shadow," Stick said as if he thought the village doc could do anything. "Fix him up. Her dah kicked him in the ribs. He's real old."

"I don't…" He cleared his throat looking from the girl to stick. "I don't fix dogs. I'm a human doctor." The devil but would he refuse to fix a black panther if one was brought to him? One of his own if the person was in cat form? *Nay,* he would have to try.

"Please just look at him. He needs you. I can't do anything for him," she spoke softly, so softly he barely heard. It was a whisper in the chilling winter air.

Snow threatened.

Cold air burned his lungs with ice.

Beneath his breath he swore. A moment of thought, with another soft curse he climbed onto the back of the wagon. He was going against training. He ran his hand down the animal's side. He touched the dog's nose. The tip was dry and hot with fever. Bending close to the animal's side, he listened. It wasn't good news he'd give the girl. The dog was going to die. When was the only question?

"Grizzly kicked him. Hard. He got in his way." She spoke again a soft sigh caught in the chill. "Can you fix his rib?"

"Grizzly?" Houston looked up. "Is that someone?" He had too many questions at the moment. He supposed it could have been the mule or a horse. Was Grizzly her dah? Did she live with a man who would kick an old dog instead of step around him?

"Her dah," Stick said offering answers before she could. He was eager where she was reticent. "Her dah gets mean drunk every night. Got to stay out of his way. Sometimes she has to sleep outside. Shadow was sleeping that's all. Didn't see him coming so he could get out of his way."

Houston wanted to hear from her even though she held back. He looked at her but his question was meant for Stick. "Were you there?"

Houston asked staring at the girl who didn't seem to want to say anything more. He found he wanted to hear her voice again. The sound reminded him of another time, another place.

He just couldn't remember.

In time he would.

"No, he wasn't," she said as she settled down beside her old dog. Her hand rested gently on his back. "He met me on my way here. I don't mind if he talks for me. Stick knows the story."

"Don't work on animals," Houston said again, wishing he didn't have to tell her no. What did he know about mending dogs? It couldn't be too different. There were basics.

I can at least try.

"Can't be much different from humans," Stick spoke again not wanting him to give up. Nervous energy abounded around the young man as he shifted from one foot to the next. "You got to do this for Leah. Shadow's one of her only friends besides me. She can't lose him. Who will she have if Shadow's gone?"

Leah, it was a nice name. Seemed to fit her. Stick was her only friend. A girl as beautiful as Leah should have lots of friends. He hadn't seen her in the village or heard of her. She swiped away tears. Maybe she was as elusive as her voice.

"I'll take a look." He was a damn fool for giving in to emotions better left alone.

Just from what little he saw of the poor animal, he wasn't going to be able to help. He didn't want to get her hopes up. This just wasn't something he needed at the moment. He swept up the dog. His foot ached as he stumbled slightly on his way to the building. Stick rushed in front, opening the door as he reached his office then standing in the way as he tried to navigate through the slight opening that was left.

After he set Shadow by the wood stove, he rubbed the dog's ears. He didn't understand how but he felt Leah's pain as if it was his own. It seemed to touch his soul. She sat next to him stroking her dog, murmuring soft endearments to the animal. She stood, looking at him, silently questioning.

Her eyes were blue, the color of a summer sky.

Next to him, she was cold, her breathing shallow. He wanted to fold her into his arms. Needed to find a means to do away with the pain freezing her. It was a task that couldn't be accomplished. It was also something that went deeper than the possible loss of her dog.

"He has two broken ribs. At least one has punctured his lung. There isn't anything I can do for him except make him comfortable. I'll give him something to ease the pain. Keep water by his side if he wants to drink."

She wasn't sobbing. Although tears were sliding faster down her cheeks, she cried without making a sound. He hated what he told her. She thanked him with that soft whispery voice he would never get used to but wanted to hear until he remembered exactly where he heard the sound before. It sounded as if it hurt her to talk. She should have someone to confide in besides a mean drunk and this young man who meant well however...

"Don't think he'll make it through the night." Houston dropped a blanket over the scruffy dog, his muzzle white with age. The animal's breathing was labored but after the small amount of opium he gave the dog, he breathed easier. Shadow would sleep until the end.

"Can she stay here with him?" Stick asked as he took her hands in his. "I'll go up the mountain to tell Grizzly she's staying so he won't be worrying none about her."

"Grizzly won't worry about me. He's not really my dah. Just my step-dah. What he will be is angry if I don't get his supper ready. I have to go."

"It wouldn't look good if she stayed. Would ruin her." Houston had the strange feeling she wouldn't care. He would though. Somehow, he understood she was special.

"She can't go home," Stick insisted, seemingly worried about her as he looked outside. It was obvious how much the young man cared for the girl. He was still standing in the open doorway. Behind him the snow began to fall. "It's too far and too cold."

"Where do you live?" Houston asked wondering how long it would take her to get home, a few minutes or an hour or two. He had a gut feeling that with the old mule pulling the wagon it would take her more than an hour.

"She lives up the mountain. Just her and her dah," Stick spoke up again looking from the darkening sky to the animal in front of the stove.

Leah placed her hand on his. The touch was light and warmed him even though her fingers were cold. Houston didn't want to think about her riding up the mountain all by herself or with just Stick beside her.

"It's alright," she spoke again sensing his fears. "I've got a pistol."

Hell, the woods were filled with predators, man along with beasts. He stood, stretching as his tired muscles pulled and ached. He thought of the lost sleep. "I'll go with you."

She shrunk away from him seemingly appalled at his suggestion. "No, no, that won't be necessary."

"I'm going with her to the turnoff," Stick offered with a lift to his shoulders. "We don't need you to go all the way to her house."

He wasn't at all sure this was the right decision. Didn't want to be afraid for her though he was. She slanted him a wan smile as she sat down on the floor next to Shadow. It seemed she intended to say goodbye. As she placed her face on the dog's head, a small sob erupted from her body, her shoulders shaking with the pain.

"I'll miss you," he heard the soft murmur of words. "You've been a dear friend."

"You can come back tomorrow," he offered believing the dog would die during the night. He told her he would make Shadow comfortable. The only thing that would truthfully ease his pain would be death. He didn't know if he wanted it to come before she arrived in the morning or after. Houston supposed she would want to hold his head in her lap when he sipped in his last breath from the air.

He found he wanted to see her again.

"Thank you," she told him before turning to look at Stick. "We should go now. What time?"

"I'm usually up by six."

She nodded. It was her invitation to Stick to follow her out as well as her commitment to return to see Shadow journey to another life. Houston lightly held her elbow as he walked her to the door then across the road to her wagon. He helped her up.

A chilling wind gust caught him by surprise. Snow fell, swirled around him. She would have a cold drive home. He didn't like sending her home by herself. He watched as the pair boarded the wagon. She held the reigns lightly in her hands as slowly the old mule started down the road, the wagon wheels crunching snow as they made their way along the deserted route.

Houston watched them as they disappeared into the night. Why he waited for a few more minutes he didn't know. He drew in a long draught of air before stuffing his hands in his pockets. He ran to the door. This time he'd neglected his coat.

Standing inside the door, he brushed snow from his trousers then rubbed his hands together to warm them. She didn't wear gloves. Her hands would freeze. He wondered if she owned a pair of gloves. The concern he felt for this ethereal woman was unusual. The sensation was something he'd never before experienced.

Shadow moaned softly. It was a ghostly sound. He shivered. He knew the old dog was ready to say goodbye to the world. Ready to face new challenges. Houston sat down beside him, stroking the rough fur. It seemed to make the dog feel better. His gaze turned toward him, his lids lowered for a moment almost as if he thanked him.

Houston tucked the blanket around Shadow before heading upstairs to his rooms. The cook left dinner for him as always. He sat down to the venison stew provided for him by one of the families. He didn't get paid much. Instead of groats, the people of the parish provided him with fresh game, some with baked bread, biscuits along with muffins straight from their ovens in the mornings. Sometimes he would find a pie sitting inside his office door. More often than not he'd find wheels of cheese in the waiting room when he walked downstairs.

It wasn't a bad life.

He needed to start over. As he slipped off his shoes and socks, he stared at his feet, his mangled foot. Rubbing his hand across the bones that had not been set well, he wondered if he could break them again, in the process making it right. The pain would be excruciating. The days of recovery too many. Was healing his foot worth the price he would have to pay in time and pain?

From the side table he uncorked a bottle of lavender oil then rubbed it on the mangled toes. The massage felt good, the scent relaxing. Once again, he thought of the girl so long ago who freed him from the steel trap. She carried lavender oil with her that day. She rubbed the medicine on his foot.

Something about Leah reminded him of the girl. That had been more than five years ago. She must have been fourteen or fifteen then...

~ * ~

Leah understood Shadow was going to die. She supposed she'd known that truth since she left with him in her wagon. There was nothing she could do for the dog so she tried the only thing she could think of.

She brought him to Doc Houston.

Thinking of Grizzly as her dah never sat right with her. He was mean. Had never treated her mother right and only tolerated her. She was nothing to him when she was younger. Now that she was older, she'd become his servant.

She never could figure out why her mother married that man. Her mother always told her she needed his protection. Leah didn't believe a woman had to have a man's protection to get on with her life. She always wished her mom had more faith in herself. The two of them would have been better off if they stayed in the highlands. The McKenna clan would have helped them with anything they needed, would have made sure they wanted for nothing. McKennas were good people.

She offered to work in the kitchen at the McKenna keep. Her mother could sew. She was an excellent seamstress. Could have supplemented their income with her work. Instead, she married a no good, mean drunk who had a hard time keeping a job.

She didn't mind living so far away from the village. It was peaceful when Grizzly wasn't around. Grizzly wasn't his real name. They used to call him Bear, but someone who went to the colonies, a trapper, came back and dubbed him Grizzly. Said it was the biggest meanest old bear he'd ever encountered. Had been lucky to get away with his life. Bear was more a grizzly than just a bear. He even had a hump on his back like she was told that a big grizzly had. Of course, Bear probably wasn't his real name either.

Leah hoped that when she got up to the cabin, he would be asleep. She didn't want to talk to him. He would want to talk if he was awake. She didn't have anything to say to him. If he would just tell her he was sorry for what happened, she could forgive him.

He wouldn't.

He never apologized for anything. He was always cursing her, telling her she was no good, telling her she should speak up. Wasn't normal for a woman to be so quiet. She didn't want to talk louder. Didn't want to talk to him at all. What she wanted was to visit her sanctuary. It would be too cold for that. Perhaps in the morning if the weather let up a bit, if it stopped snowing. From past experience she knew it wouldn't.

"What you thinkin' about. Leah? Shadow? He's going to be alright, you know," Stick asked as if her silence was getting to him. He didn't like it when she didn't talk to him. Sometimes she just wanted to think. Stick never understood any of that.

"Yes and no. Mostly thinking I'd like it to stop snowing and warm up a bit." She tugged her coat sleeves lower so they would cover her fingers. They felt like ice. Might be ice by the time she made it home. She was glad before she left, she made sure dinner was simmering over the fire. It was one less thing she had to think about.

"How come you told him you had a pistol when you don't?" Stick was rummaging in the back just to make sure, she supposed. He wouldn't find one.

Leah shrugged her shoulders pondering the question. "I suppose to make him feel better. Didn't need him taking me home or feeling obliged to do so. I'm not some fragile flower."

"You look pretty fragile to me. You *ken* you always smell like wildflowers."

She slanted him a look of reproach sending him a message that if he asked her a question, he should honor her and let her answer. "Don't want to be obligated to any man more than I have to be. He's helping Shadow just by keeping him warm and free of pain. Doc doesn't need to do anything else for me. Nothing I might have to repay. Don't have any means to repay the man."

Stick didn't have anything to say to that. He held his tongue behind his teeth simply because he couldn't refute anything she said. Men were creeps. Except for Stick. That was because he didn't think or act like a man. Didn't think like anyone but himself. Stick cared about her. As far as she could tell, she was the only living breathing person in the small village of Selkirk who cared about Stick.

She probably saw Michael Graham as well as his two buddies

before Stick sighted them only a second or two later. She squared her shoulders. Stick started quivering. He should leave now, hightail it home before Michael and his friends got closer.

"Michael won't hurt you. I won't let him. If you want, you should go now before they get too close," she told him even though she knew he didn't believe her while at the same time, she wasn't entirely sure she believed herself. Stick didn't move. He whimpered. Over the years Michael changed from an arrogant bully to an arrogant bastard. The same could be said for his friends, only worse if that was possible. She wasn't quite sure what the difference was nevertheless she knew there was a difference.

Stick seemed frozen to the seat.

When they were abreast of the men, Michael stopped the mule before taking the reins from her hand. He looked into her eyes, held her attention too long while her breath caught in the back of her throat. She didn't like the feelings that look from him generated. He wanted more from her than she was willing to give.

"What are you doing, Michael. Give those back to me. It's cold out here. All I want right now is to get home before I freeze." She found herself breathing hard, her heart ricocheting beneath her ribs. Her body trembled.

"What are you doing in the village? It's a little late don't you think?" Michael moved closer to the wagon, to her.

"Shadow was hurt. I took him to Doc Houston," she said in her paper-thin voice. "Need to be going before the snow gets falling too fast." She didn't want to talk to Michael. Didn't want to be late getting back up the mountain. She was already late. Grizzly would be swearing at her. If he wasn't dead asleep drunk.

"Not going to let you go, at least not until you grant me a few seconds of your time. Want to talk to you, Leah. It's important, you know. You've got to have a few seconds for me. Need to ask you something important. Could change your life." He set one of his large hands on her knee and squeezed. She felt a moment of fear. Pushed it aside telling herself he wouldn't hurt her. No, he wanted something else from her. Something she wasn't willing to give.

Resigned, she knew he would hold onto the reins until he had his way. She was helpless to stop him. All she could do was brace for whatever he wanted. So far, he'd not hurt her. In fact, he stopped his friends from hurting her once several years ago. It was at that time he seemed to change, at least his attitude toward her altered.

She'd been trying to walk across a bridge down by the old mill. He, with his friends saw her, teased her. Blocking her way, they kept her from the other side. She told him how mean he was. Informed him also that she thought he was better than acting the bully. It was then a strange look came over his face. He stabbed his hands into his hair. After a pause, he told his buddies to stop. With that said from the leader of the little gang, they allowed her to cross. Now, it seemed he was always trying to collect on that day. Told her she owed him.

"Can you make it fast. I've a way to go and it's cold out here. By the time I get up that mountain, the snow could be knee deep." She felt as if she was repeating herself. She was. He wasn't listening.

"Well, I'd be happy to go with you. If I was driving, I could make sure to keep you warm," he said his grin growing wider as he said the words. "I'd wrap my arms around you, let you slip your tiny little hands inside my coat. Maybe anywhere else you'd like to glide them."

She shivered and clenched her teeth. Ignoring his comment, she went on to ask, "What is it you want to talk about?"

He cleared his throat. For a brief moment, she thought he might be nervous as she watched him shuffle his feet. "My father has promoted me, Leah. I've a room of my own now. It's over the tavern. The room, well, it's not just one but a suite of rooms. Even a bathing room just for me and my wife when I have one. Just got me a big feather bed, big enough my feet won't hang over the edge when I sleep. Plenty of room for you too when you say I do to me."

She didn't know what to tell him. It all sounded very nice for him. However, Leah didn't understand what his news had to do with her or why she might do any of those things he suggested. She'd never given him a single indication she was interested in spending her life with him as his wife or in any other capacity. She was growing more and more impatient. "Michael, is that it? Are you done?"

"No," he responded quickly giving her knee another quick squeeze. "You know how much I like you. We could get married and live there. I'm sure my father will be giving me more promotions. The inn is doing well. We'll have plenty of money. I could give you things you don't have now. You wouldn't have to live with ol' Grizzly." He touched her arm as if she would like the caress. She jerked away. He scowled at her. "You shouldn't be jerking away from me, Leah. Who else is giving you an offer of marriage?" He looked to the Doc's office down the street. "Certainly not Houston Stuart the town doc."

"I can't marry you, Michael. We don't love each other." If there was one thing her mother inadvertently taught her was that she should love the man she married. Nothing else would do. Nor could she ever wed a man who made her skin crawl, even if he would be able to give her things. She didn't need monetary things. She craved an intimacy that would permeate soul deep. A relationship that would fill her heart with love.

"If you won't marry me, will you go to the dance with me on Saturday night? I would come up the mountain to get you, bring you home too if you'd like. You'd be safe with me."

"You *ken* I cannot. Grizzly would never let me go anywhere with a man." She reached for the reins. He tugged them away making it harder for her. "Michael, please, let me go. I need to get home."

"I don't know anything of the sort. You can't stay up on the mountain for the rest of your life. You need a man to protect you. Grizzly is going to make your life harder and harder. He's not going to be around for many more years. Don't turn down my offers. You might not ever get another one."

"I cannot go to the dance or anything else with you." She felt her exasperation all the way to the pit of her belly. She didn't know what to do. Didn't know how to make him understand.

Michael continued on ignoring her requests, repeating himself as if she didn't hear the first time. "Grizzly's not going to be around forever, you know. One of these days he's going to drink himself to death. You can count on that. I won't be around forever offering to make you an honest woman. You *ken* there are other women in this village, women who would like to marry me."

Once more Leah grabbed for the reins to no avail. "I am an honest woman. No man can change that fact one way or the other. Why don't you become an honest man and…" she heaved in a long breath of air searching for the right words.

"And?" One of his dark brown eyebrows arched upward in question.

She let out a long-exasperated sigh. "I don't know. Leave me alone. I can't go to the dance with you or anyone. Now, let me go. It's getting colder by the minute. I don't want to freeze before I get home. How many times do I have to say the words before you'll listen to me?"

She had stuffed her hands in her pockets a few minutes ago. They warmed. A few minutes exposed to the frigid air they would once again feel like ice.

"You boys go on to the tavern. Think I'll ride a ways with Leah. Want to make sure she stays safe. I'll catch up to you later."

His boys immediately left. They always did what Michael said. When Michael turned his attention to Stick, he leapt off the wagon intent on getting as far away from Michael as he could get as fast as possible. She watched as he disappeared down the street, the falling snow finally hiding him from view.

Michael still held the reins in his hands. He leapt onto the seat sitting close to her, closer than she felt comfortable. The mule started plodding down the road. She turned her face away from him, afraid now that they would be alone together. Leah didn't want to be alone with a man, not now not ever. Unless perhaps, it was the doc. She paused staring back the way they'd come, looked toward Doc Houston's place. A tiny quiver whipped through her belly. Heat pooled inside.

She didn't know what to make of the feeling.

"You can't stay with Grizzly all your life. You're a grown woman. I want you to think about me. Think about the proposal along with all the other things I've told you." He wrapped one of his arms around her, tugged her closer. He was strong and tall, a well-built man. She knew trying to distance herself was futile. He was right. There were other girls in Selkirk who would like his attention. She just wasn't one of those girls.

They rode in silence for a while. She heard the crunch of the snow beneath the mule's feet coupled with the wagon wheels the sound was soothing. She didn't have anything more to say. He didn't either. The flakes were freezing to the ground as soon as they fell. The weather smelled cold combined with the scent of the surrounding pines if that was possible. They passed by the MacKay house. Lights blazed in all the downstairs rooms. Brenda was pregnant again. She would be kneading bread and setting it aside to rise for the night. Her mouth watered thinking about the yeasty taste of the fresh baked bread.

He turned left toward the mountain. The winding trail in front of them would take her home. Grizzly would be angry if she showed up with a man. He told her more than once she wasn't to go gettin' herself with child. He wasn't going to pay to bring up some man's bastard. Michael would have to get off soon.

Her stepfather didn't have to worry about anything like that. She wasn't going to give herself to some man then find herself in the family way. She knew what was right from what was wrong.

"You should join your friends before they start rumors about us. You can't ride with me all the way home." She turned to Michael, for the first time looking at him, his profile.

He was a handsome man with chestnut colored hair. She couldn't see his eyes now but they were a deep, dark brown almost matching the color of his hair. His nose straight, his jaw hard and unyielding, she didn't doubt he'd make some woman a good husband. It just wasn't going to be her. She tugged in a long breath of frigid air.

"No rumors. I won't let that happen, Leah. If you haven't figured it out yet, I care about you." He pulled on the reins before hopping from the wagon. "Don't like the outcome of the conversation. Fact of the matter is, even if I don't like what you're telling me it will have to do for now. You going to be alright?"

"I won't change my mind. You deserve a woman who can love you. That isn't me." She would never lie to him, or take something she didn't want.

"I've been told love can grow when given time." He was making another argument then he'd most likely think of some other reason to present to her.

She wasn't going to argue with the man. It wouldn't get her anywhere. "Thank you for taking me this far. It only takes me about fifteen minutes now to get home. I'll be fine."

"You're welcome. I'm not going to stop asking, Leah. You can count on it. There isn't anyone else around that I'd like to be my wife." After he jumped from the wagon, he gave the backside of the mule a swat then whistling, showed her his back as he headed into town, after that on to the tavern. With a tiny shake to her head, she watched him saunter down the old trail. No, he probably would not quit asking anytime soon. She was sure, though, in time he would turn his attention to someone else.

The snow let up a minute as she moved farther into the forested area. Somewhere in the wintery sky an owl hooted. Another answered. A wolf howled in the thick stormy air. Wind shrilled through barren trees. She passed by the rundown Fletcher place. Even with the moisture cleansing the air, she smelled the garbage along with the ill-kept pens that housed the hogs. They had one horse. It's stable was muddied, mired in goop. One light burned in a back room. They had two children. Friendly little mites even if they were always dirty.

If she had children...

She stifled her laughter. She didn't think she would ever have children even though she wanted at least one. Sometimes she didn't think she would ever come down off the mountain even though she yearned to return to the highlands. She didn't suppose there would be much left of her home now after five years of emptiness. Maybe if she could save a few coins, she could return and see what was still standing. If she were lucky, no one would have moved into the abandoned home. She could clean up the dirt, make it habitable.

Leah saw the light from the fireplace in their tiny hut. The golden-red flames glowed in the darkness. Shadow would have heard the wagon lumber up the road. He would have greeted her with barks if he weren't staying comfortable in Doc Houston's office. He rested by the fire. He was warm. Comfortable.

After taking care of the mule, she walked into the house. Sincerely, she didn't want to go inside. Wouldn't if it weren't so darn cold. She swallowed hard before stiffening her shoulder to brace herself for her stepfather's spewing of his wrath. Sometime before marrying her mother and now he found religion. Of course, he was pious only when it suited him.

"Where you been, Girl?" Grizzly was sitting at the table, drinking from the jug. A dirty plate sat in front of him. At least he had dinner. She would only have to wait a short amount of time for him to sleep.

"Took Shadow to the village. Thought maybe Doc Houston could mend him." She wanted to hear an apology from the man. He wouldn't apologize. "You hurt him real bad."

"Can he fix him up?" He drank long and deep before wiping his mouth with the back of his hand. His fierce scowl told her, he'd already heard enough about her dog.

"Don't think so," she murmured as she bent over to stir the stew she left. "Have you eaten?" she asked even though she saw the dirty plate sitting in front of him. Sometimes he wanted more. Problem was he was too lazy to dish up the food himself. She would have to get it for him.

"*Aye.* You be goin' back tomorrow to bring the mangy cur home? That dog's not worth your time. He's old and worn out, good for nothin' if you ask me. Don't suppose you would be askin' though. Can't even move to get out of my way. Nearly killed myself trippin' over him." Grizzly pounded his fist on the table, rocking the spoon that was resting in his plate.

Leah ignored him as she tried to keep the evil thoughts from pounding into her head. Sometimes her mind spun in the wrong directions. At this moment she didn't have one good thought for her stepfather. She pulled in a sip of air to steady herself. Let it out slowly as she fought for the patience she needed to deal with this irascible old man.

"Yes. I've got to see Shadow in the morning." *Before he dies or help bury him if he doesn't make it through the night. From the look on Houston's face when he told her he would make him comfortable, she didn't think Shadow would see another day.*

She understood she needed to stay out of Grizzly's way. He would badger her until she would have to leave, go outside to wait until he fell asleep. She dished up a bowl of stew for herself then sat down in the tiny alcove where her bed was fastened. She ate until she was satisfied. She cleaned up the dishes. Scooped what was left of the stew into a jar before setting the container in a cold room just off the back porch.

Grizzly spent an hour mumbling and drinking before he stripped to his underwear. He settled in his bed, the jug of whiskey dangling from his fingers. When he started snoring, Leah let out a tiny sigh of relief. He would still be asleep when she left to go down the mountain in the morning.

She curled up on her bed, her hands under her cheek. Her fingers were still cold. She rose to put another log on the fire then returned to the bed.

Shadow...

Doc Houston didn't lie to her. Didn't come right out and tell her the truth either. He would keep her dog comfortable. She understood what that meant. After she thought of shadow along with the fact he would be in a better place where there was no pain and no Grizzly, all she could think about was Houston's strong gentle hands, his kind silver-blue eyes.

~ * ~

"She loves me. I can hear it in her voice." Michael sat down with his friends, Quaid and Ryan. He didn't truly understand his attraction to Leah Kennedy. The devil but he was enamored of her. Leah possessed a willowy grace along with a kindness that touched his soul, even started to heal his jaded heart. He'd always been mean. Had a chip on his shoulder from all the beatings his father administered. He thought that was the way to treat everyone, hurt them before they hurt him. As far as girls were concerned, he had no respect for them.

Until he encountered Leah.

Leah was different.

It wasn't because she was the most beautiful girl he ever set his eyes on. The amazing part of that was she didn't know nor did she seem to care. She wasn't anything like Marie Hughes who flaunted herself around all the young men. If he wanted to, he was sure he could coax Marie into bed. He was also sure she wasn't a virgin. There had been rumors last summer that her innocence had been stolen by some gent in Edinburgh. Now, it seemed she had her sights set on the doc despite his disability. He didn't know why all the ladies thought Doc Houston was a good catch. Everyone knew doctors were poor.

Leah was a virgin though. He was sure of that. He wanted her not just to bed her but to have for the rest of his life. She was his. He would make sure of that. He'd be the envy of every man around Selkirk to Edinburgh and on to Glasgow. What he didn't know was how to convince her he was the right man for her. Hell, what choices did she have here? Just the Doc. Houston Stuart wouldn't want such a fey creature.

He was educated.

More than most.

Leah seemed to be pretty smart too. He didn't know if she could read and write. Most women around these parts couldn't do either. If she married him, she could help out in the inn, wait on tables when needed. She could do the books if she could cipher numbers.

"Leah is going to the dance with you then," Quaid asked with a smirk then looked at Ryan. "You going to let the rest of the village know she's yours?"

"No, seems she doesn't want to. I'm making progress though. I think she almost said yes. The look in her eyes told me she wanted to even though she's afraid of Grizzly." Michael waved his hand in the air to get the bar maid's attention. She waltzed over then plopped on his lap. She smoothed the front of his shirt while she leaned into him, pressing her breasts against him in invitation. He liked the way she felt all warm and soft just like a woman should feel.

"Yeah, he's a mean devil, that one," Ryan said.

"What can I get for you?" she purred as she stroked his cheek. She kissed him where her fingers lingered, her little tongue lightly touching his skin.

He pulled her close. His mouth slanting over hers, he wrapped his tongue around hers. Michael liked the lady. Betsy was her name. Slept with her several nights ago. He would do so again if he wanted, if she was willing. He didn't have any doubts. Tonight, maybe if she didn't have another customer waiting for her. She didn't charge him though. Momentarily, he thought of Leah. He shrugged. A man had needs.

There were other women besides Betsy. He wasn't sure if he'd curb his desires when he married Leah. One woman was never enough for him. He didn't think that would change in the future. Perhaps Leah would prove to be so passionate in bed he wouldn't want another woman. That brought a chuckle rumbling up from deep in his lungs.

"A glass of ale along with some of that warm bread I smell baking. After that I want you, darling, that's what I want." He pinched her fanny.

She squeaked. "Me? You want me? Well, if you like you can have all your wishes."

"Later," he said as he gave her nearly barred breast a soft squeeze before putting her on the floor. "I'm starving."

"After my hours are done. You know where to find me. Don't have anyone else waiting for me."

Michael leaned back in his chair, his long legs stretched out in front of him, his arms crossed over his chest while he watched little Betsy sashay her pretty fanny to the bar to bring him his drink. He hardened thinking about later tonight. Wished it was Leah he would be bedding tonight. Damn but he was a lucky man, no denying that fact.

"So, who you going to take to the dance."

He kept his eyes on the barmaid. "Don't know. Have to do some serious thinking. Not going to show up there alone. Maybe little Elisa, if I can stand all that carrot red hair for an evening." He thought about that some more. Yes, Elisa would never turn him down, never did. He could bring her up to his rooms over the inn after the dance and make love to her. He'd had her there before. She was easy. Not like Leah.

Leah was a challenge. Maybe that was why he wanted her so desperately.

The threesome stayed at the tavern for several hours. Nearing midnight his friends left with some of the other serving maids. When Betsy served him, he pulled her onto his thighs, one hand firmly around her breast, sliding the fabric lower so he could rub his thumb over the hard tip.

"I'm your only customer now. Should we leave?" His other hand roamed the length of her leg. Giggling, she squirmed against him.

"You have to wait," she laughed then nipped him on the ear.

"Don't want to wait."

"I'll ask the boss."

He let her go, watching her again, wishing she was Leah. When he swept her off her feet to carry her up the steps to her room above, she giggled again. By the time they reached the small bed where they would sleep, she was half undressed as was he.

He let the clothing he'd taken off her fall to the floor as he set her on the bed and spread her legs. He was inside her. She was hot and swollen, slick with her need. He roared his pleasure as he left his seed inside her hot, moist sheathe.

"You can take it a bit slower next time," Betsy purred rubbing her hands along his sweat sheened back. "What had you so desperate you couldn't wait?"

"You know," he murmured.

"Leah."

Other Books by Christine Young
Available at Rogue Phoenix Press

Connal's Eternal Love
Sweet McKenna Book One

A few days shy of All Hallows' Eve Connal McKenna, Laird of Clan Chattan stands on the parapets of his castle. Bonfires line the hillsides while his clan prepares for the upcoming festivities. Drawn by the whispering of the wind, Connal McKenna feels a strange restlessness in his soul. Setting out to discover the wickedness that is calling to him, he discovers his mate. With gentle words and sensuous kisses, the auburn-eyed highlander conquers his mate, the beautiful, defiant Wynnie Adair who he comes upon during an evening ride. She must ultimately put her trust in the only man who can save her from the ruthless plans of her father and succumb to his gentle coaxing.

In Brady's Arms
Sweet McKenna Book Two

Forced to run from the only home she knows, beautiful, headstrong Lillian Townsends seeks shelter in the wild highlands where the McKenna clan live. Trying to avoid a betrothal contract signed by her stepfather to an aging lord, she is desperate to find a means to sidestep the inevitable, including a marriage to the oldest son of the laird. Lilly is enamored of the young lord who pursues her with unrelenting determination flashing his devilishly handsome charms. She is hard pressed to resist.

Besotted from the first moment Brady McKenna sees Lilly, he is determined to find a means to coax her into his arms and bed. With only the promise of carnal pleasure as his mistress, Brady relentlessly pursues the woman who has unwittingly forged a place in his heart. She is like no other woman, proud, defiant and enchanting. Despite his father's advice to stay away from her, he cannot. He boldly seeks her out and makes her his own.

Nobody but Walker
Sweet McKenna Book Three

The Highland Lass...

She was brought up, adored and loved by a doting mother and father ardently protected by her brothers. She was everything sweet and innocent until she was faced with betrayal and an unexpected and out of wedlock pregnancy. When she gave her love to a man who couldn't return her passion and commitment, she was left devastated and furious. Faced with the loss of her child if she didn't comply to his demands, Crissie McKenna followed him to Belfast then on to his country home to discover he was already married.

...The Irishman

Stunned to find out his one and only encounter with the woman he wanted to love forever created a child, Walker Endicott, Earl of Briarwood, claimed his child as his only heir. Walker threatened all her previously held values even while he thrilled her senses. From the moment he first saw her to the second she ran after him begging him to make love to her, his captivating masculinity held her fascinated. In his arms she would know tempestuous passion, bitter despair, and a soaring joy that would humble them both before the power of love.

My Sweet Broc
Bad Boys Book One

He's a bad bad boy...

Broc Wallace is a fun-loving rake who never thought any beautiful woman could melt his heart. He lives life in the present enjoying the camaraderie of his friends and the pleasures of his mistress. When Bliss races into his life, he is ill prepared to deal with her secrets or give up the tenor of his life. When the truth is revealed, he finds himself unable to forgive and forget the betrayal.

...but she's sweet for him

Bliss MacTavish knows she's playing with fire when she refuses to tell this bad boy her name. He tempts her with sweet whispers of seduction knowing her innocent nature will be unable to refuse all he yearns to give her. Deciding to follow her heart, she finds the repercussions more than she bargains for when she gives herself to this bad boy.

Crazy for Cam
Bad Boys Book Two

He's a bad bad boy...

Lord Cam MacEwen, Viscount of Rosehill, tries his best to be proper and court the lady of his dreams in the acceptable way. The feat proves impossible when the lady in question uses every means at her disposal to tempt him. He fights his jealousy for another man as well as the need to make her his own, finally giving in to her irresistible passion.

...but she's crazy for him.

Chelsea MacTavish wants the bad boy she fell in love with and kissed just before her eighteenth birthday. With feminine wiles and irresistible allure, the sensuous lady plans to best Cam at his game of hearts and make him forget his need to court her properly.

Falling for Flynt
Bad Boys Book Three

He's a bad, bad boy...

Fascinated by Hope's loss of memory yet haunted by her sultry beauty, Flynt is irresistibly drawn to the stoic miss—and into her troubles with the sultan who wants her for himself. When he discovers she is the sister of his best friend, his pride keeps him from pursuing her and making her his.

...but she's falling for him.

Raised in a harem but now penniless, alone and without her memory, Hope must discover a way to remember all that she has lost. She finds a way to continue with her life as a servant in Flynt's home. The first sight of Flynt steals Hope's breath as well as her heart. Can she overcome her fears and give herself to the man she fell in love with.

Dancing With Donal
Bad Boys Book Four

He's a bad bad boy...

Once a bad boy always a bad boy, Donal Chamberlin's carefree ways come crashing down around him when he meets the ravishingly beautiful Daryl MacTavish, the innocent little sister of one of his best friends. He is determined to win her heart as he sets his sights on marriage and an heir. His past gets in the way of his quest when a woman he once loved threatens Daryl's life.

...but she's dancing with him.

Daryl has seen the control her sister's husbands hold over them. She yearns for a life where she makes decisions for herself. No man will have power over her. But no man kisses her the way Donal does. No man can make her forget all her goals leaving her helpless to give up her dreams. Yet Donal is determined to dance through all the barriers she thrust in front of him, pursuing her until she says yes.

Loving Leslie
Bad Boys Book Five

He's a bad bad boy...

Leslie Stewart, Duke of Southcliff is stoic, set in his ways, a spy who is used to having his life well ordered. He expects life to continue on in this perfectly conventional fashion. He assumes his bad boy status while keeping mamas and debutantes at arm's length. An heir is needed but Leslie has every intention of finding a woman who doesn't covet his wealth and tittle. He is irresistibly drawn to the headstrong young lady who becomes more beautiful as she develops into a woman.

...but she is loving him.

When Leslie kisses Lacie MacTavish, she knows even at the tender age of fifteen this is the man of her dreams. Forced to wait until she comes of age, Lacie withdraws into herself. Now she is eighteen and Leslie has returned from a mission for the British Government ready to claim her as his bride. She refuses him and he must find a way to seduce her and in the process create a burning passion within her, which she cannot deny.

Pleasing Arie
Bad Boys Book Six

He's a bad bad boy...

Arie Demir has never been denied anything in his life. He takes what he wants. What he undeniably yearns for is the beautiful redheaded spitfire he sees in a restaurant in Glasgow. At every turn, she confuses him by disputing his power over her. Alison refuses to accept the fact he owns her. While Arie tries desperately with patience and tenderness to drive her wild with new sensations, his scorching kisses ignite the fires of her very soul to make her understand he is all she will ever want.

...but is she pleasing him?

Alison Fletcher never expected to find herself kidnapped and sold to a whorehouse then bought by a Turkish sultan to become his slave. She vows to never surrender to the arrogant man who believes he owns her. She is stunned by the magnificently handsome man who awaits her compliance. Unexpectedly, she finds Arie the lesser of all the evils. The hidden depths of his mesmerizing dark brown eyes hold her into their power; his muscular embrace makes her weak with desire. She is his to do with as he wishes.

Graham's Wicked Kiss
Bad Boys Book Seven

He's a bad bad boy...

Graham Chamberlin is stunned to find three young boys dangling from the trees lining the drive to Runningmead Manner. On further inspection, he is astonished at their obsession to protect a young woman who has been brutalized by her pimp. The woman he discovers hiding in a third-floor attic room is gravely injured. He takes the silver haired stowaway under his wing. Clearly, Graham's new guest is a lady with many secrets. He is determined to unlock all the mysteries surrounding her.

...But she can't resist his wicked kiss.

The years since Ria left the convent where she was raised have been a nightmare. Her secrets are dangerous—as is the powerful man determined to find her. Handsome Graham Chamberlin is clearly a gentleman with secrets of his own, but staying with him could mean the difference between life and death for Ria. With each passing day, her handsome host turns Ria's convalescence into an increasingly sensual escape. Now her greatest challenge may be imagining anything less than a future in his arms.

Feeling Etienne's Love
Bad Boys Book Eight

He's a bad bad boy...

Etienne Dubois is the son of a wealthy vineyard owner who craves the excitement of putting his life on the line. Working with the French government and as a confidant of King Charles X give him reasons for living. An encounter with a beautiful young woman in a plush bordello in Paris has him rethinking his roguish ways. Etienne never expects to become a father especially from one encounter with an innocent prostitute who whispers his name and has him rethinking his well-ordered life.

...But she can't help feeling his love.

Elisa Moreau, the only daughter of Angelique Moreau, the owner of an exclusive bordello in Bordeaux, France, has loved Etienne Dubois since she was six. Unfortunately, until an unexpected encounter at a brothel in Paris puts the two of them in the same room, Etienne doesn't even know she exists. Confused but wanting Etienne and this chance meeting to never end, Elisa gives herself to the man who has held her heart in hands for what seems like her entire life.

All I Want Is Link
Bad Boys Book Nine

He's a bad bad boy...

Merry Stewart is wildly unpredictable. Left alone to run wild over the Bordeaux and Scottish countryside she becomes impetuous and daringly bold. Over the years, she's found she can bedevil her softhearted brothers into allowing her exploits to go unnoticed. As a young woman she has learned she can do as she pleases when she pleases. Now, Merry has set her amorous sights on the Duke of Weston—a man she has never met but has every intention of marrying. No other suitor will satisfy her—especially not the exceptionally striking, horse breeder, Devlin Mathews.

...she's the woman of his desires.

Posing as commoner Devlin Mathews to escape a potentially fatal confrontation, Devlin is enthralled and infuriated by the audacious, duke-hunting dark haired vixen. Bedeviled at every opportunity, he finds dealing with the tiny she-devil exasperating as well as intriguing. Without revealing his true identify, the infamous rogue pledges to thwart Merry's plans to wed the man of her dream-never imagining the bewitching strategist would turn out to be the only woman he would ever dream of marrying.

Devlin's Angel
Bad Boys Book Ten

He's a bad bad boy...

Merry Stewart is wildly unpredictable. Left alone to run wild over the Bordeaux and Scottish countryside she becomes impetuous and daringly bold. Over the years, she's found she can bedevil her softhearted brothers into allowing her exploits to go unnoticed. As a young woman she has learned she can do as she pleases when she pleases. Now, Merry has set her amorous sights on the Duke of Weston—a man she has never met but has every intention of marrying. No other suitor will satisfy her—especially not the exceptionally striking, horse breeder, Devlin Mathews.

...she's the woman of his desires.

Posing as commoner Devlin Mathews to escape a potentially fatal confrontation, Devlin is enthralled and infuriated by the audacious, duke-hunting dark haired vixen. Bedeviled at every opportunity, he finds dealing with the tiny she-devil exasperating as well as intriguing. Without revealing his true identify, the infamous rogue pledges to thwart Merry's plans to wed the man of her dream-never imagining the bewitching strategist would turn out to be the only woman he would ever dream of marrying.

Foolish for Piper

The pickpocket...

Piper has spent her life surviving the streets of St. Giles Parish in London, a den of iniquity and crime. Masquerading as a boy she escapes the whorehouses the young girls are sent to as they come of age. The day she encounters Brett MacLachlan begins the same as every other one. When she picks his pocket, she has no idea her life is going to change irreversibly.

...and the mark

Handsome aristocrat Brett MacLachlan has come to London for his amusement only to find his world turned upside down by a thief and her dog. From the moment he spots her, Brett knows there is something intrinsically wrong. In his arms, Piper discovers passion and joy. Yet secrets of her past haunt her, and a scar will tell the true tale as well as her identity.

Taylor's Destiny

She traveled to another time and place to change destiny...

Enjoying a day of sailing, Taylor Maxwell never expected after a suffering a concussion she would wake up in another century. A resilient independent woman in the twenty-first century, the blond beauty is ill prepared for life in the 1800s. Her first sight of the naval captain who rescues her makes her heart stop, giving her hope for her future.

His life is transformed by a woman who appears from nowhere...

Born to a life of ease, Reid Stewart defies the dictates of those born to aristocracy and chooses a life of adventure in the navy and as a spy for the crown. When he discovers a nearly naked woman on the bow of small sailing ship, his heart warms. His love for Taylor and his need to protect her from a man who pursues her might cost him his life as well as hers.

Caitlin's Duke

She played a fiddle in an Irish pub...

Caitlin O'Shea Is the most beautiful woman Roc Leighton has ever seen. With her blue violet eyes and long black hair she captivates him. In turn he mesmerizes Caitlin. Caught in the power of his gaze as he watches her, she is wise enough to know he desires her but will never give his heart to her. Caitlin has vowed to never be any man's mistress.

And fell in love with an English Lord...

Roc knows the first time he watches her play the fiddle and dance around the pub, she will be his next mistress. Despite her protest, he will find a way to convince her that her place is with him. While Caitlin's determination to keep her vows, fate takes a cruel turn and she is forced to seek refuge with Roc.

Catching Meara
Book One in the McKenna Clan Series

Meara Thorton was a feisty, world-class computer hacker—cornered by the FBI and shockingly given the chance to be their newly acquired technical analyst. Brilliant and intuitive, yet aching with the loss of everyone she has cared about, her restless heart led her to discover a love she fought and a world she didn't know could possibly exist.

Sweet Sexy Sadie
Book Two in the McKenna Clan Series

From the first time Sadie's eyes met those of Brody McKenna in the hot Sierra Madre Mountains, theirs was a potent attraction—not gentle, slow, and easy, but hot, hard, and all-consuming. The daughter of a dysfunctional family, Sadie had dreams no man could wrench from her with hot sex and an all-consuming passion. She'd challenge this alpha male with all the strength she possessed. But her red hair, fiery temperament, and indomitable spirit obsessed Brody...and he knew he had to find a way to show her he was more than he appeared and convince her to make a life with him.

Sweet Misbehavin'
Book Three in the McKenna Clan Series

Cast adrift after fleeing the home of Jokul, the ice demon, Atantsi, a firestarter, grew to womanhood as she moved through time to keep the demon from finding her. Though stubborn and courageous, she was ill prepared to use powers she had not been taught. Her first sight of the intoxicating Carr McKenna left her breathless, and her second encounter gave her hope for a future she never thought she had.

A playboy, a second son and a shifter, a man who thought his life would be carefree, Carr McKenna was shocked to discover the woman he'd paid as an escort is a firestarter who is running for her life. He is the leader of all the McKennas around the world and that he has multiple powers. His passion for Margo and the need to defend her might cost him his life as well as hers.

Sweet Talkin' Sugar
Book Four in the McKenna Clan Series

Lyonesse McKenna, was dreaming, or was she? From the instant Lyn saw Deacon McClain across a black jack table in a crowed Las Vegas casino the unmistakable attraction sent Lyn's senses flying into overdrive. Her family of shapeshifters believed in soul mates. She'd always been skeptical yet she couldn't help but question the way her heart sped when he looked at her.

When Deacon appeared in Las Vegas he knew his first job was to save Lyn from a Sea Demon, but the next order of business was to convince her he would someday mean more to her than she'd ever expected. But her stubborn nature and unbendable spirit consumed Deacon...and he had to chase away all the demons real and imagined in order to win her heart.

Sweet Surrender
Book Five in the McKenna Clan Series

Ripped from her family at the top of Infinity Cliff, Kimi McKenna finds herself thrust somewhere into the future. Dark elements threaten to destroy the earth unless Kimi can work together with the white witch to stop the destruction. Confused by her mate's role in the conspiracy, she refuses to acknowledge the connection. But amidst raging fire and attacks on the people she is coming to hold dear, she allows Maska O'keefe into her heart.

Maska O'keefe has loved the beautiful shapeshifter for years. Unable to save her life years ago, he vows to watch over her as he is given a second chance to convince her that even though he is a witch and not a shifter, they are indeed soul mates. Kimi's divided loyalties between her family and the cause she is now a part of will determine their relationship. Only the part she plays as the messiah can bring this to a conclusion in the final battle.

Dakota's Bride
The first book in the Lakota/Pinkerton Series

When Emma St. John received her brother's letter imploring her to escape her stepfather's vengeful scheme and to trust Dakota Barringer with her life, she was willing to chance it. But the handsome, brooding riverboat owner Emma found in Natchez a danger of another kind. For Emma soon found herself surrendering to an unrelenting desire.

Raised by the Sioux when his parents were killed, Dakota had been betrayed once before by a white woman. He wasn't about to trust another, especially one claiming that her stepfather, a powerful U.S. senator, had framed her as a murderess. But he couldn't let Emma's intoxicating effect on him. Now Dakota would risk his very life to protect the innocent beauty who had seduced him with her tender love.

My Angel
The second book in the Lakota/Pinkerton Series

A BEAUTY IN BUCKSKINS

When her father decided to send her to a finishing school back East, Angela Chamberlain refused to be confined to stuffy drawing rooms. Instead, the daring spitfire who could shoot like a man and ride like the wind longed for a life of adventure and romance—and she knew exactly who could give it to her. Devil Blackmoor was a hired gun with a dangerous reputation. But Angela was willing to go to the ends of the earth to capture the handsome devil's heart.

A DEVIL IN DISGUISE

He'd come to America looking for excitement, but Devil Blackmoor got more than he bargained for when he encountered a beautiful rebel who answered his kisses with a wild innocence that touched his very soul. Yet standing between them were more obstacles than either ever dreamed. For Devil had strapped on a gun for the wrong man. And that made Angela his enemy. Now he'll have to choose between his duty and the woman he loves more than life.

The Locket
The third book in the Lakota/Pinkerton Series

The year is 1894. Seeking revenge for crimes against his family, Misha Petrovich follows a path that leads straight to Ariel Cameron's boarding house in Mist Harbor, Oregon. A family heirloom in Ariel's possession leads Misha to believe she is guilty. The locket has been handed down to the oldest girl in the Petrovich family for generations. Ariel is innocent of wrong doing, but her father is not. Misha is torn by his feelings for Ariel and his need for restitution against her father. Knowing that the relationship between them is fragile, Misha does everything in his power to protect Ariel's father. His efforts are to no avail when her father is shot. Ariel comes to realize Misha's steadfast courage and determination to protect her and her father despite what has happened to his family. Ariel's love and devotion heals Misha's heart.

The Talisman
The fourth book in the Lakota/Pinkerton Series

Running from a marriage that lasted one night, Dr. Moriah McKeown discovers the land she has settled on is coveted by determined and lawless men. Yet the proud young woman who once vowed never to abandon her home has second thoughts when her adopted children are threatened. Her only recourse is to enlist the aid of a dark, dangerous gun for hire.

Haunted by the past and a betrayal he will never forgive, Ian Civanovich uses his fast gun and his reckless courage to forget the faithlessness of a woman in his past. He will trust no female—nor will he rest until the threat hovering over Moriah McKeown is put to rest.

Forever His
The fifth book in the Lakota/Pinkerton Series

Struggling to come to terms with the part she played in Jacob St. John's death, Etta Barringer resigns from Pinkerton Agency and seeks peace and solace in a Rocky Mountain Cabin.

Jacob has vowed to discover the reason Etta has betrayed him, sold him out to his enemy and left him for dead.

Isolated in their cabin, they discover their love for each other and learn to trust. But the trust is shattered when Jacob learns she is married to his sworn enemy; the man who left him in the desert to die.

Allura's Secret
Twelve Dancing Princesses Book One

Allura McClellan is horrified by her father's decision to take out an ad in the Times awarding her to the man strong enough and smart enough to win her hand and uncover her secrets. She's an intelligent young woman who takes great delight in the freedom allotted to her by her father. She's well aware that marriage would effectively curtail the adventures she's shared with her sisters and cousins.

Hunter Gray is nothing like the other men who've arrived to vie for Allura's hand in marriage and everything that goes along with it. However, he is the first to refuse to concede defeat and pursue her despite her attempts to disguise her true appearance. It's her temperament that is of more concern to him than her looks. Hunter has worked all his life with the hope of someday owning his own land. Now that it looks like there's a very real possibility that everything he's ever wanted is within reach nothing is going to deter him – including Miss Allura's disagreeable disposition.

Amorica's Wager
Twelve Dancing Princesses Book Two

Amorica Hepburn was sent to London to find a husband. Finding a man was the last item on her agenda. With her two cousins, Amorica wagers she can dissuade her suitor before the others. Despite her efforts she discovers a chemistry that cannot be denied. Suddenly she is the arrogant man's wife, pledged to a marriage neither desire. But swept off to his ancestral home above the Dover cliffs and into his strong embrace, Amorica is soon possessed by a raging passion for the husband she had vowed to despise...

Damian Andrews couldn't afford to trust the emerald-eyed spitfire who happened upon his secret. Amorica's hatred of all men of his kind only inflames the war that rages between them. Still, he can not control the intense desire his stubborn bride inspires, or make her surrender to his will until he has conquered the headstrong beauty on the battlefield of love...

Ravyn's Marriage of Inconvenience
Twelve Dancing Princesses Book Three

A REGAL BEAUTY

When the duchess decides to wed her to a wastrel and a fop, Ravyn Grahm takes matters into her own hands and declares her engagement to another man. Instead of fessing up and telling her great aunt what she has done, she goes through with the pretense. Ariec Lakeland is the bastard son of an earl and has a dangerous reputation. But Ravyn is willing to do most anything to keep the duchess from discovering the lie.

A DEVIL-MAY-CARE SMUGGLER

He'd bought land in America, looking to put down roots and end his life of adventure, but Ariec Lakeland got more than he bargained for when he encountered a beautiful heiress who made a promise she didn't want to keep. But the promise could not be undone and standing between them were more obstacles than either ever dreamed. Ariec had made plans to spend the rest of his life in America and that was at odds with Ravyn's plan of living in England and running her father's estate. Now, he'll have to choose between his dreams and the woman he loves more than life.

Christel's Sunrise
Twelve Dancing Princesses Book Four

He Made Her An Offer...

Life has thrown Christel McClellan some experiences that could have devastated a less determined woman. Beautiful, self-assured and fiercely independent, she is trying to forget the loss of her stillborn child. But is the child alive?

She Couldn't Deny...

Life is carefree for Ryder MacLaren who loves to see what is on the other side of the sunrise. Laird of Clan MacLaren, he is wealthy, handsome and happily unencumbered...until stunning Christel McClellan enters his life. When he hears her story, he believes the child she thought dead has been sold to a wealthy buyer.

Storm's Passion
Twelve Dancing Princesses Book Five

SHE MADE A PROPOSAL...

Life strikes Storm Graham a shattering blow when she learns her father has bartered her to a man she detests. Storm is beautiful, self–assured and fiercely independent, and refuses to be a pawn in her father's schemes, yet she can find no way out of this bargain made in hell. Going on the offensive she asks the wealthiest man on the eastern coast of England to marry her, never believing she might fall in love.

HE TRIED TO REFUSE...

For Hadden Johnston life has provided everything he ever wanted, including a sanctuary for homeless children. He is wealthy, handsome and happily unencumbered...until stunning Storm Graham marches into his life and proposes a marriage of convenience. Yet this type of marriage to a woman who inflames his senses is far from acceptable. If he's going to be tied down, he will move heaven and earth to have this woman warming his bed.

Gotta Have Fayth
Twelve Dancing Princesses Book Six

A regal beauty with raven hair and piercing blue eyes, Fayth Graham is unwilling to parade herself in front of the wealthy Lords of England during the season. Seeking a means to dissuade any man wishing to wed her, she seeks a way to ruin herself for marriage. When she unexpectedly meets a man with sparkling gray eyes and an infectious grin, she decides this is the man who will keep her from agreeing to obey.

He returned from six months at sea, looking for a few nights of pleasure with a willing lass, but Jarret Kinsley got more than he bargained for when he met a beautiful debutant who responded to his kisses with a wild innocence that touched his heart. Yet the obstacles looming between them might rip them apart. Both had vowed never to marry, so when consequences of their dalliances got in the way, Jarret would have to choose between the life he's always desired and the woman he loves more than life.

Ella's Pleasure
Twelve Dancing Princesses Book Seven

A WHISPER OF PLEASURE
Ella Hepburn was an auburn haired debutant from the harsh Scottish coastline—a wild innocent to be seduced and tamed. A spirited beauty, she captivated Drake Montgomerie's jaded heart—while succumbing to the smoldering desire she felt for her unyielding suitor.

A WHISPER OF DANGER
In Drake Montgomerie's glittering world of money and privilege, young Ella discovered passion and desire could overcome everything she'd been taught to resist—entangling Drake, the heir apparent, in a lethal coil of aristocratic family intrigue. But grave peril would only nurse the sparks of a love that knew no limits and a magnificent ecstasy that would not be denied.

Eveleen's Seduction
Twelve Dancing Princesses Book Eight

A WHISPER OF SEDUCTION
A brutal attack on Eveleen Hepburn's cherished island off the Scottish coastline leaves her shattered and bewildered. Learning a man she once trusted can kill as easily as he can breathe even though the deed saves her life, creates questions that need answers. An innocent beauty, she enchants Logan Maxwell's cynical heart—giving in to the raging passion she feels for her mysterious suitor.

A WHISPER OF INTRIGUE

In Logan's Maxwell's world of espionage and privilege, young Eveleen discovers truths about herself she never expected, and a need for passion and love can overcome all her fears if she learns to accept certain truths. She finds herself entangled in a lethal battle for land that was once owned by French nobility, taken from them during the revolution and sold to Maxwell. But grave peril would unleash the flames of love that simmers, creating a magical union that cannot be refuted.

Tavia's Deception
Twelve Dancing Princesses Book Nine

WHISPERS OF DECEPTION

When her father decides to send her to London for her season, Tavia Hepburn resolves to see the world instead. The raven haired beauty decides to disguise herself as a lad and find employment on a ship bound for Barcelona as a cabin boy. But she never bargains on finding passion and love to a red haired sea captain who rescues her from certain death.

WHISPERS OF MURDER

For James Macmurra, the world is black and white until he meets a young debutante, who turns his world upside down. He's unable to deny Tavia's intoxicating effect on him. In a match tense with obstacles, unwillingness to divulge secrets, and unforeseen peril, irresistible desire and passion grows into undeniable love. James would risk his life to shelter and protect the innocent debutante who seduces him with her sweet love.

Larena's Fascination
Twelve Dancing Princesses Book Ten

WHISPERS OF FASCINATION

Fiery, free spirited Larena Graham never wanted to marry a duke. She is thrilled to be in love with the fourth son of an aristocrat, Gavin

Broon. But when it seems Gavin ignores her, she set her sights on politics and bettering human life. Unsuspecting intrigue and a plot against her, she continues her dangerous plans despite Gavin's wishes.

WHISPERS OF TRUST

Gavin has every intention of properly courting the beautiful Larena until he must leave the city in order to put his affairs in order. Returning to London, he finds the woman he means to make his own is embroiled in political protests that could lead to a prison ship. Larena must learn to trust the handsome Scotsman whose most pressing mission is to protect her and keep her from harm.

Tira's Education
Twelve Dancing Princesses Book Eleven

WHISPERS OF EDUCATION

Learning how to build ships is Tira Hepburn's only dream until she meets Jamie Lundin and her world is turned upside down. With her raven black hair and vivid green eyes, she tempts Jamie and pushes him to defy his vows. She never bargains on finding an irrevocable love and a passion to a man who cannot fulfill her dreams despite his burning desire for her.

WHISPERS OF A BARGAIN

Arrogant and self-assured Jamie is brought up short when Tira captures his heart. All his carefully made plans are put to the test when he decides to teach her the art of ship building if she will spend a week with him alone on his ship. He is unable to deny Tira's intoxicating effect on him. When Tira leaves him behind unwilling to live with him without the benefit of marriage, he races after her. Jamie will risk everything to shelter and protect the innocent debutante who seduces him with her sweet love.

Aidan's Love
Twelve Dancing Princesses Book Twelve

Whispers of Love

Aidan McLellan has loved since she first set eyes on him as a young girl. Spontaneous, wild and eager to grow up, Aidan haunts his waking thoughts day and night, insinuating herself into his life. With her fiery red hair and sparkling sapphire eyes, she seizes Blade's heart even while he tries to resist the innocent child until she becomes a woman.

Whispers of Courage

Blade has waited what seems a lifetime to claim the woman who captures his heart as a little girl. Claiming his inheritance before his younger brother takes what is rightfully his, Blade must convince Aidan of his sincerity after years of avoidance and wed her before his father dies so he can return home, securing his rightful place. Everything is put to the test when his life as well as Aidan's is threatened by the man who once called him brother.

Twelve Days to Love

When Archer Steele shows up at Calanthe Durand's failing plantation with an alligator over his shoulder, Cali thinks she's never seen a more handsome man. During the war she had to defend herself and her servants from both union and confederate soldiers. Independent and self-sufficient, she vows to never marry.

But Archer Steele has different ideas. The first time Archer sees Cali in town, he feels an instant attraction. He decides he will do everything and anything to convince the beautiful Miss Durand he is worthy of her love. During the weeks leading up to Christmas, he gives her twelve gifts in hopes she will fall in love with him. Yet they are faced with challenges they must overcome before Cali can commit to a marriage.

Door to Heaven

Jessica Lawrence is the stepdaughter of a woman born in the twentieth century transported back in time to the year 1868. An acclaimed suffragette, she raises Jessica to believe in the equality of women. Jess Law believes everything she was taught, and when the time is right she becomes a private investigator. Courageous and impetuous, Jess finds danger in her quest to save all women from white slavery. Her passionate mission results in a wedding to Roc Newman, a man she knows can steal her heart...

Roc can't trust the sapphire-eyed spitfire who invades his home in search of secret papers and knocks him flat with her karate moves. Jessica's refusal to obey his wishes serves to inflame the war between them. Still, he cannot control the intense desire his reluctant bride inspires, or make her surrender her independence, until he has conquered the headstrong beauty on the battlefield of love...

Rebel Heart

HER REBEL SPIRIT DEFIED HIS OUTSIDERS SOUL...She was velvet and silk, eyes the color of a summer storm and amber hair. Victoria DeMontville, because of a promise and a codicil to her father's will, was forced to marry one man to protect her from another. She hated Cameron Savage with a fierce passion. But to hold on to her genetic research and find a cure for the deadly Signe virus, she must pretend to love the enemy at her door, come with weapons of fire to melt her icy heart...

HIS OUTSIDERS TOUCH IGNITED RAGING PASSIONS... He wore a mask, disguised as the Phantom, a true legend come to life. Even as war and debate over new genetic research engulfed them all, he would find his greatest adversary in the beauty who'd branded him an outsider and barbarian, the woman he was born to possess, his soul mate.

Safari Moon

Solo St. John, a wildlife photographer, is preparing for a trip to Alaska. Suddenly, Solo finds women of all sorts invading his privacy, his home and his office, all cooing nonsense words and blatantly throwing themselves at him. Solo doesn't know why, and he has no idea how to rid himself of the persistent women. He finally decides to beg a favor of his best buddy Nyssa Harrington.

In love with Solo for the past ten years and knowing he doesn't return her feelings Nyssa doesn't want to talk to Solo. She knows if she accepts his phone call, she will not be able to resist the temptation to hope again.

Straight to Heaven

Running from demons, Alexandra McMurdie stumbles into Forbidden Ground where up is down and elements of nature are contested. Though a strong independent woman in the twenty-first century' she is unprepared for life in the 1800s. Her first site of the formidable James Lawrence makes her heart skip a beat, giving her cause to reconsider her desperate need to find a way home.

Born with a silver spoon, James' life was torn apart during the War Between the States. Moving west he vows to put the life he once knew in the past. When he discovers a half-frozen woman near Gold Hill, his heart begins to thaw. His love for Alexandra and his need to keep her from a man who has pursued her through time might cost him his life as well as hers.

A Valentine's Anthology

The Lending Library-a fantasy by Christie L. Kraemer
Faeries try to fit into the human world when the forest where they make their home is destroyed by a mysterious enemy.

Chasing Rainbows-a contemporary romance by Genene Valleau

An eccentric aunt, an inventive uncle, a mother who wears poodle skirts, and a brother who wears pearls provide a hilarious backdrop for the courtship of a young woman who yearns for a "normal" family.

The Gift-an historical romance by Christine Young

A man and a woman on opposite sides of the Civil War get a second chance at love after one final battle returns soldiers to their war-torn homes to rebuild their lives.

A St. Patrick's Day Tale
Christine Young, C. L. Kraemer, Genene Valleau

Tumble through time...

...to Ireland in 1817, when tensions are high between Protestants and Catholics and fae people guide the fate of villagers. A lovely Catholic lass stumbles upon the weakly ritual fisticuffing between Irish lads. She falls into the lap of a handsome young Protestant. Family ties, grudges, and two conniving faeries threaten their budding love. But the faeries outsmart themselves when they hijack a time machine that has mysteriously appeared in their forest and are whisked to...

...Eugene, Oregon in the 20th century, amid a property feud between the local faeries and night elves. The conniving faeries from Olde Ireland try to stir up more mischief. However, a warrior gnome convinces the magic folk to control their own destiny, and forces the intruding faeries to take refuge in the time machine again, spinning their way toward...

...A modern day castle in western Oregon. An eccentric inventor is determined to reclaim his wayward time machine and save his beloved wife from her latest misadventure. If only they can travel safely past the black hole...

a May Day Anthology
Christine Young, C. L. Kraemer, Rosemary Indra, Genene Valleau

Highland Miracle — Christine Young

HURTLED THROUGH TIME, Sean Michael Sterling, landed in the midst of a May Day celebration he didn't understand, assuming the role of Laird Sterling.

ILLIGITAMATE CHILD OF NOBILITY, Reagan Douglas searches for a way out of her half brother's house.

Defying the Odds — C.L. Kraemer

The night elves on the hill aren't happy without their magic. They concoct a plan to punish those who were involved in the act that rendered them almost human. Meanwhile, Uther, the rogue night elf, has returned to woo the Librarian to be his eternal mate.

Love in Bloom — Rosemary Indra

When childhood friends reunite it takes two fairies and a matchmaking daughter to help them admit their true love for each other.

No More Poodle Skirts — Genie Gabriel

After drifting for years in the innocent age of the 1950s, a woman struggles to join today's world by finding a career and a new love, with some help from her zany family.

Once Upon a Christmas Moon
Christine Young, C. L. Kraemer, Genene Valleau

TWELVE DAYS TO LOVE

When Archer Steele shows up at Calanthe Durand's failing plantation with an alligator over his shoulder, Cali thinks she's never seen a more handsome man. During the war she had to defend herself and her servants from both union and confederate soldiers. Independent and self-sufficient, she vows to never marry. But Archer Steele has different ideas. The first time Archer sees Cali in town, he feels an instant attraction. He decides he will do everything and anything to convince the beautiful Miss Durand he is worthy of her love. During the weeks leading up to

Christmas, he gives her twelve gifts in hopes she will fall in love with him.

BOOTS AND BLADES

An ancient evil from the old country has arrived in the high desert of Oregon. Gnome children are vanishing then re-appearing, showing various stages of traumatization. Tiamoon, warrior gnome, will put her skills to use alongside Killian, a handsome warrior, also in need of a cause.

CHRISTMAS PAWSIBILITIES

With their world destroyed and their space ship malfunctioning, the dogizens of Planet Canid have little choice but to crash land on Earth. They face tortuous experiments at the hands of the Geeks in Green...or they can trust an eccentric inventor and his zany family to deliver the Canine Queen's puppies and help them celebrate new lives.